Exodus Rising

❧ TALES OF STARLIGHT SERIES ☙

Exodus Rising
TALES OF STARLIGHT SERIES

Bryan Davis

Exodus Rising
Volume 3 in the Tales of Starlight® series

Copyright © 2013 by Bryan Davis

Published by Living Ink Books, an imprint of
AMG Publishers, Inc.
6815 Shallowford Rd.
Chattanooga, Tennessee 37421

All rights reserved. Except for brief quotations in printed reviews, no part of this publication may be reproduced, stored in a retrieval system, or transmitted in any form or by any means (printed, written, photocopied, visual electronic, audio, or otherwise) without the prior permission of the publisher.

This is a work of fiction. Names, characters, places, and incidents either are the product of the author's imagination or are used fictitiously. Any resemblance to actual persons, either living or dead, events, or locales, is entirely coincidental.

Print Edition: ISBN 13: 978-0-89957-899-6
EPUB Edition   ISBN 13: 978-1-61715-397-6
Mobi Edition   ISBN 13: 978-1-61715-218-4
PDF Edition   ISBN 13: 978-1-61715-398-3

First Printing—May 2013

TALES OF STARLIGHT is a registered trademark of AMG Publishers.

Cover designed by Daryle Beam at Bright Boy Design, Chattanooga, TN.

Interior design and typesetting by Reider Publishing Services, West Hollywood, California.

Edited and proofread by Susie Davis, Sharon Neal, and Rick Steele.

Printed in the United States of America
18 17 16 15 14 13 –BP– 6 5 4 3 2 1

Author's Note for *Exodus Rising*

Exodus Rising, published by AMG/Living Ink Books, is the third book in Tales of Starlight, a series that acts as a companion to Dragons of Starlight, a series for young adults published by Zondervan.

How to Read the Story World:

You can fully enjoy Tales of Starlight without reading Dragons of Starlight. If you read both series, however, you will gain a fuller understanding of the story world.

If you intend to read both series, here is my suggested reading order:

1. *Starlighter* (Dragons of Starlight book #1)
2. *Masters & Slayers* (Tales of Starlight book #1)
3. *Warrior* (Dragons of Starlight book #2)
4. *Third Starlighter* (Tales of Starlight book #2)
5. *Diviner* (Dragons of Starlight book #3)
6. *Liberator* (Dragons of Starlight book #4)
7. *Exodus Rising* (Tales of Starlight book #3)

You may switch the reading order for entries 1 and 2, and you may also switch the order for entries 4 and 5.

Because *Exodus Rising* ends the entire story world for both series, the story refers to events in the Dragons of Starlight series several times, so I recommend reading Dragons of Starlight in order to fully comprehend the details of this final episode.

✶ ONE ✶

DOES *a corpse care how loving hands lay her in the ground's embrace?* Adrian smoothed out the dirt over Regina's shallow grave. With no tombstone available in this uninhabited land between the southern dragon kingdom and the Northlands, no one would ever guess that the body of a petite Starlighter rested here. Only thousands of surrounding flowers would pay homage to the little blind girl, nodding their heads as the breeze whispered about her courageous acts, her indomitable spirit, and her sacrificial love.

Shellinda and Wallace knelt at the opposite side of the grave, both with tears tracking down their dirty faces and grass staining their trousers. Their rolled-up sleeves revealed grime covering their arms as well, interrupted in spots by a rash—the telltale sign of the fatal disease plaguing nearly all of Starlight. They couldn't stay here to mourn. The only possible cure lay to the north where Cassabrie had flown with Regina's spirit in tow. Dwelling within Exodus, this world's guiding "star," Cassabrie had floated away less than an hour earlier, guiding the buoyant, glowing sphere with her powerful mind.

"We'd better follow Cassabrie." Adrian swiveled, slid his hands under Marcelle's unconscious body, and rose with her cradled in his arms. Although she had spoken now and then, always in a dreamlike state and murmuring about her imagined adventures in their home world of Major Four, she had been quiet for a while. Some evidence pointed to the idea that her spirit had separated from her body, so he had to figure out how to reunite them. Maybe Alaph, the king of the Northlands, would know how to accomplish that feat. In any case, the cooler weather that lay ahead might rouse her.

Without a word, Wallace, the one-eyed preteen, led the way, his shoulders and head hanging low and a sword dangling loosely in his grip. Shellinda walked in silence at Adrian's side. The only sounds came from the south-flowing river to the left and the ever-cooling breeze from the north, each one mimicking whispers that stayed just out of reach of understanding.

As they walked through the grass-and-flower meadow, Marcelle's body bobbed in Adrian's arms. She grasped his wrist and shivered.

He held her closer to his chest. "I'm sorry, Marcelle. I know it's cold, but we lost the deerskin along the way. When we get to the Northlands castle, we'll find a soft bed and warm blankets."

Marcelle stared at him, unblinking, though Solarus cast rays of bright light across her face. She took a deep breath and spoke labored words. "The Northlands?"

Adrian nodded. "It's not far. That's why it's getting so cold."

"Your father ... is there. ... Waiting ... for you."

He studied her lips—pale and dry. Every syllable likely caused a lot of pain. "It's good to hear your voice again."

She frowned. "Look ... for him."

"My father?" Ahead, nothing but grass and flowers lay in view, though the colorful carpet seemed thinner in the distance. "Sure, I'll look for him. I saw him get healed there. I'll tell you all about it when you recover."

Marcelle blinked, her brow wrinkling. She seemed confused, worried. Her dreams had likely turned to nightmares, and delirium ruled her thoughts. Gasping between words, she said, "Have to … go back. … When it's cool. … Get the soldiers."

"When it's cool?" Adrian lowered her to the ground and knelt at her side. Wallace and Shellinda seated themselves nearby amidst the grass, their bodies still slack. Although the cooler air had made carrying Marcelle easier, sweat still trickled into Adrian's emerging beard.

After brushing a sleeve across his brow, he rubbed Marcelle's fingers between his hands. "You're already cold. You need to warm up, not cool down."

With her free hand, she ran her fingers up his tunic and caressed his face, her eyes now wide and clear. "Thank you … for taking care of me."

He rubbed her cheek with the back of his hand. "I would do anything for you. Just relax and concentrate on getting better."

"Can't … relax. … Too much … to do."

"I've heard. You've been talking about being home on Major Four, something about traveling there in spirit. I don't know if you're just dreaming or not, but no matter what happens—"

"Shhh." She touched his lips with her fingertips. "Just tell me … one thing."

He set his ear closer. "What's that?"

"Did you … mean it? … Or was I … dreaming?"

"Mean what?"

"Your question." She closed her eyes, took in a breath, and opened them again. "You asked me to marry you."

"Oh, Marcelle!" He took her hand again and continued caressing her cheek. "If it will help, I'll ask again."

She shushed him with a fingertip. "Wait. … Wait until … I return … from Major Four." Letting out a long breath, she closed her eyes. Her breathing settled, deep and even. Sleep had returned, and her dreams of Major Four would probably follow. Or maybe her spirit returned there, as unlikely as it seemed.

After folding Marcelle's arms over her chest, he wiped tears from his cheeks. She had seemed more lucid than ever, maybe a sign of recovery or maybe a signal that her wandering spirit had drawn closer. Either way, it was time to move on.

"Hurry back, my love. I will be waiting." He picked her up again and nodded at Wallace and Shellinda. "We have to go. Just do your best. Let me know if you need to stop."

They tramped across the grass, Shellinda jogging at times to keep up. Adrian focused again on the northern horizon. At this pace, it would take hours to reach the Northlands, and stops for water and other necessities would slow them further. Not only that, his arms would need rest from time to time. Every delay would bring Wallace and Shellinda closer to death as the disease ravaged their bodies. Earlier, Cassabrie had hastened their journey by a miracle, making the river reverse so they could ride a raft toward the north, but it seemed that any chance for another miracle floated away with her and Exodus.

As flowers brushed against their legs, even the spindly stems felt like a blocking force. Shellinda winced, now limping. Wallace's shoulders drooped further. If only they had the cart the flooding river had swept away, a horse to ride, or anything that might dissolve the distance to the Northlands castle and its lord, King Alaph, the white dragon. Perhaps he held the secret cure to all their ills.

✴ ✴ ✴ ✴ ✴ ✴

Marcelle clutched the spine protruding from Magnar's back as he beat his powerful wings, whipping the air with effortless strokes. Below, Mesolantrum's soldiers filed through the woods toward a clearing a couple of miles in the distance. Dressed in coats and thick trousers as they marched in balmy weather, their faces glistened with sweat. Although laboring now, they would soon find relief. The clearing hid the portal to Starlight, a passage to the frigid Northlands region in that world.

Marcelle reached under her tunic and pried a dragon's scale away from her chest, the scale Arxad had given her as a seal of their covenant. In moments, she would pass through the portal and lose the physical body her mind had conjured from the soil upon her spirit's arrival on Major Four, and this scale would fall and become lost.

She pushed the scale into a leather pouch hanging from Magnar's spine alongside her scabbard. Inside the pouch, the scale lay next to the stardrop's box. Both would be safe, at least for now.

Magnar bent his neck and drew his head close to Marcelle. "Two humans await our arrival in the clearing, but I do not think they have seen us yet. I hope to learn their identities and purpose before they learn of our presence, so I will fly lower and out of view for the time being."

"Understood." Marcelle clutched the spine more tightly. Magnar dropped to just above tree level and flew in a line that would take them to the right of the clearing. With the troops now out of sight, only greenery and an occasional glimpse of the ground passed underneath, though the soldiers' crunching footsteps and the commands of their leaders penetrated the foliage from time to time.

Soon, Magnar bent to the left and circled back. Shouts from below indicated that the soldiers had reached the clearing. Magnar extended his long neck closer to the trees, apparently listening. After a moment or two, he drew his head toward Marcelle again. "I have now identified the humans I noticed earlier—Edison Masters and Governor Orion. Captain Reed has arrived and is conversing with them."

"Interesting," Marcelle said. "I trust Edison, but Orion will do anything to keep the soldiers from going through the portal."

"I assume he fears the disease and its spread here in your world."

"And loss of influence." Marcelle leaned to the side to try to get a look at the clearing, but the rush of passing treetops and Magnar's wings blocked her view. "We need to make sure he stays on this side of the portal. If he goes alone to Starlight for even a moment, he could close our way back."

Magnar's ears flattened. "We must prevent that at all costs." He rose higher and brought the clearing into Marcelle's line of sight. Edison and Orion stood side by side. Orion glanced upward and locked stares with Marcelle, his tall form and hooked nose making him look like a long-legged hawk. He then said something to Edison and turned toward the portal.

"No!" Marcelle shouted. "Don't let him go! He'll close the portal!" She hunkered low. Magnar swooped toward the ground. Orion jumped through the invisible doorway and disappeared. Grabbing the air with his wings, Magnar leveled out and zoomed after him.

The moment they passed through the portal, sparks flew. A sizzle erupted. When everything cleared, Orion came into view, stooping between a boulder and a line of crystalline pegs in a landscape of snow and evergreens. Cassabrie stood nearby inside a shining sphere, shouting something indistinct.

Magnar thrust out his wings. With several powerful beats, he shot into the sky. Marcelle instinctively tightened her grip on his spine, but her fingers passed through it. Yet, the sudden shift in direction failed to sling her from the dragon's back. The wind in her face felt like a tingle rather than a gust. "Where are you going? We have to stop Orion!"

"Not with Cassabrie present." Magnar flew toward a castle in the distance, a familiar structure now, though clouds covered its higher levels. "She has the power to slay me and enough fury to do so without so much as the bat of an eye."

"You're flying away from a girl in a bubble? Are you a coward?"

"Your loose tongue will be the death of you," Magnar growled. "I am no coward. If I die, your human friends will die. If I live, I will fight to free them from slavery. If you wish for me to risk death at the hands of that wicked Starlighter while she is empowered within Exodus, then give the word and I will do battle with her. Otherwise, allow me to continue humiliating myself by carrying a thankless shrew to find help to solve her bodiless condition."

Marcelle drew her hands close to her eyes. As they moved, they flickered in and out of visibility. She had become a spirit, as expected, altering the effects of gravity and wind on her amorphous presence. "I apologize, Magnar. I spoke too hastily."

"As is your custom." Magnar drew his head close yet again, his brow bent but not menacingly so. "I accept your apology. I, too, am one to speak without thinking. We would both do well to bridle our tongues."

"I can't argue with that." She laid a palm on her cheek. "Can you see me?"

"Only fleeting glimpses when you move." He straightened his neck and looked toward the castle, raising his voice to be heard over the wind. "I will take you to Alaph's domain. There you may seek his counsel."

"Will you search for Adrian for me? If he's carrying my body, he might need help getting here."

"I will conduct a brief search, but after that I must travel southward to my domain."

"Did the soldiers make it through the portal? I didn't look back to see."

"Some made it. I cannot be sure how many. I saw Captain Reed, so at least they have a commander."

"That's good. And thank you for whatever you can do to search for Adrian." As a mixture of snow and rain pelted Magnar's scales,

Marcelle looked down. Patches of dirt marred the pristine whiteness of the once-frozen land. The river, now directly below, flowed freely. Perhaps this shift was part of the breaking of the curse Arxad had mentioned. He said that unpredictable consequences would result—perhaps a change in climate might be included.

Ahead, the cloud bank peeled back, revealing more of Alaph's ivory castle standing in the crook of a mountain. Although heavy mist shrouded the three turrets, the shield of vapor couldn't hide their reddish hue.

As Magnar drew closer, the doorway came into view, wide open and unguarded. A moment later, he flew inside and landed in the foyer, running a short distance before digging his claws into the wooden floor.

Marcelle slid off his side and floated down, like a leaf falling from a tree. Once she balanced herself, she ran to Magnar's front and faced him. "If you're unable to find Adrian, will you return to let me know?"

"If I find Adrian, I will bring him here. If I do not, my lack of return will inform you of my failure." Magnar angled his body and let the scabbard and pouch slide from his spine. The scabbard clattered to the floor, while the pouch struck with a thud. He then turned toward the door and took off in a run, beating his wings and lifting above the splintered wood. Within seconds, he had zoomed through the opening and into the sky.

Marcelle crouched next to the scabbard and tried to pick it up, but her hand passed through it.

"He is an impulsive dragon, isn't he?"

Marcelle straightened and spun toward the voice. A little girl stood a step away, semitransparent and shining. Although her misty body made her clothing hard to see, she appeared to be wearing wool-like trousers and tunic that fully covered her arms and legs. She ran her fingers through her short red hair and smiled.

"Who are you?" Marcelle asked. "You look familiar."

The girl bowed. "My name is Regina. And I know who you are, Miss Stafford." She grinned. "Alaph said for me to greet you."

"Thank you." Marcelle gave her a nod. "But please call me Marcelle."

"Very well, Marcelle." Regina giggled. "That rhymes."

"Yes, it does." Marcelle looked Regina over. Although semi-transparent and sparkling at the edges, she stayed visible even while motionless. "Are you a spirit of some kind?"

"You and I both are." Regina grasped Marcelle's wrist. "We can see and touch each other like we have bodies, but we don't have much weight at all. You'll get used to it in a few minutes."

"I think I already am getting used to it." Marcelle squinted at her. "So where have I seen you before?"

Regina's grin widened. "You sometimes opened your eyes while Adrian was carrying your body, and we were together in Frederick's little house in the wilderness."

"You were with Adrian?"

She nodded vigorously. "He's trying to bring your body here. I was with him and another girl named Shellinda and a boy named Wallace."

Marcelle looked out onto the snowy landscape, whispering, "So it's all true. It wasn't a dream."

"Uh-huh. All true. But I think Adrian's still pretty far away."

Marcelle refocused on Regina. "Then how did you get here?"

"Cassabrie brought me, because I died of the disease. She's inside Exodus. It's like a glowing ball, and she makes it fly. She couldn't bring Adrian and the others, though. Since they're alive, they're too heavy."

"I heard about the disease." Marcelle touched Regina's shoulder. "I'm sorry it took your life."

"Not me!" Regina ran a hand through her closely cropped hair again. "I was bald and blind, but now I can see. I like it a lot better this way."

"Well, I can certainly understand that." Marcelle turned in a slow circle. Cloud-obscured sunlight revealed the massive foyer's mysterious features. About a hundred feet above, ivory beams spanned a domed ceiling. Between the beams, leaded glass displayed a network of colorful spheres with a large reddish one at the center, likely a depiction of Solarus and its orbiting planets. A mural on the rear wall displayed a golden throne embedded with glittering gems representing dozens of colors. Below, deep scratches marred the planks, the landing zone for visiting dragons.

"Are you looking for something?" Regina asked.

"Not really. I'm just getting my bearings while I wait for Magnar to come back with Adrian—that is, if he finds him."

"Alaph said I can take you to his chambers. He's not back yet, but you can watch for Magnar and Adrian from a window." Regina reached her hands high. "It's way up there, so you can see all over the place. And when Alaph comes back, maybe he can tell you what he's seen while flying around."

"Good idea." Marcelle looked up. "Is there a stairwell around somewhere?"

Regina took Marcelle's hand. "This way."

As they walked, Marcelle caught a glimpse of her sword and pouch on the floor and stopped. "Oh, wait. I forgot about the things Magnar carried for me. I can't leave them here."

"I don't think you have any choice." Regina touched the scabbard with her toe, raising a slight sparkle. "I heard that we'll learn to move light things a little ways, but I haven't figured it out yet. I can't even move a dust bunny."

Marcelle tried to nudge the pouch with her own toe to no avail. "I suppose I couldn't stop someone from taking them even if I were here."

Regina shook her head. "Don't worry. I don't think any robbers are around."

"You're probably right. Let's go."

They walked into a side corridor, high and wide. Beams of light emanated from murals on each of the walls, following their progress. To the right, stars hovering over a dim river valley shone thin rays across their surreal bodies, like little eyes taking interest in the recent arrivals. To the left, Solarus hung over a castle very much like the one they now walked within, though the surrounding landscape of vivid green and flowered fields proved that the mural's castle had been built in a vastly different climate. Solarus cast a wide beam of reddish light that made the visitors' sparkling frames glow with a pink hue.

Regina swung their connected arms playfully. "A girl named Resolute showed me how to get to Alaph's room. There's a ladder nearby, but we won't need it." She stopped at a gap between the river-valley mural and a more abstract one of a white dragon painted on the wall several steps down the corridor. "This is where we climb."

Marcelle studied the smooth marble. "Climb?"

"You'll see." Regina laid a hand on the surface. A glow emanated from her skin, revealing tiny projections on the wall that ran toward the ceiling. She grabbed one at shoulder level, stepped on another next to her knee, and began climbing. "Follow me."

As Regina ascended, Marcelle stepped on a lower projection and followed. Normally these handholds would have been too small, but her unusually light weight made the seemingly impossible rather easy.

With every upward step, the surrounding light grew brighter. The paintings at each side ended, giving way to red plaster. The walls narrowed until the corridor became a vertical cylinder, likely one of the castle's turrets.

"Almost there," Regina called. "Just another minute."

Soon, Regina leaped forward and disappeared. "We're here!"

Marcelle climbed a few more steps until her head rose into an expansive cylindrical chamber with a high ceiling, marble floors, and curtained windows spaced at ten-foot intervals all around. Setting her hands on the floor, she vaulted to the new level, her body as light as the air itself.

Standing on an elliptical red pad at the center of the chamber, Regina looked up. "I think Alaph will be back soon."

Above, a gaping circular hole in the ceiling allowed a view of the dreary sky. Clouds raced overhead, but no precipitation fell into the chamber. "Is an invisible barrier keeping the snow from coming in?" Marcelle asked.

Regina nodded. "It's like the front doorway. People and dragons can pass through, and the bad weather stays out. But it's mostly rain now. The snow is melting."

"Because the curse has been broken?"

Regina shrugged. "I don't know. I haven't been here long enough to know much about what's going on."

"Well, it's like this …" Marcelle gazed at the raindrops sizzling on the invisible weather dome above. "Magnar wanted to break a curse that kept him bound to the southern region. Arxad said that doing so would unleash a new curse, but he didn't say what would happen." She set a foot on the pad. Since it covered nearly half the floor, it was plenty big enough for a dragon's resting place. "Maybe Alaph will be able to explain it."

"Maybe." Regina looked up again. "He's not much like the other dragons."

"And we're glad of that." Marcelle walked to a window with a southern exposure and pushed a red curtain panel to the side. In the distance, a dragon flew away, his form no more than a scarlet smudge in the midst of snow, rain, and fog. Magnar must have run into a delay somewhere, but now he would soon be out of sight. How long might it be before he returned with Adrian? Would he even keep his word to search for him?

She glided to another window and looked toward the portal. Fog hovered over the river, veiling everything except a vague sphere of light—Cassabrie inside Exodus. Magnar had mentioned that Taushin wanted to use Koren and Exodus to expose humans on Starlight to a deadly disease, but it seemed that much had developed since then. The disease had already been unleashed, and now Cassabrie rode within the sphere. This mysterious Starlighter, a mesmerizing redheaded beauty, had inhabited and charmed Adrian, foiled the authorities on Major Four, and intimidated the strongest of dragons. Not only that, she had put a certain cocky sword maiden in her place, and that took some doing. Cassabrie possessed an incredible amount of power.

The Starlighter's words came to mind like whispers on the wind. *That was part of my goal, to provide him with the experience of giving control to a powerful presence so that he would be ready for a greater test.*

What greater test? Marcelle had asked.

Cassabrie's answer echoed. *I don't know ... I don't know ... I don't know.*

The sound of a whipping breeze rushed in. Alaph settled on the floor mat, his wings beating as he balanced his sleek white body. His blue eyes locked on Marcelle, and his pointed ears perked straight up. "Welcome to my abode."

"Thank you." Marcelle bowed. "I apologize for bypassing further polite talk, but I—"

"You want to know the whereabouts of Adrian Masters." Alaph bobbed his head. "I have seen him from afar. He is on his way, though the burden he bears has slowed him considerably."

Marcelle's throat tightened. "My body, you mean."

"That is his physical burden. It makes his legs ache, his arms quiver, and his skin pour sweat, but his emotional burdens weigh down his heart, and such weight can make a man's feet drag as surely as if he were carrying the world itself on his shoulders."

She blinked at him. "What are his emotional burdens?"

"Concern for your well-being is paramount in his mind, but he also believes in the reality of the idiom I used." Alaph's tongue—narrow and blue with tiny red stripes—flicked out and back in. "Adrian is the kind of man who carries everyone's troubles. He is unable to rest, thinking that he must unlock every chain, mend every broken body, and dry every tear. Surely his shoulders are burdened by far more than they are called to bear, and his dogged determination to carry your body for untold miles is a profound symbol of his unbreakable resolve."

"But that's good, isn't it? It means he loves me. It means he cares about everyone."

"His love is unquestioned, but whether or not his method is good …" Alaph let out a frosty sigh. "I will leave that judgment for others."

Marcelle squinted. "Since you saw him, why didn't you help him? You could've carried him … or us, I guess … and he wouldn't still be trudging here with me in his arms."

"True. I could have relieved him of his physical burden." Alaph extended his neck, bringing his head within reach. "But that would have done nothing to relieve his heavier burdens, so his arrival will be delayed. His physical burden must remain in place for the time being."

Marcelle set a fist on her hip. "That doesn't make sense. The faster he gets here, the better off we'll all be."

"So you think." Alaph drew his head back. "There are other factors in play. Magnar is well equipped to bring Adrian here, and it is important that he do so for reasons that you need not know. If he fails to find Adrian or decides not to offer transport services, then Adrian will continue on his trek, and although the journey will take a great deal longer on foot, I doubt that anything can conquer his admirable resolve. Of course, he will have to cross my moat, but my servant Resolute is there to ferry him. Either way, he will come sooner or later."

"When he does, can you tell us how I'm supposed to reunite my body and spirit?"

"I know the method, but I lack the tools. When Arxad arrives, he will explain what you must do. In the meantime, it is essential that you learn a specific portion of Starlight's history." Alaph's ears rotated ninety degrees. "Regina will be your guide."

Regina pointed at herself. "Me? A guide? How?"

"You, my dear, were a Starlighter." Alaph gestured with a sweep of his ivory wing. "Take Marcelle to the white room I showed you earlier, and you will be able to tell the tale she needs to learn. Gather the story from the voices in the wind. Cassabrie and Exodus have already supplied them."

"Okay … I think." Regina slid her hand into Marcelle's. "The white room is on the main level, so we have to climb back down."

Marcelle returned Regina's grasp but kept her gaze on Alaph. "How will Adrian know where to find me?"

"When Adrian comes," Alaph said, "my servants will guide him to you. You will know when he is close. As your body draws nearer, you will be able to sense its presence, including its pain and discomfort."

"Wouldn't it make more sense for me to meet him before I go to the white room? My presence will encourage him. He'll know that my spirit is alive. Then we can listen to this tale together."

"You are a persistent one." Alaph rose to his haunches and stretched out his wings. "I have many difficult tasks ahead of me, so I must leave you for now. Feel free to do whatever you think you must to help your friend, but my advice is to wait patiently for Adrian while you witness the tale. Adrian will be better equipped if you do not intervene, and when he arrives, you will already be prepared to do what you must to reunite your body and spirit. This plan will save time so that when Arxad arrives, you will not delay his purpose."

"How will Arxad know where to—"

"Our conversation has gone on long enough." Alaph beat his wings and skittered across the room. When he reached the hole Marcelle and Regina had climbed through, he collapsed his wings and dropped into it, disappearing in an instant.

Regina stared at the hole with wide eyes. "He's gone!"

"I noticed." Marcelle crossed her arms over her chest. Wait patiently? Easy for him to say. He wasn't a bodiless spirit waiting for someone to show up with a missing body. And he didn't say she *couldn't* go and help Adrian. He had just given advice. It didn't make sense to stand around listening to a history lesson while Adrian toiled. After all, he carried her body. At least she could give him moral support.

Marcelle glided back to the south-facing window. Magnar was no longer in sight. The precipitation had changed to all rain, and the blanket of snow had receded to reveal muddy ground with splotches of ice.

No amount of bad weather could stop Adrian. He would find a way, dragon or no dragon. She could trust him. Without a doubt. When he arrived in the main entry room, he would find the scabbard and stardrop pouch and assume she was close by. He would figure everything out.

She turned toward Regina and extended her hand. "Show me the way to the white room."

✴ TWO ✴

ADRIAN dropped to his knees and laid Marcelle on the ground. As he panted, cold air swirled, and light drizzle added wetness to his sweat-drenched tunic. Wallace and Shellinda, their sleeves now covering their arms, plopped down beside him. Each sat with head tilted back and mouth open to catch the tiny drops.

"Take your time and get as much as you can," Adrian said. "We'll rest here awhile."

Wallace laid the sword on the ground. "Want me to carry her? You need a break."

Adrian rubbed an aching bicep. As he pressed a thumb deeply into the muscle, it loosened a bit, enough to ease the pain. "I'll be all right. Thanks anyway."

Wallace shrugged. "Okay, but you're going to collapse if you keep pushing yourself so hard. Then Shellinda and I will have to carry you both."

"You've got a point." Adrian sat fully on the wet ground, crossed his legs, and let his head droop low. Every muscle trembled, threatening to erupt in an avalanche of spasms. It seemed that his body shouted a warning. *Don't carry Marcelle another step or it might be your last.* Yet, maybe a few more minutes of rest would make a difference. Time would tell.

"What's that?" Shellinda asked.

Adrian lifted his head and let his gaze follow Shellinda's pointing finger toward the northern horizon. A dragon flew southward, dipping and rising as its wings beat against the misty air and battled the crosswinds.

"A male dragon." Wallace narrowed his single eye. "But I'm not sure who it is."

"Maybe you and Shellinda can get a ride." Adrian climbed to his feet, his calf muscles cramping. Once he straightened, he waved his arms over his head.

"He sees you," Wallace said. "He's coming this way."

"Good." Adrian rested his arms. "I could use a break."

Wallace rose to his feet. "Maybe not so good. It's Magnar."

"Magnar?" Adrian snatched the sword. "I'm in no shape to fight him. Let's hope he's in a good mood."

"Not likely." Wallace took a step closer to Adrian. "He might cook us all before you could swing the blade."

Magnar swept past about fifty feet overhead, turned a sharp one-eighty, and flew back in a dive.

Adrian reared with his sword, ready to strike. "No closer!"

"Have no fear," Magnar shouted. "I will not harm you." He landed in a slide across the wet grass and stopped just out of reach.

Adrian lowered his sword. "Why are you here?"

"To fulfill a promise." Magnar shuffled closer, extended his neck, and sniffed Marcelle. "She is still alive."

"We're trying to get her to the Northlands castle. It sounds crazy, but I'm supposed to reunite her body with her spirit. Even if it isn't true, maybe the white dragon—"

"It is true." Magnar lowered his body to the ground. "Get on my back, and I will carry her in my claws."

"In your claws?" Adrian shook his head. "I'll hold her while I'm on your back. Wallace and Shellinda will help me."

Magnar's eyes flashed. "The rapid change in climate in the Northlands is causing great shifts in the wind. It will take all your strength to hold yourself on. She will be safe in my claws."

Adrian let out a huff. "So says the dragon who enslaved and killed untold numbers of humans."

Magnar spat a ball of flames that rolled and sizzled on the grass. "Do not test my patience! I will not grovel for your trust. Either do as I say or continue on your burdensome path. I have more important things to do than argue with a stubborn human."

"Stubborn? How can you possibly—"

"You *are* stubborn. I have watched you long enough to recognize obstinate independence. You are fool enough to think that a few swords and chest-puffing courage will be sufficient to rescue your pathetic lot of fellow humans." Magnar's scaly brow bent. "Well, allow me to crush your hopes. You and your soldiers will rush southward in a delusional cloud of confidence, but you will all quickly learn that your bravado will burn like tinder grass along with your flaming bodies, if the disease fails to kill you first. Yours is a suicide mission. If a Creator really lives in the skies, only he can alter this disastrous course we are all following."

The dragon's words hit their mark, cutting with stinging accuracy. Adrian exhaled and relaxed his shoulders ... and his tone. "Then why are you following this course with us?"

"Because I am compelled to follow it." Magnar's voice also settled. "Though my body will likely perish in the attempt, this is the only way to save my wretched soul. For the first time in my life I am surrendering to the Creator's will and to whatever end he has in mind for me. If he does really exist, then perhaps I will find myself in better standing than what I deserve."

"Well stated." Adrian glanced at Wallace, then at Shellinda. Both stared at Magnar, their shoulders sagging. They were exhausted, ready to collapse. "Are you two brave enough to ride a dragon?"

"Not a problem," Wallace said.

Shellinda nodded. "I'm not afraid of anything …" She shivered. "Except spiders."

Adrian turned toward Magnar. "Okay, we'll go."

"Good, but the way my back spines are arranged, I have room for only two of you plus Marcelle in my claws. One of you will have to wait for me to return with your soldiers. They have arrived from your world, and they are on their way."

Wallace raised a hand. "I'll stay. I'm really the only choice. You have to be with Marcelle."

"No," Adrian said. "I can walk. Since I won't have to carry Marcelle, I'll be able to get there soon."

"Look …" Wallace lifted his shirt, revealing his rash-covered skin. "I can already feel the disease eating my insides. Shellinda's not really sick yet, so I'm the most contagious. It's better for you and everyone else if I'm not around." He lowered his shirt. "I'll get there eventually."

"The boy speaks wisdom," Magnar said, "and it would not be wise to leave an unconscious woman and two children at the castle without a human guardian. I will accept no other solution. You must go."

"Okay, okay." Adrian clasped Wallace's shoulder. "I appreciate your great courage. You are truly a warrior."

"Thanks, but …" He backed away from Adrian's hand. "You'd better get going. The more you stay around me, the more chance you'll catch the disease."

Adrian slid the sword into its scabbard and helped Shellinda climb onto Magnar's back. Shellinda sat in a gap between two spines, and Adrian settled in another gap behind her. "We're ready," Adrian said. "Be gentle with Marcelle."

"I will do what I can, but I make no promises." Magnar spread his wings. "Prepare for a rough ride."

Shellinda and Adrian each grabbed a spine. Magnar leaped into the air, his wings beating furiously. After flying in a low, tight circle, he dipped over Marcelle and zoomed upward.

Adrian looked back. Wallace stood where Marcelle once was, waving, apparently signaling that Magnar had collected her safely. Since the dragon's body wouldn't allow a view of his claws, Wallace's signal would have to be enough.

Sighing, Adrian focused on Shellinda and regripped her shirt. A gust blew Magnar hard to the side. Shellinda tossed with him, but Adrian kept her in place. His arms and fingers cramped. If the rest of the flight continued like this, it would be a rough one indeed.

After a few minutes, the air grew colder. Drizzle changed to a heavy shower, and some of the drops fell as slushy ice. Shellinda shivered hard, but it couldn't be helped. At least the effort of staying in place worked to keep their bodies active and maybe a little warmer.

Soon, the castle came into view. Below, at least half of the snow had melted away. The evergreens shook in the breeze as if shivering after casting off their cloaks of white. Adrian leaned to the side and tried to catch a glimpse of Marcelle, but she stayed out of view. How was she handling the cold and wetness? Might the brutal elements be enough to send her over the edge? Shock her system to the point of death?

Adrian straightened and blew out a long breath. The wind caught the vapor and sent stinging ice pellets into his face. The castle drew closer, along with its doorway—wide open and inviting.

A flash of white sped by in front. Magnar reared straight up, throwing Adrian and Shellinda off. They plunged toward the ground, but in another flash of white, something caught them and set them gently in a snowdrift.

Adrian grabbed Shellinda, leaped to his feet, and looked up. A white dragon flew alongside Magnar, and the two orbited at opposite sides of a tight circle, Marcelle still dangling from Magnar's claws.

"Alaph!" Adrian whispered, forcing his teeth not to chatter. "What's he doing?"

Shellinda just shivered in his grasp, saying nothing.

Alaph's booming voice rose above the thunder of beating wings. "Magnar, take Marcelle to the other side of the moat. When Adrian and the girl arrive there, transport them all to the castle's entry room."

"Why do you delay them?" Magnar shouted in return. "They are already in peril from exposure to these brutal elements."

"I need not tell you my purposes. Since you are the one who shattered the covenant, you should heed my wishes."

Magnar stared at Alaph through at least two revolutions, then snorted, broke out of the orbit, and flew toward the castle with Marcelle in his grasp. After traveling about three hundred feet, he set her down, landed next to her, and covered her with a wing.

Alaph slowed, and in a flurry of wings and wind, settled close to Adrian and Shellinda in the thinning snow, alighting as gently as a dove. He let out an icy cloud of breath and looked Adrian in the eye. "In order to gain access to the help you need in my castle, you must overcome a certain obstacle. A moat lies between us and your destination. At the moat, you will meet Resolute, one of my spirit servants, who will allow you to ride in her boat. If you cross the moat successfully, you will have free access to my abode."

Feeling Shellinda's continued shivers, Adrian scowled. "Why are you doing this?"

"It is a test, of sorts."

"A test?" Adrian resisted the urge to growl. "Marcelle and Shellinda are liable to freeze. They might have frostbite already."

"Then I suggest that you complete the test quickly, but do not react rashly to the dangers you face. Fear is your greatest enemy." Alaph vaulted into the air, and in a shower of scattering snow, he flew toward the castle.

After watching the dragon for a few seconds, Adrian shook his head. "I guess we have no choice." He wrapped Shellinda in his arms and trudged toward the castle, plowing through snow and mud. Soon, a wide swath of lumpy white came into view, as if thick clouds covered a river.

A shimmering girl stood at the edge, waving her arms. "Over here!"

"She must be Resolute." Still carrying Shellinda, Adrian churned that way. As he drew nearer, Resolute faded and disappeared. When he arrived at the spot, he set Shellinda down and crouched. "Where are you?"

"Right here." The girl reappeared only a step away, dipping into a curtsy. "I am Resolute. Alaph told me you're Adrian."

"Yes, yes. I'm Adrian." He took a deep breath to calm his voice. "We need to get across the moat. Alaph said you can take us."

"If all goes well." Holding a short paddle, she pointed at the white swath. "My boat is here at the edge." She walked onto the white swath and hovered there, gently rocking. "Come, please."

Adrian stepped to a point in front of Resolute and tested the surface. Something solid floated beneath his foot and above the whiteness. He lifted himself the rest of the way and balanced on the invisible craft. Although it swayed slightly, it felt as solid as any other boat.

Shellinda stood within reach, shivering violently. "Come." He extended a hand toward her. "It looks safe enough."

Her teeth clacked together. "If you're not sc-scared, then I'm n-not scared."

"Good girl." He hoisted her from the muddy shoreline to the boat.

"Sit here." Resolute's arm shimmered, her finger pointing. "We have plenty of room."

Adrian sat on an invisible bench, making the boat shift with every movement. Now facing Magnar and Marcelle on the opposite shore, he wrapped both arms around Shellinda and nodded. "We're ready."

At the front of the boat, Resolute set her feet wide apart and dipped the paddle into the frothy whiteness. When the boat began to drift forward, Adrian breathed a sigh. "I guess this won't be too hard of a test. Just trusting in an invisible reality, right? Sort of like faith in the Creator."

"Shhh. The moat monsters will hear you."

He whispered, "Moat monsters?"

Resolute nodded.

Adrian peeked over the side. The whiteness stayed calm and quiet, no sign of anything underneath. Still, it would be prudent to be ready.

As he slid his sword from his scabbard, the zing of steel on steel pierced the air, a much louder noise than the slow movement should have caused.

"Quiet!" Resolute hissed.

Something bumped the bottom of the boat. Adrian tensed his muscles. A clawed hand reached through the froth, grabbed the edge of the boat, and jerked downward.

Shellinda toppled over Adrian's lap. He grasped at her with his free hand, but his numbed fingers couldn't hold on. She fell over the side and disappeared.

Still clutching his sword, Adrian dove in after her. Only bare whiteness rushed by—no water, no sense of buoyancy at all. Air passed in and out of his nostrils without a problem, though it carried the stench of rotting flesh. Warmth coated his skin, and his body turned to an upright position. Pressure increased on the soles of his feet, as if he were now standing.

Seconds later, the whiteness faded to thick mist, like fog on the sea, though this "sea" appeared to be a forest at the edge of a clearing. A log cabin stood at the clearing's center. Smoke curled upward from the chimney, adding to the air's cloak. A light flickered from the cabin's single front window, probably a lantern. Maybe Shellinda went in there.

Adrian looked up. No sign of Resolute or the boat. When he fell in, it seemed that she was still safe, so maybe she made it to the other side. Since she had no physical form, that clawed creature probably couldn't hurt her anyway.

Fog shrouded the tops of the trees, likely the surface of the moat. What would it take to get up there? Climbing one of these trees? That seemed to be the only choice. In any case, finding Shellinda had to be the first step, and they would have to hurry to get to Marcelle before she froze to death.

Taking long strides, Adrian marched toward the cabin. He stepped up to the low porch and peered in the window. Near the back of the single-room dwelling, a girl sat in a claw-footed bathtub, long dark hair and youthful feminine profile giving away her gender and age. Thick vapor wafted upward from the tub, veiling the details, but it seemed that in this desolate place of mystery, Shellinda had found a friendly woman who offered her a hot bath.

Adrian blinked. But how did it happen so quickly? And what if the "friendly" cabin dweller wasn't a woman? Still clutching his sword, he sidestepped to the door, turned its knob, and pushed it open. He walked in on tiptoes, urging his feet to bend the wooden floorboards gently. After three steps, one of the boards squeaked.

Cringing, he stopped.

"Who's there?"

Adrian looked again at the girl in the tub. She didn't sound much like Shellinda, and the upwelling vapor kept her face hidden. Maybe the sudden change in temperature had altered her voice. "It's Adrian," he whispered, hoping for a volume she alone could hear.

"Adrian?" She turned her head, the mist still hiding her face. "I'm glad you're here. Come and see my new doll."

"Well, I would, but you're not dressed."

"Of course I'm not dressed, silly. I'm taking a bath."

Adrian cleared his throat. Since Shellinda had worked at the cattle camp where most of the children toiled naked or nearly naked, she had probably lost all sense of modesty. It would be okay to go to her. After all, she was prepubescent, probably barely eight years old. But why had she called him silly? She had never been so casual before.

He slid his sword back to its scabbard. "Okay. I'm coming."

He walked to the bathtub and stooped at the side. Now that he had pierced the veil of rising mist, her details came into focus. Indeed, a naked preadolescent girl sat clutching a little doll in a tub of steaming water, but her face wasn't Shellinda's.

He squinted at her. "Marcelle?"

"Of course." She splashed him with a handful of water. "Who did you think I was?"

"Well ... I ... uh."

"Never mind." She splashed him again. "Get in the tub with me. We can play swimming with the sharks like we used to." She grinned. "I mean before you decided you were too old to take a bath with me."

"Too old?" He touched his face and felt his scruffy beard. "How old do you think I am?"

"The same as me, silly goose. Six." She lifted her arms and flexed her muscles. "But my muscles are getting bigger. See?"

Marcelle's skinny biceps tightened. Then, after a few seconds, they swelled, growing in size and tone. Her face began to age, and her body blossomed, curves taking shape as she raced through adolescence.

Adrian jerked his head to the side and shot to his feet, spluttering, "I have to go!"

"Adrian! Wait!" Water splashed as if she had risen to her feet. "You really aren't too old."

"Yes, I am!" He half walked and half ran toward the door. "And so are you!"

"Adrian! Don't be scared! Please play with me!"

He ran out the door and slammed it, panting as he leaned against it. What kind of place was this? How could a moat hide such haunting magic in its depths and show only terrifying claws at its surface? The claws were real enough to nearly capsize a boat, but Marcelle's likeness had to be imaginary—maybe the manifestation of a Starlighter's tale. But why would such a tale be brought to life here?

Someone whimpered at the edge of the clearing. Adrian jumped off the porch and followed the sound, trying to see through the fog. After a few seconds, a huddled form came into view, a girl sitting against a tree with her arms clutching her legs tightly, her head tucked between her knees.

"Shellinda?" Adrian whispered. "Are you all right?"

"Spiders!" She batted at the air with her hands, her voice breaking through her sobs. "Spiders are everywhere!"

"There aren't any spiders here." He scooped her up and held her arms against her body to keep her from flailing. As she continued whimpering, he scanned the trees. Low limbs jutting from a tall oak gave evidence that it could be climbed without too much effort, though the fog hid the higher branches.

He shifted Shellinda to his back. "Hold tightly, now. I'll get you away from the spiders."

She wrapped her arms around his neck and her legs around his waist. "One, two, three, four …"

"What are you doing?" Adrian asked.

"C … counting heartbeats."

"Why?"

"I do it when I'm … when I'm scared. One of the boys in the camp taught … taught me." She took a deep breath and let it out slowly. "He said it makes what you're scared of go away by the time you get to ten."

"Let's hope it works." He jumped, grabbed the lowest limb, and swung his legs up to it. Shellinda tightened her grip, nearly choking him, but he couldn't alter her position now. He just had to keep climbing. He stood and spied the limb above. They had to hurry. Marcelle could be frozen already.

After several repetitions of jumping, grabbing, and climbing, they penetrated a thick cloud—completely white and impervious to vision. Adrian reached up for another tree limb, but felt nothing. Extending a hand, he slid along the limb inch by inch. The limb angled upward, taking him and Shellinda higher into the cloud. Soon, the limb widened and felt like solid ground. When they broke through the fog, the castle came into view, now only a few hundred feet away.

Nearby, Magnar sat on the shore next to a sign mounted on a wooden post that read DOCK HERE. "I had almost given you up for lost."

"Thank you for waiting." Adrian trudged out of the moat and set Shellinda down next to Magnar. "How's Marcelle?"

"She is alive." Magnar lifted his wing. Marcelle lay curled in the fold, shivering. "But perhaps not for long. I warmed her somewhat, but my breath can be damaging after a while."

"And Resolute?"

"I'm here, Adrian." The shining girl swayed to become visible. Standing near the docking sign, she smiled. "I'm glad you made it safely."

"Same to you." Adrian knelt at Marcelle's side and laid a hand on her throat. Her pulse raced erratically. "Let's get to the castle." He helped Shellinda climb onto Magnar's back. When they had settled, he patted Magnar's scales. "As fast as you can."

Magnar set Marcelle on the ground, stretched out his wings, and leaped into the air. After making a quick turn, he swooped low, apparently to pick up Marcelle, but his huge body blocked Adrian's view once again.

He looked back. The mud and snow were clear of any living forms, save for a shimmering girl waving near the edge of the moat. Shellinda shivered in his grasp, harder than ever. "Hold on, sweetheart. We'll be there soon."

The castle drew closer and closer, the front doorway open and enticing. After another minute, Magnar flew in, bent into a hairpin turn, nearly slinging Adrian and Shellinda off, and landed on the floor in a decelerating run.

The moment Magnar stopped, Adrian leaped off his back. When his feet hit the floor, he bent his knees, but his calf muscles knotted. He toppled to his side next to Marcelle, now on the floor where Magnar had deposited her. She shivered violently, and her teeth chattered.

With pain throttling his body, Adrian rolled and lay on top of her. "Shhh," he whispered. "I'll try to keep you warm."

Hugging herself, Shellinda slid down Magnar's side and staggered to Adrian. "Marcelle's soaked," she said. "We'll have to get her clothes off or she'll freeze to death." She knelt and began peeling Marcelle's saturated outer tunic away from the inner one, but they clung together and rode up her abdomen, exposing her waist and ribs.

"Wait." Adrian took a quick breath. After dealing with the vision of a nude Marcelle, did facing that prospect in reality have to come so soon? "I'm going to look for something to cover her with. Please wait until my back is turned before you undress her."

"Okay." She pulled Marcelle's tunic down. "Go ahead."

He struggled to his feet and hobbled toward a side corridor with marble floors and painted walls but no rugs or tapestries. "I don't see anything yet."

"Do not undress her," Magnar grunted. "I suppose it will be necessary to risk a greater dose of warm breath." He shifted toward Marcelle and blew a torrent of air over her and Shellinda. The stream began as fire at Magnar's nostrils and flamed out halfway to the target.

As Shellinda's hair whipped in the breeze, she smiled. "Oh! That feels so good!"

Adrian limped back to them and crouched in the flow. The air, hot and dry, penetrated his wet clothes and stung his skin, but the slight pain was worth it, like enduring the bite of spicy food for the sake of the flavor.

After Adrian raised Marcelle to a sitting position, Shellinda flapped Marcelle's clothes. Every minute or so, Magnar rested while they switched positions to expose other body parts to the heat. Soon, all three humans were warm and dry. Even Adrian's muscles had loosened in the hot massage.

Adrian laid Marcelle on her back, rose, and bowed toward Magnar. "I am grateful for your kindness. I spoke harshly about you earlier, and I apologize."

"Apology accepted." Magnar bowed his head in return. "Though the harshness was deserved."

Adrian straightened his tunic and belt, hoping to conceal his surprise at the dragon's humility. "Does that mean you've had a change of heart about the slaves?"

"I will speak no more on this topic." Magnar shuffled toward the doorway. "Because of your critical condition, I assume you took no notice of the items I deposited here for Marcelle's spirit." Using a wing, he pointed at a scabbard and pouch near the doorway. "Her spirit is gone now, and in her nonphysical state, she was likely unable to move them."

"Where did she go?" Adrian asked.

"I do not know." Magnar unfurled his wings. "When I departed, she was still here, but since she is such an impulsive human, it is futile to guess her reason for leaving."

"Impulsive is accurate, but her warrior instincts would tell her to stay close to a clue that might reveal her whereabouts." Adrian picked up the scabbard and attached it to his belt opposite his own scabbard. "She's probably around here somewhere."

"I leave that mystery for you to solve. I must depart immediately." Magnar beat his wings and flew out the doorway.

As the breeze from his departure swept by, Shellinda looked outside. "I wonder why he left in such a hurry."

"He seemed nervous about something." Adrian scooped up the pouch.

Shellinda scooted closer. "What's that?"

"A pouch a soldier stores valuables in—money, a locket, a key—anything he wants to keep safe and dry." He unfastened the drawstring and withdrew a small metal box. Cupping it with one hand, he opened the lid. A dazzling sphere of light lay within.

"That looks like a stardrop," Shellinda said. "Could Marcelle have gotten it from Cassabrie?"

"Maybe." Adrian closed the lid and returned the box to the pouch. "Jason used one to heal my father. If I can find the healing trees, maybe it will help Marcelle."

"But won't you need her spirit to revive her?"

"Not long ago, I thought it was a crazy theory that her spirit was wandering around somewhere." Adrian tightened the drawstring. "But I trust Magnar's word." As he attached the pouch to his belt, he laughed under his breath. "An hour ago trusting Magnar would've sounded pretty crazy, too."

"It is not crazy, Adrian Masters."

The new voice came from outside. A radiant sphere hovered over the castle's stairway, a redheaded young woman floating inside. Wearing a royal-blue cloak, she smiled, though pain streaked her countenance.

Adrian breathed her name. "Cassabrie."

She offered a half bow. "I cannot stay long, so I will say quickly what I have to say or else emotions will interfere." Her smile trembling, she gestured toward a grassy area behind her. "I left a gift for each of you on a bench in the front courtyard, though Marcelle's gift must be delayed until she is reunited with her spirit. It might appear to be somewhat morbid, but it is all I have to give. With the limited assets at my disposal, it is the fullest expression of my heart that I could manifest. I hope you understand the depth of its meaning."

"If I don't understand, then you can explain it to me." He took a step toward the doorway, but she held up her hand.

"No, Adrian."

He halted. "No?"

"I have to leave now, and for reasons I care not to explain, we must say our good-byes."

"Will I ever see you again?"

"I don't know, Adrian." Tears streaming, she shook her head. "I just don't know. Maybe when Exodus rises, you will get a glimpse of me, but until your own rising from our temporal existence, this could be our final farewell." She drifted slowly away, her voice cracking. "Good-bye, Adrian Masters. I love you. I love you with all my heart."

"Cassabrie!" Adrian ran outside and stopped at the top of the stairs. As she floated backwards over the courtyard, he laid a hand over his chest at the spot she had entered his body. The memory of her warm presence flowed—peaceful, affectionate, and feminine. "I love you, too, Cassabrie. You'll always be in my heart."

She raised her fingers to her lips and kissed them. Then, she turned within Exodus and accelerated into the snowy background.

Adrian tromped down the stairs, sweeping slush with his boots. Rain and sleet pelted his head, but collecting Cassabrie's gift shouldn't take long. He would stay dry enough.

Shellinda followed close behind. "Is Cassabrie going to die?"

Adrian swallowed to keep his voice from shaking. "She made it sound that way." He reached the bottom of the four marble steps and walked into a semicircular wedge of lush grass, surrounded on three sides by latticework and defoliated vines. On the unguarded side, a bench faced a rectangular garden plot—nothing but a bed of mud bordered by calf-high stones.

A metal box, bent and dented, sat atop the bench. A pulsing glow poured from gaps at the top seams. Adrian picked it up and opened the lid. Inside, three stardrops rolled around, bumping into each other and raising tiny sparks with each collision. As usual, the stardrops radiated brilliant light, but something new had been added—red lines running along the stardrops' outer membranes like narrow threads. The blend raised an image of Alaph and the thin red vessels that coursed across his ivory scales. Then, a new image took over—Cassabrie as she pricked her finger with the tip of his sword and instructed him to mix her blood with the stardrop crystals.

Shellinda peered into the box. "What are the red lines?"

"Blood."

"Cassabrie's?"

He nodded. "She's given us a cure for the disease."

"Why three?"

"One for you, one for Marcelle, and one for me. She must know Wallace didn't come here with us." He touched the top of a stardrop—hot and sizzling. "She is giving us life … life in her blood." His voice cracked in spite of his efforts to quell his emotions. "It's all she has to give."

"So do we swallow it, like Regina did?"

"Yes, you and I will. Like Cassabrie said, Marcelle will have to wait." He pinched one and transferred it to his palm, letting it roll to keep it from burning too quickly. "Are you ready? I'm sure it will hurt a lot."

Shellinda firmed her jaw. "I'll be brave."

"Good girl." He tossed the stardrop to the back of his throat and swallowed. As it traveled down, it burned, far more than the hottest of peppers.

Shellinda picked up a stardrop from the box and copied Adrian's motions. When she swallowed, her face turned scarlet. She reached down and grabbed a handful of snow. "Is it all right to cool it down?"

"We'd better not." He closed the box and slid it into his pocket. "I think it has to be hot to kill the disease."

She gasped, taking quick, shallow breaths. "So … so what do we do now?"

Adrian looked at the entry. "We'll take Marcelle and try to find the healing trees. Maybe we'll bump into her spirit along the way."

"Adrian!" Shellinda laid a hand over her stomach. "It's burning!"

He lifted the hem of her tunic, exposing her lower abdomen. The rash looked like it had caught fire—red and glowing. Since she had contracted the disease some time ago, her symptoms had advanced beyond his own.

Adrian scooped her into his arms and carried her up the stairs and into the entry room. He sat next to Marcelle's still-motionless body and pulled Shellinda into a tight embrace. Shaking hard, she wrapped her arms around his neck. "Oh, Adrian! It hurts! It hurts so bad!"

As his own stomach began to burn, Adrian whispered into her ear. "You're a brave girl, Shellinda. You survived that awful cattle camp. You escaped the dragons and their whips. You can survive this. Just pretend the disease is a dragon. It's burning. It's dying. And when the flames go away, you'll be free."

"Ah … ah … augh!" She pressed her sweaty cheek against his. "Burn, you wicked dragon! Burn!"

Adrian patted her back, hot and damp. Inside, flames scorched his own gut, but he dared not cry out. He just continued whispering into her ear. "Cassabrie's blood and the Creator's fire will destroy that dragon. It will be gone forever."

Adrian and Shellinda rocked back and forth. The infernos blazed within. Heat coursed through their bodies—scorching, purging. Their insides boiled. Their skin roasted.

As Shellinda's wet body squirmed in Adrian's arms, he held her tightly. Her skinny frame jerked in violent spasms. He whispered, "Creator, carry us through this fire without being consumed. You have brought us this far for a reason, and we trust that this furnace will burn only the poison within. Let it be a purifier and not a destroyer."

Shellinda moaned. Adrian let out a quiet shushing sound. "Soon … soon the suffering will be over. We have to trust. Always trust. The Creator will never forsake us."

He looked at Marcelle's body—motionless, staring, empty. He closed his eyes and whispered again, this time too low for Shellinda to hear. "Help me to believe my own prayer."

✳ THREE ✳

MARCELLE walked through a set of white double doors and into a room of pure white—floor, ceiling, and all four walls. Regina followed, her form casting a sparkling glow. As if swept by the two spirits' entry, the doors closed behind them. The moment the latch clicked, whiteness covered the knob and every gap between the door and the surrounding wall.

With only blinding white all around, the distance to every wall became vague. Was the closest surface within reach or was it miles away? It seemed impossible to tell.

Blinking at the brightness, Marcelle whispered, "What now?" The stillness of the room swallowed her voice.

"I'm supposed to tell a tale." Regina's soft reply swirled like a sonic dust devil, repeating "tell a tale … tell a tale … tell a tale."

Marcelle waited for the echoes to fade. "What's the tale about?"

Regina shrugged. "I suppose I'll listen to the voices in the wind, like Alaph said, and see what happens." Once more the final few words of each phrase reverberated.

Waiting again, Marcelle gazed at the little girl. Apparently her voice carried a unique quality here. "That's fine. The sooner we start, the sooner I can look for Adrian."

Now more visible than before, Regina angled her head this way and that. After a few seconds, her brow dipped. Tears sparkled in her eyes. She spread her arms and spoke in a hushed tone. "Back in the days when Starlight was known as Iris, when men ruled over dragons, two scoundrels, Hiram and Bodnar, cruelly mistreated their dragon slaves. They also acted unjustly toward their fellow humans, charging exorbitant rent to widows and the elderly, knowing that such tenants lacked the ability to mount a challenge in courts of law."

Marcelle drank in the thrumming. Regina's tale sounded more like a song than spoken words. The room's whiteness melted away. As if painted by a thousand brushes, a village setting took shape, surrounding Marcelle and Regina with a smooth street and bordering walkways where people strolled past various shops. Unlike in Mesolantrum's open-air markets, these shops boasted glass windows, hinged doors, and hanging signs with perfect lettering.

Cast by the light of a setting Solarus, a shadow glided across Marcelle's body. Above and to the right, a dragon flew in a low circle, carrying two men, one with a spear in his grip. Seconds later, the dragon landed in front of a nearby shop. The breeze from the wings buffeted Marcelle, making her hair sway.

"How odd," Marcelle whispered. "I can actually feel the tale."

"Shhh." Regina waved an arm. "Let's see where they're going."

As Marcelle and Regina walked closer to the shop, the dragon lowered its head to the ground, creating a dismounting stairway. The two men tromped down the neck, apparently not caring about their mount's grunts. When they reached the bottom, the man with the spear entered the shop while the other stood next to the dragon, holding a small black box.

"The man entering the shop is Hiram," Regina said, pointing, "and the one staying outside is Bodnar. They call that black object a control box, and you will learn more about it soon."

When Marcelle and Regina drew close, yellowish light from above shone on Bodnar. A glowing sphere descended and hovered about fifty feet overhead.

Bodnar looked up at the sphere, shielding his eyes with a hand as he called out, "What bedevilment are you bringing us today?"

Regina spread out her arms. "Heed my words, Bodnar." Although her lips moved, the voice flowed from the sphere, stronger and more mature than Regina's. "If you conspire with Hiram to try to destroy me, you will suffer grave consequences. You will become a wandering soul, always dry within and desperate for sustenance."

"I can't understand a word you're saying." Bodnar touched a metal collar around the dragon's neck. "Lowbred, tell that demon to go away."

"As you wish." Lowbred raised his head and looked up at the hovering sphere. "Starlighter, perhaps it would be best for you to go to a place of safety, far away from those who wish you harm. I fear that your prophecies will avail no one in this world of deafened ears."

"Deafened ears!" Bodnar pressed a button on the box. The dragon squealed, thrashing his neck and clawing at the collar.

"I will go for now, Lowbred," Regina said. "For your sake."

As the sphere floated away, Hiram ran out, carrying his spear, now with a paper-covered tube attached to the shaft. "What did he do now?"

"Another insult." Bodnar released the button. "He's the most insubordinate dragon I've ever seen."

Lowbred's neck fell limp, and his head struck the ground with a thud. His wheezing breaths provided the only evidence of life.

"Stupid dragon." Bodnar kicked Lowbred's leg.

"He'd better recover soon. I'll need him to chase down that cursed star." Hiram showed Bodnar the spear. "It's ready to go."

"Perfect." Bodnar touched the spear's tip. "Maybe we'll finally get rid of that scourge."

Regina pointed at the horizon. As she lowered her arm, Solarus set with the motion. The shoppers faded away. A few streetlamps glowed, though not with flames or even extane. Glass orbs within the lamp enclosures seemed to emanate energy of their own, like white glow sticks that never waned.

Hiram sat on Lowbred's back, carrying the spear in one hand and the control box in the other, while Bodnar looked on from the street. The sphere they called Starlight hovered hundreds of feet in the air like a small moon floating across the night sky.

Lowbred wagged his neck back and forth, as if trying to swat flies. A grimace bent his scaly face, and snorts of smoke puffed from his nostrils.

"This box," Hiram said, showing it to Bodnar, "will detonate the explosive tube attached to the spear. I just have to get close enough to drive the spear through. Too far, and the point might not penetrate, and I have to stay close for the radio signal to get to the explosive."

"What if Lowbred gives you trouble?"

"He won't. I have the collar set for a constant low-grade jolt. He knows he'll get no relief until this is over."

Regina scrambled up the dragon's tail. "Join me! Hurry!"

Marcelle followed in a trot, her bodiless form and weight apparently unnoticed by Lowbred or the two humans. After dodging Lowbred's protruding back spines, Regina sat behind Hiram, leaving a few feet of space between them, while Marcelle chose a gap behind Regina.

"You'd better get going." Bodnar swatted Lowbred's flank. "Go fetch that star!"

The dragon beat his wings and vaulted into the air toward the glowing sphere. Marcelle instinctively clutched the spine in front of her, but the bouncing ride caused only a little turbulence.

As they drew closer to the star, Hiram reared back with the spear. A girl hovered in the sphere's center. Redheaded and wearing a blue cloak, she gazed quietly at the approaching menace, her hands folded and her face serene. Although she resembled Cassabrie in some ways, she was clearly a different girl.

Now within twenty feet, Hiram threw the spear, grunting with the effort. The point pierced the glowing membrane, passed into the center, and impaled the girl in the side. White vapor spewed from the surface wound and blasted Hiram in the face. As he batted at his eyes, the star flew away like a deflating balloon.

Hiram fumbled with the control box, then pointed it at the star and pressed the button again and again, but nothing happened. The star and the wounded girl zoomed toward the northern horizon, growing smaller and dimmer every second.

Cursing, Hiram kicked Lowbred with his heels. "Land, you fool!"

The dragon angled downward. Seconds later, he fanned out his wings and skittered along the ground toward Bodnar. The moment Lowbred stopped, Hiram slid off and threw the control box, smashing it. "Stupid detonator didn't work."

"I noticed. The star shot out of range in a hurry." Bodnar nudged a fragment with his shoe. "At least you got rid of it. When the news spreads, you'll be a hero."

"I stabbed her in the side." Hiram shoved a hand into his pocket and scowled at the ground. "I just wish I could have blown her to pieces—gotten rid of her for good."

"Don't worry. She'll bleed to death. If not, she'll be scared to come back."

Snorting sparks, Lowbred again wagged his head and moaned.

Regina tugged on Marcelle's sleeve. "Let's get down. Quickly."

They rose and hustled across the dragon's back and tail, then walked close to the two men.

"Lowbred's still getting pulses." Bodnar withdrew another control box from his pocket. "Want me to shut it down?"

Hiram shook his head and whispered, "Let's dispatch him here and let Campbell pick up his carcass. I'm tired of dealing with this stupid dragon."

"Can't say I blame you." Bodnar pointed the box at Lowbred and slid his thumb over a red button. "Better stand back. He's liable to thrash."

As they backpedaled, four white dragons flew down and surrounded Lowbred and the two men. One swept its tail and slapped the box from Bodnar's hand. "Fool! How dare you try to appease your anger by punishing an innocent dragon!" The white dragon's voice carried a feminine quality, though rough and menacing. "Not only that, you have wounded the star of this world, the giver of light and truth. You must die for your incalculable stupidity!"

Another white dragon clawed through Lowbred's collar, severing it. Lowbred beat his wings and flew into the air. Within seconds, he faded into the dark sky, though the sound of his flapping wings gave evidence that he circled somewhere overhead.

Hiram and Bodnar stood stiffly. The first white dragon reared her head as if ready to blast them with her breath, but the second blocked her with a wing.

"That's Alaph," Marcelle whispered.

Regina nodded but said nothing.

"One moment, Beth," Alaph said. "If we let these two humans live, we might be able to use them in the future."

She swung her head toward him, squinting. "How so?"

"As the Starlighter prophesied, by putting them in a wretched state from which they would be desperate to escape. We will provide goals they must perform to gain freedom. Their performance will prove their worthiness to avoid the ultimate penalty."

"Understood." Beth turned toward a third white dragon. "Do you have insight, Gamal? Are these two capable of heartfelt penance?"

Gamal extended his neck and sniffed each man in turn. As his flashing blue eyes passed in front of their faces, the men shivered, but their feet stayed locked in place. "They are cruel, but they are also quite ignorant. It would take a severe penalty and an ingenious one to squeeze the evil from their hearts and at the same time infuse their minds with knowledge that will lead to genuine repentance."

"Thank you." Beth turned to the fourth white dragon. "Dalath, are you able to suggest such a penalty?"

"I do have a suggestion, but it will take years to accomplish." Dalath, smaller than Alaph and Gamal and speaking with a tenor similar to Beth's, looked toward the northern horizon. "The star has released a gas that carries a deadly disease. Although dragons are immune, it will spread among the humans until they are all dead. These two have already been infected, so they will die within days. In order to preserve them for a long-term penalty, we must alter their constitutions."

"I see," Beth said. "A separation from their bodies."

"Yes. We can make them wandering souls who must consume other souls in order to survive. They will be able to withdraw the soul from a wicked man and feed themselves with its energy. Since this will be an act of obedience, they will not plunge further into the depths of darkness, for obedience brings light and life. If they have a glimmer of light now, perhaps it will be fed, and they will eventually be able to see themselves as they are—wretched, twisted beasts who have destroyed this world's guiding star. If they do not snuff that glimmer and instead allow it to thrive, they will have the opportunity to reach out and commit a sacrificial act, and such an act could save their souls. Yet, if they turn from this path, they will become like corrupted trees that can bear no fruit. Their branches and roots will rot and disintegrate into dust."

Gamal bobbed his head. "I do detect a glimmer in these ignorant fools. Such a sacrificial act is possible."

"This punishment satisfies Justice." Beth turned toward Alaph. "Does it satisfy Mercy?"

"It does." Alaph cast a pair of blue eyebeams on Hiram and Bodnar. "I will make sure they have the opportunity to choose a sufficient act of sacrifice."

"Then we are in agreement." Beth nodded at Gamal. "Do what is necessary."

"Very well." Gamal's body began to glow, as if he had become a draconic star. He breathed a shower of sparkling ice over Hiram and Bodnar, coating them from head to toe.

The two men stood like statues, though their icy shells pulsed with radiance. After several seconds, Gamal swatted across them with his tail, shattering them. When the crystals dropped to the ground, two misty bodies stood erect, recognizable as humans, but lacking facial details. They raised their hands and looked at their flexing fingers. With each movement, the mist swirled within their nebulous bodies.

Alaph shuffled closer to them. "I will formulate a plan to save your race from the disease, and you must help me carry out that plan."

Their misty heads nodded.

Alaph nodded in return. "Get on my back, and I will take you to our domain where you will abide until the disease has finished its course. Then another dragon will arise who will carry you to a world that is free of the disease. There, after the human race is established, you will begin withdrawing souls from evil men and devouring them, thereby ridding the new world of wickedness while at the same time preserving you for a sacrificial act that I will prepare."

Gamal blinked at Alaph. "How do you know about this dragon who will arise?"

"I have already met a young dragon named Arxad. I see in him an uncommon nobility, and under my guidance, he will learn mercy toward both dragons and humans."

Regina waved an arm. Sparkles emanated from her fingers and scattered across the village landscape. Like hot embers, they burned the scene away in all directions, revealing a dim cavern. Marcelle and Regina now stood next to a kneeling man as he placed a crystalline peg into a hole.

Regina touched his shoulder. "This is Uriel Blackstone, the man who created the locks that once protected the portal to Starlight. He is the first courageous man to challenge the dragons after they began enslaving humans a century ago."

Light flashed across a thin membrane from wall to wall. When it cleared, a river appeared at the back of the cavern, flowing left to right.

From the edge of the river, the misty forms of Hiram and Bodnar glided toward Uriel. When they stopped at the portal, Hiram spoke, his voice sounding like a hissing snake. "Two villagers came to the field of flowers, but before they could go any farther, we confronted them. I took the soul of one, but the other escaped, crying out that a snatcher had consumed his fellow explorer."

"I see." Uriel stroked his chin. "It seems that you now have a label, but it is all well and good. The more frightened people are to come to the portal area, the better."

"We will continue to protect the portal, but what should we do if people come who do not have evil intent? We are not able to steal such souls."

"Then frighten them. Discourage them. Even if you cannot take their souls, your presence will scare them to the point of distraction." Uriel raised a finger. "Yet, I might want you to make an exception if I happen to wish to send an emissary in my place."

Hiram's mist darkened. "If a man comes in your name, how can we know for certain that you have sent him?"

"A secret phrase, perhaps." Uriel began pacing in a short circuit. "Something easy to remember. A verse of poetry should work, if I can just think of one."

Marcelle stepped closer to Hiram and Bodnar. The legend of snatchers in the Forbidden Zone had long been told by the elder folks in Mesolantrum enough times that many believed in their existence. Now it was clear that they were no superstition.

Uriel stopped and snapped his fingers. "I know one from an old nursery rhyme about a herd of goats that I read to my son, Tibalt, many times—not that the source matters to you." He closed his eyes as if pulling an archive from his memory. "Another question I will ask, and you'll submit to do this task."

The two snatchers repeated the phrase in concert. "It is short," Bodnar said, "perhaps too easy for others to memorize."

"I have a longer one I will teach you at another time, but this one should suffice for now."

Hiram nodded. "Will this be your last visit to Starlight?"

"I believe so. All is ready here for an army to invade, so I need only to bring a detachment to prove that humans are enslaved. I'm sure we will be able to mount a formidable attack force." Uriel knelt again and wrapped his hand around the peg. "Now please keep the portal open while I hide the peg for the final time. I will be quick about it."

"No." The swirl within Hiram's head accelerated. "Bring the peg with you. The portal will stay open long enough for you to jump through."

"But then the slaves won't be able to open it again," Uriel said. "I have told them where to find the peg. If they are able to break free from their bonds, they will know where to look for it. And

I can't leave the portal open, because Magnar hopes to come to Major Four to kidnap more humans."

"That is all well and good for you," Hiram said, "but holding the portal open drains our energy to the point of disintegration. Not only is the pain excruciating, but we risk destruction. It would be better to take the peg and hope your soldiers will be able to rescue the slaves."

Uriel's face reddened. "If the slaves can escape without a battle, there will be no need for soldiers, bloodshed, or loss of life."

"Yet you are willing to risk our existence."

Uriel stabbed a finger toward Hiram. "This is your penance. If you wish to be restored, you must be willing to sacrifice. It's for your own good."

The snatchers looked at each other for a moment before refocusing on Uriel. "Very well, but we won't keep it open for long."

Uriel nodded. "I understand. I will hurry."

The snatchers stepped into the portal plane. Miniature lightning bolts shot out from their bodies, covering the boundary between the two worlds from one side wall to the other.

Uriel jerked the peg out of its hole, ran up a flight of stairs, and disappeared from view.

The portal flickered and flashed. The lightning bolts weakened. Bodnar groaned. "This had better be the last time, but I'm afraid that when the soldiers come, they will ask us to do this hundreds of times. Our suffering will never stop."

"This will be the last time," Hiram said, his voice strained. "I know a way to keep the portal from opening on this side. It is a temporary measure, but it should work long enough to embarrass and demoralize him when he tries to open it for a military commander."

The bolts dimmed further. "What is this measure?"

"Just as the life energy we have consumed keeps this portal open, we can reverse it to keep it closed. We can enter the glass viewer and hide there. He will never know that we disrupted the energy."

"But what about our penance? Will we be disqualified if the slaves never escape?"

"Let the slaves work out their own escape. If they will summon the courage to break free from the dragons, the peg will be there for the taking. If they cannot, they are not virtuous enough to be rescued. In the meantime, we will continue working with Uriel to guard the portal from intruders. That will be our penance."

"Hold on! I'm coming!" Uriel clattered down the stairs and leaped through the portal. As the snatchers floated backwards, their bolts of lightning ceased, and they disappeared along with Uriel and the river. Now only a blank wall stood at the rear of the chamber.

Regina pointed at the wall. "Since that time, slaves searching for pheterone have chiseled out three tunnels, and they are still there to this day."

Marcelle reached through the portal plane but felt nothing. "Can we see where Uriel went and how the snatchers ruined his plans?"

Regina shook her head. "The tales I hear come from Exodus, the very star Hiram punctured. I learned that a Starlighter can see some tales in the other world through a dark glass egg in the portal, but only those tales that are happening in the present time. Since the tale you want to hear happened on Darksphere long ago, neither Exodus nor Cassabrie can tell it."

"Are Hiram and Bodnar still in my world?" Marcelle asked.

"Let's see if I can find out." Regina waved both arms. Whiteness blended in with the dark chamber walls until the cavern vanished, replaced by Alaph's white room. Setting a finger to her lips, she looked up as if listening. After a few seconds, she shrugged. "There are no answers in the air. Exodus probably doesn't see them, but that doesn't mean they aren't there."

"I think I understand." A twinge of pain pinched Marcelle's side, as if someone had pricked her with a needle. She massaged the point. "That's strange."

"What is it?"

"Pain."

"Is it bad?"

Marcelle nodded. "Pretty bad."

Regina touched the spot. "Alaph said you'd feel when Adrian got closer with your body."

"That must be it." Marcelle crouched, hoping to minimize the pain. "He also said your tale was important for me to see, but I haven't figured out why. I hoped I would get an idea of how to reunite with my body."

"Maybe if we tell Adrian what we saw, he'll be able to figure it out." Regina smiled. "He's very smart."

"Yes, I know." Marcelle tried to force a smile, but the pain spiked. A burning sensation blended with the stabs, as if she were again chained to the crystalline stake.

Images of the Reflections Crystal flashed, like pulsing photographs that grew closer and closer with each throb. Marcelle clutched her chest. Flames burned within—scalding, scorching, consuming. Had her heart caught on fire? How could that be? She didn't have a heart.

She lifted a trembling hand, gasping as she spoke. "Find Adrian! … Keep him away!"

Regina knelt at her side. "I'll take you to Alaph's chambers and bring Adrian here. I'll show him the tale."

"Good. Good." Marcelle rolled and curled into a ball. Everything burned, as if she had become a torch. Darkness flooded her vision—blackness stained with red. Somehow her body lifted into the air.

Regina's voice returned, thin and echoing. "It's a good thing you're a spirit. It won't be too hard carrying you up that wall."

Within the darkness, red blotches bounced, like globules of blood floating in an inkwell that had been jostled by a dipping pen. Every second, the fire burned hotter. After a minute or so, voices sounded—worried, frightened voices without distinct words. Her own voice penetrated her mind. "Burning … burning." Ink and blood intermixed, turning everything black. Then, her mind slid into silence … darkness … nothingness.

✸ FOUR ✸

"ADRIAN!" Shellinda pointed at a doorway well down the corridor. "Look in here!"

Carrying Marcelle in his arms, Adrian altered from a slow shuffle to a brisk march. Since every muscle again ached, allowing Shellinda to run ahead and scout the various rooms and passages had worked well. Now that the disease had been purged from their bodies, they both felt lighter and more energetic, but Marcelle's body, toned and strong, still dragged him down. "What's in there?"

"Trees," she said. "They look pretty bad, though, like they're dying."

"That must be the place." Summoning his energy reserves, Adrian broke into a jog. When he reached the doorway, he pressed his foot lightly on the floor inside, a tangled network of branches. As he applied more weight, the flooring cracked and broke away, sending wood fragments into a void below. He drew his foot back. "It'll never support me, much less while I'm carrying Marcelle."

Shellinda copied Adrian's test with her own foot. When she pressed down, the branches bent and cracked, but they didn't give way. She took another careful step and looked at Adrian. "Maybe I could drag her where she needs to go."

A girl's voice echoed in a corridor to the right. "Uh-oh!"

About thirty paces away, one of Alaph's ghostly servants walked slowly toward them, shimmering with each step, her arms outstretched. She stopped and called out, "Adrian! It's me, Regina! I'm carrying Marcelle's spirit!"

Adrian's muscles tensed. "You are?" He stepped toward Regina, but she backed away.

"No! When her body and spirit are close to each other, she feels terrible pain."

Marcelle's body grew suddenly warmer. She squirmed. Her mouth fell open. She heaved deep, hot breaths, whispering, "Burning ... burning."

Adrian looked into the tree room and spotted the closest healing bed. "Regina, take her in there and put her on that bed!" He hiked Marcelle's body higher and jogged away from the door. When he had traveled about fifty paces, he stopped and spun back.

Regina, her arms still outstretched, walked into the healing room. Although her movements made her easy to see, Marcelle's immobile spirit stayed invisible.

Shellinda held to the doorjamb and leaned into the tree room. "She's putting her on the bed now, Adrian. I saw her move. It's definitely Marcelle."

Adrian pulled Marcelle's body close and nuzzled her cheek—hot and sweaty. "I don't know if you can hear me or not," he whispered, "but if I have to, I'll move this entire castle to get you the help you need."

Shellinda stepped back from the doorway. "Regina's coming!"

The shining wisp ran into the corridor, gesturing for Shellinda to follow. As the two girls hurried toward Adrian, sparkling tears rolled down Regina's cheeks and dripped toward the floor, evaporating as they fell.

"She looks almost dead!" Regina glided to a stop, her voice squeaking. "I don't know what to do!"

Shellinda tiptoed in place. "I think the floor will hold one person, maybe even you if you weren't carrying Marcelle. We could try to drag her in there so the weight will be spread out."

Regina shook her head. "The closer her body is to her spirit, the more pain she feels. She might die before we get them together."

"A huge risk." Adrian felt Marcelle's neck pulse—fast and erratic. "She's already too close for comfort. We'll move her farther away."

"What can I do to help?" Shellinda asked.

"Go with Regina to the healing room and see if her spirit recovers." Adrian carried Marcelle's body toward the castle's main entryway, calling out as his lumbering steps rattled his voice. "You can run back and forth with reports."

While Regina and Shellinda hurried into the healing room, Adrian trudged toward the main entry. When he arrived, he sat on the wooden floor with Marcelle cradled in his arms. Her skin began cooling, and her breathing settled to a normal rhythm, though a few gasps still rattled in her chest.

He ran his fingers through her sweat-dampened hair, peeling wet locks away from her cheek. "Are you feeling better?"

She continued breathing steadily, her eyes tightly closed.

Adrian sighed. "I guess we're at an impasse. How can I put you back together if bringing your body and spirit close risks your life?"

Her left eyelid twitched but nothing more.

Adrian looked down the corridor, searching for Shellinda. With the doorway to the tree room in view and no obstacles in between, spotting her should be easy.

After a few seconds, Shellinda dashed through the opening and ran toward him. The closer she came, the clearer her wide smile grew. "She's getting better!" She stopped in front of Adrian, panting. "And I *can* walk on the branches. They're weak 'cause they're dying, I think, but they held me up."

"Then maybe I can go see her." He slid Marcelle gently to the floor and rose to his feet. "Can you stay with her body? I don't expect any trouble, but you never know."

"Sure. If something happens, I'll just—"

"Adrian!"

He spun toward the voice. At the healing-room doorway, a female spirit staggered toward him.

"Ma—" He swallowed. "Marcelle?"

"It *is* Marcelle!" Shellinda gave Adrian a shove. "Go!"

Adrian pushed his aching body into a jog. Marcelle's spirit stopped and wobbled in place. When he drew near, he skidded on the floor the rest of the way and swept her into his arms, hoping the temporary contact would last. Sparks flew everywhere. Her body molded into his embrace, and as he spun her around, her shining form left a spray of glittering dust, like a comet with a brilliant tail.

Finally, she slipped away and fell to her bottom. She laughed and reached out again, waving her fingers toward herself. "Sit with me."

Adrian sat cross-legged in front of her and slid his hands under her palms. As his fingers passed through her skin, the contact tingled, as if she were made of electrified water.

Marcelle caressed his cheek. "I have so much to tell you!"

"And I, you." He covered her hand. "I tried to talk to you, and it seemed like you could hear me sometimes, but I wasn't always sure."

She pressed her lips together. A sparkling droplet fell from each eye. "I heard you say something very precious to me."

"You mean when I asked you to—"

"Shhh!" She slid her hand to his mouth, covering his lips. "Not yet. When I'm whole. It won't make sense until then."

Adrian swiveled his head. Far down the corridor, Shellinda stood next to Marcelle's body, light from the doorway shining across them. "Do you feel any pain now?" he asked.

"Some." She shrugged, making her shoulders appear. "It's not bad."

He touched the pouch attached to his belt. "I found this. I assume it's yours."

"Yes. A stardrop's in there, and Arxad's scale from his underbelly."

"What are they for?"

"The scale is a symbol of a covenant between him and me. He said he would do everything in his power to reunite my body and spirit, and Professor Dunwoody gave me the stardrop. He thinks it might help."

"Your grade-school teacher. I remember him." Adrian touched his pocket where the metal box lay. "Cassabrie gave us stardrops mixed with her blood, and they heal the disease, but she said to wait to give you one until you're reunited with your body."

"Alaph told me Arxad is coming. We can ask him what we're supposed to do to get me put back together."

"So we wait." Adrian stretched out his arms. A sense of relief bathed every aching muscle. Just being in Marcelle's presence, seeing her smile, hearing her coherent words, provided the soothing comfort. "Did Alaph give you any idea when Arxad might come?"

She shook her head, making it visible again. "Maybe our resident Starlighter can help us."

Adrian glanced around. "Where is Regina?"

Marcelle nodded toward the healing room. "In there trying to figure out what's wrong with the trees. Maybe if we go to the white room, she can show us where Arxad is."

"The white room?"

Marcelle rose to her feet and gestured for him to stand. "I'll show you."

"But what about your body? I can't leave Shellinda in charge of guarding you, especially right by the door."

"Good point." After looking around for a few seconds, Marcelle ran her hand along his bicep. "Think you can carry me a little farther, maybe even up a high ladder?"

Adrian nodded. "I'll do whatever it takes."

"Then I'll ask Regina to show you where Alaph's chambers are so you can take my body up there. After that, we can go to the white room, and we'll tell each other our stories while we wait for Arxad."

"How will we know when Arxad gets here?"

Marcelle smiled. Her teeth sparkled like diamonds. "From what I've seen, when Regina is in the white room, we won't have to worry about anyone showing up here without her knowing about it."

* * * * * *

Drexel rode prostrate on Beth's back and grasped her body with both arms. Since she had no protruding spines to clutch, this position seemed to be the only way to keep from falling off her slick white scales. Besides, after working so hard to block the underground stream so the Benefile could bathe in its healing waters, resting his aching back felt good in spite of the need to hold on so tightly. For the time being, the three prophetic dragons had been appeased. Now if they would deliver on their promises to send him home to Major Four as a powerful Starlighter, this nightmare visit to the dragon world would soon come to an end.

After a few minutes, Beth landed next to the stairway entrance to the mining mesa. The sudden deceleration sent Drexel flying forward over her neck. He tumbled into a headlong dive, scraping his hands and knees on the rocky soil. When his momentum stopped, he turned over, sat up, and ran his hands along his tunic. His fingers bumped against the outline of Uriel Blackstone's journal, still safe in an inner pocket.

As the other two dragons, Gamal and Dalath, landed next to Beth, Drexel brushed his hands together, smearing blood-moistened dirt. "This is not a dignified way to begin my journey."

A hint of a smile crossed Beth's ivory face. "When you arrive at your destination, you should bathe and find suitable clothing."

Drexel pushed his hair back with a sweep of his hand. "I thought you weren't going to send me home until after you subdued the southern dragons."

"Your efficiency in releasing us from our snare and providing for our healing has earned you a quicker release." Beth glanced at the other two white dragons before continuing. "Not only that, I sense that you have contracted the disease. By the time we finish our quest, you might be dead, so we will have to complete your transformation now; it will rid you of the disease. Unfortunately, we cannot do this for other humans. There can be no more Starlighters."

Drexel rose to his feet. "Then I suppose you also decided to believe my story."

"Not necessarily, but verifying your story would force us to delay our purpose in the Southlands region, and that is a loathsome option." Beth turned toward Dalath. "What is your counsel?"

"We should send Drexel on his way," Dalath said, "and leave Frederick in his frozen state. It is clear that one of them lied, but they will do no harm in this world, at least for now. We can consult with an established Starlighter at another time and administer the proper consequences then. It will not be hard to hunt this man down once he is a Starlighter."

Beth nodded. "Let it be so."

Drexel resisted the urge to roll his eyes. These self-important dragons took too long to make decisions. It would be best to confirm this one before they began contemplating another. "The portal is controlled by a line of crystalline pegs, and one of them is missing."

"We are aware of this," Beth said. "We created these portals along with the crystals, but we do not have the materials necessary for replacing the missing one."

Dalath blew out a stream of ice that shattered into quickly melting pebbles. "I will create a temporary crystal out of ice. It will last long enough for Drexel to enter, and it will melt so that no one will be able to use it again."

"An excellent idea." Beth shifted toward Gamal. "While Dalath fashions the crystal, you will explain the transformation to Drexel."

"As you wish." With a swing of his head, Gamal gestured toward the stairway. "Go to the line of crystals. I will follow."

Drexel climbed down the same stairs he had ascended not long ago when he entered this world. If all went well, he would never see the planet of Starlight again, and good riddance. After his plans to rescue a pitiful slave girl, hoping to gain some well-deserved accolades, had gone awry, submitting to this new idea seemed to be the only option. Yet, the benefits could outweigh the drawbacks. Instead of taking over Mesolantrum by means of popular adulation, now he could usurp the governor's seat by force—no risk of people questioning his motives and no worry about a fickle populace. Finally at least one region on Major Four would have a governor with more than an ounce of brains, and once he could wrest control of the military forces in Mesolantrum and the neighboring regions, it wouldn't take long before the entire kingdom would be his.

After stepping off the bottom stair, he walked toward the rear of the cavern where three tunnels branched away. About halfway back, a line of crystalline pegs crossed the chamber floor from wall to wall. He stopped at a gap at the line's center, the keyhole for the portal, barely visible in the dimmer light.

He turned and faced the stairway. A shadow lumbered down the steps, then Gamal appeared, ducking his head under an arch.

When he dragged his entire body into the chamber, he extended his neck and brought his head close to Drexel. "I will use the energy from the portal to infuse you with Starlighter power. Be prepared for a significant transformation. Your hair will turn red, your irises green, and your voice smooth and pleasurable to the point that people will be mesmerized by it and easily manipulated. A simple touch from you will drain a person's energy by a slight amount, and by a proportional measure, that person will come under your control.

"You will also be able to send energy out from your body. Like an invisible hammer, this energy can knock someone to the ground. When you lock your eyes on a vulnerable person, you will be able to absorb his life energy and resupply your own reserves."

"What makes a person vulnerable?" Drexel asked.

"Anything that will drop his mental defenses—fear, trust, desire, greed. Only the strongest people will be able to resist."

"Those changes are acceptable." Drexel squared his shoulders. "I am ready."

"So you think." Gamal's eyes sparkled blue. "There is a drawback."

Drexel lifted his brow. "And that is?"

"The gift is not painless. The transformation process will be excruciating. In fact, blindness can result."

Drexel looked at the light coming in from the stairway. Eyesight never seemed as important as it did now. "If I do go blind, is it possible to be restored to my former state?"

"Possible? Yes, but the only way to do so safely is to find me and request the change."

"Safely? You mean there's another way?"

Gamal bobbed his head. "Death will revert your body to its former state."

"Death?" Drexel scowled. "That's hardly an option."

"It is an option, albeit an unlikely one since you will be nearly invulnerable. Dragon fire, however, can kill you. There are peculiar aspects to a dragon's flames, so you might want to take heed if a dragon is near."

"*Might* want to?"

Gamal's head bobbed again. "Although the flames bring danger, they can also be a benefit. If you absorb a dragon's energy, you will be empowered to the point of omnipotence."

"I see. Well, that's good to know." Drexel gave Gamal a skeptical stare. "What will other weapons do to me?"

"Spears and swords will have only a temporary effect. Your body will be able to regenerate itself, so you can physically survive any other kind of onslaught that might cut or maim you. Of course, if you were to be decapitated, you would be as good as dead. Since your ability to regenerate comes from your brain, you would be unable to repair the damage due to the separation of the healing source from your body."

Pursing his lips, Drexel nodded. "I understand."

"Yet, such healing ability would not be effective if you are blinded by the transformation process."

Drexel spread his arms. "In that case, what good could I do there? And if I can't find you, I'll be stuck in that condition."

"I agree that it is a conundrum." Gamal used a wing to point at the line of crystals. "We can send you home without any Starlighter power, but not only will you have to battle the disease, you will have to find a way to defend yourself. My prophetic vision tells me that you have been accused of murder in your home region."

"Murder?" Drexel feigned a look of shock. "Preposterous! Who could have accused me of such a vile crime?"

"Marcelle accused you of killing her mother. Her father is now governor of your region, so I think you will not be handled gently if you return in a recognizable form. I assume knives are being sharpened, and the blades will be directed at your tender portions."

Drexel concealed a shudder. "I agree. I'll have to take my chances with the potential blindness."

"There is one more caveat. Assuming you escape the blindness, much of your power will come from your ability to hypnotize people with your words and by locking them in a visual stare. Because of this power, take care not to view yourself in a mirror. If you do, you will use your own power on yourself."

"What would happen?"

"Since your vision, in a sense, eliminates guards on the minds of those who are not prepared, you might very well lose your own guard, that is, your disguise. I am not certain of this, but it is a possibility you should consider."

Drexel nodded. "That should be easy. No mirrors."

"Very well. But remember, if you are blinded, then you may return here and find me—that is, if you have a way to open this portal from the other side."

Drexel touched his tunic over the inner pocket that held Marcelle's mother's fingers. "I have a way."

"Then I will obtain the missing crystal from Dalath." Gamal turned and began ascending the stairs.

After the dragon's tail snaked up the steps, Drexel's legs trembled. Issachar would surely hang him, but only after slicing off his fingers and cutting him open from navel to nose. A man who loved his wife would have no mercy for her killer.

Soon, Gamal descended the stairs with a crystalline peg in his clawed hand, blowing cold air over it as he walked. He shuffled past Drexel and inserted it into the missing crystal's hole. Instantly, the rear wall with the three tunnels disappeared. An underground river streamed by from left to right and with it the sounds of rushing water. Light cascaded from a hole in the cavern's ceiling, and a ladder lay nearby.

"Now stand over the central crystal," Gamal said. "And we must hurry before the ice melts."

Drexel straddled the crystal. A slight tingle ran along his skin, but that was to be expected since he stood on the portal plane between two realms. "What next?"

"The transformation. As I warned, prepare yourself for pain. It will be intense but short-lived." His eyes glowing brightly, Gamal blew a stream of white gas over Drexel's face. Drexel blinked. The dragon's breath wasn't as cold as expected, though it stung, as if infused with a corrosive agent. It smelled of burning fossil fuel mixed with soap.

Drexel clenched his teeth. He could withstand the pain. Gaining the power of a Starlighter would be worth it.

As Gamal continued spewing gas, the portal plane glowed and shimmered. The stinging sensation worsened, growing from a mere irritation to an attack of invisible scorpions. Every inch of skin burned as if on fire, including his scalp.

Words shot into his ears—clanging and clawing every nerve—a billion sentences in a wild array of voices, much faster than any auctioneer could speak. It seemed that everyone in the world screamed at the same time.

Finally, Drexel covered his face with his hands and shouted between his fingers. "Stop!" He stumbled backwards and fell on his bottom, now only a few paces from the river. A bare wall stood in Gamal's place. The world of Starlight had disappeared.

Drexel scrambled on all fours to the river, crawled to hip-deep water, and dunked his head, careful to keep the current from sweeping him away. The cold wetness soothed the fiery sting. After several seconds, he lifted his head and shook it, slinging water.

That was better. In fact, the water felt very good. And best of all, he could see.

Letting out a relieved sigh, he crawled back and sat on the river's stony bank. After all the hard work chopping the trees to free the white dragons and plugging the river to provide a healing spring for them, bathing was a great idea. Showing up in the town square smelling of sweat, mold, and dirt would create a terrible first impression.

Light shone through a hole above, the rectangular opening to the outside world that took up perhaps a third of the ceiling. Rays from Solarus angled in, striking the sides of several stalactites. From the angle of the light, it appeared to be fairly early in the morning.

Drexel touched a fallen stalactite—thick, short, and covered with rough knobs. Odd that this was the only one on the floor, even after the ground pivoted multiple times to alter the river's course. They had to be firmly attached or else the floor would be littered with them.

After peeling off his wet tunic, he stood and waded into the river with his shoes still on, again resisting the swift current. His tunic tucked under his arm, he scrubbed various body parts and took an inventory. His mustache had burned off, and his hair was shorter, barely more than three inches long. Everything functioned properly—eyes, ears, limbs, and nose. In fact, every sense was sharper than ever, and his muscle tone had tightened, as if a portion of his youth had been restored. It seemed that he had escaped the blindness and instead been endowed with extra vigor.

Soon, a hissing sound crept into his ear. He turned toward the portal wall. A column of mist took shape at the river's shoreline, illuminated by the sunlight. As the mist slowly took on human form and divided into two, one of them spoke in a rasping whisper, "This man has much evil in his soul."

"True," the other said. "His energy would feed us for many months."

Drexel shuddered. These were snatchers. They could potentially cause trouble, but it would be easy to control them, as he had in the past, with a simple rhyming phrase.

He furrowed his brow. But what *was* that phrase? Something about asking a question. Uriel had written this secret password somewhere in his journal. He grabbed his tunic from under his arm and fished out the journal, but it slipped and fell into the river. The current swept it away.

"No!" Drexel dove after it, and the flow swallowed him like a hungry serpent. Flailing both arms, he battled to stay above the surface. Water surged into his nose and mouth. His head struck something hard, sending him into the depths. Consciousness drifted away. He coughed and sucked in a water-laden breath. Then everything faded to darkness.

✹ FIVE ✹

DREXEL coughed. Water spewed from his mouth. A face appeared—a woman's face, close, very close—carrying no hint of an expression, though dirt and sweat smeared her forehead and cheeks. She lifted away and knelt at his side. With long reddish-brown hair tied in two braids, youthful face, and slender frame, she was likely no more than twenty-five years old. "You have been through quite an ordeal," she said in monotone.

"I am—" He coughed again, sending a new stream of water over his bare chest. Only a few steps away, a swiftly flowing river ran past, and the grass between himself and the water lay flat. Memories of his bathing mishap flooded back to mind. Had this woman dragged him from the river? "I am grateful. I assume you rescued me."

"I did." She lifted a wet tunic from the surrounding grass and draped it over his chest. "You should cover yourself. If someone were to pass by, I care not to explain why I am kneeling close to a half-naked man." She winked at him. "Though I can't say that I kept my head turned from the view."

"Yes ... well ..." Drexel sat up and worked an arm through a wet sleeve. "I wouldn't want to put a mark on your reputation."

"Gossipers will wag their tongues no matter what I do or with whom I keep company." She rose to her feet, brushed out her calf-length skirt, and extended a hand. "Do you wish to test your legs?"

"Yes, thank you." Drexel took her hand and rode her pull to an upright stance. Pain hammered his skull. He closed his eyes and waited for the throbbing to ease. "I think I bumped my head on something."

"I'm not surprised. You flew out of Blackstone's Ridge as if shot from a bow."

Drexel opened his eyes and looked upstream. A stone's throw away, the river gushed from a hole in a nearly vertical hillside." Blackstone's Ridge? Was it named after Uriel Blackstone?"

She nodded. "He once owned this land."

"Interesting." Drexel pushed his other arm into a sleeve and pulled the tunic over his head. "Who owns it now?"

She crossed her arms over her chest. "Inquisitive strangers are not likely to find many answers, especially those who appear under such unusual circumstances."

"Then we should be strangers no longer." Drexel extended his hand. "What is your name, fair rescuer?"

"Sophia." She shook his hand. "And yours?"

His lips formed his own name, but he blocked his voice just in time. He had to come up with a pseudonym in short order. He patted his tunic, finding every pocket flat, including the one carrying Uriel's journal. The precious book was gone. "Sophia, did you happen to notice if my papers survived the water? They would have been in a leather wallet in my inner pocket."

She shook her head. "Are you having a bout of amnesia?"

"No, amnesia isn't the issue. My memory is fine." Drexel furrowed his brow. Temporary amnesia would have been a good way to buy time to come up with a name. Why had he surrendered that option so quickly? "I was simply curious as to whether or not my papers were intact. Since you questioned me, it made me think that others will, including the authorities in this place." He blinked at her. "I am in Mesolantrum, aren't I?"

"You are." She nodded upstream. "Where did you fall into the river? It's underground throughout Mesolantrum, so I thought you might be from an uplands region near the river's source. Yet your clothes are similar to those of the soldiers in Mesolantrum's military. And since your hair is a fiery red I have never seen in these parts, I haven't been able to piece together these contradictory clues."

"You are quite observant." Drexel laughed softly. "It's a long story that I'll be glad to tell you soon, but for now, I am, indeed, from Mesolantrum, though I have been on a journey to a distant land." He glanced around. "I feel quite disoriented. Which portion of Mesolantrum are we in?"

"The southeastern lowlands." She pointed downstream. "The governorship begins about fifteen miles that way." She then swung her arm in the opposite direction. "And it extends three hundred miles if you follow the path, which goes around the border of the Forbidden Zone."

"Yes, I remember. I have my bearings now." He gave her an approving nod. "You seem to know this country quite well."

"My family has lived here for ten generations, Mr. ..." She raised her brow.

Drexel searched for a good false name for himself. Robert Banes? Michael Winston? David Smith? But each time he opened his mouth to speak a name, he couldn't say it.

"Miss Halstead?"

Drexel looked past Sophia. A boy wearing short trousers, a white shirt, and suspenders ran toward them on a narrow path, calling again, "Miss Halstead?"

"Excuse me." Sophia turned. "Yes, Mitchell?"

When the boy drew close, he slowed to a stop, panting. "Since you're late ... we were all wondering ... what to do."

"And you came all the way out here instead of drilling your spelling words." She tousled his hair. "Tell everyone to read the next chapter in the primer. I will be there soon."

Mitchell glanced at Drexel and flashed a grin. "Another suitor? Are you finally gonna marry this one?"

"None of your business!" She spun him around and kicked him in the seat of his trousers. "Be off with you now!"

The boy scampered down the path, looking back every few seconds with the grin still evident.

Sophia turned again to Drexel. "You'll have to excuse Mitchell. Boys of that age are—"

"No need to explain," Drexel said, waving a hand. "I remember being that age myself. The other children called me Lips because I talked so much and …" He let his voice trail off. Memories of days long ago flooded in, people and events that had not surfaced in decades, including other names children had called him, some in endearment and some in derision—Sparky, Fingers, and Cal Broder, a rugged hero in an obscure novel he had read countless times. That name stuck for two years, two wonderful years of respect and admiration after he had tripped a bully who stole a silver coin from a smaller lad.

"Excuse me … Mister Lips," Sophia said, "but your mind seems to have wandered off somewhere. Perhaps your head wound has slowed your wits."

"Perhaps so." Drexel smiled weakly. "I did take quite a spill."

"Well, Mitchell could easily qualify for your Lips nickname. By the time he gets back to the school, his tale will have us living together without the benefit of marriage." Sophia tilted her head. "You never told me your real name."

"I have been called by so many names sometimes I prefer the unreal ones." Drexel bowed. "You may call me Cal, Cal Broder."

"I am pleased to meet you, Cal." She narrowed an eye. "That name is familiar to me."

Drexel suppressed a cringe. A schoolteacher could easily have read that old novel. "Your surname is familiar to me as well."

Her expression darkened. "That is a righteous claim. The Halstead name is known throughout the kingdom."

"I see." Drexel studied her countenance—hurt, angry, vengeful. It seemed that words flowed from her motionless lips, the sorrowful words that had turned her features downward.

Behind Sophia, an image took shape, a woman tied to an execution stake surrounded by burning wood. As smoke shot skyward, she opened her mouth and cried out, but no sounds emanated. This silent vision needed no words.

More memories flowed. Halstead was the name of the widow the counselor burned at the stake. The timing of that execution meant that this young lady must be the widow's daughter, likely ten to fifteen years old when her mother died, certainly old enough to remember the accusations as well as the pain of the ordeal.

Sophia cracked a fragile smile. "Is your mind wandering again?"

"In a way." Drexel took on a sympathetic tone. "I remember how I know your name. Your mother was burned at the stake."

Sophia's eyes seemed to flash as she spoke through clenched teeth. "The smoke of her unjust execution covered this land, Mr. Broder, and no wind or rain could ever cleanse the air of the stench. Her cries still haunt my dreams, and I hope they do the same to the scoundrels who hunted her down and sentenced her to death."

"What crime did they accuse her of committing?"

She spat out her reply. "Sorcery. Witchcraft. Divining. All malicious lies. Even the Cathedral priests lied about my mother."

"Yes, yes, I remember now." More words streamed into Drexel's mind, and they poured forth from his mouth unbidden. "Your mother saw what the clergy could not, and her abilities fueled the fires of jealousy. They preached homilies that encouraged spiritual insight but persecuted those who actually achieved it."

Sophia stared at him, her eyes wide. "Yes ... Yes, that's exactly right."

"Fools!" Drexel clenched a fist. "Such men deserve to be dragged down from their lofty perches and humiliated in the public square. How dare they hide their inadequacies in the flames of injustice! They claim to illuminate the minds of their underlings, but instead they darken the entire kingdom in a shroud of hypocrisy. Their evil knows no bounds."

Sophia grasped his wrist. "But how can we drag them down? Their power is too great."

"I will go directly to the palace. Perhaps we will learn that we have allies."

"Maybe so. The political winds are shifting wildly, and the governorship has changed hands rapidly of late." Her words quickened, nearly running together. "First we had Prescott, then Orion, then a Tark they called Leo, and now Issachar Stafford, Prescott's former banker. One of Prescott's cronies is not likely to be any better than Prescott was."

Drexel looked at Sophia's tight grip on his wrist. Prescott's injustice had lit a fire of blinding passion within her. Of course, Stafford was a much nobler man than was Prescott, but why inform her of that fact? "I will go and make inquiry about the state of affairs in the governorship. If, indeed, the palace is still rife with corruption and oppression, I will seek out allies and make a suitable plan to restore justice to this land."

"I'll come with you." Sophia pulled away and stepped backwards on the path. "Let me put my oldest student in charge, and I'll help you."

"Won't more tongues wag if you leave with a stranger like me?"

"Let them wag!" Sophia's cheeks turned scarlet. "Those biddies can cluck till sundown for all I care." She ran in the direction Mitchell had gone, making her skirt and petticoat toss up behind her. Soon, she turned on a bend in the path and disappeared into a wooded area.

Drexel exhaled. Sophia had provided a wealth of information and opened a door of opportunity, but answering her probing questions had been taxing. For some reason, he couldn't force himself to utter a single false statement. Might that be a drawback of his Starlighter essence? If so, it could pose a serious problem.

He patted his empty pocket again. The journal. Maybe it had washed up on the bank somewhere. He walked uphill to the point where the river exited Blackstone's Ridge. The water cascaded from a rock-lined hole and poured into a pebble-covered bed that wound into the distant forest. According to the journal, Blackstone had rigged this exit point to close so that the water would collect in a reservoir. He had also fashioned a huge lever under the entire foundation so that the river would reverse course if someone were to try to break through the underground gateway without authorization, and the chamber would flood and drown the violator.

Touching the edge of the hole, Drexel sighed. Such genius gone to waste. So few believed his story. If only he were here as an ally, his inventive prowess would be a boon.

As Drexel stood, his hair and clothes still dripping, a puddle collected next to his boot. He stooped and gazed at the surface. An unfamiliar face stared back at him. He touched his cheek. The reflection did the same, caressing smooth, youthful skin on a narrow, chiseled face. He ran his fingers through his hair, short locks that carried an orange tone, unusual but not unattractive. With no sign of his handlebar mustache, no one would recognize him as Drexel, head of the palace sentries.

Still staring, he lowered his hand. Stinging prickles ran along his skin, as if bees were stinging his face. He gasped. A mirror!

He jerked his head to the side and caressed his cheeks. The stinging faded.

While waiting for Sophia, he walked along the edge of the river, again searching for the journal. After a few minutes, it came into view on the bank at an elbow in the stream. He snatched it up, wiped it clean on his tunic, and pried open the wet cover. As he hurried back to his starting point, he fanned the pages—intact and mostly dry.

After a few minutes, Sophia ran along the path carrying a knapsack, her face now clean. Drexel jogged down the slope. When they met, she stopped and caught her breath, smiling. "I have …" She handed him the knapsack. "Dry clothes for you, Cal. And food. It's not much, but since you have been traveling …"

"Thank you. My travels have left me hungry." He opened the knapsack and withdrew a peasant's tunic, a suitable replacement for his sentry uniform and an excellent addition to his disguise. "Most recently I came from Dracon where I journeyed to learn the truth about the old legends."

"Dracon?" Sophia slid closer and whispered, though no one was in sight. "Are you a member of the Underground Gateway?"

"A member?" Drexel chuckled and showed her the journal. "My dear lady, I have in my possession Uriel Blackstone's personal account of how he constructed the Gateway mechanism."

Sophia touched the binding. "I heard that soldiers have recently been mustered to invade the dragon world, but I thought it might be a ploy to attack a neighboring region. Since the government constantly lies, I wasn't sure what the truth is. In the past, very few believed in the legends, but now it seems that people are unable to talk about anything else. They're gleefully expecting the soldiers to return in triumph with severed dragon heads and hundreds of liberated slaves, though I suspect that in the quiet places of their hearts they secretly fear for the safety of husbands and sons who have gone off to battle."

Drexel laid a hand over his heart. "Believe this, Miss Halstead, I have seen the slaves and the dragons, and the fear for the soldiers' safety is well founded." He tucked the journal into his new tunic's inner pocket. "A dragon is a fierce beast that can swat a man into the air with a bat of his spiny tail and fly up to catch him before he falls, only to break his body in half with a snap of his powerful jaws and razor-sharp teeth. Then he can swallow his victim's bloody remains with a single gulp."

Sophia's face turned pale. Backing away on stiff legs, she pointed over Drexel's shoulder. Her lips moved, but she said nothing.

Drexel turned. Just out of reach, a semitransparent dragon stood with a man in its jaws, his legs dangling from one side and his upper torso hanging out the other. The dragon crunched down. Bones snapped. Blood poured to the grass and spattered onto Drexel's boots, though the red droplets vanished on contact. "Fear not," he said. "It's just a vision."

Sophia shuffled to his side and curled her arm around his. "A vision?"

"Yes, creating visions is a gift I have."

The dragon slurped the rest of the body into its mouth and, tilting its head back, swallowed. As it repeated the swallowing motion, a huge lump traveled down its long neck. When the lump passed into the stomach, the dragon disappeared.

"Amazing!" Sophia looked at their locked arms, then up at Drexel. "You don't mind, do you?"

"Again, I am concerned only about your reputation."

"Have no worry about that. The hens have already splattered it with their excrement." Sophia released him and walked to the spot where the dragon had stood. "Tell me more about this gift you possess."

"I am a Starlighter." Drexel lifted the dry tunic. "Allow me to change clothes, and I will tell you about it along the way to the palace."

"Very well." Sophia turned her back.

After removing his boots, Drexel peeled off his uniform and put on the cloth-and-leather tunic and trousers from the knapsack. He then wrung out the sentry uniform, stuffed it into the pack, and slung the strap over his shoulder. "Let's go."

"What about your boots?" Sophia asked, pointing at the side of the path. "They don't match the clothes I gave you, but you might need them."

Drexel looked at his boots—military issue, specifically designed for palace sentries. Anyone among his peers would recognize them, but leaving them behind would make no sense in Sophia's eyes. He scooped them up, tied the laces together, and draped them over his shoulder. "I think it would be uncomfortable to walk in wet boots for very long."

"I hope you have tough soles. The path is not a smooth one."

"If it gets too rough, I'll walk in the grass."

She shrugged. "Suit yourself."

Along the way, Drexel told of his adventures on Dracon, or Starlight as the dragons called their world, and how the Benefile endowed him with Starlighter gifts in thanks for his rescuing efforts. The transformation endowed him with orange hair, which would otherwise be unheard of on the head of a Mesolantrum native. Of course, he left out an explanation of his occupation as sentry, his real name, or how Uriel's journal came into his possession. He did reveal that he had a military background, a fact that she had already surmised, which exposed his status as a member of the middle class rather than the peasantry. Sophia didn't seem to mind their difference in class, and she never asked for any story holes to be filled. Apparently, she was so enamored with the idea of toppling the government, she wanted to believe in this powerful, exotic stranger. There was no need to lie about anything.

The path veered to the left around a forest to the right. Signs hung on trees at varying intervals warning travelers to avoid trespassing into the Forbidden Zone that lay within the woods. The crudely drawn lettering raised more memories—the legends that old women told about the wilds, including the misty ghosts called snatchers.

"Enough about me." Drexel said as Solarus drifted past its zenith. "Tell me more about you and your family."

"There isn't much to tell. I am an only child and an orphan. Three days a week I teach primary school to the peasants who can afford to let their children leave their commune chores during the morning hours. The rest of the time I serve as a seamstress and cook in my commune."

"How did your father die?"

"It happened before I was born." Her shoulders sagged, and her voice took on a morose tone. "He refused to join the military, which was his right, mind you, because my mother was pregnant. Then one day, out of the blue, a platoon or whatever they call a group of soldiers, came to our commune's farm. They marched across one of our fields and trampled our corn."

While Sophia talked, Drexel partook of the food she had provided—a hunk of sweet cornbread and a tart green apple. He surveyed the surrounding land. The forest receded on both sides, giving way to furrowed fields bearing remnants of crops—withered brown cornstalks and specks of cotton.

"So my father ran out to investigate," Sophia continued. "When he got there, the soldiers were using our scarecrow as a target for their arrows. He shouted for them to leave, but …" Her lips pressed into a thin line. "But they wouldn't. They just kept shooting and shooting, no matter how much he begged them to get off our land and leave us alone. Then a wayward arrow hit him in the chest. The commander ordered two soldiers to carry him back to our commune, and ..." Her voice pitched up to a squeak. "And he died in my mother's arms."

As tears dripped down Sophia's cheeks, Drexel chewed quietly. The story was all too familiar. He had been in that detachment himself. One of his fellow soldiers had dared him to shoot at the plucky farmer to scare him away, but Drexel had refused, so the fellow soldier did the deed himself. "A bad shot," he had called it. "A terrible mistake." When the commander demanded to know who had shot the farmer, every soldier denied it.

Drexel tossed the apple core and sighed. Although he didn't shoot the deadly arrow himself, he could have revealed the culprit, but an unwritten code among the soldiers would never allow such betrayal.

Sophia brushed her tears away. "Since my parents were still young, and since my mother swore that she would never marry again, the people in our community dubbed her the widow Halstead. She was known by that name even to the day she burned at the stake. When she died, I was placed with another family until I was of age. I was a hard worker, so I finished my chores quickly, giving me time to explore and learn.

"One day, a boy in the noble class rode by on a horse. He was fourteen, and I was twelve. He let me borrow a book, and although I knew how to read, I had never known the true joy of it. For the next three years, he brought me a different book every week. I read of pirates on the open seas, romances in the king's palace, and biographies of members of the ruling class, though most of them seemed more fictional than the pirate adventures."

She took a breath and smiled. "I am such a blabbermouth today! I suppose I'm boring you to tears."

"Not at all," Drexel said, waving a hand, "but we should probably formulate a plan that will employ your book knowledge and my Starlighter power."

Her smile bent into a frown. "Your ability to create visions is impressive, Cal, but to the governor and his guards, a vision will be little more than a projection from a Courier's tube, a mere advance in technology. We will need more than that to clean out the corruption in the seats of power."

"A reasonable conclusion, but I have not yet revealed the, shall we say, more persuasive aspects of my power. When we get to the village, perhaps I will be able to instill in you a bit more confidence in my abilities."

"I will be glad to see this power." She slid her hand into his and smiled. "No one is around to see us."

"Indeed." The urge to jerk his hand away seemed overwhelming, but he kept it in place. "I assume someone who has read so many books must have an adventurous spirit."

She laughed. "Now you're sounding like the gossipers, Cal Broder."

"I apologize. I was merely—"

"No!" She pulled him to a stop, her cheeks again red. "Let's get this straight. No apologies. We will strike the pigs in power, and we will strike hard. And if people don't like what they see when we show affection, then let them wallow in their own filthy minds! I, for one, will be glad to give the gossiping hens reason to squawk."

"Well, Miss Halstead, allow me to ponder your words." Drexel looked into her eyes—partially glazed. Yes, she had already come under his control. He could do with her whatever he pleased, but he had to be careful to avoid taking the advantage too far. A little at a time would be best. "I agree that we should strike hard, but I will need your help. I have discovered that my power comes with somewhat of a handicap. I seem unable to speak a lie, so I will need you to help me conceal anything that I do not wish to divulge. If we are to strike with the force you desire, such secrecy is a must."

She stared at him, her eyes still glazed. After a few seconds, she nodded. "I can do that." She then marched forward with her shoulders square and her face straight ahead, not saying another word.

Drexel kept pace and copied her single-minded posture. This young woman might prove to be the perfect counterpart—intelligent, passionate, and experienced in the ways of the lower classes. She could give counsel regarding how to blend in with the peasants while he became their champion.

Smiling, Drexel touched his ragged tunic. Yes, the rise of a simple peasant to the height of power would be celebrated by the masses. If push came to shove in the palace, having thousands of people on his side might make the difference. They never need know that they had sworn their allegiance to a man in a mask.

✸ SIX ✸

DREXEL marched on, now wearing his boots again. They had dried out long ago as had his stockings. "I recognize some of these surroundings, so I assume we're getting close to the palace."

"We are." Sophia touched Drexel's sleeve. "Your tunic disguises you as a member of the peasant class. If not for your fiery hair, the noble class would pay no attention to you."

"Then I need a hat."

"Many peasants wear a beret, though it wouldn't cover your hair completely. We can find a suitable one in the village."

"It might be enough." Drexel patted his trousers. "Since I lost my wallet, I have no money."

"Then we'll barter. If you are willing to part with your old clothes, they should easily fetch a beret."

Drexel nodded toward his boots. "And perhaps these would purchase a pair of suitable shoes."

"Good idea."

As they continued walking abreast, the dirt path changed to stones. Shops alongside the path came into view, at first nothing more than shacks with peasants leaning out a front window over a shelf displaying oven mitts and copper pots. Without exception, the proprietors stared at Drexel as he passed.

He lowered his head. His hair must have been like a flaming beacon. A person suspicious of foreigners might alert a sentry, and if the sentry asked to see his papers, all might be lost.

Soon, the shops multiplied, signaling their entrance into the village's commerce district. Now in familiar territory, Drexel marched more quickly, glancing right and left in search of a shop with men's clothing on display.

Men hustled by, some pushing carts carrying shrubbery, dirt, manure, or sacks of grain or corn. Women in noble attire meandered from shop to shop, looking into windows, sampling nuts and candies, feeling swatches of cloth while chatting, though few seemed ready to make a purchase.

Drexel and Sophia passed the butcher's shop on the left, then the Royal Seamstress's window on the right. Inside, a lanky young woman draped a partially constructed white gown over a dress mannequin. She gave Drexel a sideways stare, furrowing her brow for a moment before returning to her work.

"Over there," Sophia whispered, pointing across the street.

Drexel walked that way. Inside one of the cruder shops, a man dressed in an orange tunic with black trim stood behind a table. Next to him, berets of various colors hung from a short hat tree standing on the table.

"He's a Tark," Sophia continued. "Probably a scoundrel."

"We'll see about that." Drexel chose a forest green beret and slid it over his head. "What do you think?"

Sophia stepped back and looked him over. "Quite handsome. It will do fine."

Drexel took off the beret and set it on the table. "How much?"

"Only thirty dureens," the shopkeeper said. "My dear wife made it herself. It is lamb's wool from Tarkton, the finest wool in the kingdom."

Drexel glanced at the street. Onlookers began to gather, apparently interested in how this strange redheaded man might deal with a devious Tark. He looked into the shopkeeper's eyes. "Really? The finest in the kingdom?"

"Well …" The man's chin quivered. "It is fine wool. You can see that for yourself."

Drexel ran a finger along the material. It was woolen, to be sure, but nothing special. "It's really standard grade, isn't it?"

The shopkeeper's eyes seemed to glaze over, and all emotion fled from his tone. "We bought the wool from a weaver's leftovers."

Drexel's finger paused at a flawed stitch. "But your wife still made it."

"Yes, she did." A hint of a smile returned to his face. "She is arthritic, but she is still capable."

"I believe you." Drexel pulled his uniform's tunic from the knapsack. "Will you take this for the beret?"

The shopkeeper touched the fabric. "Military grade. Rather old. It is not of equal value, especially in this condition. Twenty dureens."

"Only twenty?" Drexel again caught a glimpse of the other shoppers. More had gathered, perhaps twenty-five now, mostly peasants. He set a hand on Sophia's shoulder. "I have recently arrived from a distant land, and my friend here told me that I should trade for clothing that is more in keeping with that of the fine citizens in this region. I trust that you will not be an obstacle that will prevent me from uniting with my Mesolantrum fellows."

The shopkeeper stared straight ahead. "My mistake, sir. It is a fair trade."

Chuckles sounded from the onlookers. Some clapped their hands as whispers passed back and forth.

"Someone finally stood up to that Tark."

"This stranger certainly has a way with words."

"He's a handsome young man. It's no wonder the Halstead girl is attracted to him."

Drexel dropped the tunic onto the table, snatched up the beret, and pressed it over his head. "Now to find some appropriate shoes."

"I have shoes," the shopkeeper said, eyeing Drexel's boots. "They are Tarkton work shoes for farming, but they are similar to those made here. Few can tell the difference."

"Very well." Drexel slid his boots off and set them on the table. "Let's see them."

The shopkeeper picked up one of the boots and turned it around in his hands. "I think I have your size." He disappeared behind a rack of clothing, speaking indistinct words. After a moment, he reappeared with Drexel's boot and a pair of leather shoes. "Try these on."

Drexel slid the shoes over his stockings. They fit perfectly. He touched his own boots, both now on the table. "Will you take these in trade?"

The man pinched the leather. "They are old, sir, not new like the shoes you wish to buy."

Drexel looked him in the eye again and added a tone of firmness. "Are you telling me that these military boots are less valuable than the manure-kicking shoes you're trying to sell?"

As more chuckles sounded, the shopkeeper's glazed look returned. "No sir. The trade you offer is more than fair."

"Good. And while we're bargaining …" Drexel pulled his old trousers from the knapsack. "How much will you give me for these?"

The man ran a hand along the seam, his voice monotone. "Fine quality. Fifty dureens."

"They're yours." Drexel laid the trousers over the tunic and opened his hand. "In coins, please."

The man pulled a cigar box from under the table and counted out ten coins into Drexel's palm. When he finished, Drexel gave five to Sophia and pushed the other five into his trousers pocket. "For food," Drexel whispered. "It should be enough for a couple of days."

"Good thinking." Sophia slid her coins into a skirt pocket.

Drexel looked around. A sentry approached from the direction they had come, perhaps alerted by the growing crowd.

"We'd better go." Drexel took Sophia by the arm and whisked her away from the shop. They marched quickly toward the center of the village. Maybe they could blend in with the shoppers. Yet even with the beret covering most of his hair, the color would make him stand out. He bent low and hurried on.

"Stop!" the sentry shouted from behind them. Heavy footsteps followed.

Drexel halted and spun toward him. "Were you calling me?"

"Yes." The sentry, dressed in typical dark blues and wearing a hip scabbard, stood in front of Drexel and extended a hand. "Let me see your papers."

Keeping his face toward the sentry, Drexel looked out of the corner of his eye. Like a swarm of bees, the onlookers drew closer and hovered several paces away, their whispers rising to a loud buzz.

"My papers?" Drexel crossed his arms over his chest. "We should be allowed to walk freely without showing anyone our papers."

The sentry's eyes darkened for a brief moment, but applause from the crowd broke the hypnosis. His face reddening, he rolled his hand into a fist and punched Drexel across the mouth.

Drexel staggered backwards until several hands caught and steadied him. A man whispered into his ear, "Don't get yourself killed. It's not worth it."

"Someone has to break the chains of oppression, my good fellow." Drexel pulled away. Wiping blood from his lip with the back of his hand, he strode toward the sentry.

The sentry drew a sword and pointed it at Drexel. "Not another step!"

Drexel halted. "Allow me to go on my way, and I will not be a bother to you."

"Not until you show me your papers." The sentry extended the sword and pressed the tip against Drexel's stomach. "Now!"

"I stand here as a spokesperson for the people. It is time for this tyranny to end." Drexel lifted an arm and focused on his hand, mentally concentrating energy into his palm. Then, like a striking adder, he whipped his arm forward. A nearly invisible ball of light shot out and slammed into the sentry's chest. He flew backwards into a fruit stand, crushing it. Wood shards flew, and apples and melons rolled into the street.

While the sentry pushed to a sitting position, Drexel walked closer, keeping his arm extended. He concentrated on a connection between his palm and the fallen sentry, like a taut rope that reeled in as he narrowed the gap. With each step, energy flowed into his arm and throughout his body. The sentry curled into a fetal position and writhed in front of the fruit vendor's shop, moaning as his body slowly shriveled. A louder buzz emanated from the onlookers along with fearful whispers.

"Stop!" Sophia jerked Drexel's arm down. The energy connection broke. After a long sigh, the sentry fell limp, though he continued breathing.

Drexel glared at Sophia. "Why did you do that?"

"To keep you from killing him!"

Drexel whispered, infusing a growl. "You said to strike the pigs hard. If you want to topple the rulers of this land, you will have to get used to the idea of killing. They will not abdicate at a mere suggestion."

"With your power," she whispered in return, "maybe they will. I watched how you exposed the shopkeeper's lies and manipulated him. If we can strike with invisible swords, we won't raise as much opposition."

Drexel glanced at the Tark, now several shops away. Indeed, he had acquiesced easily. Maybe a Starlighter-enhanced suggestion would work, and the energy-sapping power could be reserved as a backup. "Your point is well taken. I apologize for my outburst."

Sophia glanced around. "We'd better go. What you've done here will soon be on the lips of everyone in the village."

"Good." Drexel straightened his beret. "Community support is an excellent preemptive strike."

"You have incited fear, not support." Sophia grasped his wrist. "Let's get out of sight and make our plans."

They hurried past the crowd, their heads low as they weaved around other shoppers who had not witnessed the display of power. Most didn't give them a second glance, though a few cast curious stares, perhaps wondering about the stranger with the fiery red hair.

When the palace came into view beyond the village's central square, they slowed to a casual walk. They closed in on a lawyer's office. Standing just outside the door, two well-dressed men with gray beards and perfectly trimmed hair conversed. A stream of thoughts flowed from their minds as if drifting on a breeze. Most of the words seemed like legal gibberish, but the word governorship popped up several times, likely because of the rapid changes in rule here. Perhaps these men could provide some valuable information.

Drexel stopped and raised a finger. "Excuse me, gentlemen."

They turned his way. The shorter of the two, a pudgy fellow with a kind smile, bowed his head. "What may I do for you, sir?"

"Seeing that you are experts in law, I thought you might be able to provide some insight regarding a legal question I have."

The taller man chuckled. "Henry, it looks like you have one last appointment today after all."

"Indeed." Henry eyed Drexel's hair. "Do you have local currency?"

Drexel dug the coins from his pocket and displayed them in his palm. "I assume this is enough to answer one simple question."

"Enough for a consultation." Henry gestured toward the office door. "Let's go inside, and we'll talk."

Drexel set a hand on Sophia's back. "Come with me. I'll probably need your expertise as well."

She drew him aside and whispered, "This man was my mother's defense attorney. I was too young to know if he really tried to defend her, but obviously he utterly failed."

"All the better. After those practice sessions in the market, I trust that I will be able to shame him into providing all the help we need."

Sophia nodded slowly. "True. But what do you have in mind?"

Drexel caressed her cheek with a soft touch. "Don't worry, my dear. Just trust me, and I will take care of everything."

"Trust you …" Sophia's eyes turned glassy again. "I do."

Drexel smiled. Since he had been able to entrance this feisty, educated woman, subduing the ignorant masses would be easy. "Good. Let's see what legal maneuvering we can add to our arsenal. Then we'll cleanse Mesolantrum of corruption once and for all."

✷ SEVEN ✷

PROFESSOR Dunwoody sat next to Issachar at a long table in the governor's office. Both wore spectacles and scanned dozens of papers that lay on the tabletop in orderly stacks. Behind them, flames crackled in a fireplace next to a tall bookshelf filled with volumes detailing old laws and contracts, poor reading for anyone except an obsessive archivist.

Dunwoody glanced at the dusty books. Someday this obsessive archivist would take time off and read every one of them, but today called for a more incisive search. Fun would have to wait.

The fire's heat warmed their backs, often too warm for comfort, but the local farmers forecasted cooler weather for the evening, so Issachar ordered the transfer of Maelstrom's imprisoning crystals from the bedroom fireplace to the office.

Dunwoody allowed himself a smile. One of the three shards held that scoundrel. Knowing that he likely cooked in his crystalline abode made the wait for the cooler air tolerable.

After locating Issachar's final audit request for the gas company, Dunwoody eyed the scheduled date and circled it on a desk calendar with a red pen. That made five requests during the past year, none of which had ever been fulfilled.

Issachar sipped from a steaming mug of hot tea and muttered as he looked at a sheet of parchment. "This proclamation concerns the height of wall hangings in the palace library." He shoved it to the side. "Have you seen anything unusual yet?"

"Everything Prescott handled could be called unusual." Dunwoody lifted a sheet of paper. "This is an order to groom his dog. It specifies that Peterkin's hair be exactly one-half inch long with a mane that is two and one quarter inches long. The mane should be dyed a darker shade so that he looks like a lion."

"Peterkin?" Issachar snorted. "That little rat dog is known for lyin' around. That's as close to lion as he'll ever get."

"Your pun is duly noted." Dunwoody stood and picked up another sheet of paper. "This is interesting."

"What is it?" Issachar adjusted his spectacles. "It looks like a requisition order."

"For extane delivery from Mikon Industries." Dunwoody pointed at a line item. "Notice the price."

Issachar's brow shot upward. "That's less than a tenth of the market."

"Which adds to the conspiracy." Dunwoody tapped his finger on the desk calendar. "Look at my compilation. Every time you scheduled an audit of Mikon Industries, you conveniently became too ill to complete it."

Issachar hummed, his expression darkening. "So Prescott really was protecting Mikon, as we suspected."

Dunwoody slid his spectacles into a tunic pocket. "With Prescott dead, the only known conspirators in this charade are at the gas company. If you're trying to root out all of his accomplices, you'll have to get more proof to prosecute someone outside of government offices."

Issachar waved a hand over the table. "So far out of all these papers, a single requisition is the only clue. If Prescott was as corrupt as I suspect, he must have hidden more evidence somewhere."

"Indeed. But where?"

Issachar scanned the office. "There must be a hidden safe, maybe a cache of—"

A knock sounded at the door.

Staying seated, Issachar took off his spectacles. "Who is it?"

"Courier, Governor Stafford. A message for you. It was sent with highest urgency."

"Come in."

The door opened. A young man wearing an all-black uniform with loose sleeves and pant legs marched in and withdrew a metal cylinder from a shoulder bag. When he had set the cylinder on the table, he folded his hands behind his back, his body straight. "Do you have any messages to send, Governor?"

"Not yet." Issachar gave him a nod. "Wait in the corridor until I give you leave."

"Thank you, sir." The Courier retraced his path and closed the door behind him.

Dunwoody picked up the tube. "Shall I project it on the wall for you?"

"Please." Issachar gestured toward a blank area next to the fireplace. "Right there will be fine."

Dunwoody looked the foot-long tube over. "I received these daily in the archives room. This is one of the newer models. I hope it doesn't have a genetic lock." He flipped a switch on the side and looked at the display screen, a square about the length of his thumb. A message appeared—*Deposit genetic material for access.*

"It does." Dunwoody pinched a stray hair on Issachar's shoulder. "This ought to do it."

"I seem to be losing too many these days." Issachar laid a hand on top of his balding head. "I'm glad you didn't have to pluck a new one."

"The lion's mane is thinning for both of us, I'm afraid." Dunwoody slid open a small metal door next to the screen and dropped the hair inside. A new message appeared—*Genetics verified*. He turned the viewing option switch to *Project* and pointed the cylinder at the wall.

A soldier appeared, looking directly at them, while hundreds of other soldiers milled about behind him, some with nervous expressions. Cold-weather clothes lay strewn here and there, the men having stripped down to trousers and thin shirts.

The soldier bowed his head. "Governor Stafford, I am Sergeant Fenton Xavier. I must inform you that we have run into an obstacle. When the portal opened, a few dozen of our men hurried through, but it suddenly closed, and the rest of us are stuck here. Captain Reed, Marcelle, and Magnar went with them. I am now in charge, but everyone who planned our strategy is gone. We would like to know if we should return to the palace or stay here and wait."

Sergeant Xavier looked up at the sky. "I estimate that we have already waited for two hours, so many of the men think Captain Reed has no way to open the portal again. It might be foolish to stay here since we have no backup plan."

After bowing again he said, "We await your orders."

The projection blinked off.

"A fair question." Issachar lifted his brow toward Dunwoody. "What do you think?"

Dunwoody stroked his chin. "The business of portals is certainly mystifying, so we need to rely on what we know."

"And that is?"

"Captain Reed wouldn't intentionally leave his men stranded. He would get a message to them if he could." Dunwoody began pacing. "I know this sergeant. He was once a pupil of mine. He is unusually ethical. He even turned himself in for accidentally cheating when he heard someone whisper a test answer."

Issachar nodded. "So his integrity is exemplary, but how does that relate to the matter at hand?"

"A poor connection at best. He is likely incorruptible, so he will do whatever he is asked by his authority. It's good that he went straight to you instead of someone else, since we don't know whom to trust."

"But I'm no military expert. I was a foot soldier for less than a year."

"That's enough to garner respect. Most of these boys are likely no more experienced than that."

Issachar stroked his chin for a few seconds before looking again at Dunwoody. "Let's order them to return, but we'll leave a small detachment there and relieve them every eight hours until we receive word."

"Excellent," Dunwoody said. "We should call the Courier in and send the message on horseback."

Another knock sounded.

Issachar called out, "Yes, Courier. I apologize for keeping you waiting. Please come in."

The door opened. A peasant girl broke away from the Courier's grasp and stumbled into the office. She took two off-kilter steps before regaining her balance. Breathing heavily, she lowered her head and folded her hands. "I beg you, sir, to hear my appeal."

"I apologize, Governor," the Courier said. "I told her to come during the next open-appeals hour."

Issachar waved a hand. "It's all right. I will hear her. Just stay close. I have a reply to record and send."

"Very well, sir." The Courier closed the door.

Issachar rose from his chair. "How may I help you, young lady?"

She curtsied in a graceful manner, her calf-length skirt sweeping the floor. "I am Sophia Halstead, daughter of the woman who burned at the stake a number of years ago."

Issachar gave Dunwoody a quick glance before returning his gaze to Sophia. "I remember it well. A tragic injustice. I assure you that I personally opposed the execution."

"Murder, if you'll pardon me, sir."

"I will gladly pardon that correction. Your term is the more accurate." Issachar cleared his throat. "Again, what may I do for you?"

As Sophia wrung her hands, apparently trying to summon courage to speak again, Dunwoody studied her eyes. They appeared to be clouded, not quite focused, and her expression took on the aspect of fear, like a waif who had been threatened or bullied.

When she finally composed herself, she gave a slight nod. "Seeing that you are a newly installed governor, perhaps you are unaware of the law concerning the rights of families who have been oppressed by government officials."

"You're right. I am unaware." Issachar turned toward Dunwoody. "Do you know about this law?"

"I have heard it mentioned a time or two. It is an old law. Never enforced in our province, as far as I know. One reason is that the government officials who oppress citizens are usually the same ones who would have to provide for their own penalty, which, of course, they would never do. And one who is oppressed rarely has an opportunity to appeal to the throne."

"Well, that will change." Issachar firmed his chin. "The law is the law, and we will follow it to the letter."

Sophia tilted her head. "You will, sir?"

"Of course." Issachar waved a hand at Dunwoody. "What is the penalty, Dawson? A monetary settlement? An individual home instead of a commune? We'll take care of whatever it is. This dreadful injustice has tainted our land for far too long."

"My memory fails me on that point, but I'm sure you have the details here." Dunwoody walked to the bookshelf and slid a huge volume from the top. He blew dust off the cover and opened it on the table to a page near the front. After flipping through it and humming to himself for a few seconds, he set his finger on a line of bold script. "Here it is. Shall I read it word for word?"

Issachar nodded. "By all means."

Dunwoody altered his tone to that of a stately town crier. "By order of King Popperell, any governorship found guilty of oppressing the citizenry will be penalized as follows: For acts of thievery, extortion, blackmail, or any other crime that oppresses monetarily, the offending governor and his accomplices will be sequestered in the dungeon for ninety days if the act was committed against a noble or for one hundred eighty days if against a commoner. In the case of an unjust execution against a member of any class, the family of the executed innocent will choose someone to replace the governor of the region. If no surviving family member can be found, the king will appoint a successor."

Dunwoody coughed, his cheeks warming. With Issachar's pronouncement that he would follow the law to the letter, he had painted himself into a corner.

"Is that all?" Issachar slid the book closer. "Has the law ever been modified or revoked?"

"It has not." Dunwoody pointed at a blank square in the margin. "The revoking law's number would have been entered in this space."

Issachar's cheeks flushed. "Well, then." He grasped the bottom hem of his tunic and jerked it down, straightening the material. "I'm not sure what to say. It seems that I have spoken hastily, and we should investigate the matter more thoroughly."

"Begging your pardon, sir …" Sophia took a step forward. "What is there to investigate? My mother's execution is a well-known fact, witnessed by hundreds, and the law is clear. Is it not?"

Issachar slammed the book closed. "As written, it is clear."

"And I am the only surviving family member," she continued. "My father died long before my mother's execution, and I have no siblings. Also, my mother's brother passed away last year, and her parents are long dead."

Dunwoody raised a finger. "I can vouch for her genealogy. Sophia is the last survivor."

"This is madness." Issachar began pacing. "King Popperell, may he rest in peace, must have meant that the *guilty* governor should be removed from office, not a governor who had nothing to do with the unjust execution. At the time, the king probably would have heard an appeal from a family member and sent troops to remove an evil governor. That is the clear intent of the law. And how can an execution be considered unjust unless the case is adjudicated by a new tribunal? We should appeal to King Sasser as soon as possible."

Sophia's body trembled. "Forgive me, Governor Stafford, but you said yourself the execution was unjust and that you would follow the law to the letter. If you try to find a loophole in order to hold on to power, then how would you differ from a guilty governor?"

"Madness!" Issachar swept his hand across the table, scattering papers everywhere. "I have been governor only a matter of hours, and the moment I set myself to rooting out corruption, this orphan comes in and shames me down to a rotten apple."

Tears welling, Sophia curtsied again, this time clumsily. "I'm sorry, sir, it wasn't my intent to bring shame—"

"Was it not?" Issachar slammed a fist on the law book. "I have been in the company of enough deceivers to recognize a well-thought-out scheme. You planned every response in advance, or perhaps you conspired with someone else, likely the person you will suggest as my replacement."

"Well, sir ..." She dipped her head low. "I do have someone in mind, and he did tell me about the law."

"Aha!" Issachar pointed at her. "I knew it."

Dunwoody raised a hand. "If I may interject a few thoughts."

Issachar ran his fingers through his thinning hair. "Yes, yes, go ahead."

"Thank you." Dunwoody hurried to the door and opened it. "If you would please wait in the corridor, Miss Halstead, we would like a moment of privacy."

"Of course." She backed out of the room and nodded demurely.

Dunwoody closed the door and whispered, "She is not here on her own accord."

Issachar sat heavily in his seat and kept his voice low. "Of course not, but how does that alter the dilemma? Whoever the mastermind is, he has surely spread the revelation about the law throughout Mesolantrum by now. If I appeal to the king, everyone will think I am trying to circumvent the law in order to hold my seat."

"True, especially if this mastermind is skillful at persuasion." Dunwoody walked to the opposite side of the table. "He will whisper from ear to ear that you require a clean house for everyone but yourself. With such a reputation, your mission to root out corruption will fail. You need popular support, and that requires being above reproach so that no one will believe the whispers."

"But at what cost? Giving in to a potential tyrant?" Issachar drummed his fingers. "Perhaps we are giving this unknown mastermind too much credit. We should interview him to see what kind of man we are dealing with. If he is a scoundrel, the two of us should be able to expose him, and if we do so in front of Miss Halstead, maybe she will forget about suggesting a replacement, and we can avoid this entire mess."

"Agreed. An examination is the best option." Dunwoody snapped his fingers. "We also have to send that message to the soldiers."

"Yes, I forgot about that. This dilemma has surely addled my brain." Issachar nodded at the door. "Bring Miss Halstead and the Courier back in."

"Good idea. The Courier can be a witness." Dunwoody hustled to the door, opened it, and gestured for the two to come inside.

When Sophia reentered, she reenacted her graceful curtsy as well as her tortured expression, while the Courier stood stiffly, clutching his shoulder bag.

"Have you come to a decision?" Sophia asked.

"Only the next step." Issachar rose and began a slow pace in front of her. "Who told you about the law?"

"A man named Cal, sir. Cal Broder."

Dunwoody blinked. That was the name of a storybook hero from a children's novel. How odd that the two names matched.

Issachar halted and looked straight at Sophia. "Are you willing to suspend your decision regarding him as a replacement until after you witness our examination of him?"

"Certainly. Far be it from me to presume that my nominee should take such a high seat of authority without scrutiny."

"Did you bring him with you?" Issachar looked past her at the open door. "Is he nearby?"

"I did, and he is. If you'll pardon me." Sophia slipped out the door, then returned a moment later, wringing her hands. "He's coming."

Issachar nodded at the Courier. "Do you have a blank photo tube?"

"Yes sir." The Courier reached into his shoulder bag and withdrew a cylinder.

"Kindly photograph the examination. Everything must be open and aboveboard."

"Yes sir." The Courier flipped a switch on the cylinder and pointed it at Issachar and Sophia. "I am ready."

The door pushed farther open, and a man wearing a beret stepped through the gap. When he locked gazes with Issachar, he swept off his beret and bowed. "You called for me?"

Dunwoody studied the man. Cal Broder's flaming red hair and sparkling green eyes stood out, and his athletic build made him

EXODUS RISING

look like an avid wrestler, or perhaps he was more acquainted with pushing loaded shovels. In any case, his face was handsome enough to attract any woman's attention.

"I did." Issachar closed the door behind Cal and gestured for everyone to make a circle at the center of the room. With Cal at the middle of the ring and everyone looking on, including the Courier with the photo tube, Issachar stood at arm's length and gave Cal a skeptical stare. "Where are you from? I don't think I have seen you before."

Cal threaded his beret through his fingers. "I was born here in Mesolantrum, but I have been away of late. I'm sure my appearance has changed over time."

"No doubt, no doubt." Issachar looked at Cal's shoes. "Where have you been? Tarkton?"

Cal lifted a foot. "Oh, these. I bought them from a Tark in the palace village. He sells berets and boots. I have not been to Tarkton in a number of years."

"I know the vendor." Issachar wobbled for a moment as if dazed. "A most disagreeable fellow."

Dunwoody leaned toward Issachar and whispered, "He didn't answer the question about where he has been."

"He didn't?" Issachar blinked. "Of course. You're right."

Cal laughed agreeably. "I apologize. I was simply assuming the reason for the question. Actually, I have been to Dracon, the dragon world."

Issachar drew his head back. "Dracon? How did you get there?"

Cal pulled a small leather-bound book from his tunic. "I came into possession of Uriel Blackstone's journal, and it provided the location of a portal and how to overcome its many obstacles."

"Did you see dragons?" Issachar asked. "Slaves?"

"Indeed. Many of both. I was unable to help the slaves, but a group of avenger dragons will soon attack the slavers and set our people free. The rescued slaves will want to open the portal in the Underground Gateway so they can come home to our world."

"And can you open it?"

Cal lifted the journal. "The instructions are here. I assume they still work."

Issachar walked to a map on the wall and pointed at a spot in a forest region. "We know of another portal that leads to Dracon's Northlands, and we heard that it has been closed and most of our soldiers are unable to pass." He lifted his brow. "Do you know anything about how to open that one?"

Dunwoody concealed a cringe. Why was Issachar giving away such sensitive information?

"I know how to open a portal from the Dracon side," Broder said, "but I suggest that we withdraw. Leave both portals closed. Let the slaves remain there."

Issachar's forehead knitted. "What? Are you out of your mind?"

"Not at all." Cal turned directly toward the Courier's video tube. "Humans on Dracon have been infected with a terrible disease. Although the avenger dragons will conquer the slavers and set the humans free, there is no cure for the disease. If the emancipated slaves come to our world, they will infect everyone here, and all will perish."

"We heard about this possibility," Dunwoody said, "but we need to be sure. We hope that our soldiers can give us a report."

"There is no need to wait for a report." Cal spread out his arms, his voice silky smooth. "I have seen these suffering souls with my own eyes. Sores ravage their skin, and I am told the beastly disease gnaws inside their bellies."

As if summoned by the words, a bare-chested boy appeared, semitransparent and sitting on the floor. Hunched over and groaning, pus oozed from hand-sized ulcers on his back and shoulders. Most of his hair had fallen out, making his scalp look like the coat of a mangy dog.

The Courier turned the photo tube toward the boy as Cal continued. "This lad's suffering is multiplied a thousand times throughout the dragon world, and if the victims come here, they will not find freedom; they will merely die in a place they have never known, and they will transport this mask of death to you and your spouses and your children. No one will be exempt from the horror."

Dunwoody squinted at Cal. Something in his cadence, his body language, his tone carried a hypnotic quality. Every word seemed to diminish thoughts of countering arguments. Yet, the arguments begged to be spoken, and someone had to break this spell and air them. "What about you?" Dunwoody asked. "Are you carrying the disease? If not, how did you escape it?"

"I had it," Cal said without missing a beat, "but the avenger dragons cured me. They had the power to cure only one human, and I have come home to warn everyone that we must protect ourselves." As he continued, more semitransparent people appeared—men, women, and children, all in shoddy, torn clothes and shuffling along in a desert-like land. Oozing sores afflicted each one. "That's why I asked Sophia Halstead to appeal for an invocation of a little-known law and to elevate me to the governor's seat. Since I am the only person intimately familiar with the Underground Gateway and the disease ravaging our people on Dracon, I am uniquely qualified to ensure our safety. Yet, without the authority to enforce what is needed, I will not be able to erect a wall of security."

"Would you leave them there to die?" Issachar asked. "That would be cruel!"

Dunwoody nodded. Issachar was fighting the influence as well. These questions had to be asked.

"Shouldn't we bring them back and quarantine them?" Issachar continued. "We'll send a research physician to them, and we'll find a cure. Surely we have more experience in medicine than they do."

Dunwoody let out a sigh. These were good points but insufficient. "Issachar, I'm afraid it's not that simple. I have the dragon's journal from the days that the disease first entered their world. Their technology and knowledge of medicine were far more advanced than ours, and their most eminent scientists were unable to cure the disease."

"Governor," Cal said, "your sympathy is a tribute to your character, but we must be sure to reserve most of our sympathies for our loved ones here." He looked directly into the camera again. "I'm sure many of you remember the unjust execution of the widow Halstead. The law says that the way to right this wrong is to allow a family member of Mrs. Halstead to choose a successor to the governor. Her daughter, Sophia, has chosen me, so by law, and for the sake of every soul on this planet, it is imperative that Governor Stafford graciously step down and allow me to protect our entire race during this time of crisis."

The Courier called out, "Yes!" Then, his face turning red, he straightened his body. "Sorry, sir. I was caught up in the moment."

"No need to explain." Issachar exhaled loudly. "I, too, have been persuaded. I have no rebuttal to this man's rational points."

Dunwoody shook his head. It seemed that cobwebs had formed inside his own skull. Something sinister was afoot here, but without a shred of evidence, how could he make such a claim, especially when his brain had gone for a swim in a whirlpool?

"Then will you step down?" Sophia asked.

Issachar gave a resigned nod. "It seems that I have no choice." He turned to Dunwoody. "Will you draw up the papers?"

"You do have a choice." Dunwoody clenched his eyes shut for a moment. He had to brush away the mental debris and think clearly. "You can send an appeal for clarification to the king. Surely no one would object to the justice of a royal interpretation of the law."

"Pardon the intrusion," Cal said, "but that would take too much time. We should immediately send word to the soldiers stationed at the portal to the Northlands and tell them to stay. They must prevent entry from Dracon at all costs. Leave half of them there, and bring the other half back to the palace to report to me."

"So let it be ordered." Issachar waved at the Courier. "Duplicate this message. Have one copy sent to Sergeant Fenton Xavier and have the other projected in the Cathedral continually. Tell the crier on duty to call everyone to see it. This crisis must be avoided."

"Very well." The Courier bowed. "And may I say, sir, that your decision to step down is the most honorable act I have ever witnessed." He turned and ran out the door.

Issachar straightened his tunic, his cheeks awash in red. "Well, I suppose I should be leaving now. If you will still have me as the banker, I will return to serving Mesolantrum in that capacity."

Cal smiled graciously. "Since I know nothing about banking, I would be glad of your service, but I have something more important for you to do at this moment." He walked to the table, crawled underneath, and looked up at the underside. He ran his finger along it, then stopped and rapped on it with his knuckles. A small door fell open. Cal reached inside and withdrew a long silver key.

When he crawled out and stood, he showed it to Issachar. "This key fits a lock in a hidden cabinet embedded in the wall behind Prescott's bed. There you will find correspondence between Prescott and the officers of Mikon Industries as well as many other documents that will prove the corruption of nearly every high official in this palace, including the conspiracy to poison you." He laid the key in Issachar's palm. "Because of your passion to clean out the corruption, I place you in charge of having these men and women arrested and locked in the dungeon. We can delay their trials until after the emergency concerning the Dracon slaves is over."

Issachar closed his hand over the key. An odd smile crossed his face. "This is an assignment I will be glad to fulfill."

"Excellent." Cal gestured toward the door. "Then let's make a public announcement about this transfer of authority immediately."

"Wait!" Dunwoody gave Cal a sideways stare. "How did you know about the cabinet and the key? And for that matter, how can a man who has been away from Mesolantrum for so long know about the conspiracy to poison Mr. Stafford, not to mention Prescott's secret deals with the gas company?"

"Does it matter?" Issachar held up the key. "We can rid ourselves of all the conspirators." He exited the room, followed by Cal and Sophia.

"Yes, it does—"

The door closed and latched.

"Matter."

Dunwoody glared at the door. Now that Cal had left, the fog was dissipating. He obviously possessed some kind of persuasive influence that mesmerized everyone, including the most skeptical hearers. And what of his ability to conjure ghostly images of diseased people? Surely that talent couldn't be natural.

In his mind, he replayed Cal's words, his delivery, his gestures. Something seemed familiar about him. With his red hair and green eyes, not to mention his power, he raised memories of Leo. If Cal really was of the same species, he could easily wrest control of the kingdom in short order, and only dragon fire would be able to stop him. Yet, with panic likely to ensue if someone were to suggest opening a portal to let a dragon in, that option seemed to be off the table, and since Cal would likely reach legendary hero status within the next few hours, no one would agree to a plan to destroy him.

Dunwoody thrust his hands into his trousers pockets. And why should they agree? Cal hadn't done anything wrong. The only accusation that might hold water would be that he participated in Prescott's shady dealings. How else could he have known about the key and the cabinet? Raising that issue, however, would likely be futile. Cal's hypnotic oratory and the aid of half of the military detachment would quickly sweep all suspicions away.

"And me with them." Dunwoody opened the door and walked toward the stairway to the archives. Although Leo's guards had ransacked the room, at least Arxad's journal still rested in a safe place. Maybe poring over those pages would provide a clue as to how to unmask this new threat to Mesolantrum. Cal Broder seemed to be a cross between Leo and someone with much more finesse. He had the sense of cunning to know how to beguile without wielding a sledgehammer. Leo had also promised to uproot foul weeds, but his tendency to rely on brute force had been his undoing.

Dunwoody descended the stairway—dark and musty. The creaking boards sounded like a crowbar prying nails from oak, an appropriate symbol. Cries for protection would be the crowbar ripping away the foundation for all freedoms in this land. With Issachar already deceived, and with fear as an ally, Broder would have the masses begging him to lead them by the proverbial hooks in their noses. They would be unaware that those who allow fear to overwhelm charity, who choose personal safety over pity for those who beg for freedom, become slaves to their fears. And such a slave master is worse than any dragon.

He stopped and looked back, whispering, "Fenton Xavier. Little Fenton Xavier." He snapped his fingers. Of course! Since the Courier had to take the time to duplicate the tube, intercepting it wouldn't be too difficult. A simple note at the beginning of the copy intended for Fenton might be all they needed to thwart Broder's plan. With Fenton's help, a wily archivist could come up with a little cunning of his own.

✷ EIGHT ✷

ADRIAN stroked Marcelle's hand, though his fingers passed through. Here in the white room, she stayed visible even while motionless. Still, her body remained semi-transparent and vaporous, like an unsolved mystery. Although she had just finished telling about her harrowing adventures as a spirit on Major Four, she had left much untold. She had related events, not feelings. Even her furrowed brow indicated she was holding back.

Standing nearby, Regina, who had helped Adrian tell his tales to Marcelle by resurrecting them in this alabaster theater, cocked her head. "I see Arxad. He's flying this way."

Adrian climbed to his feet and instinctively reached for Marcelle to help her up, but his hand grasped only tingly air.

She smiled and, like rising fog, drifted to a standing position. "There are some advantages to having no body. Being as light as a feather is one of them."

"Maybe so, but I prefer a complete Marcelle." Adrian turned to Regina. "How close is Arxad?"

"I'll show you." Regina waved a hand in front of a white wall. Colors poured in. Melting snow stretched out in every direction, interrupted by protruding trees and Alaph's castle in the distance. A whipping wind buffeted Adrian's hair and clothes. Arxad flew overhead, casting a shadow over them as he hurried toward the castle.

"He's here," Marcelle said. "Here in the Northlands."

Adrian kept his gaze on the castle. Arxad sailed through the open doorway and landed in the shadows. "Since Regina sees tales from the past, he's probably been here for at least a little while."

"Then let's see if we can find him." Marcelle took a step, but when a wide vertical crack appeared in their view of the Northlands, she halted. The crack forked in jagged lines. The entire scene shattered and crumbled until only whiteness remained, save for a dark vertical gap—an open door.

Marcelle let out a low groan.

"What's the matter?" Adrian asked.

"Pain. Worse than ever."

"But your body is in Alaph's chamber."

"I know."

Arxad extended his neck through the door. "Ah! Shellinda was correct. You *are* in here."

"Should we go somewhere else?" Adrian asked.

"No. This is the place I had hoped we would gather. Normally I am not allowed to land and walk in this area, but unusual circumstances have forced a bending of the rules." Arxad looked back toward the outer corridor. "Thank you, Resolute, for leading me here."

When the door closed, restoring the pristine whiteness, Arxad scooted toward them.

"How strange." Marcelle laid a hand on her chest. "The pain's gone."

Arxad drew close and stopped, his erect ears twitching. "Do you have the stardrop Marcelle brought?"

Adrian touched the pouch on his belt. "Right here."

"The scale you gave me is in there, too," Marcelle said. "I couldn't keep it on."

"Of course. You cannot do the impossible." Arxad curled his serpentine neck and set his head in front of Marcelle's face. "Alaph examined you and told me what must be done to perform the reunification, though I do not understand the rationale behind the process. I thought that merely coaxing your body to swallow the stardrop while in your spirit's presence would draw the two of you together, but complicating issues have presented themselves."

"Complicating issues?" Adrian repeated. "You mean the fact that her body and spirit can't be together without causing extreme pain?"

"No. That was expected, but let us not waste time in the telling. With a Starlighter here, it is best to show what I mean."

Regina spread out her arms. "What tale do you want me to show them?"

"You are accustomed to recreating tales of Starlight, but this time you must reveal events that occurred in their own world."

Regina narrowed her eyes. "How is that possible? Exodus never saw anything there."

"An experienced Starlighter is able to extract tales from the memories of those around her. Since you have already proven your expertise, I predict that you will have no trouble performing this advanced technique."

"How does it work, Arxad?" Marcelle touched the side of her head. "Are my memories locked in this pseudo-body I have or in my physical brain?"

"Both, in a manner of speaking." Arxad set a wing tip near her head. "At this time, memories reside in your physical brain, but you have maintained an attachment with your body, so your thoughts are in tandem. If your body were to die, your spiritual essence would absorb the spiritual functions of your brain. Yet, for now, a tension exists. Your functions are divided and shared, making each part like matching poles on two magnets. You repel one another, and the closer you approach, the greater the repelling force."

"So they can't get together unless the force is destroyed," Adrian said.

"On the contrary. We must keep the force intact and reverse it in one of the magnets. Then they will resemble opposite poles and attract each other."

Marcelle squinted. "How do we do that?"

"A magnet's poles can be reversed by using a technology we had in this world before the disease killed the human residents. Since that technology no longer exists, I thought I could use the stardrop to heat up Marcelle's body. Heat can destabilize a magnet, and since the stardop has spiritual properties, it can also scramble the polar attractions in the spiritual realm. The key to solving our problem is to realign Marcelle's body and spirit while she is experiencing the elevated temperature."

"That sounds like it involves pain," Adrian said.

"Without a doubt. When Alaph told me about this solution, he included a warning that Marcelle would undergo a great deal of suffering."

"It can't be worse than what I've already suffered." Marcelle glided closer to Arxad. "What's the first step?"

Arxad spread his wing around her. "To entice your body to ingest the stardrop."

Adrian patted his trousers pocket. "I have another stardrop with Cassabrie's blood mixed in. It cures the disease, but she said not to give it to Marcelle until her body and spirit are reunited."

"That is because the healing is physical as well as spiritual," Arxad said. "We will use the one Marcelle brought for reuniting purposes and dispense the other one afterward, assuming the process works." He extended his neck toward the direction he had entered. "Shellinda is just outside watching over Marcelle's body. When you are ready, you may bring both of them in."

Adrian looked that way. That was the reason for Marcelle's pain a moment ago, and somehow this magical room acted as a barrier. He turned to Marcelle and raised his brow. "Are you ready? It's going to hurt."

"I'll do my best." She nodded firmly. "Bring me in."

Adrian walked to the point where Arxad had entered. Although the door's outline had disappeared, it had to be there somewhere. He touched the wall with his fingertips. The outline appeared, and the door swung out. In the corridor, Marcelle's body lay on the floor, her head cradled in Shellinda's lap.

"I'll take her now." Adrian slid his arms under Marcelle and lifted her to his chest. "If you want, you can come inside."

"I can?" Shellinda smiled. "Thank you."

Once they entered and Shellinda closed the door behind them, Adrian carried Marcelle toward her awaiting spirit. With every step, her misty face tightened more and more into a twisted mask. She clutched her chest, then doubled over, moaning. At the same time, her body writhed in his arms, and her physical face contorted. She wheezed and tried to thrash, but he held her in place.

Adrian stopped. "What should I do?"

"Keep coming." Marcelle heaved, gasping for breath. "We have to do this."

As he continued, Marcelle's spirit slid backwards. She angled her body to stop the movement, but she kept sliding as though battling a fierce wind.

"Stop," Arxad said. "The repelling force is too strong, and she is too light and insubstantial to resist."

Adrian laid Marcelle's writhing body on the floor and, with Shellinda's help, pinned her arms and legs down. Foam leaked from one side of her mouth, and a trickle of blood oozed from a nostril.

Marcelle's spirit eased to a stop, but her spasms continued. "Next step!" As she wrapped her arms around herself, pain streaked her voice. "Please hurry!"

"The stardrop," Arxad said.

Marcelle strained her legs and trudged a step closer. "And the scale."

"That is not necessary," Arxad said. "You are not in a condition—"

"Just do it!" Mist swirled within her frame, darker and thinner. "I made a covenant with you!"

"I appreciate your fidelity." Arxad bobbed his head. "Proceed."

"Adrian ..." Background groans stretched Marcelle's every word. "Put it on my chest. You'll see the mark it made."

Adrian reached into the pouch, withdrew the scale, and laid it on Marcelle's stomach. With shaky hands, he pulled back her tunic's left placket, exposing the edge of a circle on her skin, reddened and raw.

"Go ahead, Adrian." Grimaces on the two Marcelles nearly matched. "Just press down. It'll hold."

"But I would have to—" He swallowed the next words. They were juvenile, the product of irrational fears.

"I'll do it!" Shellinda took the scale from Adrian and peeled back Marcelle's tunic. She slid the scale into place and pressed the heel of her hand over it. Marcelle's physical body's grimace tightened, but only for a moment. "One ... two ... three ..."

"What are you doing?" Adrian asked.

"Counting heartbeats." Shellinda closed her eyes. "Five ... six ... seven ... eight ... nine ... ten." She lifted her hand. The scale stayed put, tightly adhered to Marcelle's hot, moist skin. Shellinda pulled the tunic back into place and smiled. "It worked, Adrian. What you're scared of is gone."

"What *I'm* scared of?"

"Now the stardrop," Arxad said. "Put it in her mouth, well toward the back of her throat. If the connection between them is strong, her spirit should be able to help her body swallow, though it will be an excruciating process."

"It can't get much worse." Marcelle's spirit dropped to her knees. "We have to do it!"

Adrian pulled the stardrop box from the pouch. After opening the lid, he tipped the box and let the stardrop roll into his palm. The instant it touched his skin, the contact point sizzled. Grimacing, he pinched Marcelle's cheeks together and pushed the radiant ball deep into her mouth.

Her back arched and locked in place. Her face flushed crimson. She tried to spit the stardrop out, but Adrian held his hand over her mouth. "Swallow, Marcelle! Swallow!"

"I'm trying!" Marcelle's spirit clenched her fists and swallowed again and again. Finally, her body copied the motion. The redness faded to pink, and her back relaxed, though the furrows in her brow remained deep and tight.

The mist in Marcelle's spirit thickened. She released her grip on her stomach and slowly rose to her feet. "It's …" She patted her torso. "It's easing up."

"Excellent." Arxad swung his neck, bringing his head close to Regina. "Now it is your turn. Dive deeply into Marcelle's mind. You will likely have to probe both her spirit and her body to learn the secrets she holds dear."

"Secrets?" Marcelle asked. "I don't have any secrets. My life has always been an open book."

"Is that so?" Arxad shifted his head toward her, his ears rotating. "Perhaps you harbor thoughts deeper than your conscious mind can fathom. They are secret, even to you."

"After all I've been through, I'm not going to doubt anything." She nodded toward Regina. "Go ahead. I'll try to keep my mind open."

"Adrian," Arxad said, "You will sit between Marcelle's body and her spirit. According to Alaph, as Regina unfolds the mysteries, you should engage Marcelle in conversation. The topics will become clear. Our hope is that you will be a catalyst that will draw her two entities together, so make sure you absorb every sight and sound."

"I'll do whatever it takes." Adrian released Marcelle's body and patted Shellinda's back. "Think you can handle her?"

Shellinda sat next to Marcelle's body and nodded.

"If her body moves on its own," Arxad said, "let it go. Allow the reunification to commence. Just guide her path."

Adrian scooted to a point halfway between Marcelle's body and spirit, about six feet from each, and sat cross-legged.

Marcelle's spirit copied his pose and faced Adrian. "I'm ready."

He arched his brow. "How's the pain?"

"Not too bad. No worse than some training wounds I've suffered."

As he drank in her words, he stared at the space between them—only two long paces, but it felt like two miles.

Arxad spread a wing and touched Regina's back. "Now, Starlighter. Show us what you see."

"I'll do my best." Regina crouched at Marcelle's spirit's side and, craning her neck, looked her in the eye. After a few seconds, Regina rose and backed slowly away. She spread her arms and waved them back and forth. With each sweep, some of the surrounding whiteness dissolved. A forest scene took its place—tall trees with lush foliage and a circular grass-covered clearing speckled with fallen leaves.

Adrian, Arxad, Regina, Shellinda, and the two Marcelles sat or stood near the center of the clearing. A breeze kicked up the leaves and tossed them into a swirl around their bodies.

"I know this place," Adrian said. "The portal leading to the Northlands is here."

Images of Marcelle and Cassabrie appeared in the gap between Marcelle's spirit and Adrian. The two apparitions conversed, though too quietly to hear.

"Regina," Arxad said. "Concentrate on their voices. Any word might be crucial."

She nodded. Narrowing her eyes, she set her hands behind her ears. The sound of the breeze filtered in, then birdsong.

After a few seconds, Cassabrie's voice came through. "The portal will remain open." Cassabrie extended an arm to her side. Her hand disappeared. "It is very dangerous to leave it this way, but I think we have no choice. Take note, however. When you return to the Northlands, you will again be a spirit. Your army will have to march behind a ghost; prepare them for that."

Regina's conjured Marcelle slid her hand through the invisible opening. Hers, too, disappeared. As she held it in place, lines dug more and more deeply into her forehead.

"I perceive doubt," Cassabrie said. "Am I the reason?"

Marcelle nodded. "There's no use lying about it. I know what you did to Adrian."

Cassabrie looked at the ground and brushed leaves with her bare toes. "I make no apologies for my actions. I have reasons for what I did, and I cannot tell them to you now." She laid a hand on her chest. "Yet, I vow not to indwell him again. You and I are now in the same condition, spirits without bodies. Nothing matters more than rescuing our people. With all my heart, I long to be your partner in the war against the dragons and their cruelty."

Staring straight at Cassabrie, Marcelle extended her hand. "Adrian needs our help, and I will be your partner."

Cassabrie slid her hand into Marcelle's. "Until we meet again on Starlight." She then drifted away, floated into the portal, and disappeared.

Marcelle stood motionless, blinking. Every sound fell silent. She took a step closer to the portal and inserted her finger, making it vanish. As a frown crossed her face, she wagged her head. "I make no apologies for my actions." Then she spun and marched out of the clearing and into the surrounding trees. "Now if I can just find a good sword."

As Marcelle walked, Regina's scene followed her progress, keeping the image of Marcelle between her watching spirit and Adrian. Trees passed by, and leaves crunched, though they created only gentle background noise.

Adrian leaned to the side and looked at Marcelle's spirit. "What were you thinking at this moment?"

Marcelle tilted her head upward at her likeness who seemed to march in place. "I thought I was dreaming. It didn't take long before I realized that I didn't have a heartbeat, and later I found that I could dissolve."

"So you thought it was a dream the entire time you were there?"

"Most of the time, and that caused a big problem. I took some dangerous chances. I thought I couldn't die."

Adrian firmed his lips. "The Creator protected you."

"That much I'm sure of."

Regina's canvas altered from the forest scene to a small room with a bed and frayed rug. A little girl stood in her underwear in front of an oval mirror propped on a stand. She pulled a pair of oversize trousers up to her waist and fastened them. Then, staring at the mirror, she flexed her skinny biceps and frowned.

A smaller, wood-framed mirror leaned against a stack of books on a nearby dresser, a surrounding glow making it stand out in the theatrical display.

The scene froze in place. The girl and larger mirror stood so that the space between them intersected the gap between Marcelle's spirit and Adrian, allowing them to see each other clearly.

Marcelle whispered, "My mother's mirror."

"The one on the dresser?" Adrian asked.

She nodded. "It looks like it's glowing."

Arxad shuffled closer. "Then it has special significance." He reared up and pried the real mirror from his underbelly and melded it with the one in Regina's image. "Only in the great white room will this work."

The handheld mirror flashed and sparkled. Arxad carried it to Marcelle—the two mirrors joined as one—and laid it in her palms. "Now you will be able to carry it."

As Arxad slid out of sight, Marcelle gazed at the mirror. The edges of the frame crackled with tiny flames, as if set on fire by her touch.

"Read it," Arxad said.

She turned it over and read an engraving on the wooden back. "Your heart is reflected by the light you shine. How great is your light when you sacrifice all you have for those who have nothing to give."

A rumble threaded through Arxad's voice. "Now look at yourself anew."

She turned it back to the mirror side. "It has a bloody fingerprint on it."

"Yes," Arxad said. "Now pierce the physical and look into the realm of the spiritual."

"It's ..." She swallowed. "It's like I'm seeing into my soul."

Arxad's voice hummed. "Let the worries of our situation melt away. Just tell us your thoughts."

As Marcelle gazed into the mirror, she spoke softly. "My mother used to sing a lullaby." A sparkling tear dripped from her eye and vanished in a splash of sparks. "It went something like this." Her tone altered to a lilting chant. "'Tis but a glass, little one, a prayer, little one. When every dream has flown, and you're there all alone, always look for a light from above. Whenever you bleed, whenever you need, look for me in the eyes of love."

Marcelle closed her eyes and hugged the mirror. "My mother told me that she and I are reflections of each other. My heart beats in her bosom, and hers in mine. As long as I keep this mirror close, I remember her love, my father's love, and most of all, the Creator's love. Love is a shield of protection that never wears out."

Marcelle slid closer to Adrian, apparently without any effort. "Adrian, I think that's the key to everything. My lack of dependence on the Creator, I mean. I've always been independent, even to the point of being stubborn."

Adrian shook his head. "You're tenacious. That's an admirable quality."

"Let's not sugarcoat it, Adrian." She spread her palms over her lap and gazed at the mirror. "I've been a stubborn, self-protective shrew."

"No, you haven't. You just—"

"Don't, Adrian!" She clenched her fingers around the sparkling mirror. "Just don't!"

He bit his lip. It didn't take a genius to figure out it was time to shut up and listen.

She looked at him, tears brimming. "I've been giving myself excuses for my obstinate behavior for years. It's time I stopped."

He gave her a prompting nod. "Go on. Tell me what's on your heart. I want to know everything."

"Well … if you're sure. It might get uglier." Marcelle turned her tear-filled gaze back to the mirror. "When my mother was murdered, I died inside. In one moment I transformed from a little girl into a warrior. Lust for revenge consumed me, and I knew that a scrawny farm girl could never find my mother's killer, much less deliver the punishment he deserved. You know the rest. I trained and trained and trained some more. I became one of the best swordplayers in the kingdom. No one dared cross me. Men feared me. Women disdained me. I exchanged frilly dresses and dish cloths for trousers and a sword—a disguise to conceal the hate-inspired wretchedness in my soul. And I became the very witch I vowed never to be. I hated that the other women looked down on me. I found them cold and superficial, but I acted in the same way toward them. I was a hypocrite. I was so blinded by rage and lust for revenge I saw only their upturned noses and not my own."

Regina's scene again shifted. Her image of Marcelle sat on a bench in a dim room, her limbs chained to a ring embedded in the floor in front of her. Cassabrie stood beyond the ring, her smile a stark contrast to Marcelle's deep frown.

Adrian reached forward and touched the ring, cool and metallic.

"Well," Marcelle's spirit continued, "my excessive courage got me in trouble, so I spent some time in the palace courtroom's detention cell. Cassabrie visited me by dissolving and sliding under the door. She explained why she entered your body and influenced your mind for a while."

Marcelle bit her misty lip. After waiting through the pause, Adrian lifted his brow. "And?"

She pulled her tunic's placket to the side, exposing the area where the scale resided on her physical body. The circular spot turned transparent, providing a view inside. A heart hovered within, misty and swirling. "Cassabrie told me to undress my soul for you, to let you see my heart."

Adrian stared. His throat tightened. He dared not say a word.

Marcelle's face seemed to melt into tears. "Oh, Adrian, I'm so sorry for how I've treated you, for how I doubted you and Cassabrie. I don't want you to think of me as a hot-tempered witch. When I attacked that dragon at the cattle camp, I nearly got you killed, but you never lashed out at me. You never uttered a harsh word. You just dropped your sword belt and gave yourself over to the guardian dragon." Her spirit floated closer. "You saved me and the children."

The ring and chains in Regina's tale faded away. From behind Adrian, Marcelle's body slid toward him on its own, bumped against his back, and pushed him until his knees brushed against Marcelle's misty knees in front of him.

Marcelle's spirit leaned forward, stretching her tunic. "Here is my heart, Adrian Masters, a renewed heart. No matter how bad things look, I will trust you. You have proven to be a man of courage, sacrifice, and love. And I will be at your side to the ends of any world …" She released her tunic and dipped her head. "If you will have me."

Adrian slid his hand into hers. "No, Marcelle."

She stared at him, blinking through tears. "No?"

"Not until I undress my soul for you." He shifted his body and withdrew his sword. "This is what I've relied upon ever since I can remember. But while I carried you, I had to let a one-eyed boy named Wallace take it. That's when I realized that I had only one eye myself."

"I … I don't understand."

He ran a finger along the flat of the blade. "I came to Starlight thinking my sword and fighting abilities would be enough to conquer the dragons, but when I got here, it didn't take long to realize how stupid I was. The dragons are too powerful, the people are too entrenched in misery, and the disease is consuming what is left of their hopes. This rescue is simply out of our reach. I can't do it, you can't do it, and the army that's supposed to be coming from Major Four can't do it."

"So it's impossible? You think there's no hope?"

"I didn't say that." Adrian touched the edge of the blade. "Like you said about yourself, I haven't relied on the Creator much. I say the usual words everyone else says about him protecting us or guiding us. You know, the easy expressions that are more like trite idioms than heartfelt hymns. I suppose it's my way of trying to look humble and spiritual, but when it comes down to really believing my words, I've been pulling air from an empty scabbard."

"So what will you do?"

"Surrender."

Marcelle's body curled around Adrian's hip. Shellinda guided her arms and legs so they wouldn't catch on his scabbard. When her limp body lay parallel to his thigh, her motion stopped.

"Surrender?" Marcelle's spirit said. "But the slaves need us! How can you surrender to the dragons and let—"

"Not to the dragons." He laid the sword on the floor, reached to his side, and gathered her body into his arms. "I surrender to the Creator. I give up my sword, my will, and my soul to him. I am undressed. I am naked. I will charge into battle to free the slaves as a man without sword or scabbard, without belt or buckler, trusting in the Creator's purpose. To paraphrase what a wise dragon recently said, though I likely will die in the attempt, this is the only way to save my soul."

"But maybe you won't die. Maybe we'll be able to defeat them."

"Shhh." Adrian raised a finger. "I have one more thing to say, and it's ready to burst out."

Tears sparkling again, she gave him a sober nod. "Then say it."

✹ NINE ✹

I WON'T say it until you reunite." He shifted her body higher and rested her head on his shoulder. "I think you're ready."

"I am." Her spirit stretched out and flowed into her body. Her limbs quivered. She sucked in a breath. When her eyes fluttered open, she stared at Adrian. "I'm … I'm back!"

"Yes." He kissed the side of her head and held her close. "You're back."

She wiggled out of his grasp and resumed her cross-legged position, again looking at him. "What did you want to say to me?"

He pushed a strand of hair from her eyes. What a lovely sight! Gleaming pools of love and expectation. The time had finally come. "Marcelle …"

As he swallowed through a lump, she slid her hand into his and interlocked their thumbs. Her brow lifted. "Yes?"

"Well, I said something while I was carrying you, but I wasn't sure it got through."

"I heard your explanation about why you forfeited the tournament match and how you should have told me your reasons. You don't want to cross swords with me. You want to be at my side as a fellow warrior, not as a combatant." She gave him a sly grin. "But the last part is a bit hazy. I think you asked me a question."

"Actually, two questions." He cleared his throat. "First, will you forgive me for not explaining the reason I forfeited?"

"Of course I forgive you." She drew her head closer. Her eyes sparkled, and her lips pursed. "What's the second question?"

"The second question is …" He swallowed again. "Will you marry me?"

Marcelle smiled, her lips trembling. "I will marry you, Adrian Masters." As her voice cracked with emotion, tears flowed. "I will fight at your side with all my heart. Our swords will never cross, and nothing will come between us—not fear, not doubt, not even a dragon will be able to sever my heart from yours. We will be one in mind, in body, and in purpose." She drew so close, her breath warmed his cheeks. "I love you, Adrian."

He compressed her hand. "And I love you, Marcelle."

Their lips met in a kiss, gentle and warm—pure ecstasy. Every worry in every world fled away. For this single moment, they were alone in paradise.

When they pulled back, he combed his fingers through her matted hair. "You're so beautiful."

She wrinkled her nose. "I'll bet I smell like a garbage heap."

"Maybe." He shrugged. "I didn't notice."

Arxad batted her shoulder with a wing. "I noticed."

Marcelle laughed. "Thanks a lot."

"I apologize for breaking up this touching scene," Arxad said, "but there is much to do."

"The healing stardrop." Adrian withdrew the dented box from his pocket and opened the lid. "Since you're not showing any symptoms, you might not have the disease at all, and the pain might not be too bad. I think at least it'll make you immune."

"After all I've been through, this'll be like spice gum." She picked up the stardrop, popped it into her mouth, and swallowed with only a slight cringe. "Let's go."

Adrian shot to his feet and helped Marcelle to hers. She wobbled for a moment before steadying herself. She laid a hand over her stomach, let out a nearly silent burp, and smiled. "Excuse me. It's churning up a lot of gas."

"Not a problem." Adrian bowed toward Arxad. "Thank you, noble dragon. Your idea restored my beloved."

"Thank the Creator … and Alaph." Arxad picked up the handheld mirror left on the floor by Marcelle's spirit, and lodged it between his belly scales. "Speaking of Alaph, we have more of his instructions to follow, especially concerning the spiritual dwellers of this abode." He shuffled toward the door. "Come. Follow me."

After exiting the white room and arriving in the corridor next to the entry leading to the healing trees, Arxad stopped and peered in. Adrian and the others gathered around him and looked in as well.

The floor branches had given way, creating a huge hole. The trees leaned toward the center of the room, their trunks splintering and creaking.

Two beds teetered on the slope leading to the void, one of them covered with bloodstained sheets. On the mattress, a metal box marked "Medical Supplies" inched toward the edge of the bed.

"We can use that box," Arxad said. "It will be treacherous, but I might be able to fly over the bed and snatch it with my claws."

"I'll get it!" Shellinda rushed in, eluding Adrian's swiping hand.

"Shellinda!" he called. "No! Arxad will get it!"

"Don't worry." She tiptoed near the room's perimeter where the branches still appeared to be solid. "Compared to carrying rocks in a pail all day, this will be easy."

With every crunch and creak of failing wood, Adrian cringed. This was as torturous as watching the dragon hold a whip over the cattle children.

When Shellinda drew closer to the bed, she slowed to a creeping pace, spreading her arms and testing her weight with each step. After several excruciating seconds, she touched the bed's frame and reached for the box's top handle. Her fingers wrapped around it. As she slid it toward herself, she slowly stepped backwards.

A crack sounded. Shellinda froze in place. The branches under the bed snapped, sending it and Shellinda into the void.

Arxad launched into the room, plunged through the hole, and disappeared in the darkness.

Marcelle hugged Adrian's arm. Both held their breath. Regina walked in and peered over the edge of the remaining branches. Not a sound rose from the void.

After what seemed like an eternity, the beating of wings pierced the air. Arxad flew up from the hole, carrying Shellinda in his claws. She hugged the box with both arms, a smile on her face in spite of several bleeding scratches on her cheeks and chin.

Arxad swept through the entry and deposited her on the hallway floor, then flew toward the main entrance. "Meet me at the castle door."

Exhaling, Marcelle released Adrian's arm. "I'm not sure having a heart is good or not. I think mine nearly exploded."

"Mine, too."

Adrian helped Shellinda to her feet. She held out the box, grinning. "I got it."

"I see that." He pushed a hand into her hair and gently held her tresses back from her eyes, forcing her to look at him. "You're a brave girl, but every soldier needs to follow orders. We all have a duty to perform, and if we don't listen to the voice of our commanding officers, everything could fall apart, just like it almost did. Do you understand?"

She nodded, her lips tight.

"Good." Smiling, he tousled her hair and took the box. "Let's go."

Marcelle grasped Adrian's hand. As they quick marched toward the entrance, Shellinda and Regina trailing, Marcelle whispered, "You're going to be a great father."

"Thank you." Adrian's ears burned. Just the thought of fathering a child with Marcelle stoked an inner furnace—a good heat, warm and radiating from head to toe. That thought would have to stay in the background, at least for now.

When they arrived at the entrance room, the rear wall had slid to the side, revealing a stairway leading down into darkness.

Arxad perched at the top stair. "I must retrieve a weapon for the soldiers. Since the weapon might be volatile, I will need to keep it cold. While I am gone, cover the bottom of the medical box with snow." He spread out his wings and leaped down the stairwell into the darkness below. The sound of his beating wings echoed in the foyer.

Adrian edged toward the stairs and peeked down. A column of rocky steps, without rails or walls on the sides, descended sharply and disappeared into darkness. Arxad had already flown out of sight.

"Whew!" Adrian slowly backed away. "That's quite a drop!"

"Jason went down there," Regina said, "to get the stardrop for your father."

"I remember. You and I were in the healing-tree room." Adrian imagined his brother running up the stairs with the radiant sphere scalding his palm. He had done so much behind the scenes. His courage and sacrifice were amazing. "Okay, back to getting ready." He knelt on the wooden floor and opened the medical box. He, Marcelle, and Shellinda began removing the supplies—rolled-up bandages, gauze, tape, two short knives, and a few unfamiliar items.

"I wonder what Arxad means by *volatile*," Marcelle said as she examined a hypodermic needle. "Will it melt if it's not packed in snow?"

"Makes sense, but wouldn't that mean it's freezing cold wherever the staircase leads?"

"Maybe. I'm finished guessing about the mysteries around here."

Adrian walked outside, scooped a few handfuls of snow into the box, and left it in a drift. When he returned, Arxad stood in front of the plunging stairway steps, an open bag on the floor at his clawed forefeet. Large enough to hold several pumpkins, the bag appeared to be filled with a number of forearm-length gray cylinders.

"Where is the box?" Arxad asked.

"I'll get it!" Shellinda took a hard step but stopped and spun toward Adrian, grinning. "If that's okay with my commanding officer."

He winked. "By all means."

Arxad used his teeth to spread the top of the bag. "These tubes contain a compound that is unknown on Darksphere but was employed widely in this world during your race's existence here centuries ago. When the tubes are activated by means of pushing a button on a control box, they explode with enormous intensity. It would take only one to kill a dragon."

Shellinda returned with the medical box. When she set it on the floor next to the bag, Arxad touched one of the tubes with a wing tip. "Transfer them carefully. Cold helps keep them stable. Overheating or too much jostling can cause them to detonate."

Adrian let the word *detonate* roll around in his mind. Although it was a new word, the meaning was clear. "Where is the control box that would detonate the tubes?"

"We do not have one. We will have to count on their volatility when we hurl them at our targets, though I have no idea what the passing centuries have done to their potency."

"Sounds dangerous."

Arxad bobbed his head. "Quite dangerous."

"I suppose the sooner the better." Adrian waved an arm. "Everyone stand back."

"Standing back will not be enough." Arxad settled his body to the floor. "Marcelle, you and Shellinda ride on my back. We need to search for the spirits who abide here. We must gather them for a purpose I will describe later. The Starlighter can stay with Adrian. An explosion will not harm her."

Marcelle pecked Adrian on the cheek. "See you soon."

He gave her a nod. "I'm counting on it."

While Marcelle and Shellinda climbed onto Arxad's back, Adrian gestured for Regina to come closer. She glided up to him, almost nose to nose. "Remember when you helped me with your sense of smell?" Adrian asked.

She nodded. "But my nose doesn't work so much anymore."

"That's all right. I just meant I need your skills again."

In a burst of wing beats, Arxad flew deeper into the castle with Marcelle and Shellinda. When the gusts settled, Adrian continued. "Can you show me Marcelle's face when I asked her to marry me a few minutes ago?"

"I think so." Regina pulled away from Adrian and waved a hand. An image of Marcelle appeared sitting in front of him. Teary-eyed and smiling, she looked at him with adoring eyes.

"Perfect. Thank you." Using both hands, Adrian lifted one of the tubes from the bag and transferred it to the box. When he set it on top of the snow, he shifted back to the bag and repeated the process with eleven more tubes, glancing at Marcelle every few seconds. After placing the final tube, he picked up the box. "Now to cover it with snow."

Regina waved away Marcelle's image. "What do you think will happen to me, Adrian? Will I stay here with the white dragon forever?"

"That's a good question." He walked with Regina down the castle's front steps to a drift in the yard. As he crouched and scooped snow, he looked into her anxious eyes. "Do you *want* to live here?"

She shook her head. "I want to live with you and Marcelle. You said I could be your sister."

"I remember." He patted the snow down over the tubes. "A lot has changed. You were alive then, and now …"

"And now I'm dead."

Adrian closed the box. "We'll have to ask Arxad or Alaph. I don't know what is possible and what isn't."

Tears pooled in her radiant eyes. "It would be lonely here without you. You're my only friend."

He tried to brush a tear away, but his thumb had no effect. "Regina, I will do everything possible to take you home with us."

"But why? Why would you want a dead girl for a sister?"

"Because …" Adrian bit his lip. "Because I love you."

Her brow arched. "You do?"

"Of course I do. You've become very dear to me."

"No …" She fought back a spasm. "Nobody's ever said that to me before."

"Never? Not even your mother?"

She shook her head. New tears dripped and vanished. "I never met my mother. She was a breeder."

Adrian wrapped his arms around her. Although immaterial, her body felt real—tingly and substantial. "Get used to hearing I love you, Regina. If we figure out how to bring you to my home, you'll hear it morning, noon, and night."

They walked up the stairs together. When they arrived in the entry room, they sat and waited for Arxad to return. Adrian told stories about his home, tales of his father and mother, of Jason, of the commune. Regina listened with rapt attention, sometimes creating the images and animating them. She told her own tales as well, the heartaches of living in the cattle camp, of losing her eyesight, and fighting for morsels of food.

They laughed together, cried together, and even sang together as Adrian taught her some of Mesolantrum's folk songs and a few Cathedral hymns. When they hummed "Son of Solarus," the sound of Arxad's wings interrupted the tune.

Adrian rose to his feet and looked down the corridor. Arxad flew their way, Marcelle and Shellinda still riding. Behind them, dozens of radiant forms glided as if swept along in Arxad's wake.

"More people like me," Regina said. "I guess I wouldn't be lonely if I stayed here."

Adrian grinned. "Want to change your mind?"

She shook her head hard. "Never!"

Arxad landed in the entry room. When his wings settled, a plume of sparks-laden smoke spewed from his nostrils. "I think we found them all."

Seconds later, the spirits swarmed among them, smiling and laughing as they petted the physical visitors with their tingly hands.

After Marcelle and Shellinda climbed down, Arxad continued. "These are what we called the Promoted slaves. They were eaten by Magnar and his closest associates, excluding me, of course, and they now live in various parts of the castle. Since they are able to hold things for brief moments, they remove dust, repair cracks, or do whatever else they can to serve Alaph. Every evening, they gather around him and listen to his teachings, so they are knowledgeable about many subjects."

Adrian touched the top of a little boy's head. "Why did you bring them here?"

"Because Alaph will soon no longer dwell in this castle, so we are giving them a choice as to whether or not to remain."

Regina's eyes lit up, but she stayed quiet.

"A choice?" Marcelle asked. "Where else can they go?"

"They have two options, and each will require a significant change." Arxad spread a wing over a trio of girls. "They may go to be with the Creator and live in a glorious eternity; or they may have their bodies reconstituted and live here with the next lord or lady of the castle, whoever he or she may be."

"What does"—Regina formed the word carefully—"*reconstituted* mean?"

"You will receive new bodies," Arxad said. "Alaph told me that the Creator is rewarding his faithful servants, but they must never go back to the Southlands. Since their decomposed remains dwell there, they will experience the same kind of repelling force you witnessed between Marcelle's body and spirit. The pain would be too great."

"How will this reconstitution take place?" Marcelle asked.

Arxad let out another sparkling snort. "I find it amusing that you would be the one to raise that query, the very woman who created a body for herself."

She twirled a finger. "You mean they'll spin one up from the dirt?"

"In a manner of speaking." Arxad pointed his snout toward the entryway. "Before the curse beset this region, the most fertile soil in any world covered those fields. It will grow anything, and it carries healing properties, restorative magic, if you will. When you spun up a body on Darksphere, Marcelle, that soil lacked the ability to create a heart, lungs, or blood. It had no wellspring of life. It could not produce either the substance of vitality or its source. Yet, what was lacking there is present here."

An adult male spirit raised his hand. "If we were to stay, good dragon, what would we do?"

Arxad's ears wilted. "That is uncertain. I do not know who the new lord or lady of this dwelling will be."

"What about Resolute and Deference?" a girl asked. "They're not here right now. What will happen to them?"

Arxad bobbed his head. "When Resolute and Deference return, they will be offered the same options, though in a different way." He returned his gaze to the adult. "What is your name?"

He bowed his head. "Vigilant."

"Ah. A fine name." Arxad scanned the gathering. "I see one other adult, a female. Do the two of you act as leaders?"

The female, a lithe woman with long, shimmering hair, stepped forward and curtsied, her knee-length dress radiant. "I am Serenity. Vigilant and I have acted as leaders and comforters to these most industrious servants of Alaph."

"Excellent. I hope you will continue to guide those under your care as they make this difficult choice."

Vigilant gave Arxad a half bow. "Since we will no longer serve Alaph, and since we don't know who will take his place, I choose to go to the Creator."

A wave of nods crossed the radiant gathering, though Regina's head stayed motionless.

Adrian bent close to her. "What do you want to do?"

She again moved her lips slowly. "I want to be re … recon …"

"Reconstituted?"

She nodded. "Arxad said I can't go to the Southlands, but maybe I can go to Darksphere with you."

Adrian looked at Arxad. "Can she?"

"Hmmm." Arxad's head moved up and down in front of Regina's body. "Perhaps. Alaph said nothing about that possibility, but I see no reason to disallow it. If she is reconstituted here in the Northlands, there are no theoretical obstacles that I know about."

Regina clapped her hands. "I'm going to Darksphere!"

"I said no *theoretical* obstacles." Arxad looked at Adrian, his eyes flaming. "Did you lead her to believe she could accompany you to your world?"

Adrian squared his shoulders. "I didn't simply lead her to believe it. I directly told her that I would love for her to come."

Arxad lowered his voice to a rumbling whisper. "She would be better off here or with the Creator. Alaph told me that the world to which you return is not the one you left. A sinister plan is unfolding there, and I hope to bring the rest of your soldiers to Starlight before they are no longer able to come."

Adrian mimicked the dragon's low tone. "Because the soldiers will be needed on my world to stop this sinister plan?"

"Because they will be absorbed by the plan and become allies to it. If that happens, you will find yourself battling an overwhelming enemy."

"Then we have to hurry." Adrian took Marcelle's hand. "Can you give us a ride to the portal?"

"What of Shellinda and your offer to Regina?" Arxad asked.

"They can wait for us to return."

Arxad's voice lowered again. "What if you do not return? With Vigilant, Serenity, and the other spirits gone, they will be alone here with no one to look after them, at least until the new castle resident arrives. I have no idea when that will be."

Adrian sighed. "You're right. They'll come with us. We'll find a safe place for them in my world while we battle this new threat."

Arxad unfurled a wing. "Then I will go ahead of you to assess the situation while you tarry here until Regina is reconstituted. Marcelle can teach her how to collect a body in the fertile soil. When that is accomplished, you will have to find Resolute to conduct you across the castle's moat."

Adrian nodded. "And the river?"

"It is running freely, so ice no longer hides the dangerous portions. You will be able to find safe passage through a shallow area."

"What shall we do?" Vigilant asked. "What is our path to go to the Creator?"

"You and Serenity guide the others to Alaph's chambers. He will take you to the Creator himself. In fact, I think Alaph is waiting for you."

Vigilant waved an arm. "Follow me!"

With shouts and laughter, the radiant spirits hurried behind him and Serenity down the corridor. As Regina watched them depart, she stood silently, her eyes sparkling. Seconds later, they climbed up the wall protrusions and disappeared into the upper reaches of the castle.

Arxad heaved a sigh, creating a new plume of smoke. "I did not have the courage to tell them about the process they will face."

"Will you tell us?" Regina asked.

"You might have wondered why a new lord or lady will occupy this castle." Arxad glanced at Adrian before returning his gaze to Regina. "Alaph believes that he will perish today, and he will go to live with the Creator. He will be able to carry the spirits with him, but only if he eats them while he is still alive."

"Eats them!" Regina shuddered. "How awful!"

"Yes, human child. It is a troubling thought. Yet, unlike you, these young ones have already suffered that fate physically. My guess is that they will fear the great white dragon's words at first, but they will acquiesce to his gentle ways without protest. To be consumed by the vehicle that will take them to the Creator will be frightening, but when they arrive in the Creator's abode with Alaph, where they will live forever in peace and comfort, they will be blessed beyond measure."

Regina's mouth dropped open. She stared wide-eyed at the wall ladder, saying nothing.

"I will take my leave now." Arxad peered through the entryway. "Are the tubes outside?"

Shellinda nodded. "The box is in the snow, but you can see the top. Do you want me to get it for you?"

"No need. I will pick it up on my way." Arxad looked at Adrian. "If I am not at the portal when you come, look for a messenger or a sign of some kind. I will do what I can to let you know how to proceed from there."

Adrian patted Arxad's neck. "You are a treasure, Arxad. Without you, we would all be dead."

"And without you and your fellow humans, my soul would be dead." Arxad beat his wings mightily and flew through the doorway. Once outside, he dipped down, picked up the box of explosives, and elevated into the Northlands sky.

Adrian slid his arm around Marcelle and pulled her close. "So do you think you can teach Regina how to create a body for herself?"

She leaned her head against his shoulder. "I did it more than once in Mesolantrum, so I should be able to figure it out. I suppose we start by finding a patch of ground that isn't snow covered."

"First we'll visit the moat and find Resolute. If she wants to be reconstituted, you can teach her as well."

"I'll find some soil!" Regina ran out and scampered down the stairs.

Adrian extended a hand toward Shellinda and Marcelle. "Shall we follow?"

"One second." Marcelle unhitched her scabbard from Adrian's belt and attached it to her own. She slid the sword out, scanned the blade, and thrust it back in. Smiling at him, she clutched the hilt. "Now I'm ready to go."

✵ TEN ✵

ARXAD stood in the forest clearing in front of the Northlands portal, his tail aligned with the crystalline pegs. Unlike the mesa portal in the Southlands, the pegs continued around the portal plane and completed a circle on the opposite side, though mud and forest debris covered all but a dozen pegs that sat atop a low wall.

The box of explosives he had brought rested at a nearby boulder. His daughter, Xenith, waited at his side, her wings drooping as she breathed heavily. She had flown hard and fast from the Southlands to warn him about the Benefile's plan to kill the diseased humans. Their twisted logic concluded that since the Southlands dragons needed to be punished and since the human army would be an appropriate punishing hammer, it was essential to protect the invading humans from the disease.

"I feared that the Benefile might do this," Arxad said. "Sometimes they are unpredictable, but I have never underestimated their cruelty."

"So what do we do?" Xenith asked.

Arxad glanced at the portal. Only moments ago he had conversed with an officer on the Darksphere side about the plan to go to the portal in the underground-river chamber that led to the Southlands mining mesa. Traveling there would greatly decrease the time needed to march to battle. Yet, he could not leave the crystal in place while guiding the soldiers to the other portal in their world. Xenith could be the solution to the problem.

"How is your stamina?" Arxad set a wing on her neck. "Can you fly to the Southlands again?"

She took in a long breath. "I can."

"Have you heard about the portal at the mining mesa?"

"I have heard talk of it, and I know where both mesas are, but I do not know exactly where the portal is."

Arxad drew his wing back. "It is at the mine closer to the village. If you go through the secondary entry, you will see a line of crystals similar to the one here, only embedded in the ground instead of on top of a low wall. The center peg is missing." He shifted his tail and touched the center crystal with the tip. "When I return to Darksphere, take this peg to the mesa portal and place it in the open hole. If all goes well, I will already be on the other side of the portal with many more soldiers. Perhaps with your speed, you will open it in time for us to stop the Benefile."

"I appreciate your faith in me." Xenith grasped the peg with a clawed hand. "I am ready."

Arxad snaked his neck around hers. "Do you have news from your mother?"

"Only that she is at the wilderness refuge. Randall said she has a minor wound, but my concern is that she will not take care of herself. That wound or her earlier one could easily worsen."

Arxad let the report sink in. As if mesmerized by a Starlighter, he had become absorbed in Adrian and Marcelle's trials, though great battles continued in the Southlands. Jason Masters, his friend Randall, Koren the Starlighter, and others were still risking their lives to rescue their fellow humans. "Your concern is valid," Arxad said. "Your mother is not one to pamper herself. She and I are both ready to sacrifice everything to protect our race." He uncurled his neck from hers. "You are not required to do the same. You have a choice."

"Do I really?" Xenith nodded toward the portal. "Go, Father. I will see you in the Southlands."

Arxad scanned the clearing, probing trees, bushes, and boulders with his gaze. Earlier, Orion had come through the portal and closed it by removing the central crystal. Yet now Orion was gone, perhaps hiding with his purloined crystal in hand. When Adrian and Marcelle arrived, would he open the portal for them? Maybe. He wanted every human warrior to return to Darksphere. Still, he was an unpredictable human. Everyone would have to leave this part of the plan in the hands of the Creator.

"When I disappear," Arxad said to Xenith, "fly with all speed. If you see your mother, tell her …" He shook his head. "I will tell her myself when I return." He vaulted into the air, circled the clearing, and grabbed the box of explosives.

When he flew through the portal, sparks splashed everywhere. He burst into a forest glade, warmer and dimmer than the one he had left, and zoomed upward. A soldier with multiple stripes on his sleeve ducked just in time to avoid the dangling box.

As Arxad circled about, the soldier shouted commands. Dozens of other soldiers leaped to their feet and ran to form lines. Arxad swooped low, deposited the box, and shouted, "Do not touch that box!" Then, he dropped to the ground and skidded across the grass. A trio of soldiers dove out of his way and rolled while other soldiers laughed.

Arxad whipped his wings and slowed to a stop. When he settled, he curled his neck and faced the first soldier. "Are you ready to travel to the other portal?"

The soldier crossed an arm over his chest, completing the gesture with a thump of his fist. "Sergeant Fenton Xavier at your service. We are ready."

"Good. I need a messenger to stay here. I expect two of your warriors to come through the portal. They will need to know where to find us."

"What should our messenger tell them?" Fenton asked. "We don't know where we're going."

Arxad scanned the soldiers. Which one looked the part of a courageous volunteer? After a few moments, a shaggy-haired young man came into view only a few steps away. As he stood at attention, his square shoulders, firm jaw, and excited eyes gave him the aspect of an adventure-seeking human.

"You!" Arxad shot his head forward, stopping the motion just before his snout bumped the man's nose. "I am Arxad, high priest of dragons. Are you brave enough to ride a creature such as I?"

The man flinched, but only slightly. "I am."

"What is your name?"

"Heath. Heath Mannix."

"Very well, Heath." Arxad withdrew a few inches. "I will take you to the portal and bring you back here. Then you will guide your fellow soldiers there while I wait here for the other two warriors. When they arrive, I will carry them to the portal, and we will all go to my world together."

Heath bowed his head. "I am at your service."

"Gather your courage. You will mount my back soon." Arxad whipped his head toward the sergeant. "What news do you hear from your governmental officials?"

"News?" Fenton glanced around as if looking for another human to answer. "What news are you expecting?"

"I have word from a prophet that someone here is hatching a plan that will transform your world into a land of tyranny."

"Well, Issachar Stafford is our new governor. I suppose he's strict, but he's trying to clean up the corruption. He doesn't appear to be a tyrant."

"Perhaps not." Arxad looked into the sky. Thin clouds passed overhead—nothing ominous. "According to my prophet, the schemer will be someone who has the power to manipulate minds with hypnotic influence."

"Hypnotic? A magician, perhaps?"

"A magician is easily unmasked," Arxad said. "This man does not rely on illusions."

"Hail, soldiers!" The shout emanated from the forest.

Fenton took a step and called, "Who goes there? Show yourself!"

A man dressed in a loose-fitting black tunic and trousers led a horse into the clearing. When he noticed Arxad, he halted and stiffened. "I …" He swallowed. "Sergeant Xavier, I have a message for you from Issachar Stafford."

Fenton held out his hand. "There is no need to fear the dragon. Arxad is an ally."

The messenger reached into the horse's saddlebag, his stare still on Arxad. He withdrew a silver tube and laid it in the sergeant's palm.

"Is it genetically locked?" Fenton asked.

"It is. At first we did not lock it, but the head of the archives insisted. He said the contents should be viewed only by you."

"I understand." Fenton plucked a hair from his head, deposited it into a tiny hatch in the tube, and looked into its end. For the next several minutes, he stayed in that position, sometimes lifting his brow, sometimes cringing. Finally, he pushed a button on the tube and gave it back to the messenger. "I erased it. There will be no response."

He pushed it back into the saddlebag. "Not even an acknowledgment that you will obey the order?"

"I will obey the order to the best of my ability."

The messenger nodded. "Very good, sir. I will tell the new governor." He pivoted and hurried away, again leading the horse.

"The new governor?" Arxad bent his brow. "Does he speak of Governor Stafford?"

Fenton shook his head. "According to the message, we have yet another new governor—Cal Broder, a man who claims to have recently visited your world. It seems lately that we change governors every time a cock crows." He shuffled close to Arxad's ear and whispered, "We have been ordered to guard this portal and not allow anyone to come through it. The new governor wishes to protect the people of Mesolantrum from the disease that is spreading through your world."

"That is a noble desire," Arxad whispered in return, "but the two who are coming have been cured and are immune. They pose no threat."

"All the same, I have been given an order." Fenton tapped his chin. "I can send a messenger to the governor and ask for an exception, but I'm not sure whom I can trust at the palace, and waiting for a reply would take a great deal of time."

"Time we cannot spare," Arxad continued in a low tone. "Shall I assume that you believe this new governor to be the fulfillment of the prophecy I mentioned earlier?"

Fenton nodded. "The message showed this new governor using hypnotic power. If you had not warned me in advance, and if an old teacher of mine had not added a warning message at the beginning, I might have been taken in myself."

"What did your teacher say?"

"During my school days, we called him Professor Dunwoody. He said that he read a journal you left here centuries ago. He thinks this new governor has the powers of what he called a dark Starlighter."

Arxad hissed the words. "A dark Starlighter."

"I assume this is a troubling development."

"A corrupt male Starlighter is practically omnipotent. The power to defeat him is beyond the ability of anyone in this world."

"Then what should we do?"

"Permit me to think for a moment." Arxad closed his eyes. He could fly to the governor's palace and do battle with the usurper, but that would greatly delay the delivery of soldiers to Starlight, and even then, since a powerful Starlighter could easily add military might to his forces, the chances of winning such a battle against him were slim. No, even though this Starlighter would become more powerful during the delay, that confrontation would have to wait. "I need to send a message to your teacher."

"Very well. I can choose a runner from my—"

"No. It must be you. I deduce that you will not be easily influenced by this Starlighter, and since your teacher has thus far resisted his influence, you and he must be the only ones who know my plan."

"What is this plan?"

"I am still formulating it." Arxad blew twin plumes of smoke from his nostrils. "A Starlighter's power depends on the focus between himself and his intended victims. The best way, therefore, to defeat him is to distract him, to make him believe that all is well and his victory is already won. His own arrogance and overconfidence will be our allies."

Fenton nodded. "I see what you mean. We create a pretense that we are all under his control."

"Might you be able to have a celebratory festival that will honor this new governor? Even if he is suspicious of your intent, a corrupted Starlighter will not be able to resist public adulation, especially if he believes it will further his goal of worldwide domination."

"Worldwide? Will he seek to usurp the king?"

Arxad bobbed his head. "Undoubtedly, which means that you should invite the king to the affair. His presence will surely keep the Starlighter distracted until I can return and do battle with him."

"Invite the king?" Fenton blew through pursed lips, releasing a breathy whistle. "That will be a feat. King Sasser hasn't visited Mesolantrum in years."

"Then you will have to entice him in some manner. I leave that up to you and your teacher."

"But wouldn't putting the king in the presence of this Starlighter also put him in jeopardy?"

"He is already in jeopardy. Perhaps making him understand this will be the best way to persuade him." Arxad blew out two new black puffs of smoke. "Give us as much time as you can. We will join you at the festival by stealth."

"What if you lose the battle on your world?"

"Then both worlds will perish." Arxad laid a wing on Fenton's back. "We must keep this dire possibility in mind; it will motivate us to be courageous."

Fenton scanned the soldiers. "I will have to come up with a way to explain this to those under my command."

"Explain nothing. They are soldiers. They will obey their superior."

"As must I. I was given an order." Fenton backed away from Arxad and spoke in a commanding voice. "Because of my lack of experience in dealing with dragons and their world, in my absence I direct you all to follow Arxad's orders."

"In your absence?" Heath stepped closer. "Where are you going?"

"I am resigning." Fenton stripped off his uniform's shirt and let it drop. "Do whatever Arxad tells you. That is my final command."

While the other soldiers looked on, some with mouths agape, he marched away along a path that meandered through the forest.

When he disappeared from sight, Heath swiveled his head back to Arxad. "A dragon is now in command?"

"You heard him." Arxad lowered himself to the ground. "Let us make haste."

While Heath mounted, Arxad scanned the soldiers again. With few exceptions, they appeared to be skeptical, hesitant. "I realize that many of you lack trust in a dragon," Arxad said, "but let it be known that I will treat you exactly as you deserve, as soldiers, as warriors, as valiant men who have come here to risk their lives in order to save their fellow humans. As such, I know that you are anxious to get on with the business of rescue. You crave the conflict. You relish flexing your muscles and exercising your stout hearts as you charge into battle. You dream of leading home a band of liberated Lost Ones, as you have called them. Yet now you are answering to a member of the race that has been the source of your trials. You have been commanded to obey one of the creatures who enslaved those you hope to deliver, and the foundation upon which you stand threatens to crumble. It is as if the Creator has handed the mantle of authority to evil itself."

A man bearing wrinkles and gray hair whipped out a sword from a hip scabbard. "You talk too much!" He stood directly in front of Arxad and looked up at him, his face as hard as granite. "We are not so faint of heart that we need a sermon from the likes of a dragon! By obeying you, we obey our sergeant. You need not worry about us." The man kicked the dirt, sending a light spray over Arxad's forelegs. "Get along with you now! Do what you have to do, and we will follow our orders."

Arxad suppressed a chuckle. "Very well. I will get along." He stretched his wings and launched into the sky. Heath let out a gasp that sounded like a human's cry of exhilaration rather than fear.

As Arxad flew over the trees, he and Heath shouted back and forth about the landscape below, making sure Heath learned the way. They passed over the field of flowers and the hole leading to the underground portal, then traveled back to the forest clearing and landed where they began.

After planning a route that would keep them undetected, Heath led a march toward the other portal. Men lined up amidst shouts of command. Feet tromped on underbrush. After a few minutes, their voices died away.

Arxad stood alone in the clearing. Except for a breeze rustling the branches, silence reigned. He turned toward the portal and extended a wing. Instead of disappearing, the tip stayed in Darksphere. The passage to Starlight was closed.

He reared up, curled his neck, and looked at Marcelle's mirror, still embedded between two belly scales. His own face stared back at him. The leaves seemed to whisper the conversation with Marcelle that brought this keepsake into his possession.

✻ ✻ ✻ ✻ ✻ ✻

Marcelle spoke in a hushed tone. "It has a verse from the Code on the back. It says, 'Your heart is reflected by the light you shine. How great is your light when you sacrifice all you have for those who have nothing to give.'"

"I have heard these words before," Arxad replied. "They are great wisdom."

"Yes ... yes, they are. The mirror reflects what is physical, and the verse reflects what is spiritual, so I suppose you should place it so the mirror faces outward and the verse faces inward."

"More wisdom. I will do as you suggest."

✻ ✻ ✻ ✻ ✻ ✻

Arxad settled to the ground next to the box of explosive tubes and stared at the portal. On the other side, a battle ensued. His own mate and daughter risked their lives in the midst of that battle, and here he sat in safety waiting for a pair of humans who might or might not be able to find Orion and the necessary crystalline peg. At the time, the possibility of locating and persuading Orion seemed high, but now it seemed less likely than finding a dragon tooth in a mountain of bones. Yet, the former governor was no fool. He had nowhere to go. The prospect of returning to his own world had to appeal to him. It would certainly be better than staying in the cold Northlands, especially with night approaching.

Arxad mentally nodded. They would come. Still, what good was this assurance? He was on Darksphere doing nothing. He was a dragon who had sided with humans, a traitor to his own kind, a priest who failed to elevate the spirits of his race beyond the level of selfish savagery, a father who had sent his daughter on a dangerous journey to open the Southlands portal, a mate who had abandoned his beloved in a time of danger.

He let his neck flop to the ground, making his head slap the grass. Failure had been his life's story. His brother Magnar had become a child-eating monster; Starlight had deteriorated into a land of darkness, both physical and spiritual, easily overthrown by an even darker dragon; and now Darksphere had succumbed to a different manipulating usurper. This new world he had hoped to nourish with intelligence, wisdom, and honesty had fallen prey to a deceiver. He had left them woefully unprepared to resist the charms of a corrupted Starlighter.

Arxad closed his eyes. As he rested, words from his own prayers came to mind, prayers he had written in journals now stowed somewhere in the Zodiac. *Creator, in the midst of my turmoil, be my peace and comfort. Let me know that you honor my willingness. Though feeble, my efforts are all I have to give. If I fail, come to my aid. Show me that you are something more than a hopeful dream, a fool's wish for solace beyond this mortal coil, this cycle of endless life, suffering, and death. I need to know you are there.*

He opened his eyes and looked up. "Yes, Creator, I humbly request that you make yourself known to me. I ask for a sign, hoping you will not be offended by my lack of faith. If Adrian makes it safely through this portal to join me here …" He shook his head. "Perhaps that is too easy. The Creator of all can do much more." He stared at the sky for another moment before continuing. "If Adrian comes through the portal with Orion following in a penitent posture, then I will know that you are intimately involved with the affairs of dragons and men, that you are helping us in these impossible quests, that you graciously care to listen to a poor dragon's faithless request for a sign." He heaved a deep sigh. "Restore my faith, and I will no longer be a doubting dragon."

✸ ELEVEN ✸

Standing near the river in a field of dark moist soil, Adrian held Regina's hand, a physical hand. He kissed her knuckles and looked into her eyes. "Can you see?"

She nodded, her smile as bright as Solarus. "I can see. I can hear. I can smell." She bounced on her toes. "Everything works!"

With Shellinda looking on wide-eyed, Marcelle laid a hand on Regina's chest. "I feel a heartbeat. It's racing along." She ran her fingers through Regina's short red locks. "It's all so amazing!"

"*You're* amazing," Adrian said. "You showed her how."

Marcelle kicked a clump of soil. "All I did was show her how to spin in the dirt. She did the rest."

"I love your humility." Adrian offered a warm smile. "It looks good on you."

"Charmer." Displaying a smile of her own, she swatted his arm. "No time for flirting. We'd better get to the portal."

Adrian scanned the landscape. A cool breeze sprayed misty rain across his face and formed tiny droplets on his eyelashes. In the distance, Resolute paddled an invisible boat toward the castle, navigating the moat. Now this radiant spirit would go home and wait for Deference to return. Then the two of them would reconstitute their bodies. Only moments ago, she had watched Regina's restoration and announced her confidence that she could do the same, though she wanted to wait for Deference. The new lord or lady of Alaph's castle would soon have two flesh-and-blood tenants waiting.

Adrian turned in the opposite direction. The portal lay in the forest several hundred paces ahead and up a slope. It seemed so long ago that he and his father rolled an extane gas tank down that slope and tried to cross the ice-covered river with it. Where was Father now? Marcelle had seen him with the soldiers, so he might be marching southward with them into danger. At his age, the journey promised to be long and hard, but Edison Masters would find the stamina.

"Let's go." Adrian scooped up Regina and set her on his shoulders, grasping her ankles at his chest as he marched toward the slope. Holding hands with Shellinda, Marcelle strode at his side, still somewhat unsteady as she trudged across the mud-and-snow ground. At times, she had to clutch Adrian's arm, but every step seemed surer than the last. She would be herself in no time.

After more than half an hour, they reached the top of the slope, passed through a cluster of evergreens, and entered the portal clearing. Orion sat atop a boulder, his long legs dangling. With his shoulders slumped, he stared at a crystalline peg in his hands. "I've been expecting you."

Adrian lifted Regina from his neck and set her down. "What kind of meeting are you expecting? One of cooperation or resistance?"

"First, one to express my shame." Orion pushed himself off the boulder and stood upright on the muddy ground. "I have been listening to many conversations taking place on both sides of this portal. I have heard the soundings of courageous hearts; of sacrificial minds; of fathers, sons, and daughters, both human and dragon, who are willing to die for the sake of those who cannot help themselves."

Adrian crossed his arms over his chest. "That's a pretty speech, Counselor."

"I have had more than a few hours to formulate it." Orion slid the toe of his boot through the mud. "I am nothing like those brave souls. I am ashamed that I ever held the office of counselor. I lack the integrity or strength of character to counsel anyone."

Marcelle let go of Shellinda's hand and drew a step closer, giving Orion a skeptical stare. "So what will you do?"

"I will take my leave." Orion extended the crystal to Adrian. "It is yours. Open the portal. I will come with you and try to help in the fight against the new menace our people face. It's the least I can do."

Adrian glanced at Marcelle. She gave him a go-ahead nod. Although the change in Orion appeared to be too sudden to believe, his willingness to hand over the crystal meant a lot.

"Very well." Adrian took the peg. "I suppose since we're all going, we'll have to leave the portal open."

"I see no other choice." Orion pointed at a hole in a line of crystalline pegs standing atop a knee wall. "It goes there."

While Marcelle watched with a hand on the hilt of her sword, Adrian bent close to the wall and inserted the peg. A few paces ahead, light flashed across a vertical plane, then vanished. "I'll go first, then Orion, then Marcelle, Shellinda, and Regina."

"Agreed." Orion spread out an arm. "After you."

Adrian strode through the portal. A shower of sparks flew in all directions. When they settled, Arxad appeared only a few steps away, sitting on his haunches.

The moment Orion shuffled into the clearing with his head low, Arxad's brow shot upward. He wrapped a wing around Adrian, and pulled him close. "Your presence here is most pleasing."

"I can see that." Adrian patted Arxad's scales. "Thank you for the … uh … warm greeting."

Marcelle and the two girls walked into the clearing hand in hand. Marcelle grinned and spread out her arm. "May I join in?"

"By all means." Arxad swept her in with his other wing. "It is a pleasure to embrace the noble woman who persists in wearing my scale in spite of the difficulties."

She grasped his wing's mainstay to keep her balance. "Why the sudden show of affection?"

"I, too, have a covenant to keep. It is a private matter." Arxad released them and blew warm air across their bodies. The two girls walked into the flow, giggling as the dragon-breath breeze batted their hair and clothes.

Orion shoved his hands into his pockets, his scant hair matted by rain. "This buoyancy is a pleasing sight, Arxad, but may I suggest that we have much to do?"

When Arxad took in a breath, he looked at Orion. "Of course. But we do not want you to catch a cold." He extended his neck and blew a warm blast over Orion's body.

As his clothes and hair dried out, his frown eased into a weak smile. "I appreciate your graciousness, good dragon."

"We should go." Adrian scanned the ground and spotted the box of explosive tubes. "Can you carry all of us and the box at the same time?"

"That would be a challenge, but I can try to—"

"No." Orion held up a hand. "I do not wish to go with you. I cannot be of service in physical battle. I hope to go to the palace to see how I can help there by stealth."

Adrian glanced at Marcelle, then at Arxad before returning his gaze to Orion. "What's your plan?"

"I know enough secrets to persuade a few people to provide help." Orion walked toward the edge of the clearing, waving a hand. "Don't worry about me."

"Find Professor Dunwoody," Arxad called. "He is familiar with the situation and can likely use your help."

"I will find him." Orion waved again and walked out of sight. Soon, the forest quieted to a hush. Without a word, Arxad lowered his body to the ground.

Adrian dropped to one knee in front of the two girls. "Shellinda," he said, taking her hand. "You have been courageous and a huge help, but now I think it's time for you to rest. I will take you home to my mother and ask her to adopt you."

"Adopt me?" Shellinda smiled. "Do you really think your mother would want me?"

"Definitely. She always wanted a girl but never had one." Adrian kissed her forehead. "I would love it if you would be my sister."

"Yes! Yes!" Shellinda threw her arms around Adrian. "Thank you! Oh, thank you!"

Marcelle nudged Adrian's arms with her knee and cleared her throat. She nodded discreetly toward Regina.

Regina stared at his embrace with Shellinda, a tear trickling down her cheek.

"And now I need to talk to this brave girl." Adrian reached out for Regina and folded her in. Eye to eye with her, he whispered, "We already talked about you being my sister, and you will live in our home, but first I think we'll need a Starlighter to go with us. Is that all right?"

Sniffling, Regina nodded. "I want to go wherever you are." She took Shellinda's hand. "And when I come back, we'll be your sisters together."

"That'll be perfect." He kissed Regina's forehead. "My mother will be thrilled to have you both."

Adrian, Marcelle, Shellinda, and Regina climbed onto Arxad's back—Marcelle and Shellinda seated together in one gap between spines and Adrian and Regina in another. Once they settled, Adrian provided directions to his commune, and they took off into the air. Carrying the explosives box in his claws, Arxad flew just above the treetops, high enough to keep the box from hitting the branches yet low enough to avoid detection.

Along the way, Arxad explained what he had learned from Sergeant Fenton Xavier by means of the messenger and how a dragon had become the commander of the soldiers. The news about the usurper, Cal Broder, sounded ominous, all the more reason to keep out of sight for now.

By the time he finished the tale, the trees gave way to furrowed fields. Adrian searched the ground below. Withering cornstalks stood in even rows along with yellow stubs that were once flourishing beanstalks. Cotton remnants sprinkled white specks in a trail from a field to a one-story house at the center of the rich farmland. Beyond the house, sheep grazed in a fenced-off pasture along with Primus, the commune's plow horse; two cows; and a few goats. One of the cows stood in the long shadow of a small barn. She looked up at them for a moment, then returned to grazing.

The communal bathhouse stood at the opposite side of the main house. Buckets and barrels lined one exterior wall, some filled and some empty—nothing unusual.

A wagon filled with cotton sat within a few paces of the main house's front door, and partially unraveled balls of baling string lay on the ground nearby, but no one stood anywhere in sight.

Adrian adjusted his scabbard. Something was wrong. Normally, the commune families wouldn't leave raw cotton unattended, especially with so many men away from home. Theft hadn't been a problem lately, but with troubles mounting all around, desperate people might try anything to gain an advantage.

He pointed at the house. "Three families live there, so everyone is accustomed to making room. Two hardworking little girls will be welcome."

Arxad angled his body into a slow descent. "But are they accustomed to a visit from a dragon?"

"I'd better give them some warning." Adrian cupped his hands around his mouth and shouted, "Mother! It's me, Adrian! Are you in the house?"

A breeze blew across the cornstalks, making them wave. Otherwise only the livestock provided any sign of life.

"I don't like the looks of it," Marcelle said. "When I lived here, someone was always working out in the fields during daylight hours."

Adrian forced a confident tone. "Maybe they're all inside eating. We can join them."

"Maybe." Marcelle's tone dripped with skepticism. "We'll see."

"Any idea how much my mother knows about where we've been?"

"Probably quite a bit. I saw Randall while I was here in spirit, and he visited your commune afterward, so I'm sure he got her up to date."

Arxad landed in a run on the cotton-laden path and stopped close to the wagon. Adrian leaped off and helped Marcelle and the girls down.

After they stretched their legs, Marcelle set her hands on her hips. "Isn't it odd that the front door's closed?" She sniffed the air. "And I smell something … rotting, I think."

"Maybe you smell something from the mudroom," Adrian said. "The children might have tracked something in after feeding the livestock or milking the cows and goats."

She nodded. "That was my job when I was little, but those are morning chores. They would have finished long ago and cleaned everything up."

"Good point." Gesturing for her and the girls to stay back, Adrian walked toward the front door. A dead chicken lay at the side of the well-beaten path, its body fully intact—no sign of trauma.

He stopped a few paces from the threshold where a motionless gray cat sprawled across the path. When he nudged it with his toe, it slid a few inches, somewhat limber though rigor mortis had begun to set in.

He stepped over the carcass and halted on the welcome mat. After wiping his feet, he lifted the latch and pulled, but the door wouldn't give way. As he pulled again, a scratching sound rose from below. Someone had wedged an angled stone in the gap at the bottom of the door.

He kicked the stone out of the way and pulled once again, but the door still wouldn't budge, as if the locking bar on the other side had been laid in its brackets.

Something white caught his attention. He touched a nail that attached a scrap of paper to the center of the door. Apparently this scrap was all that remained of a larger sheet, perhaps a message on parchment.

Looking down, he scanned the area for the parchment but found only the doormat, the dead cat, and ground-crawling vines from the pesky figgeraut that grew under the house. Even Mother's home-brewed herbicide wouldn't kill it.

Marcelle joined him, her nose wrinkling. "Well, the cat and chicken explain one mystery."

"Maybe." Adrian kicked at the figgeraut. "I don't think the animals have been dead for very long."

"Could everyone have gone to the village?"

"Not likely." A small green bird landed on Adrian's shoulder and chirped. Adrian angled his head and looked at it. "One of mother's parakeets. What's it doing out here?"

"Is it normally caged?" Marcelle asked.

"Along with its mate. This is the male." The bird pecked at Adrian's fledgling beard.

"It seems quite tame."

"They both are." Adrian walked to a front window and peered into the communal kitchen area. A cooking pot sat on the woodstove, but no fire burned underneath it. Beyond the opposite side of the kitchen, dishes sat neatly stacked on the dining table, and no one occupied the surrounding benches. A bird cage hung from a pole near the fireplace—empty, its door open. A breeze lifted a parchment from the table and blew it to the floor, making its torn edge easy to see.

"The pasture door must be ajar." Adrian strode around the house, followed closely by Marcelle. Arxad and the girls stayed put near the cotton wagon. The parakeet flew from Adrian's shoulder to the roof and perched there, watching.

As Adrian approached the back of the house, his shoes crunched glass shards littering the muddy walkway. Ahead, a fist-sized hole had been punched through the door's glass pane, and a shovel lay in front of the threshold. A trail of footprints led toward the pasture before disappearing in the grass.

Adrian picked up the shovel and propped the metal blade under the door's latch. It would work perfectly as a wedge to keep someone in the house.

He tossed the shovel to the side and looked through the hole. Still no sign of movement. He lifted the latch and walked into the mudroom, keeping his footfalls quiet.

Marcelle followed. With her foot, she nudged a child-sized pair of muddy sandals, one far more worn than the other. "No stench in here."

"Must have been the dead animals then."

They passed through the commune's gathering area, an open room with a few padded chairs, a wicker bench, a short table with a pile of books on top, and a rug covering the wood floor where the children usually sat. Padding on the balls of his feet, he entered his family's quarters, a two-room suite, one for Mother and Father and one for their sons. He peeked into both rooms and found neat sleeping pads and clean chamber pots. All was quiet.

Still shadowed by Marcelle, Adrian walked back to the gathering room and turned into the kitchen and eating area. He picked up the parchment and, with Marcelle looking on, read silently. *All ye herein are commanded to appear at Cathedral for a mandatory viewing of a video presented by our new governor, Cal Broder, who is implementing rules to prevent a deadly disease from entering our region. Anyone who disobeys will be punished according to Statute 143, Section C.*

"Any idea what that statute says?" Marcelle whispered.

Adrian nodded. "I guarded Prescott's backside long enough to remember that one. He threatened people with it all the time. It's a suspension of property rights. They would close down our commune, take the land, and send the families to the tenements."

She set a fist on her hip. "Which explains why no one is here."

"Probably." He laid the parchment on the table. "I just can't believe my mother would leave the baling string like that. It would take only a minute to put it away."

"Maybe a palace guard made sure everyone left. Your mother wouldn't stop to pick up string with a spearman watching her."

"You don't know my mother. And besides, the broken window is suspicious." When Adrian returned to the gathering room, his leg knocked over a small crutch that had been leaning against a chair. He picked it up and showed it to Marcelle. "This is Jonathan's. He's five."

Marcelle ran a finger along the word *Jon* burned into the uneven wood. "They wouldn't leave this behind."

"Exactly. It's all adding up." Still holding the crutch, Adrian marched out the rear door and jogged toward the pasture, his eyes locked on the barn, Marcelle keeping pace. "Mother!" he called as he pushed the gate aside and hurried on. "It's Adrian!"

Fifty yards ahead, the barn's main door opened enough to reveal his mother holding Jonathan in her arms. As her face twisted, she cried out, "Adrian?"

"Yes!" He ran faster, but she held up a hand.

"Stop!"

Adrian slowed to a halt, now only ten paces away. "What's wrong?"

Tears flowing, she set Jonathan down on his bottom and wrung her hands. "We heard something about a disease on Dracon. Is it true?"

"It's true." Adrian gave the crutch to Marcelle and spread out his arms. "But we're all in good health. We found a cure, and we're not carrying the disease. There's no danger."

Wiping tears with her apron, she limped toward him. "Oh, Adrian!"

Adrian met her halfway, wrapped her up in his arms, and spun her in a slow twirl. When he set her down, he brushed her tears with his thumb and kissed her on each cheek. "I'm sure you want news, so I'll tell you what I know right away."

While Marcelle carried Jon and his crutch, Adrian laid his hands on Mother's shoulders. "First, the best news of all. I found Frederick! He's alive!"

She gasped. "Praise the Creator!"

"Yes! And he's still on Dracon, taking care of rescued slaves—a bunch of children. No surprise, right?"

She brushed away a new tear. "Yes, that's Frederick. He always loved the children."

"Father and Jason are still on Dracon as well, and they were fine when I last saw them. Father was injured for a while, but Jason found an amazing way to heal him. If you had seen it, you'd be so proud."

"I have no doubt of that." She grasped his arm tightly, her hands trembling. "Is … is that a dragon?"

From the direction of the house, Arxad skittered toward them, Shellinda and Regina riding on his back.

"Don't worry," Adrian said, laughing. "He's a friend."

"I'm not worried." Mother swallowed. "At least that's what I'm trying to tell myself."

Arxad's wings beat, and his legs churned, his claws scratching at the ground. He leaped over the pasture fence and flew the rest of the way, then landed in a graceful slide.

"Mother," Adrian said, extending an arm, "allow me to introduce you to Arxad, a priest of Starlight who wants our people to be set free." Adrian bowed toward Arxad. "Good dragon, this is my mother, Estelle Masters."

Arxad lowered his head. "It is a pleasure meeting the woman who reared such a gentleman as Adrian. I have met very few with such integrity and sacrificial character."

"I appreciate your generous words, Arxad." Mother's voice carried a slight tremor. "Since you brought my son to my arms, you are welcome here."

"I regret that I brought only one of your sons home. If it is in my power, I will see to it that all your men are restored to you."

The girls slid down Arxad's side and stood with their arms crossed, fidgeting. Adrian winked at them. Introducing them could wait for the perfect timing.

"And that brings up the bad news." Adrian took a half step back. "Our work isn't finished yet, so I have to return to Dracon. You understand, don't you?"

"Of course you have to return." As she brushed dirt from his tunic, her chin quivered. "You went to Dracon for a purpose that isn't finished, and your father and brothers are still there, so if you tried to stay here …" Her voice cracked. "If you tried to stay here, I would have to sweep you out of our house and send you back with the dragon you came on."

"Speaking of our house …" He nodded toward it. "I saw the message from the palace, but what happened back there? Were you locked in?"

She clutched her apron tightly. "Two sentries ordered everyone to go to the Cathedral. They said the new governor could protect us from the disease that would arrive from Dracon. We didn't have time to unload the cotton and hitch the horse to the wagon, and Jack already had to carry Olivia, so I hid with Jon. The sentries were suspicious that someone was still inside, so they blocked the doors and shouted that the house was now under quarantine, that they would return to seal it more securely. I had to break a window to escape, and I carried Jon out here."

"I guessed something like that." Adrian clasped his mother's shoulder. "Some bad news. Smoky is dead."

"I know." She looked down. "I saw him through the window."

"And I noticed a dead chicken." Adrian lifted her chin and looked her in the eye. "Any idea why the sentries would do that?"

"They didn't do it. Or at least they claimed they didn't. They said dead animals were a sign that the disease was in the air, so we had to get protection right away." Mother wrinkled her nose. "They smelled rotten sooner than they should have. I think the sentries sprayed them with something deadly."

"That explains a lot." Adrian furrowed his brow. "But killing animals just to scare people? That's insane."

"If you had seen the sentries, you'd understand." She touched her cheek. "They had a splotch right about here, like a bruise, maybe the size of a walnut, and they acted like it would be the end of the world if we all didn't comply right away. They had a look about them, as if they were, well …"

"Obsessed?" Adrian asked.

"Yes. Yes, that's a good word for it. I was about to say fanatical."

Adrian scanned the countryside beyond the house—desolate and quiet, probably safe … for now. "You were right to hide. Good thinking. But I also saw that the bird cage is open, and one of the parakeets is flying around the house. What happened?"

"With all the talk of slaves in chains, I just couldn't stand to see them caged. I decided to let them go."

Marcelle set Jonathan down and hugged Mother. "It's good to see you again, Mrs. Masters."

"And you, dear." She kissed Marcelle on the cheek. "I trust that you kept Adrian out of trouble."

Smiling coyly, she folded her hands behind her back. "Well, I don't know about that. Considering what he did, you might be in for a lot of trouble."

"What?" She gave Adrian an admonishing-mother look. "What did you do?"

"I think what she means is …" Adrian pulled Marcelle to his side. "I asked her to marry me." He lowered his voice to a whisper. "And she actually said yes."

"Well, of course she did." Teary-eyed again, Mother gave Marcelle another kiss on the cheek and held her hand. "I'm thrilled, dear. I've always admired your strength and courage."

"And there's more." Adrian gestured for the girls to join him. When they drew close, he guided them in front. "Mother, I want you to meet Shellinda." He laid a hand on her head. "And Regina." He shifted his hand to her head. "These two girls were enslaved in a place called the cattle camp. We brought them here thinking you might want to adopt—"

"Yes!" She stooped and gathered the girls into her arms. "Oh, yes, yes, yes!"

Adrian smiled at Marcelle. "That was easy."

She laughed. "As if you were worried about it."

Mother leaned back and compressed Shellinda's arm. "Why, dear child, you look like you haven't eaten anything for weeks!" She did the same to Regina. "And you, too!" She straightened and, taking each girl by the hand, led them toward the house. "Come with me. I have some bread and butter and corn on the cob ready to eat. We'll start fattening you up right away."

The girls tagged along, glancing back with wide grins. Regina gave an "Is it all right to go?" kind of look.

Adrian nodded. "Mother, Regina needs to come with us, so please pack her food and send it with her."

Mother stopped at the pasture gate. "You're not taking this child back to that slave planet!"

Arxad shuffled closer. "We need her gifts to see beyond the portal boundary. She should not have to set foot in my world at all, and if she does, we will keep her far away from any battles and bring her back safely."

After petting Regina's head and looking at Arxad skeptically, Mother nodded. "Very well. She will wash and return with a bundle of food."

"We should wash, too." Marcelle sniffed her underarm. "I probably smell worse than the dead animals."

"Let's go." Adrian scooped up Jonathan and carried him toward the house with Marcelle again keeping pace.

Arxad skittered along as before, more slowly this time. His wings flapped just enough to help him stay above the ground.

"Does he bite?" Jonathan asked.

"Well, Jon, that's a good question." Adrian turned toward Arxad. "Do you bite?"

"In certain circumstances." Arxad settled to his haunches and lowered his head. "But in the interest of friendship between your world and mine, I will submit to satisfying the curiosity of this child."

"What does he mean?" Jon asked.

"That you can ride on him. He's harmless."

Jonathan's eyes bulged. "Can I really?"

"Just hold on tight." Adrian lifted Jonathan to Arxad's back, then climbed up and sat behind him.

Jon patted Arxad's broad shoulder. "Wow! He's just like in the storybooks! So big and strong!"

Arxad bent his neck and looked at Jonathan, a nearly undetectable smile bending his scaly face. "Would you like to see me breathe fire?"

Jonathan clapped his hands. "Yes! Yes!"

Arxad extended his neck toward the sky. Starting with a puff of sparks-laden smoke, he blew a vibrant stream of orange fire from both nostrils, then followed with a fireball from his mouth that fell to the ground and rolled, spitting and hissing until it disappeared with a loud pop.

Jon let out a whoop. "That was amazing!"

Adrian laughed. "Arxad, by tomorrow you'll have achieved legendary status in Mesolantrum. Everyone will be talking about what you did."

"In a good light, I hope." Arxad spread his wings. "According to my sense of distance and time, I think the soldiers will be closing in on the portal in less than an hour. I will drop you and the boy off at the house, and then we should be on our way as soon as possible."

"Marcelle and I need to wash up and fill some flasks."

"Bring empty flasks," Arxad said. "A river flows near the portal, and the water is clean."

"Good to know."

Marcelle patted Arxad's flank. "I'll get started." She ran ahead, carrying the crutch on one side while her sword whipped her leg on the other.

Adrian helped Jonathan wrap his hands around Arxad's protruding spine. "We're ready!"

"Hold tightly!" Arxad jumped into the air and flew toward the house. Jonathan squealed with delight. With every bump and bounce, he bounced as well, as if riding an unbroken horse.

After orbiting the house once, Arxad landed near the back door, lowered his body again, and waited for his passengers to slide down. Adrian carried Jonathan into the house, deposited him on the gathering room's wicker bench, and returned to the mudroom where he washed his face and hands in a basin.

While he scrubbed a wound on his forearm, Marcelle, her face now clean, draped a towel over his shoulder. "I'm wondering if your commune members will return at all," she said. "Knowing Meredith, she might say something that'll get them all in trouble."

Adrian dried his hands with the towel. "She and Elyssa are a lot alike. They say whatever's on their minds."

"Let me see about this cut." Marcelle took the towel and dabbed Adrian's cheek with a clean corner. "Your mother should stay in hiding until we come back. The sentries might return to take possession of the land."

"They'll just padlock the doors and stop up the well. I can fix those later."

"True." Marcelle draped the towel over the basin. "I'm just worried. Something smells rotten, and it isn't me or those dead animals."

"I know what you mean. Like I said, killing animals to scare people is insane, and the idea that this new governor can protect them from disease has to be some kind of ploy."

"Not to mention the fanatical looks on the sentries."

Adrian heaved a sigh. "We'll get my mother and Shellinda and Jonathan situated in the barn and cover their tracks. They should be okay for a while."

After they finished preparations, including packing extra bread and corn for the departing humans and several dried fish for Arxad, they said their good-byes at the barn. Adrian, Marcelle, and Regina took their places on Arxad's back and launched into the air, the box of explosives again in his claws.

Soon, they passed over a forest that acted as a boundary to the Forbidden Zone. Beyond that, a field of flowers came into view. Most appeared to be dead, though a few yellow blossoms peeked out from among brown petals and withered stems.

A hundred yards or so into the field, the surface gave way to a sinkhole that plunged into darkness. Several hundred paces farther on and down a slope, a dark rectangular hole scarred the ground, too squared off to be natural.

"That is the access to the underground portal," Arxad said. "Magnar and I have flown through it, but the passage is tight and too dangerous for riders. I will set you down, and we can enter one by one. And we must act as quickly as possible. Since we are in a more temperate region, I assume the snow you packed in the box melted long ago. The explosive tubes are getting warmer, and I have no idea how long they will remain stable."

✹ TWELVE ✹

AFTER Arxad carefully deposited the explosives box on the ground, he landed next to the rectangular hole. The three passengers dismounted and looked over the edge. Solarus gave light to the chamber below, a square room with a river running through it on one side. A ladder lay on the floor, perhaps ten feet down.

"I see no soldiers," Marcelle said as she scanned the field. "It has been an hour."

Arxad pushed his head deep into the hole, then drew it out again. "They were supposed to take a circuitous route in order to avoid detection by Cal Broder's allies. My lack of knowledge of your forest paths likely caused me to misestimate their time of arrival."

"While we're waiting for them," Adrian said, "I'll get the ladder." He sat at the edge of the hole with his legs dangling.

Marcelle touched his shoulder. "That's quite a drop. No use taking a risk when we have a dragon here."

"Good point." He looked up at Arxad. "Care to offer some help?"

Arxad bobbed his head. "You may hold to my neck, and I will lower you as far as I can. Then I will take flight to watch for the soldiers."

"Sounds good." Adrian grasped Arxad's neck with both hands. Arxad swung him out over the hole and lowered him slowly through the opening.

"When you get down there," Arxad said, grunting, "face the wall on the opposite side of the river and look for a black glass egg embedded in the stone. It is a viewing window Regina can use to watch for my daughter's arrival on the Starlight side of the portal."

"Will do." As Adrian descended into the dimness, a rush of water echoed in the chamber. To his left, the river ran by at a rapid clip, maybe twice the speed of a double-time march. Foam rode atop some of the waves and splashed over the edge and onto the floor. To his right, an eerie glow emanated from a wall, though the surface appeared bare.

Marcelle and Regina watched from above. The rectangular hole took up roughly a third of the ceiling's surface space. Adrian winked at them. "I guess I get all the fun, don't I?"

"You're welcome to it." Marcelle took Regina's hand. "We'll wait for the ladder."

When his feet came within five feet or so of the floor, he let go of Arxad's neck and landed on flat stone. Arxad withdrew and shifted out of sight. Seconds later, the sound of beating wings blended with the rush of water and slowly diminished.

"What do you see?" Marcelle asked, still at the hole's edge.

He scanned the ceiling. "A few stalactites here and there, maybe a foot long." He set a hand under one of the stalactites. Gray water dripped and collected on his palm. "Water's leaching in. It probably rained here recently, so the ground might be fragile. We'd better not let too many soldiers walk over this place at one time."

Marcelle nodded. "Good thinking."

Adrian walked to a side wall and touched a rusting scabbard hanging vertically in one of three metal brackets. The other two brackets were empty. "Someone's been storing weapons. One sword's still here, but it's rusted pretty badly. Must have been here for a while."

"So it's damp down there?"

"Very damp." Adrian touched the wall with a fingertip and rubbed it against his thumb. "Almost like it's rained, even in the sheltered areas."

"Maybe the river floods when it rains."

"Could be." He walked to the wall opposite the river. At waist level, eight finger-sized holes lined up in a row at equal intervals except for a wider gap in the middle. A couple of feet above the holes, something shimmered. At eye level, Adrian ran a finger along a glassy surface—an egg-shaped orb embedded in the wall, about the size of his own head. "I found the glass egg Arxad was talking about."

"Good. We'll get Regina down there to look at it."

Adrian picked up the ladder and heaved one end toward the opening. "Grab this."

A voice hissed, "Begone, intruder!"

The ladder slipped from Adrian's hands and clattered to the floor. He searched for the source of the voice. A dark figure approached from the riverbank, mist swirling in its frame.

"Adrian?" Marcelle called. "What's wrong?"

Adrian forced himself not to shudder. "I have company."

Steel sliding against steel sounded from above. "Do you need help?"

"No! Wait!" Adrian held up a hand. "He's kind of … immaterial. I don't think a sword will do any good."

A second misty phantom appeared and walked in tandem with the other. "Let us see if this intruder has a soul we can steal," one said to the other.

Adrian nudged the ladder with his foot. "More company."

"I'm coming!" Marcelle leaped from above and landed in a tumble and roll. She bounced back to her feet and joined Adrian at his side, her sword extended. She whispered, "Hiram and Bodnar!"

"Who?"

"Snatchers. I forgot to tell you about them." She slid her sword away. "You're right. Our blades won't do any good."

The two snatchers paused. As they stared at Adrian and Marcelle, low hisses passed between them.

Marcelle whispered, "They're here to protect the portal from intruders. They can steal a soul from an evil person. I'm not sure what they can do to us."

"Are you all right?" Regina called from above.

Marcelle looked up. "So far. Watch for Arxad and let us know when he's coming."

One of the snatchers said, "No dragon will be able to help you if you stay here."

Water broke over the river's edge and began flooding the floor. In seconds, the level rose to their ankles. The snatchers floated above it, their spinning fog becoming darker. "You have less than a minute, intruders. Leave now or die."

Adrian grabbed the ladder and stood it upright. "We can get out of here, but if they flood the portal—"

"There's a secret phrase." Marcelle lifted her wet boots in turn. "Uriel Blackstone told them to honor the person who spoke it."

Water lapped against Adrian's waist. He jerked the ladder toward the hole and propped the top end against the edge. "Any idea what it is?"

"I heard it only once. I don't remember."

He pulled her to the ladder. "Think fast or climb."

"I remember it," Regina called out. "Another question I will ask, and you'll submit to do this task."

Still hovering above the water, their bodies compressing, the two snatchers looked up at her. "What did you say?" one of them asked.

She took in a shaky breath and shouted, "Another question I will ask, and you'll submit to do this task."

"Is that it?" Water splashed into Adrian's face. "Is that the phrase?"

"It is the correct phrase," a snatcher said, barely audible above the water's rush.

Adrian guided Marcelle up a few rungs. He stood on the bottom rung and lifted his mouth above the surface. "Then why isn't the level going down?"

Rising with the flood, one of the snatchers pointed at Regina. "She uttered the phrase. Not you. She may come to the portal, but you must leave or drown."

Adrian pushed Marcelle's back, spewing water. "Go! Go!"

They hurried up the ladder and climbed out. When they planted their soaked boots on solid ground, Adrian spun back, knelt at the hole's edge, and clutched the ladder to keep it from getting swept away. Water dripped from his hair, and a cool breeze cut through his wet clothes, raising a shiver. "She can't come unless you drain the chamber!"

Marcelle knelt beside him. Her saturated trousers clung to her body. "We can't send her down there alone."

"When the portal opens," Adrian whispered, "they can't flood the chamber. The water will flow out into Starlight."

The sound of beating wings returned. Arxad descended and landed in a slide, uprooting some of the dead flowers. "The soldiers are coming. They are massing at the border of this field."

"Tell them to gather about fifty paces away." Still clutching the ladder, Adrian laid a palm on the dirt. "I'm not sure the ground will hold them, and besides, if the snatchers see them, they might get spooked and not trust Regina."

"Ah! So the snatchers are still haunting the portal. I did not detect their presence earlier."

"Do you know how to get rid of them?"

"Unfortunately, no. We will have to come up with a way to circumvent them." Arxad peered into the hole. "Did you see the viewer?"

Adrian nodded. "Regina is too short to look through it, but we'll figure something out."

"Very well. When Regina sees Xenith, we will begin sending the soldiers down."

"What if Xenith doesn't come?" Adrian asked.

"The only other way to open the portal is with a genetic key, and we do not have one. We would have to return to the other portal." Arxad blinked, a sparkle evident in one eye. "She will come."

"Of course she will." Adrian regripped the ladder with both hands. "Hurry back. We still have the tubes to worry about."

"The air temperature is dropping," Arxad said. "Perhaps the risk is lessening." He launched into the air once more and flew toward the field's boundary. Gusts from his takeoff blew more water from Adrian's hair.

Below, the flood began to recede. One of the snatchers floated closer to the hole and spoke in a low hiss as he descended with the retreating water. "Send the girl down."

Adrian laid a hand on Regina's red-topped head. "Do you want to go?"

Her stare fixed on the hole, she nodded, though not with conviction.

"I don't think they'll hurt you," Marcelle said. "They're supposed to serve whoever Uriel sends."

"I'll go." With Adrian's help, Regina mounted the ladder. He kept a hand on her as long as he could, but as her foot passed the fifth rung down, he had to release her.

When she reached the water level, she slowed to the flood's receding pace. Each time the surface dropped below a rung, she stepped down to it and looked up, her eyes revealing a blend of fright and excitement.

With every glance, Adrian gave her a reassuring nod and whispered, "You can do it!"

After several more seconds, she stepped off the ladder and set her feet on the puddle-strewn stone floor. One of the snatchers pointed at the wall. "If you are truly Uriel Blackstone's emissary, then you will know what to do."

Regina looked at the wall, then at Adrian, her expression begging for help.

Adrian set his hands on the edge of the hole and leaned in. "She's too short to see into the portal's viewer. Can I give her a boost?"

A snatcher looked up at him, its expression indiscernible within its misty mask. "Your request is reasonable."

Adrian swung onto the ladder and hurried to the bottom. The snatchers drifted closer but not quite within reach. Their wheezing breaths blew across Adrian's wet skin, carrying a vile stench.

Resisting a shiver, he knelt in front of the portal wall and hoisted Regina to his shoulders. "Look through that black egg thing," he said in a soothing tone, "and tell me what you see."

She squinted at the glass. After a few seconds, she whispered, "I see an empty room that's pretty dark and stairs that lead to light."

"So Xenith's not there yet."

"I hear voices, though."

"Do you recognize them?"

"No. It's like when I saw the girl in the star. She's talking to me. She's telling me a story."

"Exodus," Adrian said. "I suppose since you're looking into Starlight, you can communicate with Cassabrie."

"I think so, but … but it feels like she's …" Her voice altered to a lower pitch. "Like she's speaking through me."

"Regina?"

She tapped him on the head. "Turn to face the snatchers, please, Adrian."

Adrian held his breath. Could it be? Cassabrie's voice?

When he pivoted, Regina spoke with a resonating tone. "Hiram and Bodnar, hear me. Exodus, the guiding star that you conspired to destroy, commands you to allow my fellow travelers access to this chamber. They must witness the great resurrection, the final triumph that has been planned ever since you struck the star with your feeble spear according to the darkness of your corrupted minds."

The two snatchers looked at each other. Then, with a hissing growl, one of them pointed a smoky finger at Regina. "What proof do you offer that you speak with the star's authority?"

"Proof?" Regina laughed. "How long will you act like fools? You refused to listen then, and now you threaten your own restoration by clinging to your stubborn ways."

One of the snatchers drifted closer, turning darker as he spoke. "We are not fools. Our restoration depends on guarding this portal. If we become lax in our duty and allow access to those who did not know Uriel's phrase, we will be blamed for the breach."

"You speak from fear rather than from faith, but your point is valid." Regina stroked Adrian's hair as if petting a cat. "The proof you seek will become manifest in a moment. I ask only that you allow Marcelle to join us until the demonstration is complete."

"Only until then." The darker snatcher looked up at Marcelle. "You may enter."

Marcelle slid down the ladder and joined Adrian. "Regina sounds like Cassabrie," she whispered.

"I know." He raised a finger to his lips. "Let's see what happens."

Regina patted Adrian's cheek. "Turn me toward the portal again, please."

When he turned, the glass egg faded from black to white and displayed the scene she had described earlier, a dim chamber with a stairway leading up toward a source of light. The viewing window spread out, as if the egg had cracked and spilled its contents across the wall. Soon the entire chamber in Starlight came into view, though it revealed nothing significant, just the boundaries of the room on the other side of the portal.

Marcelle touched the wall, still solid. "The portal's not open."

"It is merely a viewing window," Regina said with Cassabrie's voice. "I cannot open it." She waved her hand. "Hiram and Bodnar, watch and see what your foolishness has wrought."

The chamber vanished, replaced by a view of the great barrier wall where the river flowed northward out of the Southlands. Alaph landed on the north side at the river's edge, his white wings brilliant against the gray sky. A redheaded girl wearing a blue cloak and an elderly man rode atop his back. As the girl slid down, her cloak billowed, revealing calf-length trousers underneath. The man tried to dismount by crawling backwards, but he slipped. The girl caught him and helped him steady himself on the ground.

Regina pointed at the wall. "Koren and her father, Uriel, also known as Orson, rode Alaph to the Southlands, hoping to provide a way for the soldiers from Darksphere to breach the barrier wall. I will now allow them to speak for themselves as you watch what took place not long ago."

In the Starlight scene, Koren reached into her pocket and withdrew a box with a red button on one side. After looking at it and sliding it back in place, she picked up a bag about the size of a saddle pack. "You wait here and rest. I'll place the tubes."

With the bag forcing her to lean to the side, she marched to the base of the wall. Then, touching the wall with her left hand and extending the bag with her right, she tiptoed through ankle-deep water on a walkway that abutted the base and followed it toward the river's center where a gate lay open, allowing the river to pass through.

When she reached the gate, she swung around the wall's corner and skulked through the opening, again walking along a narrow path that lay under the water's surface. The portal viewer followed her progress inside and dimmed as she passed through the gate. She stopped, turned slowly toward the way she had come, and looked up at the inside of the inner wall. The viewing window turned as well, as if standing behind her and watching whatever lay in her field of vision.

Well above Koren's head, a mechanism with two wheels and a belt between them sat on a stone shelf that ran parallel to the wall and over the river's spillway to the left. Sliding her feet, she closed in on the wall, then turned right and followed another path until she reached a ladder.

She pulled the box from her pocket again, reached high, and set it on the shelf. With the bag still in hand, she grabbed a rung, scaled the ladder, and sat on the shelf with the bag in her lap.

After resting for a moment, she withdrew a metallic cylinder from the bag.

"That looks like one of our explosive tubes," Marcelle whispered.

Adrian nodded. "Identical."

Still holding the bag, Koren rose to her feet, bent low, and walked on the shelf toward the wall's river opening. Every few seconds, she withdrew a tube from the bag and set it down. When she reached the opposite side of the river, the last tube slipped from her hand and lodged in a crack on the shelf. It let out a sizzling sound but stayed intact.

Koren hurried back toward the ladder, stepping over the other tubes she had placed. When she arrived, she snatched up the box, hurried down the ladder, and sloshed back to the river's gate, then to the north side of the wall, shouting, "I think one of the tubes might explode!"

Uriel rose from a kneeling position at the river's edge and looked at the top of the wall. "Alaph! Did you hear?"

While Koren slid closer and closer to the riverbank, Alaph flew down from the top of the wall. "We must mount quickly!"

A boom sounded. Koren stopped, still short of the bank, and held her breath. Uriel ran along the wall's base and threw her into the water. As Koren flailed in the current and drifted northward, more booms thundered.

Stones flew everywhere. One crashed into Uriel's neck, snapping it. A sharp-edged rock severed his leg. As he collapsed, a cascade of boulders fell over him, and a cloud of dust hid his body from view.

Marcelle gasped. "Poor Uriel!"

Koren swam toward the wall, struggling against the current and screaming, "Daddy!" Another explosion sent a jagged flat stone hurtling out of the cloud straight toward Koren. Alaph swooped down and blocked the stone with his body. It cut into his ivory skin and impaled him. His wings flapping wildly, he snatched Koren out of the water with his back claws and lifted into the sky.

He flew haphazardly downstream, away from a series of billowing clouds, and descended toward the water. Finally, he and Koren plunged into the river. They splashed with wings and arms until they fought their way to shore. Koren crawled to the shallows first, and Alaph dragged his body to the bank farther downstream.

Koren ran to Alaph and knelt close to the flat stone protruding from his flank. Although it appeared to be a deep wound, no blood flowed. Alaph clamped down on the stone with his teeth and slung it away.

The image froze. Regina lifted an arm and spoke again in Cassabrie's voice. "Alaph died, and following his instructions, Koren used stardrop crystals to release his spirit to fly to the Creator."

The scene animated again. Koren now stood well away from Alaph's body. She walked to the corpse while prying a lid from a crucible. She pinched a dab of sparkling crystals from the crucible and rubbed her thumb and finger together, sprinkling the crystals over Alaph.

Like gnawing fireflies, the crystals crawled along his body, growing as they consumed his flesh, both along the surface and deep inside. White smoke rose in a line, like the trail of a raging meadow fire. The crystals left behind nothing—no skin, flesh, or bones.

After a minute or so, a wispy mist flowed from Alaph's body— dragon shaped with beating wings. As it rose, it faded from view. More misty shapes followed, Vigilant and Serenity, then a boy, then three girls, then another boy, all following the dragon into the sky.

Koren backed away, weeping, apparently not noticing the departing spirits. When the crystals reached the end of Alaph's snout and the tips of his wings, they flashed and popped, then disappeared. Only a scorched circle remained.

As she turned toward the barrier wall, the viewing window turned with her. A pile of rubble stretched from the left edge of the river to near the opposite bank. Water poured over the center through a channel that gradually widened as the river forced its way through the debris.

Again the scene froze, this time with Koren staring at the devastation.

"Koren succeeded," Regina said in Cassabrie's voice, "but at great cost. The soldiers are even now crossing the remains of the barrier and will soon mount an attack against the Southlands dragons, though they are unaware that a greater danger awaits. Not only will they be exposed to the deadly disease; they will also face the remaining Benefile—the three white dragons of Alaph's race. Without Alaph there to temper their sense of justice with his merciful ways, many humans will likely die as the Benefile attempt to punish the Southlands dragons for their crimes."

Koren and the rubble disappeared, replaced by a radiant sphere. Cassabrie hovered within, her red hair and blue cloak flowing. "Adrian," she said, now without Regina speaking for her, "I am on my way to the Southlands, and I will do what I can to alleviate the suffering there. I have a plan …" Her face quivered, and her voice began shaking as it rose in pitch. "If it works, not only will I be able to provide a cure for the disease to everyone, I will also rid the land of the Benefile. Without Alaph in their midst, their terror will be great, so they must be eliminated."

Adrian stepped closer to the wall. "What is your plan?"

Cassabrie gave him a tremulous smile. "When you cross into Starlight, wait in the portal area until you see the plan unfold. Only then will it be safe for you to come to the dragon village. And come you must, for the Benefile are the only force keeping Taushin and the Southlands dragons from continuing their rule over the slaves. If I succeed in eliminating the Benefile, the slaving dragons will take out their fury on the remaining humans. The slaves' rescue depends on your army."

"Have you seen Xenith?" Marcelle asked. "She needs to open the portal for us."

Cassabrie closed her eyes for a moment. When she opened them again, she nodded. "Xenith is in flight in a southerly direction, but since so much of the land between the north and the south looks alike, I am unable to tell exactly where she is."

"So if Xenith doesn't show up in time," Adrian said, "we'll have to rely on the soldiers who are already there."

"They are not enough, Adrian. The dragons who side with Taushin are too powerful. The soldiers will surely fight with courage, but their valor will not overcome scorching flames and tearing claws. They need your help."

"I think Magnar's on our side now," Adrian said. "At least he appeared to be."

Cassabrie's cloak settled around her. "Magnar has transformed into a powerful ally, but he is one dragon against many, and he will be the Benefile's main target. His crimes were conceived in evil, and the Benefile will show no mercy."

"I understand. We'll charge like raging bulls."

"I know you will, Adrian." Cassabrie turned to Marcelle. "Exodus showed me your restoration, my dear friend, and I heard Adrian's proposal." Tears trickling, Cassabrie smiled. "I am blessed. I now know that a woman of passion, beauty, and honor will always be at my beloved's side. Since his heart will be filled, mine is filled, though because of the path I have chosen, I will not be able to be physically present for your coming together, though I trust that I will be there in spirit."

"I'm sorry to hear that." Marcelle reached for the wall, but when her fingers touched the surface, Cassabrie and Exodus began fading away.

"Good-bye, my friends," Cassabrie said, her voice becoming thinner. "When you see Exodus rising, you will know that my journey is complete."

The wall darkened to stone. Only a glimmer from the black glass gave evidence of the Starlighter's tale.

Marcelle sighed. "Cassabrie's going to do something dangerous."

"No doubt," Adrian said. "If we could get through before Xenith comes, maybe our invasion could take away her need to do whatever she's planning."

"If," Marcelle repeated. "My mother used to say, 'If's are like wishes that rise to the sky; they make a child dream of blueberry pie. When the sheep need a shearing and a hem needs a thread, you will find all the iffers asleep in their beds.'"

"You sound like Uriel Blackstone," one of the snatchers said.

Marcelle blinked at him. "What?"

"Your voice. Your cadence. And the rhyme you spoke reminds me of a pass phrase he gave us."

"Okay," Marcelle said, stretching out the word. "What does that mean?"

"It means that we should help you." The snatcher glided next to Adrian. "There is another way to open the portal."

"Bodnar!" the other snatcher hissed. "What she said was not the pass phrase. Do not reveal Uriel's secrets!"

"Uriel is dead." Bodnar pointed at the wall. "A Starlighter's tales are always true. It is obvious that Uriel was aiding the soldiers, so if we are to honor his efforts, we should help her achieve them."

"You take great risk." Hiram's mist swirled around his eyes. "A failed attempt will flood the chamber again."

"Perhaps not," Bodnar said. "Since you opened the reservoir only moments ago, it has not had time to refill."

Hiram floated to Adrian's other side and looked him over. "He has no resemblance to Uriel Blackstone, so he is likely not a relative, but if you wish to explain the procedure to him, I will not protest."

Bodnar passed a smoky hand below the window of black glass. "The only way to open it from this side is for a descendant of Uriel Blackstone to insert his fingers into the locking mechanism. Your brother Jason went through because Tibalt Blackstone accompanied him and used his fingers to unlock the portal. Jason tried to do it himself with his own fingers, but he failed and instead flooded this chamber."

Marcelle lifted her hands. "It all adds up. Drexel killed my mother so he could cut off her fingers and use them as a genetic key. She and I must be related to Uriel."

"But how?" Adrian asked. "If Uriel is in your lineage, wouldn't you know it?"

"I heard that my great-grandfather was a traveler very few people knew about. The gossipers say his wife used more than one surname and that she had multiple lovers, so I suppose it could be true without me knowing it."

"The gossipers lie," Bodnar said. "Your great-grandmother had only one lover, her devoted husband."

Marcelle cocked her head. "How do you know?"

"When Uriel Blackstone returned from enslavement on Dracon, he found that his wife had died giving birth to Tibalt Blackstone. He married Laurel, who had escaped from Dracon with him. Assuming you are who we think you are, Laurel gave birth to a girl who became your grandmother, so you are Uriel's great-granddaughter."

Marcelle wiggled her fingers. "So maybe I *can* open the portal."

"If you plan to try," Bodnar said, "do so now. Since the reservoir is refilling, there is little danger if you fail, but the danger will increase quickly if you wait."

Marcelle set her fingers in front of the eight holes, palms up. "Like this?"

"Correct."

She slid her fingers into the holes until her knuckles bumped against the surrounding wall. Everyone stared at the entry points, their voices hushed. The rushing water seemed louder as it continued its cascade through the chamber.

Marcelle whispered, "Nothing's happening."

"If you were not a genetic match," Hiram said, "the floor would have pivoted and reversed the river. Something else must be amiss."

Adrian nodded at Marcelle. "Pull them out. I want to check something."

When she withdrew her fingers, Adrian set his palm against her palm. His fingertips extended a half inch beyond hers. "Uriel might not have thought about fingers that are too short."

Marcelle pulled her hand away. "Like mine."

"Maybe we can do something about that." Adrian slid out his sword and pressed the point against the rightmost hole. "This might take a lot of work, but it'll be worth it."

"Use the right tools," someone said from above. "You can't skin a bear with a penknife."

Adrian looked up, squinting. A narrow-faced man dressed in military garb knelt at the hole's edge, his face shadowed by his hand. "Who are you?" Adrian asked. "You look familiar."

"Joseph Olivet, a lowly private sent by Arxad to check on your progress. He wanted a skinny guy to come in case the ground up here is fragile."

"Ollie?" Adrian laughed. "I haven't seen you since primary school."

"That's because I've been hiding from you ever since you took up the blade. I didn't want to get skewered."

"Because of the inkwell incident?"

"Yep. By the time I figured out you weren't mad at me anymore, I had already been transferred to the training school in Tarkton."

Adrian winked. "Well, I am still mad at you, so you'd better give me more than advice."

"Yes sir!" Ollie saluted. "What can I do for you?"

"Do you have a hammer and maybe some stakes?"

"Plenty of stakes for our tents. I might be able to find a hammer or two amongst us." He disappeared from sight, calling, "I'll be right back."

After a few moments, Ollie called, "Look out below!" Something clanked on the stone next to Adrian's feet. "Our smithy sharpened the stakes before we left," Ollie said. "They ought to work."

Adrian collected two hammers and a pair of metal tent stakes from the chamber floor. "Where's Arxad?"

"Our draconic commander is lining up the troops about fifty paces away."

"Perfect." Adrian set the point of a tent stake at the edge of one of the finger holes. "Come on down here and help. We'll take turns chiseling out these holes until Marcelle can open this portal. You can make up for the inkwell incident by spilling some sweat with me."

✸ THIRTEEN ✸

PROFESSOR Dunwoody paced on the walkway in front of the Cathedral's entry steps. People streamed up the stairs to wait for the next scheduled showing of the video. Those who had viewed the most recent showing had cleared the stairs and now began their trek home or to their businesses, convinced that the charismatic Cal Broder was the rightful governor of Mesolantrum. These had marched down with starry looks in their eyes and smiles on their faces, and a purplish-brown splotch on one cheek gave new arrivals reason to pause and ponder.

Chatter abounded. Dunwoody stopped at times to dodge people and listen to their conversations, but frenetic talk of magic touches and temporary immunities made no sense at all.

He halted and searched the sea of faces, dim now in the waning daylight. What was taking Fenton so long? If they were to put Arxad's plan into action, they couldn't afford to dally.

"Professor!"

Dunwoody swiveled toward the voice. Fenton jogged from a street leading toward the palace. When he arrived, now dressed in the garb of a Tarkton noble, he touched his lapel, leaned close to Dunwoody, and whispered, "It's one of Leo's. I found it in the palace. I think it will help with the deception."

"Well played." Dunwoody looked him over. Although the Tark garments provided him with a new aspect, he wouldn't fool anyone who knew him. "My main concern is that someone will recognize you. Broder has probably never met you, but surely someone in the crowd has."

"Oh, yes. I was in such a rush, I forgot." Fenton reached into an outer tunic pocket and retrieved a handful of hairy black items. He ducked low and began applying the items to his face. Dunwoody stood over him to block him from view. A moment later, Fenton rose again, now sporting sideburn extensions along with a thin mustache and goatee. "How do I look?"

Dunwoody nodded. "Surprisingly authentic. Even your own mother wouldn't recognize you."

"Good." Fenton flashed a boyish smile. "Then I'm ready."

Dunwoody pulled Fenton's sleeve and guided him up the stairs to a secluded spot on one side of the Cathedral's porch. "Let's watch Broder for a moment. My understanding is that a Starlighter maintains influence over a person as long as that person is within his view, but judging from what I see of the people leaving this place, I think he is doing something that extends his control. What we learn might alter our plans, and we will have to guard our own minds with all diligence, as if we were tortoises with protective shells, though we have two legs instead of four and no ability to—"

"It's all right, Professor," Fenton said. "I understand."

"Then let's go." Dunwoody led the way through a side entrance and down the main sanctuary's right-hand aisle. As they passed rows of seats, most of them empty since the people gathered near the center, the video began playing on a portable screen that had been set up next to the priest's rostrum, slightly elevated from the floor.

Dunwoody stopped near the front, shielded by a wide column, and set a hand on Fenton's chest. "Let's watch from here. Remember. Guard your mind."

As the video replayed the recent events in the governor's office, Dunwoody scanned the sanctuary. No sign of Broder, only his accomplice, the young lady Sophia standing to the side of the screen. Whether or not she was an unwitting victim of Broder's charms remained unclear. In either case, it would not be wise to trust her.

Broder's recorded voice carried in the Cathedral chamber, resonating as he appealed to the audience. "For the sake of every soul on this planet, it is imperative that Governor Stafford graciously step down and allow me to protect our entire race during this time of crisis."

Some in the audience smiled. Others wept. When Issachar announced his decision to resign, many applauded.

Finally, the video finished, and the onlookers sat with an eerie hush. Sophia stepped in front of the screen and called out, "Please line up in the center aisle to receive a touch of immunity from our new governor. He will press two fingers on your cheek. You will feel a twinge of pain, but it will subside in mere moments. This will temporarily protect you from the disease that threatens to invade our land."

Fenton gave Dunwoody a questioning look and mouthed, "Touch of immunity?"

Dunwoody whispered, "Let's watch and learn."

Dozens of people rose from seats in the two middle sections and collected in the aisle. When they had all lined up, Sophia waved a hand toward the back of the stage. In the relative dimness, Broder sat in the priest's high-backed chair, reading a small book. When he noticed Sophia's signal, he tucked the book into a pocket and strode to the front, his head high and his shoulders square. An excited buzz erupted from the onlookers as they craned their necks or rose slightly on tiptoes to get a look at the new governor.

Broder jumped down to audience level, as nimble as a deer, and held up a hand. "Silence, please."

The chatter instantly subsided. Broder smiled in an agreeable way, no apparent pretense in his manner. "Citizens of Mesolantrum," he said in a resonant tone, "as Sophia said, I will touch you on the cheek. A slight discoloration on your skin will be a sign to all that I touched you, an effectual symbol that you care about your family and friends enough to avoid transmitting the disease. You see, since the power of my touch is temporary, the mark will eventually fade, so I ask that you return here once each week for another application."

"How many weeks?" a lady near the front asked.

Sophia stepped forward. "Seven. By then, all who have the disease on Dracon will be dead, and the danger will have passed."

Smiles and nods rippled through the crowd.

"There is a troubling issue," Broder continued, still addressing the crowd. "Some people fear coming to me to receive the touch. What do you think will happen if not everyone receives it?"

"They could transmit the disease to us," a man in overalls said.

A woman next to him added, "When our protection wears off, we could catch it."

Sophia scowled and spiced her tone with anger. "They would be a danger to all of you during those vulnerable times, so their refusal is tantamount to an assault on your spouses and children. Because of their selfish fears, they will be a constant threat."

Grumbles passed from mouth to ear down the line.

Broder looked at Sophia. "So what should we do with such people?"

Sophia set her hands on her hips. "Considering your desire to be a governor who listens to the will of the people, I say let the people decide."

"Ah! A jury of their peers. Who could argue with that?" Broder folded his hands. "I only appeal for mercy. Fear is a powerful influence. Not as powerful as love, of course, and all who love should want protection, but let us not forget that we all have fears at times that cause us to do what is not exactly wise."

"Isolate them," the man in overalls said. "At least until the seven weeks have passed."

"A quarantine." Broder nodded slowly. "Safe to all and merciful as well."

"What if they escape?" Sophia asked.

The man in overalls spoke up again. "Then they should be locked up in the dungeon. Even there, seven weeks isn't like a death sentence."

Murmurs and nods of approval passed through the line.

Broder raised a hand again. "Then it is agreed. We will write this decision in a proclamation and see to it that all are aware."

"We had better begin the immunity touch," Sophia said. "We shouldn't keep the next group waiting."

"Yes, yes, of course." Broder gestured for the first person in line—a mother with two children in tow. He touched her cheek with two fingers. She winced briefly, then smiled. When Broder pulled his fingers back, the now-familiar discoloration appeared.

Dunwoody grasped Fenton's arm and pulled him behind the column. "Oh, he is a sly one, isn't he?"

Fenton nodded. "His voice is spellbinding. His logic is sound. If I were not prepared, I would have fallen for his appeal."

"Yet there is something taking place that is far from sound." Dunwoody peeked at the line. One by one the people took their turns receiving the touch, and with each application, an almost imperceptible aura around Broder seemed to expand and brighten.

Dunwoody pressed his back against the column and shifted Fenton directly in front of him so Broder wouldn't be able to see either of them. Leaning close, Dunwoody whispered, "They were acting out a play, a planned dialogue. Those under Broder's spell wouldn't notice that Sophia's interjections were scripted. They acted as if these people were the first to consider what to do with those who refuse to accept the touch, but they likely recited the same dialogue with the previous group, and if we stay longer, we will see a repeat performance."

"I think you're right." Fenton wrinkled his brow. "But what if people in one group compare what they heard with people in another group? Won't they grow suspicious?"

A new voice emanated from somewhere close by. "You underestimate the willingness of people to believe in whatever enchants them."

Dunwoody spun toward an alcove in the wall. Counselor Viktor Orion stepped into the light, dressed in his official robes, black and silky. "To people who are enamored with something that provides comfort and security," Orion said, "evidence means nothing. They will not believe a fire is coming even if they smell the smoke."

Dunwoody narrowed his eyes. "How much of our conversation did you hear?"

"Enough to know that you are plotting against our new governor." Orion grasped Dunwoody's upper arm and whispered, "Fear not. I am your ally. I have been to Dracon and back, and I have pledged in front of Arxad himself to amend my ways. Now I don these robes for the purpose of trying to curry Broder's favor and learn more about him. Tell me your plan, and maybe we can combine our efforts."

Dunwoody pulled back and crossed his arms tightly. "Considering your past alliances, I prefer that you tell me your plan first."

"A fair counter." Orion brushed a hand along his robe. "As counselor of Mesolantrum, I can claim the right to see Broder's genealogy. Learning a man's origins is the best first step in discovering his goals."

"Good, good," Dunwoody said. "And after that?"

"I have no further plans. I thought I would decide the next step after I accomplished the first one."

"Unfortunately that is our dilemma as well, but this Broder is not a man you can scheme against one step at a time. He is too crafty." Dunwoody reached into an inner tunic pocket and withdrew a small notebook. As he thumbed through the pages, he mumbled, "Starlighter facts. Where are they?" He squinted at a page title that looked like *Drinking Nuts*, but it must have said *Dragon Notes*. "My scribblings are so rushed I can barely read them myself."

"What are they?" Orion asked.

"I jotted down some facts about Starlighters from Arxad's journal. Cal Broder is a male Starlighter." Finally the heading *Starlighter Musings* flashed by. Dunwoody turned back to the page and read the list of notes. "Let's see. A Starlighter reveals what has happened on Starlight, which was called Iris long ago. Both males and females are able to hypnotize unwary listeners. The power of the female to hypnotize is stronger than that of a male, but the male is also able to drain energy from a target by focused concentration or by touch."

"By touch?" Fenton said. "That means Broder is draining the people."

"I know. I know. Listen." Dunwoody pointed at the bottom of the page. "The tales a Starlighter tells are always true. Although a female Starlighter has been known to be deceptive when not delivering a tale, no male Starlighter has ever been known to utter a falsehood of any kind."

Fenton peeked around the side of the column. "Then the touch to the cheek really provides immunity."

"No, no, no." Dunwoody pulled him back into hiding. "Don't you see? The staged dialogue was designed so that Sophia would be the one to speak the falsehoods. If we were to stay for the next session, you will hear every word that Broder speaks to be unarguably true. She is his lying puppet, which allows him to avoid this encumbrance. He can use the power of a Starlighter without worrying about the essential integrity that his gender and species demand."

Fenton nodded. "A convenient combination. Difficult to overcome, I think."

"Perhaps." Dunwoody tapped his chin. "Unless this handicap can be exploited somehow."

"The solution is simple," Orion said. "We need to force him into a position where he has to utter a truth that would expose him."

Dunwoody nodded. "Exactly what I was thinking. Though I haven't yet thought of a scenario to spring such a trap."

Fenton set a finger against his own cheek. "So if the touch drains energy, then he is really trying to gain more power for himself."

"Yes, yes, of course." Dunwoody flipped through the notebook pages again, though looking for nothing in particular. "Soon he will acquire so much power no one will be able to conquer him. He could be counting on the hypnosis in order to seize what power he can immediately. This charade is likely a temporary measure."

"So you will have to execute your plan quickly," Orion said.

"Without a doubt." Dunwoody returned the notebook to his pocket. "I have a way for you to participate without telling you the plan. If you go along with it, you will prove that you are my ally."

"What should I do?"

"I have known you for a long time. You are a master at the art of deception. You will figure it out."

Orion nodded. "Thank you. ... I think."

Fenton straightened his body and brushed a wrinkle from his tunic. "I'm ready."

"Just remember, you're Elias Tryon, the king's herald, not Fenton Xavier." Dunwoody set a finger to his temple and nodded. "And put on your tortoise shell. He is sure to test his power on all of us. You can pretend to be influenced, but don't let him touch you."

"I understand."

"Wait for my signal." Dunwoody set a hand on Orion's back. "Let's go."

Dunwoody and Orion walked out from behind the column and eased toward Broder, approaching at floor level parallel to the front of the stage. They stopped a few paces away and waited for the final citizen to receive the mark—a middle-aged peasant woman, likely a commune dweller. When Broder touched her cheek, she closed her eyes and gasped. Then, smiling, she turned and ambled toward the exit.

When the door closed, shutting out the awaiting new arrivals, Broder clapped his hands. "I've never felt better in my life! Every touch makes me feel—"

"Like you're saving the world?" Sophia asked as she hurried to stand by his side. "Look. We have visitors."

Broder swiveled toward Dunwoody and Orion. "Ah! Professor Dunwoody! Have you come to receive immunity?" He extended a hand, but Dunwoody dodged his touch.

"No, no. I make it a point to demonstrate chivalry by being last." Dunwoody laid a hand on his chest. "Far be it from me to use my familiarity with nobility to avoid standing in line while women and children wait at the door."

Broder half closed an eye. "An interesting form of chivalry."

"Many have thought me eccentric, but I am what I am." Dunwoody touched Orion's shoulder. "This is Counselor Orion."

Broder extended his hand. "I'm pleased to meet you."

"Ah!" Orion backed away. "I washed with holy water, and you have touched many faces today."

Sophia growled. "Holy water is better used on swine."

Orion gave her a shallow bow. "Miss Halstead, I hope you will accept my apology for my role in your mother's death. I was wrong. I repent of my evil actions, and I ask you to forgive me."

She leaned toward him, her cheeks fiery red. "Raise her from the ashes, you rabid wolf, and cut your own throat as penance. Then I will accept your apology."

"That's enough, Sophia." Broder grasped her arm and pulled her away. "Open the door and let the newcomers in."

Muttering under her breath, she hurried toward the anteroom.

"Now to the reason we have come." Dunwoody withdrew a small scroll from an inner pocket. With two ornate wooden ends and a wax seal, it seemed to fit the majesty of the Cathedral. "Have you seen a royal invitation before?"

"I haven't received one myself, but I have seen one." Broder leaned closer. "Who is the recipient?"

"You are, but I cannot give it to you yet. A herald has arrived from Tarkton, and he is awaiting an introduction. According to custom, when a king's herald visits a new governor, he must be introduced by the governor's chief officer. Since I held that office for Governor Stafford, and since you have not replaced me, I am taking on that role." Dunwoody bowed his head. "Assuming you approve."

Broder nodded. "I do."

Dunwoody cleared his throat and spoke loudly enough for all to hear. "Cal Broder, governor of Mesolantrum, allow me to introduce Elias Tryon, the king's herald, who has come with salutations and glad tidings."

Fenton walked out from behind the column, marched to them with stately pomp, and bowed low. "Greetings, Governor Broder.

King Sasser sends his best wishes and hopes for a mutually beneficial relationship."

Broder bowed in return. "I honor the king, and I appreciate his kindness."

"And," Fenton continued, "the king also sends a special request."

Dunwoody handed Fenton the scroll.

While Fenton broke the seal and unrolled the parchment, the arriving crowd shifted in their seats and craned their necks to listen. Sophia walked closer, now within arm's reach of Broder. When Fenton stretched out the page, one hand holding a dowel high and the other low, a chorus of shushes sounded.

"By order of King Sasser, the royal palace will host a festival to welcome the new governor of Mesolantrum. All officers and members of the court are ordered to attend, and invitations will be delivered to men and women of all classes throughout the kingdom. We will have a feast, music and dancing, and formal addresses from the king and the new governor. This event will take place at eight o'clock in the evening on the seventh of this month."

"The seventh?" Broder's forehead wrinkled. "That's tomorrow night."

Fenton bowed his head. "It is, sir. If that is too soon, I will send the king your regrets and—"

"No, no." Broder cleared his throat. "Please tell King Sasser that I am humbled by his kindness and honored by this recognition. I am happy to accept his invitation and look forward to meeting him."

"Excellent." Fenton rolled up the scroll. "I will return to the royal palace immediately with the good news."

Broder glanced at the crowd before leaning close to Dunwoody, Fenton, and Orion. "How is it that the king learned of my ascension to the governorship so quickly?"

Dunwoody raised a finger. "I immediately sent a rider with the appropriate papers for your ascension as well as a copy of your video. It arrived in Tarkton in three hours."

"Three hours?" Sophia said, her tone still sour. "No horse can make it to the royal palace in three hours."

"Well ..." Dunwoody's cheeks turned hot. "My guess is ..."

Orion chuckled. "Since our good archivist has spent so much time in the bowels of the palace, I assume he is unaware of the relays we have instituted. The rider changes mounts at the transfer stations. With a series of fresh horses, three hours is the normal delivery time for an expedited message. I have sent several myself, and the method is quite efficient."

Sophia's face flushed again. "I apologize. I was unaware of the transfers."

"In any case," Dunwoody continued, "since it has been only seven hours since I sent my messenger, that means King Sasser arranged this festival and prepared the invitation in less than one hour, which is decidedly fast."

"Yes," Broder murmured. "Very fast."

"You should be pleased. I assume your video made quite an impact on the king."

Broder raised his voice. "I am pleased. In fact, I am ecstatic that the king would arrange a festival in my honor at all, let alone so quickly."

Dunwoody scanned the gawking crowd, already under this usurper's spell. Now would be an excellent time to test Broder's theoretical weakness and perhaps even reveal a secret about this mysterious man. "Counselor Orion, you mentioned that you wanted to ask a question of our new governor."

"I do." Orion gave Broder a probing stare. "As counselor in Mesolantrum, it is my duty to keep a record of your genealogy, but it is possible that the record is already stored somewhere if you have worked in the palace in another capacity. Have you ever held a position under a previous governor here in Mesolantrum?"

"Here in Mesolantrum." Broder shifted his weight. "Actually, I—"

"No, he hasn't." Sophia stepped in front of Broder. "May I suggest that you allow our governor to finish this life-saving ministry to the people before you conduct an interview for a log book that will be buried with the other dusty and forgotten archives?"

"Yes, my lady." Orion bowed. "You're right, of course."

Sophia took Broder's arm and guided him toward his seat on the stage.

Dunwoody whispered, "Let's go," and marched up the center aisle with Fenton and Orion, then out the door. After hustling down the Cathedral's front steps, Dunwoody stopped at the edge of the street and whispered, "Did you notice that dodge?"

"I did," Fenton said. "It was quite obvious."

Orion looked back at the Cathedral. "She is guarding him like a mother hen."

"A mother hen guarding a fox," Dunwoody said. "Once he no longer has use for her, she might find herself plucked and skewered over a spit." He scanned the building's four towering spires, barely visible now in the growing twilight. It seemed that a shadow had drawn a curtain across all of Mesolantrum. "So now we know that Broder used to be in the governor's service. I already conducted a cursory search on his name and found nothing, but I can employ a few sets of fresh eyes to search more diligently. They will pore over every photograph of every person who has held a position in the palace during the last …" He blinked at Orion. "How many years, would you think?"

"He appears to be younger than thirty, but we shouldn't rely on appearance."

"You're right. We'll say the last thirty-five years. Our researcher will try to find a match with Broder. The pretext, of course, is gaining information for the Cathedral's genealogy records, so that should allay suspicions."

"Perhaps we should *raise* suspicions," Orion said. "You and I already have enough motivation to try to topple him from power. We know he is a fraud, but the people lack the willpower to see through his charade. Sprinkling doubt will help our cause."

Dunwoody shook his head. "Doubt sprinkled among believers leads only to backlash. Only incontrovertible proof will break the spell he has over the people, and even that might not be enough. We will keep evidence to ourselves until we have an avalanche instead of a sprinkle."

"To publicly bury him," Fenton said. "Without overwhelming evidence, I'm sure the military will be hesitant to make an arrest."

"Exactly, but if that doesn't work and Broder succeeds in seizing control, we will have to take care of the problem in another way." Dunwoody let out a long sigh. "I can't believe I am even thinking such thoughts."

Orion lowered his voice to a whisper. "Assassination?"

"You said it. I didn't."

"Merely as a question," Orion said, "though it has happened quite recently without much of an uproar."

"Yes, yes, I know. Prescott." Dunwoody stroked his chin. "This new governor is far more popular. Not only that, research and past experience indicate that only dragon fire can destroy him."

"Then the plan should proceed as follows," Orion said. "Our herald here will take a message to the king that Broder has accepted the invitation."

"But the invitation isn't real. It's just a ploy to get him out of Mesolantrum."

"Actually, the king's calendar already shows a festival taking place to open the grand ballroom after several months of renovations."

Dunwoody rolled his fingers into a fist. "Excellent. Divine providence is on our side."

"It's not a surprise, really. There is a festival of some sort nearly every week. I will simply write the message with a plea to combine the festivities." Orion touched his silky robe. "I know how to persuade King Sasser. I will send along a few bottles of special wine from my collection and request that everyone from the protocol officer to the king's chef be ordered to forget the original purpose of the festival. No one will ever know the difference."

Dunwoody nodded. "Good, good. Then we can try to expose Broder in front of the king and everyone at the festival. We can separate him from Sophia somehow."

"Exactly what I had in mind," Orion said, "except that I should stay here and begin work on unhypnotizing the people, if you will. We need to take advantage of Broder's absence."

"Ah! A good ministry. Perhaps I can persuade Issachar Stafford to accompany me. I would like to work on unhypnotizing him as well."

"What about me?" Fenton asked. "What do I do after I deliver the message to the king?"

Dunwoody firmed his lips. "Well, it is an unsavory and brutish method, but for the good of the kingdom …"

"Say no more." Fenton held up the scroll. "If your plan doesn't work, on the return trip from the palace, a certain herald will have to arrange an ambush."

"Do you have the ability to hold him captive until you can arrange for an execution by dragon fire?" Dunwoody asked. "And could you betray someone of such high office? I know of your duty-bound principles."

"I swore an oath to protect Mesolantrum, not the governor." Fenton straightened his body. "Broder is Mesolantrum's enemy, and I will do what I must to conquer him."

✸ FOURTEEN ✸

ADRIAN drove the hammer against the tent stake. Tiny stone fragments chipped away from a finger hole and fell to the floor. Sweat trickling as he maintained a crouch, he nodded at Ollie. "Ready to take a break and have Marcelle try again?"

"Definitely." Ollie lowered his own hammer. "This rock is harder than your skull."

"I'm not the one who cracked the chalkboard with his head." Adrian straightened and touched Marcelle's arm. "Ready?"

"Sure. My part is easy." Marcelle set her hands in front of the holes. "I think you chiseled out plenty. You'd better get a drink. Then we'll see what happens."

"Sounds good." Adrian turned toward the river where the two snatchers hovered at the water's edge. Regina knelt a little ways downstream, filling one of three flasks she carried. "Careful, Regina," Adrian said. "I don't want you getting swept away by another flood."

Hiram let out a hiss. "As long as no one experiments with the finger holes, these waters are completely under our control. Since the reservoir is again full, we can flood the room in seconds and empty it again just as quickly. If we had wanted to sweep any of you away, we could have done so long before now."

"Not a slight against you. I'm just trying to keep her safe." Adrian knelt with Regina and filled one of the flasks. While they drank, Ollie joined them and dunked his entire head into the water. When he drew it out, he gave it a shake, slinging water everywhere.

"Ahhh!" Ollie brushed his wet hair back with both hands. "Now that feels good!"

Regina laughed. "That's a funny way to get a drink!"

"I think his dog taught him how to do that." Adrian took her hand and led her back toward Marcelle. A few of the stalactites still dripped, but as wet as he was from sweat, he didn't bother to dodge the droplets. At least all the work kept the chill away. When they joined Marcelle, he gave her a filled flask. "Let's give it a try."

After taking a few drinks, she gave the flask to Adrian and pushed her fingers into the wall, filling the eight holes. Clicks sounded. Pinpoints of light glowed on the wall, and dozens of colors painted a mosaic across the surface. Directly in front of Marcelle, two dragons faced each other, their clawed hands splayed below her fingers. Letters appeared over the dragons' heads—
Where only courageous hearts may brave the river's flow.

Scarlet light pulsed around the finger holes and blended with the multicolored pinpoints, projecting rainbowlike arcs across every surface. Even the river glowed with shades of orange and purple. Warm air wafted by from invisible sources and dried Adrian's sweaty skin.

From the dragons' mouths, a line of red lights connected with the glass egg. The glass swelled, and its blackness spilled over the lights, like a shadow overwhelming dots of radiance.

Soon, the egg's darkness faded. The wall became clear and transformed into a wide doorway leading to an extension of the chamber. At the opposite side of the room, dim light filtered in from a staircase that ascended out of sight. A row of crystalline pegs stood in a line in front of Marcelle's feet, the center peg missing.

"You did it!" Adrian grasped Marcelle's shoulder. "Uriel would be proud of his great-granddaughter."

Marcelle gave him a tired smile. "So now what? Should everyone go through while I stand here?"

"I think so. If you go to Starlight, the portal will close, and you can't open it from that side."

"So I have to stay put for the entire battle?" Marcelle furrowed her brow. "I'm not liking this plan."

"Don't worry. You won't miss the battle. Xenith will show up eventually."

"Let's at least see how long it stays open." Marcelle withdrew her fingers. The other chamber remained in view for a few seconds, then began to darken. Like stars appearing at twilight, the dragon pinpoints returned one by one.

As soon as the holes appeared, she reinserted her fingers. The darkness dispersed, revealing the other chamber once more.

"It doesn't stay open long," Adrian said.

"Long enough for me to jump through."

"I know what you're thinking." Adrian tapped her on the head. "Just concentrate on holding the door open."

Ollie pushed a hand through to the other room. "I'll give Arxad a report. He'll probably start sending the men down one at a time."

"Good," Adrian said. "Also ask him to send one of the men back to the Northlands portal to get the central peg and bring it here. If that man can't take it and jump back through the portal before it closes, tell him to return with the news."

"Got it." Ollie gripped the ladder and bounded up the rungs, leaving Adrian, Marcelle, Regina, and the two snatchers, who still hovered near the river's edge.

"If necessary," Bodnar said, "we are able to hold the portal open for a short time."

"A very short time," Hiram added. "We would do so only in an emergency situation. The pain is excruciating."

"I appreciate that, but I hope it won't be necessary." Adrian took a step across the portal plane and scanned the room. "It looks safe."

"Do you want me to ask Exodus for news?" Regina asked.

"That might help." Adrian took her hand and led her across the portal. "Let's see what Cassabrie has to say."

Regina walked slowly toward the chamber's exit steps. "I think I'll hear better if I go outside." She looked up the stairway, blinking at the light.

A scream pierced the chamber. Adrian pulled Regina away from the stairs and stood in front of her.

"That sounded like a dragon!" Marcelle called.

"I know. I know." Adrian whipped out his sword, making the blade sing. "Regina, go back to Marcelle!"

Dragon fire shot into the chamber and engulfed Adrian's clothes. He threw himself on the floor and batted at the flames, his vision warped by smoke, fire, and pain. Regina screamed. Marcelle shouted, but another dragon scream garbled her words. Wetness rushed in. Strong arms rolled him into the flow. Sizzles erupted and quickly ebbed.

After a few seconds, soothing words followed. "It's okay, honey. The fire's out."

"Honey?" Adrian opened his eyes. Marcelle straddled his abdomen, splashing water over his charred sleeve from a shallow pool on the floor.

"Yes. *Honey.* That's you." She tilted her head and gave him a hurt look. "Don't you like it?"

"Sure. It's nice. I just haven't heard you say it before." He looked at the stairway. Regina stood against a wall a few paces to the side, her eyes tightly closed. "What happened to the dragon?" he asked.

"No sign of it." Marcelle rose and, gripping his wrist, hoisted him to his feet. "We'll have to check it out together." She snatched his sword out of the water and handed it to him, then withdrew her own. "Ready?"

Adrian turned toward the portal. The river and the two snatchers were gone, replaced by three tunnels leading into darkness. Water trickled between the crystalline pegs and collected in wider streams as it flowed toward the stairway. "Did the snatchers open the floodgates?"

She nodded. "They're becoming quick-thinking allies. But I guess they couldn't get to the portal in time to keep it open. As soon as the water rolled in, I jumped across to douse your flames. Besides, I thought a dragon was coming down."

"Thanks. I did, too."

She touched a raw spot on the back of his hand. "Any bad burns?"

"Nothing worse than that one." He brushed damp ash from his tunic, revealing small holes here and there. Fortunately, the flames hadn't burned through more than one layer. Wearing extra clothes for the journey to the Northlands had paid off. "I guess we're on our own until Xenith arrives."

"As long as we're together we should be fine." Marcelle marched to the stairway and looked up, her hand tight on the hilt of her sword. "I hear more dragons—screams and beating wings. They're getting closer."

"They're fighting." Regina waved her arms. "They're in the air, and they're shooting fire and ice at each other."

"Ice?" Adrian asked.

Regina nodded. "White dragons are shooting ice. The others are shooting fire."

"Stay here while we check it out." Leading with his sword, Adrian kept his head low and crept up the stairs, Marcelle at his side. As they ascended the dozen or so stone steps, their shoulders brushed against the rocky sides. Light increased. Dragon screams sharpened. Wings beat heavily, as if a storm whipped a hundred blankets.

When they reached the top, a dragon came into view only a few paces away. It sat on its haunches at an awkward angle, its neck extended horizontally as if mimicking a clothesline. Water trickled down its gleaming scales and dripped to the ground.

"I think he's frozen," Marcelle said.

Adrian stepped forward and tapped its foreleg with the flat of his blade, making a slight crack in a sheet of transparent ice. "Frozen stiff."

The dragon shifted and let out a quiet moan. Adrian backed away a step. A shadow swept by. Above, a white dragon swooped toward them, its toothy maw wide open. A stream of white shot out. Adrian and Marcelle dove behind the frozen dragon's rear quarters and hunkered down.

Ice crystals splashed across the inert dragon's back and arced over Adrian and Marcelle. The white dragon bent into a one-eighty turn, swept past again, and whipped its tail against the dragon's elongated neck, breaking it and sending the frozen head skidding across the ground.

Beating its wings, the white dragon lifted back to the sky. "Stay hidden!" it shouted. "The battle is too dangerous for humans!"

Adrian rose slowly to his feet and helped Marcelle to hers. The dragon still sat in a frozen state, though headless. A trickle of blood fell from the break point, but nothing more.

New screams pierced the reverie. Directly above a forest line in the distance, white and dark dragons flew to and fro, clipping each other, clawing and snapping, and shooting rivers of flames and ice. Beneath them, trees burned, and more frozen dragon statues dotted the landscape in front of the forest.

Marcelle set the tip of her sword on the ground. "Why would the white dragon protect us like that?"

"I was wondering the same thing."

"I know why," Regina said as she stepped up to the top stair. "They're punishing the slave-master dragons, and they're protecting humans who don't have the disease."

Adrian slid his sword back to its scabbard. "How do they know we don't have it?"

"Cassabrie says they just know." Regina shrugged. "Maybe by smell?"

Adrian scanned the battle scene. The white dragons flew with spectacular speed and agility. They had hemmed the darker dragons in and seemed to be herding them toward the north where the dragon village lay. "Has Cassabrie said anything about the humans in the village? Do they have the disease?"

"They do, and the Benefile want to kill them so your soldiers can attack the slaving dragons. Cassabrie thinks the white dragons are guided by some kind of strange rules. They want to use the slaves' race to punish the slave masters. She calls it irony, whatever that is."

"Irony is …" Adrian shook his head hard. "Never mind." He picked up a stone and squeezed it to release some tension. "Does she think it's possible to stop them?"

"She says she has a plan to cure everyone and destroy the white dragons. Then it will be up to you to battle the slave masters. But she says to wait here for now. Xenith is on her way."

"A plan." Adrian dropped the stone. "That's not exactly comforting. People are dying while we wait."

Marcelle crouched next to Regina. "Did she say anything else about the plan?"

Regina shook her head. "I wish I could ask her questions, but I don't think I can. I tried once, but she didn't answer."

"With Cassabrie …" Adrian sat on the ground next to Regina, his back to the descending stairway. "You just never know. She speaks her mind quite often, but not always when you want her to."

"Maybe I just don't hear her all the time." Regina closed her eyes tightly. "Sometimes she sounds like she's standing in front of me, and sometimes her voice is like a whisper, and if I move around, it gets louder."

"Maybe a change in elevation?" Adrian nodded at a series of boulders that resembled stair steps near the mining mesa's steep side. "How about up there? It looks easy to climb."

Regina opened her eyes. "I'll try."

While Regina ambled toward the boulders, Marcelle sat next to Adrian. "So you're content with waiting?"

"Content?" Adrian folded his hands tightly. "I won't be content until we set every slave free, but what choice do we have? We can't battle all those dragons. Two swords against a thousand teeth and a flood of fire."

"How about a recon mission? One of us could check out the village while the other waits here for Xenith." She nudged him with an elbow. "But when it comes to a battle, we need to stay together. We have to watch each other's backsides."

"I'd better not touch that comment."

"Is that so?" Marcelle winked. "Have you already been watching my backside?"

"Another one I'd better not touch." He gave her a half-hearted smile. "Sorry to cut the flirting, but we have to get back to business."

"Business." She slid a few inches farther away. "If you say so."

Adrian focused on the battling dragons, still spewing fire and ice all around. Yes, waiting was the only option … an annoying option, especially with Marcelle sitting with a cloud over her head. "Did I say something wrong?"

"Not really." She kept her gaze straight ahead. "I think I'm just expecting too much."

"Okay, that's a loaded statement." He slid toward her, closing the gap. "What's on your mind?"

"Well, if you really want to know." She looked his way, her expression wary. "When you look at me, do you think of me as a fellow warrior …" Her cheeks flushed. "Or something more?"

"Definitely something more," he replied without hesitating. "I wouldn't have asked you to marry me otherwise. You're the most perfect woman I have ever met."

"That's exactly my point." She looked away again. "I'm far from a perfect woman, and I don't want to be a goddess on a pedestal to you."

"A goddess on a pedestal? I don't—"

"Just listen." She set her fingers over his lips. "You're always trying to gloss over my faults. I'm your perfect little angel. And I know why you do it. When you love someone, you always assume the best about them." She lowered her hand. "But I'm not perfect. I'm too introspective, and I try to deduce what others are thinking. And whatever I deduce becomes true in my mind, and I react according to my perception, never thinking that I might be wrong. So I need someone to kick me in the trousers sometimes, because I get so sure of myself about something, I can't see any other options."

"Like about Cassabrie?"

Marcelle nodded. "Like about Cassabrie. And not only her. Also about the women in Mesolantrum. In my mind, they either scorn me, or they're jealous of me, when in reality they probably don't give me a second thought beyond that I'm a silly girl who needs to grow up."

"Is it possible that you're being too hard on yourself now? I mean, if you tend to deduce negative ideas about others, could you be doing it to yourself?"

"There you go again, Adrian. Here I am spilling my guts about how I've been misjudging people, and you won't even believe me. You put a positive twist on everything about me."

"But isn't it possible that you're being too hard on yourself?"

"I don't know." Marcelle let out an exasperated sigh. "Maybe."

After several seconds of awkward silence, Adrian again checked on the dragon battle as it continued drifting northward. Very soon it would be safe to go on a recon journey. He unbuckled his scabbard and set it on the ground, making it easier to sit comfortably. "As long as we're confessing our faults, I suppose I should tell you some things about me that irritate my mother. After all, you're going to have to put up with me for as long as we both shall live."

Another few seconds passed in silence, then Marcelle bit her lip. "Yes, I know."

"Well, Mother always scolded me for not taking off my boots in the mudroom. I'd get wrapped up in something, maybe an idiotic statement from Prescott a few hours before, and I'd forget about everything else. So I would track mud from one end of the house to the other. Then when she made me clean it up, sometimes I would use a towel that she had just washed and—"

"Stop it, Adrian!"

"Is something wrong?"

Her lips now a thin line, she nodded. "I don't want to hear it."

"But you just said—"

"I know what I said. Just ..." She covered her face with her hands. "Just give me a minute."

Adrian folded his hands in his lap. An urge to again ask what he had done wrong welled up in his throat, but he swallowed it down. That question could wait. Better to allow a little breathing room.

After a few silent moments, Marcelle lowered her hands and stared straight ahead, quiet and contemplative. Soon, tears sparkled, and one fell to her cheek. "I'm sorry. I shouldn't have brought this up. We shouldn't talk about our stupid little shortcomings."

He gazed into her wet eyes. No need to say anything. Not yet.

Her chin trembled as she continued. "I mean, I love you, and you love me, and neither one of us will ever do anything to intentionally hurt the other. So what if one of us says or does something that's a little annoying? As long as it's unintentional, we can let that kind of stuff roll off our backs. And even if it takes a while for you to see me in a more ..." She looked away again. "Well, never mind about that." She sniffed, obviously trying to suppress a sob.

Adrian slipped his hand into hers, and she clasped it gratefully. After another silent moment, she returned her gaze to him. "You see, while you were carrying my body, you had no idea whether or not I would ever recover. Yet you still asked me to marry you, knowing that you might be caring for an invalid the rest of your life."

Her grip on his hand tightened. "That's love, Adrian. That's real love. And you never stopped showing it to me. I could've died that very day, or the next or the next, and those thoughts had to enter your mind, but they never altered your stride. You marched on, not thinking about yourself, only about me and the children in your company."

As more tears dripped, her voice cracked. "We never know how long we're going to live, Adrian, so we have to celebrate every moment together without thinking about your muddy boots or my overanalyzing. Whenever I see you doing a little something that annoys me, I'm going to think about those strong arms carrying me on and on and on, never slowing, never faltering, and that will remind me of how much you love me." She kissed his cheek and let her lips linger. "Your way is better. Keep seeing me as a perfect angel, and I won't care about mud on your boots or which towel you use to clean up your messes. You'll always be my knight in shining armor."

Adrian intertwined their fingers. "Then you will always be my perfect angel." Smiling, he added, "An angel who knows how to kick butt with a sword."

After another moment of silence, Marcelle drew back and looked Adrian in the eye. "There is one thing I have to ask of you, one part of your character I want you to change."

"Okay. I'm ready. I think."

Her aspect turned serious … somber. "When it comes time to go to battle or march into danger, I want us to be together. I need to be with you, and *you* need me to be with you."

"No matter the circumstances?"

"No matter the circumstances. We draw our swords together."

Adrian slid out his sword and set the blade in front of his face. In the glimmering surface, his eyes stared back at him, darkened by a shadow. "It won't be easy putting my protective nature to the side. I'll do the best I can."

"I guess that's all I can ask." She massaged his shoulder. "I trust you, Adrian. You'll do what's right."

"Thank you. I trust you, too." Adrian glanced at the nearby tree line once more. The battling dragons had moved on. He rose to his feet and reattached his scabbard to his belt, then slid his sword back into place. "It looks like the dragons have all gone to the village, so—"

"Adrian!" Regina called from atop a boulder. "Something's wrong! Cassabrie's in trouble!"

✵ FIFTEEN ✵

ADRIAN pulled Marcelle to her feet and looked toward the village. Smoke rose in billowing clouds, and fire raged across a structure, maybe part of the Zodiac, but it was too far away to be sure. "What's Cassabrie saying?"

Regina jumped down and ran to his side. "She's talking to Koren. She's in pain."

"Can you show me?" Adrian waved his arms. "You know, make it come to life around us?"

As tears welled, she nodded. "I'll try, but I think I can't show what's happening right now."

Marcelle pushed Regina's hair out of her eyes. "That's all right, sweetheart. Just do the best you can."

Regina stepped past Adrian and faced the dragon village. Staring intently, she swept a hand in front of her body as if brushing dust from a wall. A streak of light followed her motion, transforming a section of their view into another scene. As she continued brushing, colors spread out and painted the inside of the Zodiac's domed room, complete with the Reflections Crystal sitting on its pedestal at the center.

The Exodus star perched atop the spherical crystal, balanced perfectly. Cassabrie sat within Exodus, her red hair moist, stringy, and dangling across her face. Above, Taushin, the usurping black dragon, flew across the apex of the open dome and then out of sight.

Adrian turned toward the Zodiac's entry corridor. Koren sat with her back against a column, manacles on her wrists. A chain fastened her to a ring embedded in the floor.

Regina pointed at her. "I think Taushin chained Koren there, but it's hard to be sure. Everything happened so fast."

Koren rose to her knees. She looked at her hand. Her blackened fingers trembled.

"She's been burned," Marcelle said. "The poor girl!"

Koren swallowed and called out in a squeak, "Can you see Deference? Is she inside the crystal? We need someone to move the lid again."

Inside Exodus, Cassabrie lowered her head. "I already tried to look." Her own tunic muffled her voice. "I can't tell."

"So what do we do now?" Koren asked.

"We?" Cassabrie lifted her head and stared at Koren. "I can do nothing. I am trapped here, and I am dying. You are the only one who can set us all free."

"You mean …" Koren set a rectangular box in her lap.

Adrian walked closer to her. The box was the same one Koren had at the barrier wall.

"Yes," Cassabrie said. "Even if Elyssa managed to concoct more medicine, it will ultimately fail, as you well know. There is only one cure possible, and when the real cure is made manifest, the false cure will become worse than the disease itself. Those who choose the pretender and refuse the authentic will perish within moments. And like rain from the sky, the real cure will purge the very air of the disease, so that its scourge will inflict no one else." Still sitting, Cassabrie straightened and reached behind her cloak. Her hand reappeared clutching a metallic cylinder.

"Is that an explosive tube?" Adrian asked.

Marcelle leaned close to Exodus and peered in. "Definitely. I can see the lettering on it."

Tears cascaded down Cassabrie's cheeks. "Push the button, Koren. You have proven that your mind is free from Taushin's influence. Do what you must before it's too late."

Koren covered the button on the box with her hand. "But I can't kill you. That would be murder."

"My life is an offering, Koren. Yes, my death will come by your hand, but that is all part of the plan."

As the conversation flew back and forth, Adrian, Marcelle, and Regina swiveled their heads to keep up.

"But why?" Koren's chains rattled. "You could have kept the box and destroyed yourself. Why did you send it to me?"

"Because those who need liberation must make a decision to value freedom. You are the last Starlighter, and as such, you will begin the process. Your decision will set off a chain of decisions among your fellow slaves, whether for good or for evil. If I made the decision myself, if freedom were to be given without the sacrifice of heart and mind, it would be cheap. It would be of no value to the ones whose chains have been loosed. They would soon return to their bondage."

A dragon shrieked somewhere beyond the exit corridor. A woman screamed, "No! Don't kill my baby!" The sounds of war ensued outside—yelling, clanging, grunting, and the crackling of fire.

Cassabrie's brow furrowed. "The battle has come to our very doorstep, Koren. What will the last Starlighter do?"

Koren held the box tightly, her hands shaking. Exodus dimmed while the Reflections Crystal brightened.

Clutching the tube with both hands, Cassabrie rose to her knees. "Koren, I beg you. You must push the button. I am weakening. The battle is raging outside. Your fellow slaves are dying. We have only seconds before ultimate disaster can no longer be avoided."

"But Jason and Elyssa might come and—"

"This is *our* world, Koren! Our friends from Darksphere are here to help, but time has run out, and they cannot be the guiding light the people need. Only you have enough knowledge and wisdom to see this through. Only you will be able to apply the prophetic words, the true meaning of 'The slaves must take her blood and bone.' When you push the button, you will understand."

Koren closed her eyes and wept.

Marcelle grabbed Adrian's sleeve. "Those tubes destroyed the barrier wall. Can you imagine what one would do to Cassabrie?"

He nodded. "She would be torn to pieces and scattered to the wind."

"Push the button, Koren," Cassabrie said.

"I can't."

"You have to."

"I won't."

"You must."

"There has to be another way."

An explosion shook the ground. Regina's vision of the Zodiac vanished. Adrian grabbed Regina's hand, then Marcelle's and helped them balance as they rode out the shake.

At the village, billowing clouds of dust shot up from the Zodiac, now a heap of rubble in the distance.

Marcelle gasped. Regina's mouth hung open. "Did she push the button?" Marcelle asked.

"I … I don't know." Adrian stared at the sight. Both Cassabrie and Koren must have died in the explosion.

Marcelle pointed. "Adrian! Look!"

At the explosion site, glowing fragments flew in every direction. The pieces rained on the dragons, apparently causing no harm to the darker ones, but every fragment that touched a white dragon burst into flames. As the Benefile shrieked and faltered in the air, fire crawled along their bodies and devoured them.

Above the Zodiac, a radiant girl rose into the air, her arms spread and her face toward the heavens.

"Adrian," Regina said in Cassabrie's voice. "Exodus has risen. The disease has been vanquished. Bring your soldiers quickly and fight with all your heart."

The rising girl faded, and along with her, Regina's echo of Cassabrie's voice. "I love you, Adrian, and you, Marcelle. My life is over, so I can no longer be at your side. Yet, if you need help, call to the Creator. He answers every desperate cry. Perhaps he will send my spirit to your aid."

Cassabrie disappeared. Regina dropped to her knees and wept. "She's gone!"

As if shot from the cloud, a tawny dragon appeared in the sky. Smaller than most dragons, it flew toward them at high speed.

"That must be Xenith," Marcelle said. "It looks like Cassabrie had everything planned to the last detail."

Adrian kept his stare fixed on the point where Cassabrie disappeared. A tear crept from his eye, but he quickly brushed it away.

As the dragon hurtled closer, Adrian stooped near Regina. "Can you show us what's happening? Can you tell if Koren survived or if Frederick's anywhere around?"

Regina shook her head, tears flowing as her voice squeaked. "Exodus is gone. I can't hear anything."

Adrian drew his sword and nodded at Marcelle. "Get ready for battle."

"Right." Marcelle slid hers out with a ringing note.

"Hail!" Xenith called from the sky, breathless. "I come ... as a friend ... of humans!"

Adrian waved at her and shouted, "Fear not! We draw our swords as your allies in battle!"

Xenith dove toward the ground, fanned out her wings, and landed in a quick trot. When she stopped, she collapsed to her belly, her wings limp as she gasped for air. "I heard only ... allies. Since two of you ... do not ... look like slaves ... I assumed the best."

"We're not slaves, Xenith. Let's save explanations for later." Adrian reached out a hand. "Do you have the crystalline peg Arxad gave you?"

Xenith pried her foreleg from under her body and extended the peg in her claw. "I fear that it has cracked slightly. An explosion sent me crashing to the ground, and I was unable to protect it in time. In fact, my ears are still ringing, and my hearing is impaired."

"Let's hope it's only temporary." Adrian took the crystal. A jagged line cut across one facet from top to bottom. "It's still pretty much intact."

"Since you are so informed," Xenith said, her breaths coming more easily, "I assume you know how to use it."

"I think so." Adrian ran down the steps to the portal chamber. He leaped to a crouch in front of the line of pegs and pushed Xenith's into the center hole. He stared through the portal plane, but the three tunnels stayed in view—no river rushing by, no soldiers ready to charge, and no snatchers staring from their misty frames.

He slapped the ground. "It's not working!"

Marcelle rushed down the steps and joined him. "The crack ruined it?"

"Probably." Adrian twisted the peg, keeping it inserted. As he turned it, the plane flashed and crackled, showing bits and pieces of the Major Four chamber. With each flash, snippets of rushing water and murmuring men passed through. A few muted shouts grew clear.

"I see something!"

"So do I!"

"Get ready, men!"

Adrian turned the peg this way and that, trying to find the clearest setting. Finally, the pieces gathered together and revealed the other chamber. The sound of the river stayed constant, and about twenty men stood densely packed, all staring into Starlight.

As Adrian kept pressure on the peg to hold it in place, the crystal's top half broke away.

Marcelle leaped through the portal. "I'll open it!" Within seconds, she and the men vanished. After a few more seconds, they appeared again, this time with Marcelle holding her fingers within the portal plane. "Okay. Get them marching!"

"Come through!" Adrian barked. "Line up in rapid-march formation at the top of the stairs. A dragon ally named Xenith is there. She'll tell you what's going on."

As the men ran through the portal, Adrian squeezed past them and Marcelle. He looked up the ladder and shouted, "Arxad! Send everyone down as quickly as possible! I need the explosives first … and some rope."

While Adrian waited, the two snatchers hovered near the river. They conversed with each other, their hissing whispers too quiet to discern.

The ladder rattled. A lanky man tromped down the rungs with the explosives box.

"Thank you." Adrian nodded at the portal. "Set it down over there and join the others."

As more men hurried down, Marcelle stepped closer. "What do you have in mind?"

"I'm thinking about how to use the tubes. All Koren had to do was set them in place in the barrier wall. We have to use them against flying reptiles. It won't be so easy."

"Good point. We can't just throw them."

"Actually, we can, but we have to prepare them."

A soldier with a coil of rope hustled into the chamber. When he reached the floor, he handed the coil over to Adrian. "Will this be enough?"

"Let's hope so." Adrian withdrew a dagger from a sheath on the man's belt. "I have need of this, too."

The soldier nodded and followed the others across the portal and up the stairs.

Adrian reeled out a few feet of rope and sliced it off. "I assume you've heard of bolas."

"Sure," Marcelle said. "We had a class on how to use them."

"I'm thinking about tying a section of rope to a tube and adding some other kind of weights on the ends. That should allow for easy wrapping."

"Around a dragon's neck?"

"Right." Adrian cut off another section of rope. "But it'll take the best throwers we've got."

"And I assume you're as good with bolas as you are with a sword."

Adrian smiled. "I've thrown a few in my day."

"We don't have time to test to see who else can do it," Marcelle said. "We'll have to trust their own evaluations."

A man jumped to the chamber floor. "I'm the last one." He pulled the ladder away from the hole and set it down. "Arxad's coming. Gotta make room."

Carrying the rope, Adrian followed the soldier to the Starlight side of the chamber. Seconds later, in a flurry of beating wings, Arxad dropped through the hole and settled clumsily to the floor. When he righted himself, he snaked his neck past Marcelle and looked at her face-to-face. "By your stance here, I take it that Xenith did not come."

"She's right out there." Adrian pointed over his shoulder with his thumb. "We'll explain later, but tell all the men that we believe the disease is gone. They don't have to worry about getting it."

"I will learn the tale from Xenith and inform the men." Arxad folded in his wings and squeezed past Marcelle. Then he lumbered up the stairway and out of sight.

Keeping an eye on Marcelle, Adrian draped the coil and rope sections over his shoulder. Only she could open the portal now, and only from the Major Four side. She was stuck until they could return.

"I know what you're thinking." Marcelle gave Adrian a scolding look. "You're not going into battle without me."

"But what about the portal? It'll close, and the crystal is broken."

"So we'll go back through the Northlands portal if we have to." Her voice took on a tremor. "Just don't leave me behind."

"But the crystal might not be at the Northlands anymore. We sent a man to retrieve it. And besides, what if …" Adrian lowered his head.

"What?"

He looked directly at her. "What if you died in battle? Here you're guaranteed to be safe."

"You don't know I'd be safe!" Marcelle bit her lip before continuing. "Adrian, you promised." A tear rolled down her cheek and fell to the floor. "We'll figure out a way to help the children. Trust me."

Adrian gazed at her contorting face. How could he deny her plea? Since he planned to trust her for the rest of his life, to keep her at his side until death, it didn't make sense to cast her away now. "Okay. You're right." He extended a hand. "I was wrong. Come with me."

A trembling smile appeared on her lips. "Okay, I'll have to jump through as soon as—"

"Wait!" Hiram floated close to Marcelle. "Allow us to hold the portal open for you."

"Didn't you say the pain is excruciating?" she asked.

"It is nearly intolerable, but if we each take turns and alternate when the shock threatens to destroy us, perhaps we will be able to keep the portal open until you return."

"Thank you," Marcelle said. "We'll return as soon as we can."

"You would be wise to do so." Hiram drifted forward. The instant the edge of his misty body touched the plane, tiny lightning bolts shot out in every direction.

Marcelle jerked her fingers from the holes. "Ouch!"

"Jump," Hiram said, his voice crackling as his mist swirled and pulsed. "Your pain will be short-lived."

She lowered her head and leaped. As her body hurtled through, light flashed across the plane. When her foot landed on the Starlight side, Adrian caught her arm and steadied her. "Are you all right?"

She shook her hair back. "Fine. Let's go."

Adrian picked up the explosives box, and they hurried up the stairs side by side, then ran between two columns of men and stopped at the front where Arxad stood next to Xenith. At least three hundred soldiers lined up in an array of sweaty bodies, the expressions on their faces a blend of battle-readiness and anxiety. The most dangerous adventure of their lives lay ahead, against beasts they had never fought before.

"Sorry for the delay." Adrian set the box down, opened it, and withdrew one of the tubes. He wrapped the middle of a rope section around its center. Since it had no notches or other protrusions to hold the rope in place, the binding wouldn't be secure. "This will have to do." He held the rope by an end and let the tube dangle. "I need experts in the use of bolas."

Several men raised their hands.

"Excellent." He lifted the tube. "Tie something to each end. I don't care what you use—rocks, your boots, or whatever it takes to attach this tube to a dragon's neck. It will explode in a way you have never seen before. Imagine a balloon popping but with such force that it would sever a dragon's neck."

As Marcelle quickly passed the tubes around, Adrian cut off more sections of rope and moved the volunteers to the front line.

"What will make it explode?" one of the men asked.

"Impact, we hope. The tubes are not stable, so be careful. Since they're still pretty cool, they shouldn't be dangerous while we're carrying them, but once they're wrapped around the dragons' necks, we hope they'll explode."

One of the older soldiers laughed. "So carry them gently, but throw them hard!"

"That's the idea." Adrian picked up a stone and began tying it to one end of his rope. "If the impact doesn't set them off, the dragons' thrashing should do the job."

While the soldiers tied their ropes to their tubes, Adrian stooped next to Regina. "This battle will be no place for a girl. Go back to the river chamber and wait for us. I'll assign two soldiers to stay with you."

"Okay." Regina hugged him and kissed his cheek. "I love you, Adrian."

"And I love you, precious girl." Adrian returned the kiss. "I'll be back. I promise."

After choosing two men to take Regina through the portal, Adrian ran to the front of the lines. When Marcelle joined him, he nodded at Arxad. "Commander, I await your orders."

"As much as I hate to say this," Arxad said, "be prepared to kill every dragon you see except for my beloved Fellina and, of course, myself and Xenith. I will point out Fellina as soon as I see her." He flapped his wings and leaped into the air. "Charge!"

Xenith launched after him. Adrian and Marcelle sprinted ahead, each carrying a rope and affixed tube. As they ran, the soldiers marched double time behind them, while the two dragons circled back to allow their human allies to keep up.

Holding the dangling rope while running, Adrian glanced at Marcelle every few seconds. She ran with her face set like stone, her eyes wide and fiery. She was a woman on a mission.

Soon, the details ahead clarified. At least a dozen dragons stood in front of the demolished Zodiac, their wings still fluttering as if they had just landed. No white dragons stood or flew anywhere in sight. A sea of fallen humans lay strewn among the dragons, some in soldiers' garb, apparently the detachment that had marched from the north. Some struggled to get up, but a quick snort of fire from a nearby dragon discouraged any further movement.

Koren stood at the edge of the Zodiac's rubble, a blue cloak fanning out behind her. She appeared to be dirty but uninjured as she conversed with a smaller black dragon standing close by.

Adrian squinted. That had to be Taushin.

"The dragons aren't reacting to us," Marcelle said, puffing in time with her footfalls. "I know they've seen us."

"Strange. They're not hypnotized."

Arxad called from above. "Fellina is the smaller dragon lying on the ground. Magnar is the largest one, and he appears to be guarding her. Attack every dragon except for those two."

Marcelle swiveled while running. "The six soldiers closest to me will help Magnar guard Fellina! Make sure no harm comes to her!"

"On my signal!" Adrian shouted as he lifted his bola. "Pick out a dragon and throw. I'll take the one with a greenish tint in its scales at the center. The rest of you quickly decide amongst yourselves which dragon to take. Men at the left throw to the left. Right throw to the right." After giving them a few moments to choose their targets, he heaved in a breath. "Now!"

He slung his bola at the dragon near the middle. Marcelle's and several other bolas flew in tandem. As they sailed, they whistled, flopping through the air like wounded birds.

Without altering stride, Adrian drew his sword and yelled, "Ready your weapons and attack!"

A bola slung around each dragon's neck including the black dragon near Koren. The weights at the ends whipped around until they fastened the tubes against the dragons' throats and held them in place. The dragons clawed at the ropes to no avail, but the tubes didn't explode.

Adrian leaped at a thrashing dragon and plunged his sword deep into its belly. Marcelle jumped and latched on to a dragon's spine. Using the spine as leverage, she swung up to its neck and plunged her sword into one eye, then the other. Hundreds of other soldiers joined in the fray, thrusting and slashing.

Several dragons, including Taushin, frantically beat their wings and lifted over the hacking weapons. The Major Four invaders, now joined by those who marched from the north, swarmed over the other dragons while the assigned soldiers guarded Fellina.

Adrian vaulted onto a fallen dragon's body. "Arxad! Xenith! Let them fly but keep them close! We want to account for them all."

While Arxad and Xenith flew around the escaping dragons, blowing fire and snapping their teeth, Adrian slid his sword away. With all the thrashing and shaking, the tubes should explode at any second, but time was running out. If they didn't detonate soon, this battle would turn against the humans in short order. Even the element of surprise would be lost, and a barrage of flames from a host of angry dragons would fry them all in mere seconds.

✦ SIXTEEN ✦

WHEN the final group of Mesolantrum citizens filed out of the Cathedral, Drexel stood in front of the stage and waved at Sophia. "Come quickly."

She scooted to his side. "What is it, Cal?"

"We have a lot of work to do." He grabbed her wrist and led her toward a side exit. "First, I need to get a report from the portals, then I have to prepare for the king's festival. If we're going to be on time, we'll have to make haste."

"We, Cal?" she asked, her voice bouncing as they hurried along.

"Yes, of course." He stopped at a door between two columns and smiled. "I apologize for my lack of courtesy." He bowed low. "My dear Miss Halstead, would you do me the honor of accompanying me to tomorrow night's festival at the king's palace?"

She curtsied. "I would be delighted, kind sir."

Drexel patted his tunic. "We'll need to find better finery for both of us."

"I'll take care of that, Cal. I assume Professor Dunwoody will put in a good word for me to Mr. Stafford so I can access the necessary funds."

"Excellent." He opened the door to a village side street where twilight had blanketed the area in dimness. Cooler air wafted in along with the odor of wood smoke. "Go and procure the best carriage you can find and the finest horses to draw it. We will leave in the morning."

"In the morning?"

"Yes, to ensure our arrival well before evening. I want to have time to make friends at the palace before the festival begins."

"I guessed that, but where am I to go tonight? If I return home, it will be very difficult for me to get here early enough. I sent a messenger to find a substitute teacher for tomorrow, but I haven't made any other arrangements."

"If you mean lodging, I haven't even learned where *I'm* staying yet, but I'm sure there are palace rooms aplenty for both of us. I will likely take residence in the governor's suite."

She looked at him hopefully. "And where will I stay?"

"Allow me to think for a moment." He stared into her eyes. Sophia had either come under his control to the point of discarding her morals, or she possessed lower standards than he had previously thought. In either case, such cohabitation was distasteful. She was physically attractive, to be sure, but stooping to the level of a libertine would be detestable. "I have heard that the captain of the sentry guard, Drexel by name, has been away on a long journey. He has quarters in the palace—humble, to be sure, but adequate for one night's stay. I will have a servant make the arrangements, and I authorize you to purchase whatever you desire for your toiletry and linen needs."

"Are you sure?" Sophia glanced out at the vacant street, then ran a hand along Drexel's sleeve. "Governor Prescott was married, so I'm sure his suite is accustomed to a woman's presence."

"No doubt. No doubt." Drexel drummed his fingers against his thigh. "Here's what we'll do. Proceed with finding a carriage, horses, and clothing immediately. We will leave as soon as we are ready and sleep in the carriage. I will summon Dunwoody, and he will be our chaperone as well as our liaison in Tarkton so that I will be properly introduced to the royal court tomorrow."

"Well, if you're sure." She straightened his lapel. "Perhaps another time."

"Yes, yes. Another time." He grasped her shoulder. "Go. You have much to do."

"I will go." Without another word, she strode out the door, her head low.

Drexel exited behind her and strolled toward the palace. At the end of the side street, a woman wearing a peasant dress and shawl waved and scurried toward him. "Your Excellency! Wait!"

Drexel spun and hurried into an alley between a livery stable and a smith's shop. If he stopped for every fawning female in the village, he would never get to the palace.

Dodging waste pails and mop-water puddles, he jogged to the opposite end of the alley and turned away from the village square. This route would take him to the palace's rear entry, but the guard there would let him in. By now everyone knew of his ascension to the governor's seat.

He entered the palace gardens and followed a path that led him to the rear courtyard near the dungeon. With darkness falling, lanterns in the yard cast long shadows over this enforcement area. Burnt remnants of the gallows and pillories lay strewn about along with kindling fragments and scorch marks around the pyre. Apparently something drastic happened here quite recently. An execution by fire and then an uprising by the populace in protest? Perhaps Issachar decided to demolish and burn the instruments of punishment, though since he had always been a law-and-order kind of fellow, such a move didn't fit his philosophy.

A guard at the dungeon's trapdoor entrance saluted. "Governor, I'm glad to see you. I have an urgent question."

Drexel stopped close by and nodded. "Very well."

"While Leo was governor, he ordered a hundred prisoners from Tarkton to be transferred here. They're in the dungeon now. A nasty lot if you want my opinion."

"An interesting development, but why are you informing me?"

"Well, we don't know what to do with them. Leo said he had a purpose for them, but now that he's gone, we were wondering if you want them sent back to Tarkton. They're unruly cusses. Most of them would slit their mothers' throats for a night with a silk stocking, if you know what I mean."

"I know what you mean." Drexel stroked his chin. So this Leo had a goon squad sent here to help him with enforcement. Ogres like these could come in handy if put under hypnotic control.

The palace's rear door banged open. The Courier who had sent the video tube ran down the stairs, his black uniform and his hair disheveled. "Governor! I have an important communiqué!" He halted in front of Drexel and reverted to his ramrod-straight pose. "Your scout reports that the forest portal has been abandoned by the soldiers. He saw them marching toward the Forbidden Zone on the east side."

"The Forbidden Zone?" Drexel lifted his brow. "Is he certain?"

The Courier nodded vigorously. "It seems that they have defied orders, sir. He also thinks he saw a dragon flying in the same direction, but he wouldn't, as he said, bet his life on it."

"Hmmm." Drexel glanced between the Courier and the dungeon guard. The soldiers appeared to be heading toward the other portal. But why? With a dragon ally, might they believe they could launch an attack from the mining mesa? Maybe events were progressing on Dracon much more quickly than anticipated, which might mean that emancipated slaves could soon stream into Mesolantrum. An unwanted distraction. Hero worship for the rescuers.

Delays. And Marcelle and the Masters family might return to ruin the takeover plans.

Drexel looked at the palace—tall and stately, the image of achievement … yet not the greatest achievement. Perhaps the idea to depart as soon as possible would turn out to be a better solution than he had thought. Even if the worst happened, he would lose Mesolantrum tonight but gain the kingdom tomorrow. Staying here and facing a dragon could cost him everything. Still, it would be best to prepare for events that would take place here during his absence.

"Thank you for the timely message." Drexel patted the Courier on the shoulder. "Now arrange for swords, spears, torches, and plenty of thick rope to be brought immediately."

The Courier pointed at the ground. "Here, sir?"

"Yes. And hurry."

"Yes sir." The Courier turned and ran toward the palace.

Drexel walked directly to the dungeon guard and locked him in a stare. "Now, tell me more about these unruly cusses."

* * * * * *

Still standing on the fallen dragon, Adrian looked up at the vortex of flying dragons. When would those tubes explode? With the impact and all the flapping and thrashing, surely they would self-detonate soon. Could they have lost their potency?

Magnar flew past Arxad and bit through the rope binding a tube to one of the dragons, then forced that dragon to a thudding crash on the ground. Koren withdrew her control box from a pocket and pointed it at Taushin, the black dragon. "It is time for the hatchling from the black egg to meet the Creator," she said calmly.

"What?" Taushin hovered in flight, beating his wings furiously. "No! Have mercy!"

"Sometimes justice triumphs over mercy." Koren then whispered something too quiet to hear and pushed the button. The tubes exploded. The ground shook, sending soldiers and slaves toppling.

Adrian tumbled off the dragon's body and dropped to his seat. Marcelle fell over his lap. He threw his arms over her and ducked to avoid flying dragon parts—heads, wings, and claws spinning and smoking across the field.

After a few seconds, the tremors settled. Nearby, Jason rose next to Koren and helped her up. They both appeared to be fine, just a bit wobbly with a few streaks of dirt and blood on their faces.

Holding Marcelle's arm, Adrian climbed to his feet, hoisted her to an upright position, and steadied her. "Are you all right?"

She nodded, her hair in disarray. "That was quite a jolt. I guess it took longer than we thought for the tubes to get shaken enough."

"Shaking didn't make them explode." Adrian grasped the wrist of a soldier and pulled him to his feet. "Koren used her control box."

While Adrian and Marcelle helped others rise, Adrian kept his eye on Jason. He and Koren walked into the battlefield, helping people to their feet as they passed.

Adrian crouched and picked up a little boy, no more than four years old. As he brushed dirt from his torn tunic, he whispered, "Are you all right?"

The boy nodded and waved both arms. "The dragons went boom!"

"They sure did." Adrian looked again at Jason. He crouched next to two seated men who had rolled up their trouser cuffs. As Adrian stared, the identities of the two men became clear in spite of the dirt and blood covering them from their bare legs to their faces—Father and Frederick. Elyssa crouched next to them, applying a salve to one of Frederick's leg wounds. Dirty from head to toe and her hair cut raggedly on one side, she looked like she had been in a wrestling match against a pair of dull shears.

Adrian gestured for Marcelle to come along, then broke into a run toward the gathering. When he arrived, he wrapped his arms around Jason. "It's about time you showed up here!"

"Me? I've been here for ages!" Jason pushed Adrian away and punched his arm. "Where did you come from?"

"To make a long story short, the portal at the mining mesa." Adrian ran a hand through Jason's hair. "The rest will have to wait. There's a lot to tell."

"That's an understatement," Marcelle called. She jogged to their side, twirled her sword, and thrust it into her belt scabbard. "Probably more than you'd ever want to hear."

"Soon we'll have time to tell everything." Jason grasped Adrian's forearm. "For now, though, there's still a lot to be done."

When Jason left, Marcelle hooked her arm around Adrian's. "He's right. Let's go help the wounded."

"We will," Adrian said, "but first …" He knelt and hugged Father, then Frederick. "I see you had good seats for the battle."

They both laughed. Frederick nodded toward the battlefield. "You made quite a mess out there, brother. Make sure you use the right towel to clean it up."

"Oh, you're so funny!" Adrian pinched Frederick's trousers. "Wait till Mother sees all the blood. She'll have you beating your clothes against a rock to get them clean."

"Speaking of clean," Frederick said, gesturing toward Elyssa, "you'd better check with our field nurse about getting cleansed from the disease. We might have a problem."

Elyssa touched Adrian's shoulder. "When the Zodiac crumbled, stardrops flew everywhere. They're the cure for the disease, but they're gone now."

Adrian took her hand. "Don't worry. Marcelle and I have already taken stardrops. We'll be fine."

"And the soldiers who came with you?" Elyssa asked.

"Cassabrie said that the disease has been vanquished, but Captain Reed might want to be cautious and keep the soldiers here for a while. I'll check with him."

"Captain Reed is in the village butcher shop," Elyssa said. "We converted it into a hospital."

"Then I'll ask him myself." Adrian rose and extended a hand to his father. "You look like you need to visit the hospital."

Edison grabbed Adrian's hand and hoisted himself up while Marcelle pulled Frederick to his feet. When they all stood comfortably, Adrian hugged Elyssa. "Thank you. We'll take it from here."

"You're welcome. It's good to see all the Masters men in one place." Elyssa smiled and clasped Adrian's hand. "The butcher's shop is just a little ways past where the Zodiac used to be."

"Before we go," Adrian said, "maybe one of you could answer a question. Why was it so easy for us to attack the dragons? They seemed to be just standing around waiting for us to lasso them with our bolas."

Elyssa smiled. "The power of a Starlighter. Before you got here, Koren created a lot of phantoms for the dragons to fight. That fooled them for a while until Taushin set them straight. So when you came charging toward us, they thought you were phantoms and ignored you. Koren's plan worked perfectly."

"She created phantoms ..." Adrian looked at Koren. The diminutive Starlighter appeared to be nothing more than a dirty waif wearing a cloak. Yet she was so much more—a strategist, a warrior, a heroine.

When Elyssa left, Adrian and Marcelle walked with Edison and Frederick toward the shop. Along the way, they helped wounded soldiers and slaves rise. Some seemed relatively uninjured, while others needed medical attention. Adrian picked up a little girl and carried her with one arm, while Edison and Frederick worked together to help a middle-aged man hobble to the makeshift hospital.

Wallace joined them, carrying a squirming little boy who bled from a gash across his leg. Adrian mussed Wallace's already tangled hair. "In the middle of all the action, as usual."

He shrugged. "I didn't want to get bored."

"How did you make it all the way from where we left you?"

Wallace grinned. "I rode a dragon. What else?"

Inside the butcher's shop, Captain Reed, his arm in a sling, stood next to a table where a girl sat with a blood-smeared bandage around her head. Slaves and soldiers sat or lay on mats spread across the floor. After Adrian, Marcelle, Wallace, and the others helped the wounded sit or lie down at bare spots on the mats, Wallace guided Adrian and Marcelle to a skinny old man with scraggly gray hair who lay on a mat that had been pushed away from the others. His closed eyes, bluish lips, and motionless chest proved that he had perished in the battle.

"This is Tibalt Blackstone," Wallace said. "He died saving Fellina's life."

Marcelle crouched and pushed a strand of hair from Tibalt's eyes. "He was Uriel Blackstone's son. I met him in the dungeon. I had no idea that he and I were related."

A tear trickled from Wallace's eye. "He's a hero. His father would have been proud."

Adrian clasped Wallace's shoulder. "Many heroes were revealed today. Young and old alike."

"I know." The tear dripped from Wallace's chin. "I wish more of them had survived."

"Me, too, Wallace." Adrian patted his back. "Me, too."

Adrian and Marcelle weaved around the wounded and people who hustled in the shop bringing water and makeshift bandages to those lying on the mats. When they reached Captain Reed and Edison, Adrian gave them an across-the-chest salute. "Did you leave some of your men behind to give the dragons a chance?"

Captain Reed returned the salute with his good arm, though weakly. "I decided my men needed a challenge." A smile wrinkled his weary face. "Thanks for the reinforcements. Without those exploding weapons, we would have lost the battle."

"Thank the Creator. Those weapons very nearly failed." Adrian gazed at the wounded men, women, and children. Although their burns and lacerations inflicted a great deal of pain, at least they would heal over time. "Captain, are you planning to accompany the slaves back to Major Four?"

He shook his head. "We have to gather our dead and tend to the wounded. It might take a day or two. And waiting will give us a chance to make sure no one is infected."

"I know a way to help with the wounded." Adrian pointed toward the south. "There's a healing river in the wilderness area in a certain glade. I'll tell Koren where it is. Maybe she'll know some shortcuts for getting there by foot."

"Or by dragon?" Reed asked. "Perhaps Arxad will fly some of the most seriously wounded there."

"Good thought. Arxad knows where the glade is. We should ask him right away."

"I'll ask him," Marcelle said. "I need to head out anyway. I have to hurry back to the portal and keep it open in case they couldn't get the peg from the Northlands portal. Hiram and Bodnar can't last forever."

"You'll go without me?" Adrian asked.

Marcelle punched his arm. "The battle's over, big guy. I think you'll be safe for a while."

"I'll come with you," Captain Reed said. "We'll get our wounded heading to the river right away."

The two hurried out of the butcher shop. When the door closed, Edison cocked his head. "What was that about Hiram and Bodnar?"

Adrian leaned his aching body against a wall. "It would take a long time to explain what they're all about, so I'd better focus on the most important issues."

"Very well. Let's hear them."

"We have a problem at home. A man named Cal Broder has taken over as governor of Mesolantrum. Arxad thinks he is a male Starlighter who has the power to usurp the king's throne."

After Adrian provided a few more details, his father described how Frederick escaped from a prison of ice as well as how they battled both white and dark dragons all the way from the forest to the village.

When they finished exchanging stories, Adrian exhaled. "Sorry I missed the action."

"We managed." Edison limped toward the shop's exit. "I'd better let Jason know about this Cal Broder character."

The moment Edison opened the door, a cry rose from the demolished Zodiac. "All hail, Queen Koren!"

Adrian stood at the doorway with his father. After the cheer repeated twice, Edison let out a satisfied sigh. "Exodus has risen over the land of Starlight, and its glow now radiates from a girl named Koren."

"Koren is Exodus?" Adrian asked.

Edison nodded. "Something Alaph told me gave me a clue. He said, 'The Exodus star came to shine a light from above, and those for whom it came destroyed it because they preferred darkness over the light. But a day is soon coming when a liberator will demonstrate that the light of love must shine from within. Only in that manner will the slaves be set free. Like a flaming torch, she will spread the fire of freedom from one heart to another, and Exodus will burn brightly within everyone who cares to receive the light.'"

"So Koren is that liberator?"

"No, Son. Koren was merely the first to receive the flame from the liberator's torch, and now she will light other torches." Edison spoke in a musical cadence. "The light of love has risen, and now we must all spread it until it is a blazing fire, illuminating the heart of mankind and destroying all deception in its path."

"That's what we'll need back home," Adrian said. "There's a lot of deception going on."

"Right. I will be on my way."

Adrian grabbed his father's arm. "I have something to tell you."

"Yes?" Edison looked at him expectantly.

Adrian tried to smile, but his lips wouldn't cooperate. "I asked Marcelle to marry me. We're engaged."

Edison's mouth dropped open, but he said nothing.

"I know I should have discussed it with you first, but we weren't exactly—"

"No, no! It's fine!" Edison laughed. "You and Marcelle, huh?" He patted Adrian's shoulder. "Believe it or not, your mother said you two would get together. I thought it was impossible, but that'll teach me to doubt her intuition."

"I suppose we aren't exactly … well … a predictable match."

"Predictable?" He lowered his voice to a whisper. "Son, if you can handle her temper, I think you're in for the ride of your life … in a good way, I mean. She'll be passionate in every way imaginable."

Adrian's cheeks flushed hot. "That's a bit more than I expected to hear from—"

"Come now, Adrian," Edison said, chuckling. "You'd better get used to the idea. Marcelle is a passionate—"

"I know. I know." Adrian forced a smile and gestured toward the battlefield. "Weren't you going to talk to Jason?"

After staring at Adrian for a moment, Edison nodded. "I'll see you soon."

The moment he left, a shimmering girl ran in. She stopped in front of Adrian and smiled. "It's good to see you again."

Adrian focused on the quickly fading girl. "Deference?"

She curtsied, reenergizing her sparkling form. "I came to help with the wounded. Since I'm not physical, I can probe bodies and see what's going on inside."

"Great. That'll be a big help." Adrian passed a hand across her sparkling cheek. "By the way, we discovered how you can recover your body if you want to."

Deference's eyes lit up. "Really?"

Adrian nodded. "We showed Resolute how it's done. She's waiting in the Northlands so you can do it together."

"Hooray!" Deference clapped her hands. "I'll go as soon as I can!"

Another cheer erupted, louder than ever. At the Zodiac, people embraced, some danced, others just knelt and wept. The fires of liberation were spreading.

During the next hour or so, the liberated slaves gathered their few belongings, collected food from the homes of the dead dragons, and distributed it freely to everyone. Arxad, Magnar, Fellina, and Xenith carried the most seriously wounded to the healing waters while the healthy soldiers hiked to the river leading to the demolished barrier wall and washed there.

After making sure the wounded had been cared for, Adrian walked toward the barrier river, following a chorus of splashing sounds. When he arrived, he found several soldiers bathing, including Ollie.

"Hey, Adrian!" Ollie tossed a square fragment of soap. "Word has it you're engaged to Marcelle!"

Adrian caught the soap. "News gets around fast."

Another soldier rubbed lather into his hairy chest. "She's a fiery one, to be sure. But if anyone can tame her, you can."

"Uh … thanks … I think."

The men laughed. A few whistled. One howled like a wolf.

"If you guys knew Ollie like I know him, you wouldn't want to bathe anywhere close by." Grinning, Adrian turned and walked away. He sneaked a look back. The other men were now washing upstream from Ollie.

Adrian followed the riverbank to the south until the sounds of laughter subsided behind him, replaced by splashing water ahead. Soon, the river bent to the right where a sudden rise in elevation created a head-high waterfall and a pool at the spill point.

After dropping his sword belt to the ground and taking off both his outer and inner tunics, he waded in to chest level with his tunics in hand. Water soaked through his trousers, raising a chill, but it soon passed. He ducked his head under the waterfall and began lathering his body and the tunics with the soap. After a few minutes of scrubbing and rinsing, a voice sounded from the nearby forest.

"How's the water?" Marcelle walked from the trees toward the riverbank, stripping her outer tunic over her head. "Save some soap for me."

"No problem." Adrian slogged to shore and handed her the remaining soap. "I'll make sure no one comes." His entire body dripping, he picked up his sword belt. "Call me when you're finished."

"No need for that." She draped her outer tunic over his shoulder. Her bare arms glistened, and her sweat-dampened inner tunic pressed close to her athletic frame. "You can watch."

Adrian's cheeks heated up again. "I think I'd better not. I know we're engaged, but—"

"Don't get so worked up." She waded into the river. "I'm not stripping any further than this."

Glancing between the ground and Marcelle, Adrian fastened on his belt and wrung out his tunics. "What happened at the portal?"

"Good news and bad news," Marcelle said as she lathered her arms. "When I got there, Hiram and Bodnar were both in the portal trying to keep it open. Neither one had enough strength to do it alone. When I jumped through, they fell back into the Major Four side. Their smoky bodies sizzled and thinned out, but they said they would recover. Hiram added something about not having a purpose at the portal any longer, so he and Bodnar would leave and search for an intruder who came to the portal earlier, that this man had enough evil energy to feed and restore them. I remember these words. 'Every evil soul leaves a trail. We need only follow it wherever it leads.'"

She shivered hard. "Then, their bodies just stretched out and blew down the river channel."

"I hope that's not the good news."

She ducked under the falls, then pulled out, shaking her head and slinging water. "It's not. Just a few minutes later, the soldier arrived with the other peg. So when I reopened the portal, he put the peg in place, and now it's wide open. We can go back anytime we're ready."

"Perfect."

"And Regina's fine. She and the two soldiers had climbed the ladder and were playing in the field. Evening's coming, though. I'm not sure where they'll be when we return."

"I'm sure she's in good hands."

Marcelle lifted her tunic, exposing her toned abdomen, and scrubbed her face with the hem. "More bad news, though." The material muffled her voice. "Broder probably knows by now that we crossed him."

"How's that?"

She lowered her tunic and pushed her hair back, squeezing out water. "The soldier who brought the crystal reported that three palace guards were heading toward the Northlands portal clearing, probably to check on our soldiers who are supposed to be watching it. He was able to elude them, and since he had already picked up the peg, they didn't enter Starlight, but they're sure to report back to Broder."

"Do we have any idea if Broder knows about the mesa portal?"

"No clue, but I sent the soldier to Professor Dunwoody to give him an update."

"Dunwoody? Not your father?"

"Yes, Dunwoody." Marcelle crouched in the water, now neck deep. She appeared to be scrubbing her body under her tunic, but soap bubbles hid the view. "I love my father, but I have to admit that he is easily deceived. I mean, it took him forever to believe that Prescott was poisoning him."

"So he'd be an easy target for Broder."

"Exactly. But Professor Dunwoody is an incurable skeptic. If anyone can resist Broder, he can." Marcelle rose and extended her hand. "Toss my shirt. I need to wash it."

"Oh. Sure." Adrian pulled the tunic from his shoulder and threw it to her.

She caught it, set it under the falls, and lathered it up. After a few moments, her eyes rotated toward him, though she faced the tunic. "Adrian, do you remember way back when we used to bathe together?"

His cheeks warmed once more. "Actually, I was thinking about it recently. What were we? Three or four years old?"

"Something like that." She refocused on her hands. "Perfect innocence. We splashed each other and played games. We didn't realize we were different … or we didn't care."

The heat spread to his ears. "Things have changed, haven't they?"

"In a way." She stood under the falls, letting the water flow over her shoulders and chest. "When we're married, I hope we can play again, not caring that we're different."

Adrian swallowed. "Are you worried about that?"

"Actually …" She stepped out of the falls. She stared at him for a moment, then, tightening her lips, she nodded.

"Because I'm so …" He raised his brow. "Uptight?"

She nodded again, her eyes sparkling with tears.

"I understand. Uptight. Serious. Stick-in-the-mud. I've given you plenty of reasons to worry." Adrian loosened his belt and let it fall to the ground. Keeping his face slack, he waded into the water.

She blinked at him. "What are you doing?"

"Checking for sharks." He swam underwater, grabbed Marcelle's ankles, and pulled her under. They wrestled, entangling arms and legs, and sent plumes of bubbles flying upward. Finally, they surfaced under the falls. With their arms wrapped around each other, water cascaded over their heads and shoulders. He drew his head close until their noses touched. "The shark's gone. It's a good thing I was here to rescue you."

She grinned from ear to ear. "But you never know when it might come back." She reached down and pinched his buttocks.

"Hey!" Adrian scooped her up and carried her toward shore. "We'd better get out of these shark-infested waters."

Holding to his neck with both arms, she kissed his cheek. "My hero!"

"Is that so?" When he walked up to dry ground, he set her down but kept a hand on her shoulder and brushed a strand of hair from her eyes. "Marcelle, you're *my* hero. You've vanquished my fears. I can't imagine a woman who could surpass you in courage, sacrifice, and—"

"Adrian." She pressed a finger on his lips. "Just tell me that you love me. That's all I want to know."

"I do love you, Marcelle." He drew her close. With their bodies pressed together, her heartbeat pounded against his chest.

Marcelle whispered, "One ... two ... three ..."

"What are you doing?"

"Shhh. ... Four ... five ... six ..." When she reached ten, she pulled away, her hand caressing his cheek. "Counting heartbeats. To chase away fears."

"Like Shellinda said?"

She nodded, her eyes somber and moist. "For both of us."

While Marcelle put her outer tunic on, Adrian pulled both of his tunics over his head and again retrieved his sword and belt. He raised and lowered his legs in turn, making his boots squeak. "I hope a dragon will be available to dry us off when we get there."

"No harm in asking." Marcelle slid her hand into Adrian's, and the two walked toward the village on a path that wound through the forest. As they drew closer, the sound of cheery voices drifted by. Soon, it would be time to march back to the portal with the rescued slaves, yet they had no cogent plan in mind to conquer Broder.

"Let's think about this." Adrian let go of Marcelle's hand. "Since Cal Broder can manipulate people's minds, and since most people will be vulnerable, maybe we should make him think we stayed here for a while so we can go back without his knowlege."

"Easy enough. We can send a message that we stayed to make sure we don't have the disease."

"Right, but we have to make everyone else think we stayed. Otherwise, Broder might use his power to pull the truth from them."

Marcelle shrugged. "So we'll stay behind long enough to give everyone a chance to leave. Then we'll sneak back to Major Four behind them. We'll tell your father and brothers to get with Dunwoody right away, and they'll keep Broder busy while we see what's going on behind the scenes."

Adrian touched the side of Marcelle's head. "With a brain like yours, how am I supposed to think you're not perfect?"

"You haven't eaten my cooking."

He laughed. "I remember my mother chasing you out of the kitchen when you burned the soup. You were put on garden duty for a month."

"Adrian!" Jason jogged from the direction of the village. When he arrived, he set a hand on Adrian's back and walked with them. "Everyone's gathering. We're getting ready to leave."

"How many are going, and how many are staying?"

"I'd say about half and half. And the soldiers who came with you are staying, since they didn't swallow stardrops."

"We'll stay with them for a while just to be sure."

Jason narrowed his eyes. "But I heard you two did take stardrops."

"They were different. Not the ones that came after the Zodiac exploded."

"Well, Father told me what's going on at home. We'll need you there."

"Don't worry. We'll come as soon as we're certain. Just be sure you and Frederick and Father go straight to Professor Dunwoody for instructions."

"The old archives curator?"

Adrian nodded. "He probably has the best handle on what's going on."

"Okay. If you say so."

When they arrived at the village, Magnar used his hot breath to dry Adrian and Marcelle. A crowd gathered between the ruins of the Basilica and the Zodiac—men, women, and children laughing and chattering as they packed their food and belongings into carts.

Soon, Adrian, his brothers and father, Marcelle, Elyssa, Koren, and Randall had gathered on the south side of the crowd and faced the mesa. Captain Reed, his arm now free of the sling, ran to the group and clasped Adrian's shoulder. "I visited the healing river, and my arm is as good as new. Since my men are being cared for, I decided to accompany this group back to our world in case they run into some resistance. One of my privates will be joining us as well."

"Good idea," Adrian said. "A bit more muscle won't hurt."

Jason laid a hand on Edison's back. "We have a lot to be thankful for. Will you do the honors?"

"Gladly." Edison looked toward the sky. "Creator …" His voice trembled. "You have brought us this far. There are many broken bodies and broken hearts, and we ask that you mend each one. We look forward to seeing our lost loved ones again in our heavenly home, and we trust that slavery in both worlds has come to an end. Thank you for guidance, protection, and most of all, for freedom."

Edison lowered himself to his knees and thrust his dagger into the ground. "The battles are over. Let the suffering be forgotten, and let the rejoicing begin."

After a moment of silence, Adrian and Marcelle hugged Edison, Frederick, and Jason, then walked slowly away from those lining up to march toward the mesa portal.

Koren broke away from a second crowd of emancipated slaves. "Adrian! Marcelle! Wait!"

They stopped. "Yes?" Adrian said.

"Just a second." Koren turned to one of the closest slaves, an elderly woman wearing a tattered gray shawl. "Tell everyone who is staying here to go to their Assignment homes and prepare for a journey northward. Gather the cattle children or anyone else who doesn't have a home and provide food and clothing for their journeys as well. Find Wallace. He'll help you."

"I will!" The woman kissed Koren on both cheeks. "Bless you, child!"

As the woman led the other slaves down a street toward the outskirts of the village, Koren turned back to Adrian, making her cloak spin. Although dirty and torn, the portrait seemed appropriate, beauty in the midst of a torn world and a promise for a brighter future.

"You mentioned the cattle children," Marcelle said. "I assume they're all free now."

Koren nodded. "Every one of them. Xenith is in charge of transporting them to the healing river." She gestured toward the street the others had followed. "Let's go to Arxad's cave and talk. We'll need the privacy."

Adrian extended his hand. "I'm glad to finally meet you."

"The pleasure is mine." Koren reached out, then drew her hand back and looked at her fingertips, blackened and raw. "Sorry. Dragon fire."

Marcelle grasped Koren's wrist and studied the wounds. "Do you have any medicine and bandages?"

"In Arxad's cave, and I can go to that healing river myself when we're done." Koren gestured with her head. "Come. We have a lot to talk about."

✹ SEVENTEEN ✹

BREAKING into a quicker walk on the cobblestones, Adrian, Marcelle, and Koren hurried down the street, passing several dozen slaves. Because of their excited chatter, Adrian stayed quiet. Questions could wait.

They descended a slope that dropped from the village's plateau to a plain that expanded for miles and miles, ending far to the south at a range of high mountains, barely visible in the distance. After a few hundred paces on a stony path, they came to a high wall with several cave entrances, one yawning arch after another at intervals of about a hundred feet. Koren entered one, picked up an oil lantern, and struck flint stones together until the wick blazed. "Arxad and Xenith are caring for Fellina at the river. No one is home."

Koren led Adrian and Marcelle through the cave's wide, rocky corridor. "Arxad's family has a padded sitting area at the back." Koren's words echoed. "We'll be comfortable there."

From behind them, the faint sound of cheers and laughter drifted in—confidence, jubilance. Soon, they faded out of range. The stone floor gave way to a cushion that looked like some kind of tanned animal skin with straw protruding from holes here and there. The ceiling rose to perhaps thirty feet, plenty of room for a dragon to stretch. "Are you hungry?" Koren asked.

The word *hungry* incited a grumble in Adrian's gut. He laid a hand on his stomach. "Well, actually …"

"I'm starved," Marcelle said. "I'm not sure when I last ate. We brought some food, but I think we left it at the portal."

Koren smiled. "I'll get something for you."

"We need to put medicine on those burns first," Marcelle said.

"I'll do it. You two rest."

Adrian and Marcelle sat cross-legged opposite each other. As Koren trotted away with the lantern, the huge chamber slowly dimmed. Clattering echoed in the corridor. She called, "Don't worry. I'm all right." The walls repeated her words.

"Are we sure we have time to talk with Koren?" Marcelle asked.

"That horde will take a while to get out of the portal chamber. We have time." After a few seconds of silence, Adrian took Marcelle's hand. "You know, it really feels strange."

"What feels strange?"

"Being with Koren," Adrian said. "I had never met her, but I feel like I already know her."

"Or she knows us."

"Right. She's a Starlighter. She's probably seen everything we've done here."

Marcelle nodded. "I could see it in her eyes. Wisdom and pain crackling in an emerald fire. She's seen so much."

"Maybe too much. She reminds me of when Cassabrie was …" He licked his lips. That topic might still be too raw.

"Inside you?" Marcelle compressed his hand. "Go on. It's all right."

"Well … I don't know how to say it. When Cassabrie was inside me, it wasn't like she had taken over my mind. I could still think, but not without her influence. She infused herself into my entire being so that I thought I was thinking independently. She was so thoroughly embedded, I couldn't even tell that she was bending my thoughts."

"A Starlighter's power," Marcelle said.

"So now I think I know why she did it. She wanted me to be ready to do an impossible task."

"You mean carrying my body all the way to the Northlands?"

"That and more. Now that I've been immersed in the full force of a Starlighter's power, maybe I can resist the Starlighter in our world, at least better than I could have before."

Marcelle nodded slowly. "That makes sense."

Koren called from the darkness. "And I can help prepare you, too. I'll be there in a second."

"How could she hear us?" Marcelle asked. "I could barely hear you from a foot away."

Adrian grinned. "Starlighters see everything."

"I wonder if she saw us playing sharks in the water."

"Don't ask. She might make it come to life right here."

Footsteps clopped in the corridor, drawing closer. Light crawled along the side walls and expanded into the chamber. Koren appeared, the lantern in one hand, her fingers now bandaged, and a tray balanced on the other. When she arrived, she hung the lantern on a wall hook and sat with the tray in her lap. Sliced bread and meats covered the center. "Since most of the dragons are dead, we'll have plenty to eat for a while." She nodded at the food. "Please. Eat your fill."

Marcelle picked up two pieces of bread and pressed a hunk of meat between them. "Thank you."

"Yes," Adrian said, copying Marcelle's choices. "Thank you."

"Now to explain how I heard you." Koren set the tray to the side. "In a manner of speaking, I am now Exodus, so I know everything the star knew, and I am still gathering tales from the air."

"Okay. We assumed that." Adrian bit off a hunk of his sandwich.

"And there's more." Koren leaned close. Her eyes sparkled—shimmering obsidian in the midst of brilliant green as she spoke in a hushed tone. "It is very difficult to hide open conversations from me, so I know about your plans to return to your home world by stealth."

Marcelle lifted her brow. "Then no one has privacy here?"

"Not exactly." Koren laughed. "But I will make a covenant with everyone. I will never look into their homes, businesses, or private messages. We'll learn to trust each other."

"So how can you prepare us?" Adrian asked.

"I have insight into this male Starlighter's weaknesses, and I wanted to tell you about them here in private so your plan will remain a secret."

"Weaknesses?" Marcelle repeated. "More than one?"

"Two actually." Koren lifted a finger. "First, a male Starlighter can never lie, so you might be able to use that to trap this Starlighter into saying something that will expose him." She lifted another finger. "The second one is simply a piece of information that should work to cripple him. Exodus saw this Starlighter come to be, so I can show him to you before one of the Benefile transformed him."

"Transformed him?" Marcelle's brow furrowed. "You mean he was someone else before?"

"Someone else physically, but his cruel heart stayed the same." Koren rose to her feet and spread out her arms. "Let me show you."

As she backed away a few steps, she waved a hand toward the lantern. The flame doubled in size, and a phantomlike figure rose from the fire. Amorphous at first, it slowly took the shape of a dragon and turned as white as snow. Seconds later, another figure appeared in front of the dragon. It, too, clarified in form and details, taking on the frame of a male human wearing a palace sentry's uniform. A mustache formed on his face and slowly curled on each end.

"Drexel!" Marcelle hissed. "I should have known!"

Adrian nodded. "Everything's coming together."

A line of crystalline pegs took shape at Drexel's feet. The dragon breathed a cloud of frost that enveloped his head. His face tightened, and his teeth clenched. Like slithering snakes, orange streaks crawled through his hair until the hue covered his scalp. His facial features morphed until he transformed into an unfamiliar man.

As the portal plane behind him brightened, Drexel covered his face with his hands and shouted, "Stop!" He then staggered backwards and disappeared.

Koren waved the image away. "Before that tale, the white dragon said he was giving Drexel Starlighter powers. I also know that Drexel came here to take a slave child home with him so he could gain praise for his efforts, though along the way, he killed some children in the mines. He is an evil hypocrite of the worst sort. And one more important warning—the white dragon told Drexel that absorbing a dragon's power would make him omnipotent."

"So he might seek to capture a dragon," Adrian said. "Good to know."

All three sat quietly as they finished their bread and meat. When Adrian swallowed his last bite, he spoke up. "Cal Broder will be even more dangerous than we thought. Drexel knows secrets. He can use them to blackmail people in power."

"And with his Starlighter gifts," Marcelle said, "he'll soon take over Mesolantrum … or the entire kingdom."

Adrian rose to his feet and reached down a hand. "But now we can exploit his weaknesses."

"Right." Marcelle grabbed his hand, pulled herself up, and brushed off her trousers. "He won't be able to lie about his real identity."

Adrian helped Koren rise. "Do you have any other advice for us?" he asked.

"You should take Arxad with you. Make sure he's well nourished with pheterone. He will be a powerful ally."

"We will ask him. But now that you mention pheterone, how will the remaining dragons survive here without slaves to drill for it?"

Koren's green eyes glimmered in the lantern light. "The only reason the gas was there to mine is because the Exodus star was trapped in an underground chamber and leaking gas into veins that ran under Starlight. Now that Exodus is gone, that supply will be no more." She pulled on Adrian's sleeve. "Let me show you something you might not have noticed on the way over here."

She led them out to the front of Arxad's cave and knelt at the side of the path leading to the village. "You see this?" She pointed at a calf-high white flower. "A stardrop landed here, and no one picked it up."

"It became a seed?" Marcelle asked.

Koren nodded. "Smell it."

Adrian and Marcelle knelt with Koren and bent close to the flower. The blossom had four petals with thin red lines, raising a memory of Alaph's skin. Adrian inhaled deeply. Although the air carried no odor, it coated his tongue with a bitter film. "Extane?"

Marcelle smacked her lips. "No doubt about it."

"I call it the Benefile flower." Koren touched one of its four delicate petals. "This is the mercy petal. It has the most red lines, and it's velvety soft."

"And this one?" Marcelle touched a petal on the opposite side, then jerked her hand back. "It stings like a bee."

"That's the justice petal. It's a bit prickly." Koren plucked one of the flowers and rose to her feet. "When it produces seeds, we can harvest and plant them. Soon we'll have plenty of pheterone-generating flowers. The remaining dragons will thrive."

"How will they repopulate?" Marcelle asked. "Will Arxad and Fellina have an offspring for Xenith?"

Koren pinched off the justice petal and let it drop to the ground. "You might have noticed that Magnar rescued a female dragon from your explosive tubes. She is his mate. It's a long story, but I hope they'll produce a suitable mate for Xenith."

Marcelle and Adrian rose with her. "How did the dragons survive all the years before they kidnapped humans and forced them to drill for pheterone?" Marcelle asked.

"For the first couple of centuries, they were fine. Exodus had emitted enough to last that long, but as the density lessened, the dragons created a mechanism to capture air and concentrate the pheterone into an inhalable form."

"I get it," Adrian said. "Like an oxygen tank."

Koren cocked her head. "What's an oxygen tank?"

"I'll have to send you a photograph later. It's hard to explain."

"Anyway …" Koren slid the Benefile flower into her hair, taking a moment to make sure it stayed put. "This pure form allowed the dragons to survive for many more years, but when pheterone continued to diminish, even that device failed, so that's when Magnar decided to go to Darksphere to bring humans back to Starlight."

"If he would have come in peace to trade for labor," Adrian said, "maybe we could've saved a lot of lives."

Marcelle let out a huff. "Not with the governors we've had. They would've tried to capture Magnar, stuff him, and put him on display in a museum."

"You're probably right." Adrian looked toward the mesa. No one stood or walked anywhere in sight. "I think our escapees have a big enough head start. Let's see if Arxad's willing to come with us."

"I know where to find him." Koren led them back to the village and to the Zodiac's ruins. Arxad sat near the top of the heap, clawing at the fragments and poking his snout into the rubble. "How is Fellina?" Koren called.

"Quite well." Arxad burrowed his snout farther down, muffling his voice. "She bathed in the healing waters, so I left to attend to this urgent matter."

Koren walked partway up the rubble. "What are you looking for?"

Arxad lifted a hefty stone with his teeth and spat it to the side. "Any shards that once belonged to the Reflections Crystal."

Adrian jogged up the pile and crouched next to Arxad. "What good will broken pieces do?"

"Even a tiny shard works as a lie detector."

"You have need of a lie detector?" Adrian shoved a head-sized stone out of Arxad's way. "We were just talking about trying to expose the male Starlighter by cornering him with his own words."

Arxad pushed his snout low again, his eyes darting. "Yes, Koren told me her theory, so I thought I would provide you with a tool. You see, a male Starlighter can speak words that are technically true when his intent is to deceive. Such words cannot fool the crystal. Even the pieces will turn black—" His ears perked up. "Ah! Here is one!" He pointed with a claw. "If you are willing, Adrian, please use your opposable digits and pick it up for me."

Adrian looked into a hole in the debris. An octagonal piece of glass glittered in the midst of gray, crumbling stones. He picked it up and fingered the smooth corners and edges on the wafer-thin crystal. "Are all the shards shaped like this?"

"Not likely. This is an intact facet, and such pieces covered the crystal's exterior. When Exodus exploded, the crystal burst. I assume many of the individual pieces shattered while some remained intact."

Adrian stared at the transparent wafer. "Speaking of crystals, where did those portal pegs come from originally? And what about the black crystal in the mesa portal?"

"The Benefile provided all of them." Arxad heaved a sigh, sending two plumes of white smoke skyward. "To make a long story short, Alaph conceived of the portals, knowing that we needed a way to help your race survive. The pegs actually create the portals themselves, while the black crystal is a lock as well as a viewport for the Major Four side of the Southlands gateway. Alaph did not want a method of gaining entrance or looking into the Northlands side from your world."

"Why is that?"

"He never told me, but I have some theories. I leave it to you to speculate. For now, we should return to the business at hand." Arxad touched the crystalline wafer with the tip of his wing. "It is good to have this piece. It would be better to have more in case we each need to carry one, but we might search for days and not find another."

"We? Does that mean you plan to go with us?"

"Of course." Arxad curled his neck and brought his snout even with Adrian's nose. "I made a covenant with Marcelle to bring justice to our worlds and to set every captive free. From what I heard, justice has fled from your world, and your people are being oppressed and will soon be held captive, so I still have work to do."

Adrian patted Arxad's neck. "Thank you. We'll be glad to have you with us."

As Adrian and Arxad climbed down to ground level, a cooling breeze blew across the ruins, raising dust and spinning it in a slow twirl. Arxad gazed at the debris for a moment, a despondent look on his face, but he soon turned away.

Koren raised her cloak's hood. "I bid you farewell, but please let me know about your wedding plans. I would like to come."

"Of course," Marcelle said. "Consider yourself invited. We'll send you the details as soon as we know."

"One more word of caution." Koren's lips quivered into a grin. "Watch out for sharks." She spun and hurried toward Arxad's cave.

"Sharks?" Arxad said.

Adrian winked at Marcelle. "Just a joke between us humans."

"Someday perhaps I will understand your strange humor." Arxad lowered his neck. "Climb onto my back. We should be going."

Once they settled in their spots between spines, Arxad flew toward the mesa. To the west, Solarus sank near the horizon, its rays highlighting the clouds in streaks of red and pink. Darkness would soon fall on the land, but it seemed that the coming night would be the best this world had seen in centuries.

When they arrived and dismounted, Adrian walked to the stairs leading to the portal chamber and looked down. All was quiet except for the river's rush, a comforting sound. The portal was still open.

He signaled for Arxad to wait, took Marcelle's hand, and tiptoed with her down the steps. At the bottom, the chamber had darkened, too dark to see the river. No matter. The way had to be clear.

Marcelle slid her arm around his and whispered, "I guess everyone's gone."

"Good. Our secret's safe. We can make some noise." He turned and called up the stairway. "All clear, Arxad!"

Arxad lumbered down the steps, barely visible. "I detect the odor of other humans, fresh and close by."

"What's this?" Marcelle held a garment in the stairway's dim light. "A soldier's uniform."

Adrian touched an insignia on the shoulder. "A captain's tunic."

She ran a hand along three squares stitched onto the cuff. "It's Captain Reed's. I would know it anywhere."

"Very strange. Why would he leave it here?" A chill ran up Adrian's spine. "Arxad, something's wrong. Give us some light."

"I concur." Arxad blew a stream of fire. The chamber lit up, showing the river in the background and several human bodies dangling from ropes just beyond the portal. When the flame extinguished, darkness again swept over the chamber.

Adrian whipped out his sword, making it zing. Marcelle did the same. "Arxad!" Adrian shouted. "Give us more light! And keep it going!"

Arxad let out a slow stream of fire from both nostrils and shuffled forward, expanding his light into the Major Four part of the chamber. Adrian and Marcelle charged ahead, both with their swords leading the way.

Adrian stopped at the closest hanging body and sliced a rope over its head. As the body fell, its wrists bound, he caught it and let it drop gently to the floor. Arxad brought his fire closer, illuminating the face of a man, swollen and blackened, but still recognizable. Adrian breathed, "It's Ollie! He's dead!"

Marcelle batted at sparks on Ollie's uniform. "It looks like he's been set on fire!"

"Cut them down! All of them!" Adrian jumped up and swung his sword over body after body, no longer catching them. Another man fell, then a woman, then a little boy. Shouting a guttural cry, Adrian charged around the room, hacking ropes with fury. Finally, when the last body fell, he stood with his shoulders sloped, panting. A hundred obscenities flew through his mind and begged to be spewed, but his throat had clamped shut.

He nudged a little girl's body. Limp arms and charred clothes. Long hair. Not Regina. A wave of relief surged within, then nausea boiled. He swallowed down burning bile and let out a scream, loud and wild.

"Adrian!" Marcelle leaped to a writhing male body. "This one's alive!"

Adrian swallowed again, both to quell the nausea and another scream. As he staggered closer, she turned the body to its back, revealing a teenager with a puffy reddened face, too smeared with char to recognize. His fingers were jammed in his noose in an apparent attempt to escape its strangling hold. "Water!" she shouted.

Adrian stripped off his tunic, dunked it in the river, and brought it back, dripping. He swabbed the boy's face and let water drain between his parched lips. The water bubbled, giving evidence of respiration, but it was weak and shallow.

For a moment, the chamber darkened again. Arxad took in a breath and tromped closer. He sent a jet directly over the boy. With much of the char stains now wiped away, a familiar face broke through.

"Jason!" Adrian dropped his sword, scooped Jason into his arms, and held him close. "Jason! Can you hear me?"

A bare whisper blew through Jason's lips. "Adrian?"

"Yes! Yes!" Adrian's voice squeaked. "It's me! What happened?"

Marcelle sliced the noose away, revealing a deep purple bruise encircling Jason's neck.

Jason groaned. "My throat. I feel like I'm on fire."

"He *is* hot," Marcelle said, touching Jason's cheek. "Take him to the river."

While Adrian carried Jason and stepped slowly into the current, Arxad shot a ball of fire that splashed over a rag-topped stick next to the fallen ladder. The flames caught the fuel and burned steadily. "I will fly out and search for any sign of captives or their captors." With a beat of his wings, Arxad shot upward and zoomed through the hole in the ceiling.

Marcelle snatched the torch and leaped from body to body, checking each one for signs of life. As she moved, her words stormed back to Adrian's mind. *You don't know I'd be safe!*

He shuddered. Maybe she wouldn't have been safe. If she had stayed here until he returned, he might have found her corpse dangling from a rope.

Casting off the dark thoughts, Adrian lowered Jason into the flowing water and let a trickle wash over his throat. "Recognize anyone?" Adrian called, his voice competing with the river's rush.

"Ollie. Two other soldiers, probably the ones we left to guard Regina. Maybe eight slaves. Two are women. Two are children."

"Do you see Frederick or my father?"

"No. I'd recognize them."

"Are they all dead?"

"All but one of the soldiers. He's a goner, though. The rope sliced into his jugular but kept it from bleeding. Now it's gushing. I can't stop it."

"Jason," Adrian said into his brother's ear, "can you tell me what happened? Do you know where Father and Frederick are? Or Elyssa?" Regina's name begged to be included, but Jason wouldn't know her.

"They—" He coughed and spat out a wad of bloody mucous. "They took the rest … the rest …" He opened his eyes, wide and terrified. "Adrian! They tried to set us on fire! They hanged us! From the stalactites! And now they're going to hang everyone else! Not enough room to do it here! Not enough rope!"

Adrian shouted, "Where? Where did they go?"

"Back … back to the dungeon. They want to burn everyone to … to …"

"Shhh … shhh … Settle down. You're all right. We'll figure out how to save them, but I need you to calm yourself and try to remember some details." Adrian scooped water and moistened Jason's lips. "How many were there, and how long ago did they leave?"

Jason inhaled a deep breath through his nose and let it out slowly. His brow slackened, and his respiration eased into a steady rhythm. "Seventy or more. … Most up top." He coughed, again spitting up blood. "I don't know … when they left. … I kept … blacking out. They didn't know … how to close the portal, so …"

"Shhh …" Adrian wiped the blood from Jason's cheek with his thumb. "Just stay quiet. We have to get out of here and catch up with them."

Marcelle threaded a noose through her fingers. "Thick rope. Whoever tied this knot didn't do it in a hurry. They planned the hanging in advance."

"Strange place to do it, though." Adrian looked up at one of the stalactites—short and knobby. "Someone knew the stalactites could hold a rope and the weight of a body."

"Drexel." Marcelle threw the noose on the floor, growling. "I want one minute alone with him. Just one."

"You and me both." He shifted his gaze to the hole in the ceiling. "They had seventy men. Plenty to capture my father and brothers."

"And Captain Reed and Ollie," Marcelle added.

"Right. They were probably forced to disarm."

"The ambushers grabbed women and children and threatened them?"

"That's my guess." Adrian looked back where Captain Reed's military tunic lay. "I'm trying to imagine a scenario that would cause the captain to leave this behind."

Marcelle touched the cuff again. "If the attackers would hang children, you know they would hang the highest-ranked officer. Maybe Reed dropped this to save his own skin."

Adrian winced. "Marcelle, that's pretty harsh."

"Not harsh. Just realistic. He already cracked under pressure once before and gave my plans away to Maelstrom."

"To save his sister's life." Adrian exhaled. "Maybe he wanted to survive so he could go along with the prisoners hoping to help somehow. He probably shrugged the tunic off and let it fall while the ambushers were choosing who to hang."

Marcelle nodded. "I guess that's the best scenario."

Adrian trudged out of the river and laid Jason on his back. "How are you feeling now? I can have Arxad fly you to the healing river and—"

"No!" Jason wiped water from his eyes. "I'm all right. I'm going with you."

Adrian gave Marcelle a weak smile. "Remind you of anyone?"

"He's just like his brother," Marcelle said. "A stubborn warrior."

"Okay," Adrian said to Jason, "you have about two minutes to recover while I ask you a couple of questions. If you're not able to stand on your own by then, you're going back to Starlight."

"Fair enough." Jason took in a deep breath and exhaled slowly. "Let's hear your questions."

"Something's not adding up. If your attackers believed in the disease enough to try to burn you and the others, why were they willing to touch them at all? They could've speared everyone from a distance and burned the bodies, but hanging someone requires a lot of touching."

"I know." Jason grabbed Adrian's wrist. "Help me up."

Adrian pulled him to a sitting position.

"Four of their thugs did the hanging." Jason took another deep breath, making his chest rattle. "They talked about some kind of immunity. I'm not sure what they meant. I got the feeling most of them didn't believe in the disease at all."

"Scare tactics," Marcelle said. "The hanging bodies are a warning to keep anyone else from entering."

"Like you and me?" Adrian looked up at the ceiling hole. "They must have noticed we weren't among the others."

"They noticed." Jason caressed his throat. "They checked everyone closely. They decided hanging me would be enough to prove they'd hang anyone, but they spared Father and Frederick, something about orders from the palace."

"Two minutes are up." Adrian helped Jason rise to his feet and held his arm. "Can you stand?"

"I'll manage." Jason wrung out the hem of his tunic, his expression somber. "Fortunately my clothes didn't burn very well. I finally broke my hands free, but I couldn't slide out of the noose. I guess I passed out trying."

"You did enough to save your life." Adrian embraced him and patted his back. "Thank the Creator you survived."

The beating of wings returned. Arxad flew into the chamber and landed with a thud. Once he settled, Adrian filled him in on Jason's story. With every piece of information, the dragon's head bobbed, his eyes dark red in the torch's flickering light.

Arxad growled. "Much has changed in a short period of time. Our enemies are ruthless. Perhaps they spared most of their prisoners for their value as bait to draw the two of you into their clutches, but they will likely kill anyone who is too slow or causes any trouble."

"Did you fly close enough to recognize anyone?" Adrian asked.

"I did not. I stayed high to avoid detection."

"We'd better go." Marcelle pointed with the torch. "The bleeding soldier is dead. There's nothing more we can do here."

"Right." Adrian grabbed his sword and shoved it into its scabbard. "It's time to cut Drexel into pieces."

"If I may offer some counsel," Arxad said.

Adrian nodded. "But please make it quick."

"By all accounts, your upcoming battle will be one of mental discipline, discernment, and focus. You have already lost the physical battle, so you have to strategically employ your remaining assets."

"Which are?"

"Wisdom and stealth. Create a decoy. Since your brother is not able to march at your pace, I will fly with him to Mesolantrum's palace and create a stir. They will think he is you, so you will be free to infiltrate. If they really are using your father and brother as bait, they will not be quick to kill those two."

"Do you think they'll kill the others?" Jason asked. "Their threats to hang them later might have been a bluff."

Arxad bobbed his head. "I see no reason for them to keep the others alive. They are witnesses to the crimes, and preventing their escape and feeding them will be taxing."

"Whether or not they eventually hang the prisoners," Adrian said, "they'll throw them into the dungeon first. That's where Marcelle and I will go."

"If the captives are in the dungeon, then that is where the captors will expect you to go. Therefore, Jason and I will fly over the dungeon area to ensure that the guards are distracted."

"You've flown so much in the past few hours." Marcelle stroked one of Arxad's wings. "You look exhausted. Are you sure you can do this?"

Arxad blew a weak plume of sparks. "I will do what I must."

"Koren said to make sure you get plenty of pheterone," Marcelle said. "We have some in the dungeon area."

"I know where to find it. The maze at the rear entrance of your dungeon should be easy to penetrate. I will go there first to energize and await your arrival. Perhaps I will learn more about what is afoot."

"And there's another way into the dungeon." Marcelle drew in the air with a finger. "There's a pipeline tunnel leading from Professor Dunwoody's archives room. Leo discovered it, but he's dead. Maybe we can use it safely."

"We'll see." Adrian set the ladder against the edge of the hole above. "That passage could be the perfect place for them to ambush us."

Holding the torch in front, Marcelle climbed first, followed by Jason with Adrian helping from behind. Once they reached the top, Adrian pushed the ladder down. From below, Arxad guided it to the floor, making sure it missed the corpses. Then, he flew up and settled on the field of dead flowers. Clouds veiled the moon but allowed enough light to see the surrounding area.

"How far of a head start do they have?" Adrian asked.

"Using human measurements?" Arxad looked up. "Perhaps a mile or so. They are not moving quickly. I assume the children slow them down."

"Can you carry all three of us?"

"If I were not already nearly spent, I could. Even so, I will take you as far as I can."

Adrian searched the darkness for any sign of distant torchlight. "If we can get to the palace before the prisoners are thrown into the dungeon, maybe the passage from the archives won't be guarded yet."

"I can carry you far enough to overtake the others. Because you will be able to proceed at a rapid pace, you will surely arrive before they do." Arxad lowered his head to the ground, making his neck a staircase. "I suggest that you help Jason. He still looks unsteady to me."

Adrian nodded at Marcelle's torch. "Better douse that first. We don't want them spotting us."

She tamped out the flame, tucked the torch under her arm, and guided Jason up Arxad's back, then sat behind him. Jason clutched the spine in front with both hands, apparently able to maintain a strong grip.

"Do you have room on your back for me?" Adrian asked. "Or would you prefer to carry me with your claws?"

"My spines are spaced so that three can ride, but since you ask …"

"Carry me with your claws." Adrian spread out his arms. "I'll get a better look at what's happening on the ground."

"As you wish, but I think I am too weary to catch you while flying by, so I will have to grab you now." Arxad hooked his clawed forefeet around Adrian's upper arms and jumped into the air, jerking Adrian up with him.

Adrian let out an *oomph* but quickly adjusted to the pressure. As they flew higher, Arxad's wings beat erratically, and gasps intermingled with his breaths. He wouldn't last long with so much weight dragging him down.

Below, the forest edge, barely visible in the darkness, drew rapidly closer. In the distance, a stream of orange light came into view, bobbing on a path like lanterns floating on water. When Arxad flew near the procession, Adrian tried to count the mass of slow-marching humanity, but they had pressed too close together. Men with spears and swords, perhaps fifty on each side of the line, guided the prisoners, occasionally prodding them with the points of their weapons.

Shouts and cries drifted up from the throng. These poor souls thought they had been set free, but they had, as the old saying goes, jumped from the bear's den into the tiger's jaws. And so accustomed to slavery, they likely lacked the spirit to try to overwhelm their captors. With children at risk, even Father, Frederick, and the other rescuers wouldn't rebel.

Arxad veered away from the line. After flying a few hundred feet past the marchers, he descended to a clearing in the forest and set Adrian down gently, allowing him to run until the momentum eased. Arxad settled on a flat slab of granite and lowered his neck to the ground. "Quiet now," he whispered, though a wheeze escaped with the words. With every gasping breath, enough fire flared through his nostrils to guide their movements.

Marcelle scrambled down his neck, hopped to the ground, and joined Adrian. After relighting the torch, Arxad took off again, his claws brushing the treetops at the edge of the clearing. Soon, he and Jason flew out of sight.

A rustling noise sounded in the trees far to the rear. Adrian set a hand on Marcelle's back. "Hurry!"

"This way!" She grabbed his wrist and led him to the edge of the clearing, then pulled him into a crouch behind a hedge. "Let's watch them go by," she whispered. "We'll see how your father and brother are doing and maybe get some clues about what Drexel's thugs are up to. We can still get to the palace first."

"But they'll see the torch."

Marcelle tamped it out. "We won't need it. I know this path."

"Marcelle!" Adrian hissed through clenched teeth. "You need to ask me before making decisions like that. When they get past us, we'll have to go through the underbrush to overtake them."

Now in darkness, he stared at her, trying to guess her expression. Her silence could mean anything from anger to remorse. Finally, she whispered, "You're right. I'm sorry."

"It's okay. I know you're doing your best." As the rustling noises heightened, he locked arms with her. "Just remember. We're watching, not attacking, no matter what."

Her tone sharpened. "I'm not making that promise, and neither should you."

Adrian inhaled deeply. She was right. Making a decision before seeing the circumstances didn't make sense. Still, they had to be careful. "Fair enough, but don't charge to the rescue without my okay."

"If that's the case …" She tightened their arm curl. "Don't let go. You never know what might happen when my blood gets boiling."

They hunkered low and looked through a gap in the hedge's thick foliage. Since the path led straight through the clearing, the slaves and captives had to come this way. More rustling sounded, followed by barked commands to hurry up, some laced with profanity.

Adrian's heart thumped. If these so-called guards would hang and burn his brother along with women and children, they had to be beasts of the lowest order. They deserved to die, but, like Arxad said, patience had to rule. They would pay for their crimes soon.

A man bearing a torch stalked into the clearing from the left side, a sword in hand. As he swept the torch from side to side, the firelight illuminated his unkempt beard and scraggly hair. His narrowed eyes followed the torch's smoky trail. After a few seconds, he waved the sword and called, "Let's go!"

A second man followed the first, an infant clutched in one arm and a dagger poised near its throat. The baby hung limply over his muscular forearm, likely either asleep or unconscious. The guard favored a peg leg, and a wide rip in his tunic revealed a scar in the midst of a hairy chest. "Garth," he called to the lead guard. "We had to double tie and gag the Masters men. They were making plans to escape."

"If they keep it up …" Garth slashed a hand across his throat. "We don't have time to waste dealing with troublemakers."

"Gladly."

Several children of various ages scrambled into the clearing, guards with spears at their backs, each guard bearing one or more of the same haggard traits as the first two. Some children whined or staggered as they tromped by, though one child remained calm, a girl with short red hair and eyes so bright, the green hue shone even from a distance. She looked all around as if studying every detail, her hands folded in front.

Adrian mouthed, "Regina," but stayed quiet.

A boy tripped and fell. The guard behind him drove a spear into the boy's back and flung him toward Adrian and Marcelle. He rolled to a stop facedown just a few steps away.

The spearman laughed. "Garth, that's one more for the vultures."

Marcelle lunged. Adrian jerked her back. A low growl rumbled in her chest, but she stayed put. The boy groaned for a moment, then heaved a sigh and made no other sound.

As the next slaves in line entered the clearing, a teenaged girl broke away from the earlier group and ran toward the wounded boy.

"Come back here!" Garth bellowed.

The girl knelt at the boy's side and pressed her hands on his wound. A wooden pendant dangled from a thin chain around her neck, glowing eerily.

"I said come back here, or we'll skewer another little rat!"

"I'm coming!" the girl shouted. "I just want to see if he's alive!"

She looked straight at Adrian, her eyes sparkling. Dirty tear tracks covered her cheeks. Rips marred her red vest and flowing white shirt. Yet, the battle scrapes couldn't disguise the daughter of Meredith Cantor.

"Elyssa?" Adrian whispered.

She gave Adrian an almost imperceptible nod, then whispered in return, "They killed Jason." Her voice cracked. "But this boy's still alive."

"Well?" Garth stalked toward her, his torch bringing light to the hedge. "Is he dead or not?"

"He's dead." Elyssa rose and glared at the guard who speared the boy, her fists clenched at her sides. "You manure-sucking jackal! You murdered him!"

He pointed his spear at her. "If you don't get back in line, you'll be next!"

Her head down, Elyssa sauntered toward the others, but when the lead guards turned, she broke into a run, dashed past them, and disappeared in the brush at the opposite side of the clearing.

Garth pointed at the spearman and another guard. "Kill her! You can catch up with us later."

"I have to help Elyssa," Marcelle whispered.

"I'll check on the boy." Adrian released her arm. "Be careful."

Just as the two guards rushed away, Marcelle ran to the right, staying outside the clearing, and disappeared in the darkness. Garth marched into the woods, still following the wide forest path. With everyone looking either to the front or to the side Elyssa had run, Adrian dropped to his belly and elbow-crawled toward the boy. Shouts and rustling rose from the woods, hiding his own sounds and probably Marcelle's.

By this time, many adults had filed into the clearing, walking in a four-person column with guards at intervals on either side, each guard carrying a child and a sword or spear. Even more unkempt and haggard than the lead guard, these couldn't possibly be highly trained men nor even proper guards at all. Threatening the children was their only means for keeping their prisoners in check.

When Adrian reached the boy's motionless body, he rose to his knees and glanced at the line to try to locate Father and Frederick. He lifted the boy and cradled him in his arms. Blood oozed from his lips and nose as he gurgled through shallow breaths.

Adrian shuffled on his knees to the edge of the clearing, rose to his feet, and backed through the underbrush. Father and Frederick came into view, Father at the right-hand side of the column, both gagged and both with their hands tied at their backs. Another scan revealed that many of the male slaves had been bound but not gagged. Randall and Captain Reed were probably among them, but their faces didn't come into view.

Adrian strode toward the castle, pushing hard to get through thick, thigh-level brush. With the able-bodied men tied up, attempting a rescue now would be foolhardy. He would have to stay with the plan, but with the added weight of this wounded boy, could he get to the palace ahead of the guards? And what of Marcelle? Knowing her, she could dispatch the guards who chased after Elyssa, but would she be able to get to the palace quickly with Elyssa in tow?

Marching on, Adrian let out a quiet sigh. *Creator, I said I would rely on you ahead of my sword, so I'm asking for your help now. We're going to need it.*

✸ EIGHTEEN ✸

MARCELLE ran around the perimeter of the clearing, hopping over logs and low bushes. With flames from the guards' torches providing just enough light, and other guards giving sound cover with their shouts and noisy tromping, stealth didn't matter.

She reached the path where the line of captives would soon travel, rushed past it, and ran on. Well ahead in the thicket, a single torch bobbed in the darkness, moving slowly from left to right.

A man shouted, "I think I see her!"

Another called, "I'll be right there."

Marcelle slowed to a furtive pace, following the torch's path as she slowly withdrew her sword. Straight ahead, two guards followed the torch and closed in on a hedge. To the right of the hedge, Elyssa crouched low. Firelight washed over her, increasing in radiant pulses in time with the guards' approach. With each step, Elyssa glanced between her pursuers and Marcelle, obviously aware of everyone around her, even though Marcelle stood in darkness.

Dropping to a crouch of her own, Marcelle eyed Elyssa. Why didn't she run? Was she hurt? Too scared? Not likely. Their short meeting in the dungeon proved that she was a plucky girl, and her daring escape just now confirmed her courage.

One of the guards poked at the hedge with a sword. "I see you, wench."

"Don't kill her yet," the other guard said. "We can have a little fun with her first."

Marcelle leaped at the closer guard and whipped her blade through his throat. The sword and torch fell from his hands. As he gargled his own blood, Elyssa let out a scream, loud and long. With a quick spin, Marcelle plunged her sword into the other guard's stomach and ripped the blade upward between his ribs. He shouted, "Garth!" but his call faded as he slumped to the ground and keeled over.

Elyssa's scream immediately stopped. She jumped to her feet and grabbed the fallen torch. "Do you think I covered the sounds?"

"Ah!" Marcelle set her foot on the guard's chest and yanked out her sword. "So that's what you were doing."

"Of course. And the plan worked perfectly." Elyssa held the torch close to her face. "I escaped. Two guards are dead. And the others won't figure it out for quite a while. They'll think I screamed because the guards caught me."

"Good thinking." Marcelle grasped Elyssa's arm. "First things first. Jason's not dead. Adrian and I rescued him."

"Not dead?" Elyssa's lips wavered as if trying to form a smile. Flickering light sparkled in her eyes. "Where is he now?"

"Flying on Arxad toward the dungeon. He's hurt, but he'll make it." Marcelle slid her sword to its scabbard. "Adrian and I guessed that you were being taken to the dungeon, so we had planned to get there before you did. Now we're behind schedule, and we'll have to try to overtake them while traveling in the brush. It won't be easy."

"Especially if we have to travel without a light." Elyssa nodded at the torch. "If we stay anywhere close to the path, they'll see it."

"Good point. I was planning to follow the path, which is possible even in the dark, but now that we're behind …"

"Don't worry," Elyssa said. "I can see in the dark, and I can feel changes in the air—chemicals, moisture, even emotional tension. I'm a Diviner."

"I heard the rumors." Marcelle withdrew her sword again and extended it to Elyssa. "Think you can hack through the vines and underbrush?"

"After what I've been through with Jason?" Elyssa took the sword. "Not a problem."

"You can tell me your story, and I'll tell you mine." Marcelle nodded toward the palace. "Lead the way."

"Warrior?" Elyssa asked, grinning.

Marcelle cocked her head. "What?"

"Never mind. It's a joke between Jason and me."

"You're joking at a time like this?"

"Jason's alive, so I'm in a giddy mood." Elyssa touched the torch with the edge of the blade. "Better snuff that flame."

Marcelle crouched and rolled the torch along the ground until the flame died and darkness flooded the forest.

"Hold on to me," Elyssa said. "I'm going to walk as fast as I can."

Marcelle felt for Elyssa and clutched the back of her shirt. "Ready."

"Then let's go!"

❋   ❋   ❋   ❋   ❋   ❋

Adrian broke through a hedge into a clearing, the wounded boy still in his arms. The cloud-veiled moon cast a dim glow, a benefit absent in the forest thicket. A few steps to the left, the path the captives had taken ran through the clearing and continued, too narrow here to walk four by four. Judging by the footsteps and crying children still resonating in the forest, they had marched past only moments ago.

Cold air had descended, locked in the woods by the trees. Adrian shivered. Even his multiple layers of clothing couldn't ward off the chill. The wounded boy had only a thin tunic and short trousers, not nearly enough to shield him from the falling temperature.

Breaking into a jog, he hustled onto the path and followed the sounds. At least he could make good time for a little while. In spite of the rapid progress, it seemed that ropes pulled from behind. Somewhere back there Marcelle likely labored through the forest. When Elyssa screamed, he had retreated to look for them but found only two dead guards—no sign of Marcelle or Elyssa. Marcelle had won that battle, but where could she and Elyssa be now?

As he drew nearer to the sounds, he slowed his pace. The path crossed another path, the two meeting at perpendicular angles. He stopped and stared to the right. Where did this one lead? Hustling through the forest had disoriented his mental compass, so simply following the sounds instead of watching for familiar landmarks had been the quickest option. But now? It was time to get his bearings.

He inhaled through his nose. The air smelled familiar, a particular type of wood burning somewhere. Poplar? Yes. A typical fireplace choice for the poorer folk. One of the communes had to be close by.

A little bird alighted on his shoulder and chirped in his ear. Adrian craned his neck. One of Mother's parakeets. The nearby commune was probably his own. Taking the boy to Mother, hopping on Primus, and following the meadow route to the village would get him there in time.

He turned to the right and jogged down the new path. The parakeet flew alongside, sometimes landing on branches as it seemed to wait for him to catch up. The boy jostled and bounced. Adrian hugged him closer. Warm liquid oozed through Adrian's tunic and down his chest, but it couldn't be helped.

Soon the path opened into a field. Lantern light came into view through a distant window. Adrian picked up his pace. When he arrived at the commune, he slowed and looked through the window. The glass lantern shone on the dining table, high and bright, freshly trimmed with oil. Yet, no one sat around it. Very strange.

Still holding the boy, Adrian tiptoed to the door and pulled the handle. It opened easily. He peered inside. The parakeet flew by and alighted on top of the cage next to the fireplace, but no fire burned in the brick recess.

He backed up a few steps and inhaled again. The aroma of burning poplar came from somewhere, but where?

He circled the house and strode toward the barn, the moon's dim glow still guiding his steps. After entering the pasture gate and passing by Primus and a goat, he slowed. No one had put Primus in his stable. Again, very strange. The smoky odor thickened. Someone had to be in the barn, perhaps Mother, Shellinda, and Jonathan. Only a fool would leave a fire burning there unattended, and Mother was no fool.

When he arrived at the barn, he eyed the partially open door. Smoke wafted through the gap. Holding the boy with one arm, he swung the door open with his free hand. More smoke poured through. Inside, Mother stood on the far side of a wood fire, fanning the smoke with a blanket. Jonathan stood beside her, leaning on his crutch, while Shellinda swept with a broom, pushing straw out of reach of the flames.

Mother looked up. "Adrian?"

"Yes." He jogged in, holding his breath through the smoke. When he passed the fire, he laid the boy on his stomach on the dirt floor, close enough to the flames to keep him warm. "Mother, he's been speared in the back."

Mother dropped to her knees and pushed the blanket into Adrian's hands. "Keep fanning the smoke away." She pulled the boy's tunic up to his shoulders and peered at the wound. "The spear might have punctured a lung. I'm surprised he isn't dead already."

"Can you do anything to help him?"

"Nothing that won't hurt like the devil's pitchfork, but since he's unconscious—"

The boy gurgled. Blood spilled from his mouth and nose.

"He's drowning in his own blood!" Mother stabbed a finger toward a shelf between two stables. "Fetch the branding tools and shoeing nails!"

Adrian dropped the blanket, dashed with Shellinda to the shelf, and grabbed a branding iron, tongs, and handfuls of nails.

"Never mind." Mother heaved a deep sigh. "He's gone."

Adrian let the tongs clatter to the floor. Words of lament caught in his tightening throat. The poor boy.

Shellinda dropped the nails, fell to her knees, and wept.

Adrian shuffled to the fire and laid the blanket over the boy's body, covering all but his head.

Mother petted his thin hair, matted and interrupted by bald spots. As tears flowed, spasms fractured her words. "I'm trying ... trying to keep children safe." She sniffed hard. "Jonathan ... Shellinda. ... Trying to keep them warm. ... Fool any sentries who might be looking for us. ... But I couldn't ... couldn't help this little one."

As if moving on their own, Adrian's fingers rolled into fists. Sadness boiled into fury. A growl rumbled in his throat. "I have to go."

"I understand." Mother sniffed again. "Someone has to stop this madness."

"I'm riding Primus to the village. I don't know when I'll be back." He kissed her, Shellinda, and Jonathan, then hurried out the door.

After finding Primus and leading him through the pasture exit, he grabbed a fistful of the horse's long mane. "Listen, boy," he whispered, "just stay calm. Carrying me won't be any harder than pulling the wagon."

Still holding the mane, he reached over Primus and vaulted to his back. Primus reared up and whinnied, but Adrian held on. "Steady, boy! It's all right!"

When Primus settled, Adrian leaned close to his ear. "I know you don't normally travel at night, but we have to get to market." He nudged the horse with his heels. "Let's go!"

Primus began with a trot. As Adrian urged him on with successive kicks, he sped to a rapid gallop. The commune's grassy field raced by, looking like a dark blur in the dim moonlight. At this rate, he could easily overtake the others, cross the bridge at the Elbon River, and follow the path into the shopping district before the others arrived.

One problem remained—how to find the passage to the dungeon through the archives room without Marcelle. He would have to leave that to her and instead head straight for the rear entrance to the dungeon. Maybe Arxad would be there.

Yet, how could Marcelle manage such a feat? Somewhere in the forest, she and Elyssa hurried toward the palace in the dark, unable to take the path without running into the fake guards. They would have to go around them without the benefit of a torch.

Adrian lowered his head and let his body bend with Primus's gallop. If anyone could figure out how to get there in time, Marcelle could.

* * * * *

Marcelle and Elyssa pushed through an opening between two thorny bushes and emerged on the path to the palace. Now in dim light, they stopped and brushed burs and clinging seeds from their hair and clothes.

On the path behind them, shouts and chatter filled the woods. Marcelle swiped a thumb-sized bug from Elyssa's back. "Well done. I'll take it from here."

She gave Marcelle her sword. "We'd better get moving."

Marcelle sheathed the sword and ran toward the palace, looking back every few seconds to check on Elyssa. The lithe young woman kept up beautifully at first, but her steady gait soon regressed to limps and fitful lunges. Not being a trained warrior, she wouldn't last much longer.

After another minute, they drew near the market district. Pole-hanging lanterns lined the street, giving light to the shops. The simpler ones had hinged boards covering their wares, and the fancier ones boasted signs dangling from door hooks announcing when they would open the following day. A few gaps between shops gave evidence of carts that had been pulled away by horses, sure to return at dawn.

As Marcelle passed Mrs. Longley's seamstress shop, a light glimmered somewhere within. Marcelle halted and peered through the window. Who could be inside at this time of night? Investigating would give Elyssa a much-needed breather.

Elyssa stopped beside her. She braced her hands on her knees and panted. "Thanks for the rest."

"Not a problem. They're far behind us now." Marcelle tried the door latch. It opened. She swung the door out and stepped inside. "Mrs. Longley?"

"Who is there?" came a call from the rear of the store.

"Marcelle Stafford."

"Well, if this isn't divine providence, I don't know what is. Come to the back room."

Marcelle motioned for Elyssa to follow. After closing the door, they weaved through a maze of dress dummies, some with partially completed dresses and others bare. When they reached the rear of the store, they entered an open door to the back room. Bolts of fabric lay piled against one wall; a board filled with dowels holding spools of various colored thread covered another; and three sewing machines lined a third wall, each with a foot pedal on the floor, pin cushions sitting near partially spent spools of thread, and lacy ribbons draped here and there.

Mrs. Longley knelt on the floor, pinning the hem of a white gown hanging on a dress dummy, her stare locked on her work and two bright lanterns illuminating her busy fingers. "One moment, please."

Marcelle reached toward a lacy sleeve but pulled her hand back. She was much too dirty to touch it. "Oh, Mrs. Longley, it's gorgeous!"

"Your father said to spare no expense." She rose to her feet. "I planned to send for you tomorrow to try it on so I could check the hem length, but since you're here, we can do it now. This way I'll have it ready for delivery tomorrow. Your father is paying extra to have it finished quickly."

Marcelle spread out her arms. "You don't want to put that lovely dress on this filthy body."

Mrs. Longley picked up a lantern from the closest sewing table and waved it in front of Marcelle. "My goodness, girl! Whose pig sty have you been wallowing in?"

"Let's just say I got lost in the woods. It's a long story."

"I don't understand why you insist on denigrating our gender." Mrs. Longley shifted the light toward Elyssa. "Elyssa Cantor?"

She nodded. "Yessim."

"I thought you were—"

"Dead. I know." She glanced at the door. "I don't mean to be rude, but we need to be going now."

"Not so fast." Mrs. Longley snatched a tape measure from the floor, set one end at Marcelle's shoulder, and extended it down to her ankle. Then in the blink of an eye, she measured Marcelle's waist, shoulders, hips, and torso length. "Good. Your measurements haven't changed since your order last year for the … ahem

... trousers and military tunic, so I used those numbers. I will finish the gown tonight and have it delivered to your father in the morning." Her brow suddenly furrowed. "But since he is no longer governor, shall I send it to your old room?"

A horse galloped by, its hooves pounding the cobblestones.

Mrs. Longley looked past Marcelle. "Whoever could that be at this time of night?"

"A Courier, probably." Marcelle turned toward the front window, but the horse was already out of sight.

Elyssa pulled Marcelle's sleeve and hissed quietly, "We have to go!"

"You're right." Marcelle walked backwards. "Sending it to our old room will be fine." She bumped into a dress dummy and grabbed it to keep it from falling, smearing dirt on a silk dress.

"Marcelle! How could you be so—" Mrs. Longley pointed at the door, her arm rigid. "Just go!"

"I'm trying!" Marcelle turned with Elyssa and hurried through the store, dodging the remaining dummies. After running out and closing the door, Marcelle looked toward the forest. Lights flickered, bobbing and drifting their way. "Ready to run again?"

Elyssa took a deep breath and nodded. "I'm with you all the way."

✱   ✱   ✱   ✱   ✱   ✱

Adrian slowed Primus to a walk. The clop of his hooves rebounded off a bathhouse and lawyer's office on one side and the royal smithy's workshop on the other. Getting past the vacant marketplace had been easy, but sneaking around the village square on horseback without being seen would be impossible.

He dismounted and led Primus to Old Pete's blacksmith's stable. After tying him and providing hay and water, he walked alongside the main road toward the palace, letting his eyes dart from the street to the alleys to the sky. No sign of Arxad and Jason. No sign of the tumult their presence was supposed to incite. Maybe they were still at the back of the dungeon where Arxad could inhale extane.

A man dressed in the distinctive Courier uniform ran from the opposite direction, sweat dampening his hair.

Adrian ducked toward an alley, but the Courier called out, "Wait!"

Keeping his head turned slightly, Adrian stepped into a shadow. "What is it?"

The Courier, a male teenager, spoke breathlessly. "Have you heard the news about the slaves returning from Dracon?"

"Rumors abound," Adrian said, disguising his voice. "What news do you have?"

"They carry a deadly disease! Return to your home until further notice from Governor Broder."

"Then aren't you risking your life being out here?"

"I am immune." The Courier touched a discolored spot on his cheek. "Because of the possibility of direct contact, we're not supposed to take any risks, but someone has to spread the news."

"Thank you. I'll hurry to finish my business."

"Where is your immunity mark?" The Courier grabbed Adrian's arm and pulled him into the light. "You don't have one!"

"Yes, that's why I need to hurry. Thank you again for—"

"You look familiar." The Courier squinted. "Weren't you a palace bodyguard?"

"Actually …" Adrian embraced the Courier and held him close. "I just came from Dracon where I contracted the deadly disease. You'd better hurry home and wash with hot water and lye soap."

The Courier jerked away, his eyes wide. He spun and ran in the opposite direction, brushing off a sleeve as if it were on fire.

Adrian hustled back to the blacksmith's shop and scanned the anvil, a table with tongs and stacks of horseshoes, a partially completed rail leaning against the table, and a farm plow with wheels. He ran his finger along the plow's axle, collecting some dirty grease. He dabbed a bit on his cheek, grabbed a horse blanket from a head-high partition next to the stall, and draped it over his head.

Stooping like an arthritic man, he limped toward the palace. Since the captured slaves and soldiers weren't in the dungeon yet, it made no sense to go there. Heading straight to the archives room seemed to be the best plan. Maybe Marcelle and Elyssa were already waiting inside.

He continued an exaggerated limp until he reached the sentry leaning against the guardhouse at the front gate. As soon as the sentry took notice, he straightened. "May I help you?"

Adrian mimicked the tone of an elderly man. "I'm Marcelle Stafford's grandfather. She was visiting me and left for the palace not long ago. She forgot something, and I'm bringing it to her. Is she home yet?"

"I wouldn't know, sir. I haven't seen her. Maybe you could check with the guard at the rear door."

"Thank you, son. I will do that." Adrian hobbled away on a path leading around the palace. When he reached a shadowed area, he picked up his pace, then, when he came in sight of the rear door, he slowed again. The path ended at the Enforcement Zone, now void of the gallows and the pillories. Only flat stones and scattered debris raised any reminders of the cruel punishments that took place here under Prescott's regime. He crossed the dimly lit area and ascended the stairs slowly, again limping.

A hefty guard walked away from his station at the door and stopped at the top of the stairs. "No need to keep climbing, old man. The governor is not accepting poverty pleas at this time of night."

Adrian halted and reprised his disguised voice. "I'm looking for Marcelle Stafford. She left my home only moments ago and forgot her sword." He touched the sword at his belt. "I was hoping to give it to her."

"She didn't enter this way. Did you check with the front guard?"

Adrian nodded. "He said to check with you."

"Then perhaps she stopped somewhere along the way. A Courier probably warned her to get inside. We're expecting detainees from Dracon to arrive at any moment. We suspect that they have a fatal disease or are at least carrying it."

"I heard about the disease. It sounds terrible!"

The guard pointed across the Enforcement Zone. "They'll be quarantined in the dungeon, so you need not worry as long as you stay far away from here."

"What about those who are detaining the detainees? Won't they catch it?"

"Governor Broder brought in a special unit from Tarkton. They have been immunized. I for one am thankful for their courageous efforts." He touched a discolored spot on his cheek. "Immunized or not, I wouldn't want to be close to anyone with the disease. I'm not ashamed to say that I value my good health … for the sake of my wife and children, you know."

"Oh, I understand. I am a father, too." Adrian laughed. "Then I assume you'll stay well away from the dungeon when they arrive."

"To be sure. My post is already too close for my liking."

"And the dungeon keeper? Will he leave his post?"

"Not likely. He never married. He is willing to take the risk."

Adrian looked that way and spotted the guard sitting on a flat, waist-high boulder at the dungeon entrance, his back turned toward them. "I see. I see. He must be a fine man."

"Well, it's been nice talking to you, sir, but like I said, you should go. I wouldn't want you to catch the disease."

Adrian nodded. "Would you mind leaving a message for Marcelle telling her that I came by?"

"Not at all. I'll write a note and take it to her room now."

"Now? What about your post?"

The guard laughed. "You're the first person to come at night since I've been assigned here. I'll just lock the door and hurry back."

"Well, thank you, young man." Adrian turned and began limping down the steps. At the dungeon, the guard still sat on the flat stone, his head low. Wearing a hooded long-sleeved tunic, he looked ready to stay there through the chilly night.

As soon as the palace door opened and closed, Adrian looked back. The sentry was gone. Adrian tiptoed quickly to the dungeon guard, wrapped an arm around his throat, and cut off his air supply. Gagging, he flailed his arms and tried to buck Adrian off but to no avail. After several seconds, the guard fell limp.

"Sorry, my friend." Adrian snatched the ring from the guard's belt and tried a key in the trapdoor's lock, then another. The third key, a long brass one, slid in and turned the locking mechanism. He grabbed the door's iron handle, lifted the thick slab of wood, and let it fall open.

Adrian dragged the guard down, supporting his shoulders and letting his boots thump on the stairs. At the bottom, with only dim light from above illuminating the chamber, he stripped the guard's tunic and put it on, then hauled him through the middle corridor. With every step, the passage grew darker, but there was no time to find and light a lantern.

When Adrian reached the corridor's end, he turned right and pulled the guard down the stairs to the total darkness of the lower level. Breathing heavily, he laid the guard on the floor and felt for a cell door. His fingers brushed along a thick crossbar. He jerked it out of its brackets and threw it to the side.

He found a metal latch and opened the door. After dragging the guard inside, he pushed him to a sitting position at the back, then slammed his head against the wall. "Sorry again. Call it insurance."

Adrian hustled out, closed the door, and briefly scanned the darkness for the crossbar, then scolded himself for tossing it out of sight. He tried the keys until one fit into a hole in the latch. He locked the door and ran toward the main entrance, racing up the two flights of stairs. When he arrived at the trapdoor, he raised the tunic's hood, walked out with his back to the palace, and let the door fall. With a thud and a click, it locked on its own.

"Hey!" the door guard called from somewhere closer than the palace steps. "I was wondering where you went."

Adrian altered his voice. "I thought I heard something down there. It was nothing."

"Are you all right? You sound hoarse."

"Cold weather." Adrian sat on the stone. "Go on back. I'll be fine."

"All right. ... If you say so."

As the sentry's crunching footsteps faded, Adrian kept his head low. In many ways, this plan was perfect. He had the keys to the dungeon entrance and to every cell. The guards from the Tarkton unit wouldn't recognize him, and the prisoners who knew him wouldn't give him away. All he had to do was wait for everyone to be locked up, and when the Tarks left, he could free them all without a fight.

Only a couple of potential snares remained—the dungeon guard in the lower level cell might wake up, and the prisoners lacked the necessary weapons to purge Mesolantrum of the phony governor and his minions.

Adrian stared at the dungeon's trapdoor. A third problem came to mind. He was now stuck at this post. How could he communicate this makeshift plan to Marcelle and the others? Since she hadn't entered the palace yet, maybe she went straight to the dungeon's rear entrance. Maybe they were all there waiting for Arxad's strength to return. Or maybe she and Elyssa were still in the forest trying to find their way to the village. In any case, he couldn't leave this spot to help them.

Sighing, he shifted on the cold stone. Trust Marcelle. Her sharp mind would figure everything out.

"Creator," Adrian whispered, "once again my sword feels powerless, and I humbly rely on you. Like the bird that led me home, guide my path once more."

✸ NINETEEN ✸

MARCELLE ran toward the palace, Elyssa at her side. The shops breezed by. With the streets vacant, no more physical obstacles remained, just nagging worries. Where might Adrian be? Would he show up at the archives?

When they neared the palace, they slowed to a walk and stopped at the front gate where a sleepy-looking sentry leaned against the tiny guard station. Extane-powered lanterns at the top of head-high poles lined the walkway surrounding the palace, providing just enough light to illuminate the palace's sculpted marble columns and white stairs guarded on each side by stone lions and wolves.

Marcelle cleared her throat.

The sentry perked up and stood at attention, accentuating his towering height and lanky build. A discoloration marred his cheek, but that didn't mask his identity—Ben Nottley, one of Marcelle's former students.

Blinking, he leaned toward them. "Miss Stafford?"

"Yes. You're Ben Nottley, correct?"

"I'm glad you remember me. I was in your sword-training class two years ago."

"And a good student as I recall." She nodded at the gate. "Please let us in quickly. I am on an urgent errand."

He shifted from foot to foot. "Miss Stafford, I have orders from Governor Broder not to allow any unauthorized entries until dawn."

"Unauthorized? I live here!"

"Curfew for palace residents is midnight except for pre-authorized exits and entries, so unless you have a pre-authorized—"

Marcelle forced a firm tone. "Listen, Nottley, you know me. You know I live here. Don't be so stupidly rigid with the rules that you'll get in trouble because you forced me to sleep in the streets tonight."

Nottley pulled on his collar. "I see your point, but what about this girl?" He nodded at Elyssa. "Does she live in the palace?"

"Tonight she does." Marcelle gripped the hilt of her sword. "You said you see my point, so I suggest that you avoid a closer look. You know what I'm like when I get angry. I believe you suffered a case of severed suspenders one day."

His face reddened. "I will let you in, but I will have to report your postmidnight entry in the log."

Marcelle rolled her eyes. "Yes, yes. Whatever. Just let us through."

Nottley unhooked a key ring from his belt and unlocked the gate. "By the way, your grandfather came by looking for you. He said you left something at his house, and he was bringing it to you."

"My grandfather?" Marcelle cleared her throat. "Oh, he did? Where did he go?"

Nottley gestured with his head. "Around back to check with the rear guard. I'm sure he's gone by now. It was several minutes ago."

"Okay. Thank you." Marcelle led Elyssa through and walked side by side with her at a casual pace. "If we hurry," she whispered, "he'll get suspicious."

"What was that about your grandfather?" Elyssa asked.

"I'm guessing Adrian was checking to see if I made it."

"If the guards all said they haven't seen you, then he'll assume you're not here."

Marcelle glanced back at Nottley. He again leaned sleepily against the guard station. "So he probably went on to the dungeon to wait in hiding. When the prisoners arrive and get locked up, he'll be ready for Arxad to cause a distraction."

"Perfect. It's all falling into place in spite of the problems."

When they reached the palace's massive oaken doors, Marcelle heaved one open and stepped onto the huge foyer's marble floor. No interior guard patrolled the area, but his rounds would probably bring him by soon. Walking quickly, they passed a statue of former Governor Prescott's father and entered a dark, narrow corridor. As the light faded, they slowed. Marcelle reached out a hand. Her fingers touched the archives' wooden door.

She pulled it open and hustled down the stairs, touching the wall on each side to guide her way down the dark squeaking steps. "No lights here," she whispered.

When she reached the bottom, she turned the knob and opened the door slowly, peeking through the gap as it widened. At the back of the room, Professor Dunwoody sat in his cushioned chair reading an old book, a pair of spectacles resting on his nose and a lantern burning on a table next to his arm. As before, books, scrolls, and papers lined the wall shelves in haphazard array, a worse mess than when she visited as a poorly embodied spirit but far better than the disaster Maelstrom's goons left after searching the place.

The hinges squeaked. Professor Dunwoody jerked his head up and removed his spectacles. "Ah! Marcelle! It's about time you arrived!"

She walked in, Elyssa tagging close behind. "You were expecting me?"

"Of course." He slid the spectacles into his tunic pocket, rose, and laid the book on the table. "And I see by the color in your cheeks that your body and spirit successfully reunited."

She touched her cheek. "Right, but that's a long story. For now, I have to get to the dungeon passage before—"

"Before Governor Broder's guards seal it off. I know. You should go into hiding immediately." He pushed the chair away from the wall, revealing the escape passage's access panel. "I assume you remember how to use it."

"I do." Marcelle dropped to her knees in front of the panel and its painting. This time the artwork took on a new meaning. Before it was just a redheaded girl standing with her arms spread inside a glowing sphere. This time, her green eyes and blue cloak seemed vibrant, alive. She was now Cassabrie the liberator, though the original artist could never have captured her beauty, wisdom, and nobility even if he had a photograph in hand.

"Why the hesitation?" he asked. "You touch the—"

"I remember. I was just thinking about something." She pressed her finger on the girl's mouth. A three-by-three-foot door popped open, hinged on the left-hand side. "So how did you guess that we were coming?"

"Deduction." Dunwoody crouched next to her. "I heard a Courier's report that a platoon of Broder's thugs captured the liberated slaves as well as the Masters men with the exception of Adrian. Since there was no mention of you, I assumed you and he were together and you would have learned that Broder issued an order to incarcerate the captives in the dungeon. Logic combined with your passion demands that you would try to rescue them by entering the dungeon through this passage. My only mistake was in assuming Adrian would be with you. I see Miss Cantor has accompanied you instead."

"Adrian and I got separated. I think he tried to check on me here at the palace, but I hadn't arrived yet, so he's probably waiting for Arxad and Jason at the dungeon's rear entrance."

"Arxad is here as well?" Dunwoody stroked his chin. "Very interesting. I should have deduced that."

Marcelle crawled into the opening. "Let's go, Elyssa."

When the two reached the other side, Marcelle turned and looked back. Professor Dunwoody slid his lantern through the opening along with four finger-length glow sticks. "I'm not sure how dense the extane is around the pipeline and in the dungeon's lower levels. You wouldn't want to blow yourselves up."

"Right." Marcelle took the lantern and handed it and a glow stick to Elyssa, who crouched behind her. "Is there anything else we need to know before I tell you what I know?" Marcelle asked as she slid the other glow sticks into her tunic pocket.

"Oh, yes. A briefing."

For the next few minutes, Professor Dunwoody explained that Cal Broder, a male Starlighter, had already subdued most of Mesolantrum with his hypnotic powers and that only dragon fire could kill him. He related his plan to accompany Broder to an improvised festival in Tarkton, hoping that Broder's absence would allow time for the citizens to break away from the hypnotic spell. While in Tarkton, he would try to publicly trap Broder with his own words, since, according to Arxad's journal, a male Starlighter cannot lie.

Marcelle then revealed that Cal Broder is really Drexel, transformed by a white dragon. Since he murdered her mother, she wanted him to be exposed in front of the entire kingdom.

"Brainstorm with me," Marcelle continued. "How can we make sure that hundreds of nobles come to this festival? A ballroom dedication isn't enough to draw a crowd, nor is a welcome party for a new governor. The more people we have, the more likely we'll catch Drexel off guard."

"True. True." Dunwoody drummed his fingers on the floor. "What occasion could raise the interest of so many people so quickly?"

"Well, nothing spreads faster than gossip. Put out a juicy tidbit, and wagging tongues will fan the flames."

"I see. A scandal. But of what nature?"

"A wedding!" Elyssa prodded Marcelle's shoulder. "You'll be the bride—the woman who could never be conquered by a man. The woman who would wear only trousers will glide down the aisle in a beautiful, lacy gown, which is as good as ready right now. Every woman in the city will want to see the man who charmed Marcelle Stafford out of her trousers."

"That's a scandalous way to phrase it," Professor Dunwoody said. "Such word choices will draw attention."

Marcelle shook her head. "It's not enough. Women in Tarkton read that kind of nonsense in smutty novels all the time, and, besides, they don't know me very well. The trousers-to-gown angle won't work."

Professor Dunwoody snapped his fingers. "I know just the thing. Let's say that you and the groom are coming from a distant, exotic land, which will be true, of course, since you recently arrived from Starlight. We won't tell them your identities. Mystery is quite an allure."

"Okay," Marcelle said. "That's good so far."

"I will add more details as I consider the idea, but I'm sure we can attract a sizable audience. When you finish your business in the dungeon, try to find a good place to rest with Arxad and Adrian until morning. Then collect your bridal gown and fly on Arxad to the royal city. I will send a Courier to the king's chief protocol officer right away so that word of the foreign couple will begin spreading and purchases can be made.

"When I arrive there, I will make sure the wedding arrangements are in order. The festival will have a dual purpose—a recognition of the new governor of Mesolantrum and a wedding between two exotic visitors." Grinning like a schoolboy, the professor rubbed his hands together. "Oh, yes! The city will be abuzz before noon! We will have such a throng at your wedding, we will have to turn people away."

Marcelle gave him a hopeful look. "But it will be a fake wedding, right? I mean, I've been hoping for a ceremony here at home."

"Don't worry," he said, waving a hand. "It will be like a rehearsal. Perhaps I will dress as a Tarkton monk. I have no authority to conduct an authentic wedding ceremony, so no real union will take place, but as one who until recently spent years alone in the archives, I think I can pass for an oft-secluded cleric."

"What about my father?" Marcelle asked. "Are you going to tell him our plans?"

Dunwoody's lips thinned out. "I suppose I will ask him to accompany us in order to authorize purchases, but I'm not sure how much I will tell him."

"I take that to mean he's not resisting Drexel's influence."

"Not too well, I'm afraid. Since Broder … I mean, Drexel … has given your father full authority to clean out government corruption, he has no motivation to resist. When a man's passion is unleashed, it is difficult to divert his attention."

"True." Marcelle heaved a sigh. "If only he could have seen Drexel's transformation, but you don't have a Starlighter available to show it to him."

"No, but I hope that I can put his mind back on track. I found a photo of your mother in a box with her wedding gown. I can take the photo along with us and use it to keep his focus where it ought to be—to expose, capture, and prosecute her murderer."

"My mother's wedding gown? He told me he lost track of it during our move to the palace."

"Ah. Well, I discovered it in this very room while I was cleaning up the mess Leo's guards made. It is safe and in excellent condition. It is a peasant's gown, to be sure, but it is quite lovely. I'm sure your father really did misplace it, and the box was simply redirected to me."

Tears welled in Marcelle's eyes. "Thank you, Professor. You're a great friend."

"Well, no more time for chitchat. You had better get started." He closed the panel, muffling his voice. "I'll see you in Tarkton!"

Marcelle rose to her feet. "Elyssa, you carry the lantern. I'll need my hands free in case we meet resistance."

Elyssa held up the lantern by its handle. "I already have it."

"Right." Marcelle took a deep breath. Thinking about her mother had fogged her brain. She had to clear her mind and focus on the path ahead. "Follow me, and stay close."

Marcelle strode into the tunnel, passing Arxad's eggshell trunk, the water barrel, washing implements, and rations box she and Captain Reed had found to aid the children they rescued from the dungeon. She paused at a pile of wood chips and grabbed a handful. "Manna bark," she whispered as she poured half of the chips into Elyssa's free hand. "We'll probably need it."

Marcelle stuffed the remaining chips into her pocket and continued into the narrowing passage. When they reached the hole leading to the gas line tunnel, still a gaping cavity in the dividing wall, Marcelle scaled the rubble, crawled through the hole, and hopped down to the tunnel floor. After Elyssa made her way through, Marcelle climbed over the waist-high pipeline and waited for Elyssa to join her. Once they settled, Marcelle pointed to the right. "That way."

As they walked alongside the pipeline, they bent to keep from scraping their heads on the tunnel's ceiling. The lantern's flame sizzled and popped, spiking in height with each sound but not enough to worry about … yet.

Elyssa touched Marcelle's back. "When I was in the dungeon's lower level, the extane was thick enough to explode with just a spark. I thought it would be even thicker here."

"Maybe they found the leak and patched it."

"Which means a repair crew was down here," Elyssa said. "So why didn't they fix the hole leading to the archives?"

"Hard to say." Marcelle stopped at the section of the left wall that separated the tunnel from the dungeon. She laid a hand on the masonry—newly stacked bricks, solid and impenetrable. "Now I know why."

"They weren't worried about anyone getting into or out of the dungeon this way," Elyssa said.

"And that means no extane for Arxad in the maze. He was already exhausted. He'll never be able to fight to rescue the slaves or carry us to Tarkton." Marcelle pounded the wall with a fist. "I'm not sure we could break it open even with a sledgehammer."

Elyssa ran a hand along the pipe, holding the lantern over her fingers.

"What are you doing?" Marcelle asked.

"Searching for the patch. I can see imperfections in the metal, even inside the pipe. I can also feel extane on my skin. Every element has a signature, so I can detect the slightest leak. I've never seen a perfect patch on anything." She stopped. "Here it is."

"Okay. How will that help us?"

"I'm not sure it will." Elyssa set the lantern on top of the pipe. The flame sparked wildly. "You see? A slight leak."

"Too slight to do any good."

"Can you pry the patch open with your sword?"

Marcelle touched a tiny crack in the metal. "It's too small for the blade." She withdrew the sword and pounded the hilt against the patch. Clangs echoed throughout the tunnel, but the patch didn't budge. As she looked farther down the pipeline, listening to the fading sounds, a Y-junction came into view as well as a metal wheel attached to the side, the valve she had opened to release the flow to a collection tank in the forest. "I have an idea. Bring the lantern."

They walked about a dozen paces to the junction. Marcelle sheathed her sword and gripped the wheel with both hands. "Help me close it."

Elyssa set the lantern on the ground and grasped the wheel. "Which way?"

"Make the top of the wheel turn to the right."

They planted their feet and pushed, grunting with the effort. As the wheel slowly rotated, it emitted a grinding noise that became a squeal. After several seconds, it stopped and wouldn't budge another inch.

Marcelle brushed her hands together. "That should increase the pressure back at the patch, and the leak will release more gas."

"To create an explosion and break down the wall?"

"That's not what I had in mind ..." Marcelle looked up at the timbers supporting the ceiling. They appeared to be sturdy, but who could know how sturdy? "We'd risk a tunnel collapse, and it might not break the wall."

"True." Elyssa picked up the lantern. "Then why do you want to increase the leak?"

"To get extane into the dungeon for Arxad." The two walked toward the blocked access. "He needs the energy."

"But won't the gas company employees notice the pressure increase and adjust the flow?"

"Eventually, but maybe not right away. They probably have only one or two people working this time of night, and they wouldn't expect anyone to shut off any valves."

When they arrived at the dungeon barrier, Elyssa balanced the lantern on the pipeline near the leak. "Okay, but there's still the brick-wall problem. Right now you're just building up gas in this tunnel."

"Since you're able to find a tiny crack in the pipeline, I thought you could find a weak spot in the bricks. Maybe we can at least open a hole."

"Maybe, but if we can't break it soon, we'd better open that valve again." Elyssa reached high on the wall and ran her hands along the masonry, sweeping across from left to right, then back again as she shifted downward. "It was obviously built in haste. There are several fragile points."

"I'll get something to pound with." Marcelle hustled to their entry hole and lifted two stones double the size of her fists. She hurried back to Elyssa and laid one in her palm. "Where do we hit it?"

Elyssa touched a chest-high spot. "I think—"

The lantern hissed. Its flame jumped several inches and burned with vibrant sparks and crackles, alternating between orange and green.

Marcelle grabbed the lantern and set it on the ground. The flame shrank but continued popping.

"Right here," Elyssa said, pointing at the spot.

"Get your glow stick out."

They both withdrew their glow sticks, shook them, and set them on the pipe. Marcelle's glowed red and Elyssa's blue.

After extinguishing the lantern, Marcelle reared back with her stone and rammed it against the wall. A fragment broke loose from her hammering stone, but the wall showed no sign of budging. "Let's take turns pounding it. Me first, then you, then me again without stopping."

Elyssa set her stone near the target. "Ready."

"Now." Marcelle pounded the wall again. Elyssa followed with a blow of her own. Marcelle hit it once more, then Elyssa struck it. Again and again they pounded. A brick chipped. Mortar cracked and crumbled. Marcelle spoke between grunts and blows. "Keep it up. … Just a few more."

A chunk of mortar flew from the wall, creating a gap between two rows of bricks. They attacked the gap with their stones. Bits of mortar flew past their faces. Finally, bricks shifted inward and fell, and the gap became a ragged, fist-sized hole.

"Stop!" Marcelle dropped her stone.

Elyssa did the same, panting. "We're breathing a lot of extane."

"It'll help in the short term." Marcelle reached through the hole and grabbed a brick that hadn't yet separated from the wall. "We'll chew some manna bark when we're done."

"The gas is giving me a boost," Elyssa said. "I'm already recovering."

Marcelle jerked the brick toward her. It broke away, loosening the bricks around it and revealing the dungeon's floor at a level about three feet above the tunnel's floor. She pulled one brick after another until she had made a gaping hole big enough to crawl through. "That should let the extane flow."

Elyssa nodded. "I sense the dungeon drawing it in, like it's inhaling from the tunnel."

After they collected the lantern and the glow sticks, Marcelle set her back against the wall and vaulted herself to a sitting position with her legs dangling over the tunnel floor. She then slid backwards, her hips moving wall debris until she had fully entered the dungeon.

Elyssa copied her entry, and the two stood side by side. Their glow sticks painted the walls red and blue. Where the lights converged, they colored the air with a purplish glow, creating an eerie aspect.

"Let's see what we can find." Marcelle pulled out a few manna chips, popped them into her mouth, and strode forward on the upward-sloping floor, chewing rapidly. Elyssa trailed by a step or two. Her chewing sounded like a hungry rat gnawing at a tree.

After several seconds, they reached the stairway leading up to the dungeon's main level. Marcelle spat the chips into her hand. "Quiet now."

"I hear something," Elyssa said, her words muffled by the chips. "Erratic breathing."

"Coming from where?"

Elyssa walked back to the cell area. She leaned her head one way, then another. Finally, she pointed at a cell door. "Someone's in there."

"I thought they emptied the dungeon." Marcelle grabbed a bar in the door's window and looked inside, but the cell was too dark. She withdrew one of the glow sticks, shook it, and tossed it between the bars. Glowing green, it bounced once and settled near the center of the cell.

A man in a palace guard's uniform lay against the back wall, his body twisted in an uncomfortable position. "He must be unconscious," Marcelle said. "I doubt anyone could sleep like that."

Elyssa peeked in. "He's not chained. I was told they always chain prisoners on this level."

"And what about his clothes? Could he be a rebellious guard, someone who resisted Drexel?"

"Which would mean he might be on our side. But how can we help him? Once the extane fills this place, he won't be safe."

"I'm against helping him unless I know who he is." Marcelle retrieved the fourth glow stick and threw it inside. This time, it rolled close enough to the guard to illuminate his unfamiliar face. "I don't recognize him."

"Me either," Elyssa said as she peered in again. "But we can't just let him die."

Marcelle pulled a few more manna chips from her pocket and tossed them as close to the guard as she could. "We'll just have to hope he wakes up and finds them. There's nothing else we can do until we take control of the dungeon and get the keys."

"I suppose you're right."

Marcelle pushed her partially chewed chips back into her mouth and began gnawing on them again. She and Elyssa scurried up the staircase on tiptoes and paused at the top. To the left, the dungeon's main-level corridor led to the exit where a guard likely stood on duty since the escaped slaves were expected to show up soon. Ahead just a step away, another staircase led down into the maze.

Marcelle held up her glow stick and scanned the dank corridor, though the light faded after only a few paces. All was quiet except for a steady drip somewhere in the darkness. A musty odor filled the air along with hints of sweat and urine, not as pungent as during her earlier visits here.

She gestured with her head to continue, and the two hurried quietly down the stairs. When they reached ground level, Marcelle used her tongue to push the chips to the side and whispered, "We'll need your gifts again to get us through this maze. I've made it before, but it wasn't easy. I don't remember all the turns."

"Not a problem. A Diviner can find her way through any maze." Elyssa stepped in front of Marcelle and, with her glow stick extended, strode to the right. Marcelle added her stick to the light and followed through a series of turns, sometimes one way, sometimes another. Dripping sounds multiplied. Rats scurried here and there, and cobwebs lined the joints between walls and ceiling.

Although the path often split, sometimes in two and sometimes in three directions, Elyssa never paused. She just marched on and on.

Finally, the corridor bent, and the dimmest of lights came into view, likely the dungeon's rear exit. A lump sat between them and the light, heaving and rumbling.

Marcelle pulled Elyssa to a stop and called out, "Arxad? It's Marcelle and Elyssa."

A draconic head rose from the lump. "Yes." His voice labored through his words. "I broke the entrance open. Jason and I are resting."

"Jason!" Elyssa ran ahead.

Marcelle followed at a slower pace. "Not Adrian?"

"I have not seen Adrian," Arxad said.

Marcelle shone her glow stick over Arxad. He lay with a wing over Jason's legs. Elyssa stroked Jason's hair, her smile quivering. "He's just sleeping."

Arxad bobbed his head. "His injuries nearly killed him, and his body is trying to repair itself. I, too, am near total exhaustion, and I hoped to ingest pheterone here in order to regenerate, but I detect only a minuscule amount."

"More is coming." After spitting out the manna chips, Marcelle gave Arxad a summary of their recent journey through the pipeline, her errant supposition that Adrian would be waiting here, and the plan to stage a festival at the royal palace, complete with a faux wedding. Early on in the summary, Jason woke up. Elyssa helped him sit against a wall, allowing him to catch the crucial points of Marcelle's briefing.

When Marcelle finished, Arxad let out a long sigh. "This plan hangs by a fragile thread. With Adrian's absence, I am concerned that he, too, has been captured. If so, your festival plans are endangered."

"That's putting it mildly," Marcelle said.

"I hoped the understatement would ease the blow." Arxad inhaled deeply. "I assume it will take a lengthy amount of time for the extane to make its way to this area, so I will not be able to assist with the rescue of former slaves from the dungeon for at least a few hours. At this point it is best to wait until after Drexel leaves for Tarkton. Once we free Adrian's relations as well as Randall and Captain Reed, they will be able to put things in order in Mesolantrum while we fly to the king's abode."

"So be it." Marcelle sat next to Arxad and caressed one of his wings. "At least I can sneak upstairs from time to time and see when the slaves arrive or if Adrian is with them."

"Rest, Marcelle." Arxad guided her head against the wall with his wing. "Sleep. When Adrian arrives, we can adjust our plans. In the meantime, if you do not rest, you will be unable to think, unable to fight, and unable to look like a beaming bride tomorrow."

Jason and Elyssa joined her, Jason in the middle. "My brother will get here," he said. "You know he will. Nothing's ever stopped him before."

"You're right." Marcelle leaned against Jason's shoulder and closed her eyes. He carried his brother's smell and spoke with the same tenor. It would be easy to pretend he was Adrian. Maybe that would help her fall asleep.

Arxad began humming a gentle tune, soft and rumbling. Words mixed in now and then, too few to make sense of the song.

Keeping her eyes closed, Marcelle whispered, "What are you singing, Arxad?"

"I am composing a song to match a melody I know. The original lyrics are in my language, so the meter and rhyme would not translate to your tongue. Therefore, I am improvising by creating words you can understand and with gender references that apply to your situation."

"I look forward to hearing it."

"I think it is ready to be aired. It is simple—a lullaby of sorts. I hope it will provide some comfort." Arxad cleared his throat with a hearty cough, then crooned in a deep bass.

Beloved friend, I pray for you,
So far away in some strange land.
The space beside me feels so cold;
Come warm it now and hold my hand.

I grew accustomed to your touch,
The way you gently dried my tears;
When shadows lurked within my room,
You chased away my darkest fears.

Without you I am half a heart;
I wander lost, I cry, I roam.
My empty house feels strangely cold
Without you here to make it home.

Creator grant him light and peace,
Escape from tempters' lies and charms,
Success in quests that prove his love,
A path that leads him to my arms.

And grant me rest while I await
The answer to my tearful prayer,
And let my waking eyes behold
My love, my hero, standing there.

When the final note faded, Marcelle bit her lip, trying to stifle a sob. When she regained her composure, she whispered, "Arxad …" Her voice trembled. "Arxad, that was perfect. I love it."

"Thank you. It comes from my heart, for I long to be with my beloved Fellina."

"Your love for your mate is beautiful to behold."

"As is yours for your future mate."

Marcelle let out a sigh. Yes, Adrian would come. The Creator would guide him. He didn't need a worrying fiancée pacing the floor and watching out for him every second. He was a warrior, a hero, and he trusted in the Creator. Nothing would keep him away. Nothing. Because he loved her. And that was all that really mattered.

✴ TWENTY ✴

ADRIAN rose from the stone and stretched his back. Joints popped and muscles trembled. After nearly two hours of waiting, everything had stiffened. There had been no sign of Marcelle or Arxad, and the former slaves had obviously been delayed. Could Father and the other warriors have tried an escape plan? If so, whether it succeeded or failed, their arrival might still be hours in the future.

After a few more minutes, Garth's voice pierced the silence. "Clear the way! Diseased people coming through!"

Adrian resisted the urge to turn. Exposing his face to the sentry would ruin everything. The voice sounded fairly close, perhaps on the path leading around the palace toward the Enforcement Zone.

The sentry called from the steps. "What happened? We expected you long ago."

"We lost a couple of our men in the forest," Garth said, "so we sent scouts to look for them while we waited outside the village."

"Did the scouts find your men?"

"They were both dead. Slashed. Murdered."

The sentry shouted toward Adrian. "Better open the dungeon and get away!"

"I'll open it," Adrian replied in his disguised voice, "but I'm staying here."

"Suit yourself. It's your life."

Adrian detached the key ring and unlocked the trapdoor. As he pulled it open, Garth shouted again. "Lock up the troublemakers first."

Adrian held the door open, his back toward the palace. Garth shoved two men to the edge of the entrance. Keeping his head low, Adrian gave them a quick glance—Father and Frederick, both still gagged and bound, scowls bending their faces.

"Give me the keys," Garth said, holding out a dirty hand. "I'm taking these two to the lower level."

"I'll take them." Adrian held up the key ring, again disguising his voice. "And I'll need these for a few minutes. You'll be busy enough with the other prisoners." He found the key he used to open the lower-level cell and held it separate from the others. "I'll be back to help."

"Not afraid of the disease?"

Adrian slid out his sword, intentionally making it zing. "I'm not afraid of anything."

"Ha! Some courage in Mezoland!" Garth shoved Frederick, making him stumble downward. After a few awkward steps, he leaned against the stairwell wall and regained his balance.

Garth pivoted and strode toward the palace. "Let's move them in!"

Adrian gave the Enforcement Zone a furtive glance. Garth joined dozens and dozens of men, women, and children waiting in the same array in which they had marched on the forest path, mangy-looking guards still poised with daggers and other weapons at children's throats. Yet, Regina was now nowhere in sight, probably standing in the midst of the throng.

Near the front, Captain Reed and Randall stood close together, their heads low, though their moving lips indicated a stealthy conversation.

Adrian set the tip of his sword at his father's back and whispered in his own voice, "Don't react at all. Just go down."

Edison walked slowly on the crooked, wooden steps, raising dull squeaks. Once below ground level, Adrian grabbed a lantern hanging on a stand as well as a pair of flint stones. When they reached Frederick, the trio continued until they dismounted the stairs at the bottom. Adrian whispered, "Go to the end of the middle corridor, turn right, and then down another set of stairs. I'll cut you loose there."

They marched quickly single file into the darkening passage. Loud footsteps clopped behind them along with the sound of crossbars clattering to the floor.

"Where are those keys?" Garth bellowed.

Without turning, Adrian called, "Give it a rest! I'll be back in a minute to help!"

"Hurry up! I'm tired and hungry!"

The three picked up their pace to a quick jog and rushed down the stairs toward the lower level. When Adrian reached the bottom, he felt for a gag and sliced it off with his sword.

"Good work," Frederick said.

Adrian turned Frederick and cut his bonds. When they broke free, Adrian felt for his father and repeated the process.

"What now?" Edison asked.

"You'll stay in a cell down here, but I won't lock you in. When those thugs leave, we can unlock all the cells and make a break for it. The real dungeon guard is already in your cell. I knocked him out, but if he wakes up, you might need to keep him quiet."

"Good plan," Edison said. "Where's Marcelle?"

"I don't know. No time to explain." Adrian set the flint stones together. "Let me get this lantern lit so I can find the lock."

"No." Frederick grasped Adrian's wrist. "Too much extane. I can taste the bitterness."

"Then I'll just feel for it again." After one unsuccessful try, Adrian pushed the key in and threw the door open.

"There's light in here already," Edison said. "Glow sticks."

Now awash in green light, Frederick picked up one of two glow sticks and lifted it high. The glow provided an eerie view of the cell. Straw and feces covered the floor, and chains dangled from the rear wall, ending at loose manacles. The guard lay on his side, his eyes closed and his chest moving in time with his rattling breaths.

Adrian eyed the glow stick still on the floor. "Those sticks weren't here when I locked him up."

"Guard!" Garth shouted. "Where are you?"

"I have to go." Adrian hustled up the stairs and through the corridor, jogging into the dim light where Garth stood at the bottom of the entry stairs holding a torch.

"What took you so long?"

"A lot of extane down there, so I couldn't light the lantern. It's not easy searching for a key while watching troublemakers."

Garth grunted. "You really *are* a brave one. Or stupid. At least you got it done."

"Of course I did." Adrian lifted the lantern's glass and set the wick against Garth's torch, adjusting the wick's height to create a vibrant flame. "We'd better keep the other prisoners on this level. We'll have to cram them in."

"Then open the cells, and we'll bring them down. I already dislodged the crossbars."

"Will do." Carrying the lantern, Adrian hustled through the corridor and opened each cell along the way. The image of the glow sticks in the cell came to mind. Maybe Marcelle had thrown them in to see who was inside. Maybe she had entered the dungeon through the wall leading to the pipeline and then ventured down to the maze and the rear exit. Even if so, there was no time to search for her.

When he opened the final door, he extended the lantern into the stairwell leading to the maze. Air upwelling from the dungeon's lower level breezed across his cheeks and down toward the maze, making the flame crackle with orange and green sparks. Extane had probably flooded that area as well, and the vacuum action from the maze kept the majority of the gas from entering the rest of the dungeon.

At the other end of the corridor, Tark guards, still holding children, escorted slaves down the stairs into the first two cells and slammed the doors behind them. Randall tromped down next. With daggers poised at young throats all around, he allowed himself to be herded into the next cell. There was no sign of Captain Reed.

After pulling the hood over his head and ducking low, Adrian walked that way. He stopped near the entrance end of the corridor and locked a cell, then the one across the way. As he walked from cell to cell, Tarks and former slaves pushed by. He stole furtive glances at each child. After a minute or so, Regina shuffled past, a Tark's spear prodding her back.

When they reached Randall's cell, the Tark shoved Regina inside, sending her stumbling out of sight. Another Tark guided several men and women into the same cell and slammed the door.

Adrian sidled to the door. Holding the lantern near the window, he peered in. Regina sat next to Randall, both staring straight at him. Her brow shot upward. He set a finger in front of his lips, then jerked his head away and lowered the lantern. Aside from a few whimpers, the cell remained quiet.

Lifting the ring, Adrian set the key close to the lock. Maybe he could get away with pretending to lock it and—

"Hurry up!" Garth shoved Adrian and pulled the door open. "Why isn't it locked yet?"

Adrian lifted the key. "I was just about to."

"I'm keeping my eye on that young man in there." He closed the door and picked up a crossbar from the floor. "Lock it."

When Adrian locked the door, Garth dropped the crossbar into its brackets. "That should keep him out of trouble."

"He looks like a troublemaker to me, too." Continuing down the corridor, Adrian kept an image of the two faces in his mind. Randall had been stymied by threats to children, but what about Regina? What might she be able to do? Use her Starlighter power to aid the rescue effort? If so, what power could she try? With no Exodus to call upon, she might be a normal little girl now.

After several minutes, every captured slave had been stuffed into a cell. When Adrian locked the last one, he lifted the lantern and let the glow spread down the corridor toward the dungeon's front entrance. Tarks shuffled that way, some mumbling about going to bed or getting food. Garth pushed past them and strode toward Adrian, a torch in hand. "Let's put the other crossbars in place, and then we can lock the trapdoor."

"Sounds good." Adrian set the lantern down and picked up the closest crossbar. Since the other Tarks were leaving, maybe he could smash this beam against Garth's head and start releasing the prisoners.

As Garth drew near, Adrian's lantern sparked and flashed. Garth's torch did the same. He glanced between it and the lantern, just out of the beam's reach. "I heard that extane can burn," Garth said.

Adrian nodded. "Like I told you, the lower level's thick with the stuff."

"But not up here." Garth stroked his chin, mingling dirty fingers with his unkempt beard. "And the first two troublemakers are down there breathing it."

"Serves them right," Adrian said. "If they don't chew manna bark, the gas will eventually kill them."

"Then we wouldn't want them to suffer, now, would we?" Garth grabbed Adrian's arm, pushed him toward the front entrance, and threw his torch down the stairs.

"No!" Adrian threw the crossbar at Garth and sprinted down the steps. Flames erupted from below and raced up the stairwell. Adrian stopped halfway down, turned his back, and ducked his head. The fire swept by and ran across the upper level.

Adrian batted at his clothes, snuffing tiny flames, and hurried the rest of the way down. At the lower level, another wave of fire hurtled farther into the corridor and disappeared through a hole in the wall. That had to be Marcelle's way of entry ... and maybe his own escape.

He looked up. The other wave of flames probably continued into the maze on its way to the rear entrance. Now it would be far better if Marcelle and company hadn't made it there. The corridor would become an inferno in mere seconds.

He snatched open the first cell door, and jerked his fingers back from the handle. *Hot!* He stepped into the room, now illuminated by several piles of burning straw. His father and Frederick knelt with the unconscious guard between them, both brushing flames from their clothes.

"We're exposed!" Adrian hissed. "Let's get out of here!"

"We can't leave this man!" Edison said.

Adrian scooted to the guard and lifted him to a sitting position while Frederick batted Adrian's back. "I see you encountered the same fire."

"I did." Adrian grasped the guard under an arm. "Who's strong enough to carry him?"

Frederick lowered his shoulder. "Put him on me."

Adrian and his father hoisted the guard over Frederick. Once Frederick had stood and balanced, Adrian grabbed the glow sticks and hustled to the door. "This way!"

They jogged farther into the lower-level corridor and stopped at the end where a ragged hole led into a gas pipeline tunnel. "This is how Marcelle gets in and out," Adrian said. "The passage leads to the archives room in the governor's palace."

"Are the slaves locked in cells upstairs?" Edison asked.

"Yes." Adrian shook the ring on his belt. "I have the keys. We'll circle around and get them out."

"Too slow and dangerous." Edison pointed upward. "We have access from here. The Tarks won't be coming back for a while."

"One of them was still up there, but we can fight our way past him." Adrian prodded Frederick's arm. "Take the guard to the archives. Find some weapons and meet us outside." He pushed a glow stick into Frederick's hand. "Just follow the pipeline. I'm sure you'll figure it out."

Frederick nodded. "Got it." He laid the guard down, hopped to the pipeline level, and dragged the guard onto his shoulder again. After heaving a tired sigh, he trudged to the right and disappeared in the darkness.

Adrian clapped his father's shoulder. "Let's go."

As they marched quickly toward the stairwell, the remaining glow stick guiding their way, Edison whispered, "One concern, Son. That fire probably ran up the pipeline toward the gas company. I'm not sure what kind of safeguards they have to keep it from igniting their supply. If their tanks explode, the fire could ignite the entire pipeline system."

"And bring an explosion here." Adrian picked up the pace. "Faster."

He leaped up the stairs two at a time and halted at the top. Ten paces down the corridor, Garth stood, wielding a sword with three other Tarks behind him, all swords at the ready. A pair of lanterns sat on the floor near the trio, shining undulating orange light over their bristly faces.

Edison joined Adrian, breathless. "It doesn't get any easier, does it?"

Garth pointed his sword at Adrian, his beard and hair singed. "I noticed that Mezoland has its share of rats scurrying up from the sewers. I think it's time to exterminate a couple."

✳ ✳ ✳ ✳ ✳ ✳ ✳

Marcelle walked barefoot through a flower-filled meadow. Wearing only a sleeveless tunic and short trousers, she was a child again—happy, carefree, at peace. As the blossoms brushed against her knees, a hundred fragrances flooded her senses. A clear sky allowed Solarus to bathe her bare arms and legs with luxurious warmth.

She lowered herself into the midst of the flowers and lay on her back. Of course this had to be a dream, but it didn't matter. Whatever was really going on in the outside world could wait. For now the delicious scents acted as her chains, and she surrendered as their willing prisoner. Let the dawn's bugle call take its time.

After a few minutes of bliss, a new odor crawled into the mix, something foul that painted the back of her throat with a bitter film. She sat up. Adrian stood over her and extended his hand. "Marcelle, I need your help."

She fluttered her eyes open. Adrian, Solarus, and the flowers melted away. Darkness held sway except for two glow sticks—red and blue—that seemed to hover in midair, bobbing as if floating on the tide, their lights almost spent. Yet the glow painted the outline of a dragon directly underneath, supporting the sticks as they rose and fell with his respiration.

She angled her eyes to her left. Her head still leaned on Jason, who appeared to be sleeping. Smacking her lips, she gently lifted her head. Extane saturated the air, coating her tongue with its telltale bitterness.

From her dream, Adrian's words echoed. *Marcelle, I need your help.* Were they simply a reflection of her anxieties, or did they really mean something?

She reached for Arxad's wing and gave it a gentle pull. "Are you awake?"

"I am." A hearty rumble rode the air. "I have been intentionally inhaling deeply to ensure that I receive as much pheterone as possible. I already feel greatly invigorated, so I need no sleep."

"I won't be able to sleep either." Marcelle rose and stretched. "I had a dream that worried me."

Jason's lips smacked. "I'll join you in sleeplessness."

"Too much pain?" Marcelle extended a hand.

"Mainly around my neck." With her help, he rose to his feet. "It's getting better, though."

"Where's Elyssa?"

"I'm over here." Barely visible, Elyssa stood several paces farther into the dungeon. She rubbed a thumb and finger together. "Something's wrong."

Marcelle walked toward her. "Extane, I know."

"Something more. The air temperature is rising sharply, and its velocity is increasing."

"Get behind me!" Arxad jerked up to his haunches and spread his wings. "Quickly!"

Marcelle, Elyssa, and Jason hurried to him and hid behind his wings. Arxad curled his long neck and pushed his head between Marcelle's and Jason's. "Don't breathe. The air will be too hot."

Marcelle peeked around a mainstay. A wall of flames hurtled toward them, rolling like a tidal surge. She ducked back. Fire slammed against Arxad's canopies and arced over their heads, roaring and crackling in shimmering hues of green and orange.

After a few seconds, a *phoom* sounded. The flames flashed, then died away. Arxad lowered his wings and gave them a shake, scattering tiny embers. "That was quite painful, but better for me to take the brunt than you."

"Thank you, Arxad." Marcelle stepped around him, licking her lips. The bitter taste in the air had vanished. "The extane's gone."

Elyssa walked farther into the corridor, again rubbing a thumb and finger together. "It is, but ..."

Marcelle joined her. "What is it?"

"Troubling sounds. Stampeding feet, distant cries of anguish."

"Prisoners in the dungeon?"

"I don't think so. Farther away. Panic instead of despair."

"We had better take to the sky," Arxad said as he turned toward the exit. "We will be safer there and gain a better vista."

All four hurried through the opening. Arxad lowered his head to the ground. "With the pheterone boost, I should have no trouble carrying all of you."

"One second." Marcelle quickly passed manna chips around, popped two into her mouth, and began chewing. Then she, Jason, and Elyssa walked up Arxad's neck and chose a gap between spines, Marcelle in front and Elyssa at the rear. With Jason still somewhat unstable, Elyssa reached around a spine and held his tunic with both hands.

Arxad beat his wings and leaped into the air. After ascending a hundred feet or so in tight orbits, he straightened and flew toward the palace. Well lit by gas-powered lanterns, its glimmering ivory turrets stabbed the dark sky. Directly below, several torch-bearing Tarks milled about in the Enforcement Zone, some gripping spears tightly.

As Arxad flew in a wider orbit over the Tarks, he bent his neck and drew his head close to his passengers. "What does the Diviner sense?"

Elyssa spread an arm and let the wind buffet her hand. After a few seconds, she bent her brow. "Anxiety. Pressure. Like something is about to—"

A loud boom sounded. A few miles to the right of the palace, fire and smoke erupted. Below, Tarks dropped to the ground.

"Hold on!" Arxad folded in his wings and dropped. Just as he fanned out again to land, a concussive wave slammed into his body and tossed him into a spin.

Marcelle flew off and rolled on the ground until she bumped into a fallen Tark. She leaped to her feet, whipped out her sword, and pointed it at him, though the entire world seemed to twirl around her. "Don't move!" she barked, her chips now wet splinters on her tongue.

She glanced around. Arxad slid to a stop near the dungeon entrance, while Jason and Elyssa rolled together toward the palace, their arms locked around each other.

When the trio had regained their bearings, they climbed to their feet. The ground continued shaking. One Tark fell, then another. The rest stood with their eyes wide and their limbs trembling.

Marcelle balanced against the tremor. "Elyssa! What's going on?"

Elyssa knelt and set a palm on the ground. "Fire is shooting through the pipeline below. It's setting off explosions along the way."

Marcelle fought to calm her breaths. "The line is shut off at the dungeon's lower level. What will happen when the fire reaches that point?"

"Probably another explosion." Elyssa's voice quaked. "Maybe the biggest one yet."

Marcelle set the point of her sword against the closest Tark's throat. "Did you put the freed slaves in the dungeon?"

He nodded. "A ... a few moments ago."

"Villain!" Marcelle slashed the blade across the Tark's calf and spun toward the dungeon. "Arxad! Open that door!"

✵ TWENTY-ONE ✵

ADRIAN whipped out his sword. Shouts rang from the cells, pelting his ears. At the closest cell to the right, fingers protruded between the window bars, reaching. "Help us!" a man called. "The straw in here is burning! We're running out of air!" Smoke filtered past his fingertips. "Hurry!"

Adrian unhooked the key ring and gave it to his father. "Unlock the doors while I beat these Tarks back."

Garth laughed. "The rat's courage has swelled his head."

"Then pop the boil," a bald Tark said. "Let's see the pus splatter!"

Garth pointed his sword at Adrian's father. "One of you slide past me and make sure he doesn't open any cells."

"I will." The bald Tark squeezed past Garth at the side of the corridor, his sword extended.

Adrian lunged at him and slashed. The Tark blocked the blade with his own. With a quick twist, Adrian wrenched the Tark's sword away, then hacked at his wrist, slicing halfway through it. The Tark screamed and fell to his knees in a pool of blood.

Lunging again, Adrian stabbed at Garth, but he dodged with a nimble backwards leap. With a leap of his own, Adrian kicked the fallen sword toward his father and flew at Garth, his blade swinging.

Garth parried the blow, and the two locked swords, the metal blades zinging as they slid up to the hilts. The other two Tarks pushed around Garth on either side and thrust their swords at Adrian. Adrian threw himself toward his father, rolled into a backwards somersault, and vaulted to his feet.

From deeper in the corridor, three copies of Adrian ran toward them, each with a drawn sword. Bearing fierce expressions, they let out bone-chilling screams.

When the Tarks turned that way, they stiffened. Adrian launched at them. With a series of thrusts, spins, and hacks, he sliced into each Tark until they all lay bleeding on the floor.

"Got it!" Father unlocked the cell door and threw it open. Smoke poured out along wtih coughing women and children. Several men followed with babies in their arms.

The three copies of Adrian waved in sync and called, "This way! Hurry!"

Adrian took the keys from his father. "Lead these folks out. I'll unlock the others."

Stepping over and around the fallen Tarks, the released prisoners followed Edison and the trio of Adrians. After a few seconds, the copies faded and disappeared.

Adrian unlocked and opened the cell across from the smoking one. More prisoners spilled out and followed the others.

A man caught Adrian's arm. "We'll need the key to the dungeon exit."

Adrian looked at the man's dirty face, bearded and blood-smeared. "Captain Reed?"

"Yes." He extended his hand. "Hurry."

Adrian slid keys along the metal ring. "I'm not sure which—"

"It's one of the longer ones," Reed said. "I used to work dungeon detail."

A loud boom rocked the corridor. Adrian, Captain Reed, and the escaping prisoners toppled over. Adrian dropped his sword and key ring and slapped his hands against the ground to break his fall.

When the quaking subsided, groans and crying drifted through the corridor. A single lantern remained lit, its feeble flame barely providing enough light to see.

A tremor ran along Adrian's palm and up his arm, growing in intensity. An image flashed to mind—the fire disappearing into the pipeline tunnel. As Father had guessed, those flames must have caused a chain reaction. Soon the entire dungeon could explode.

He leaped to his feet, pulled Captain Reed to his, and shoved the ring into his hand. "Give me the entrance key, and you unlock the rest of the cells. This place is going to explode."

Reed popped a key loose and gave it to Adrian. "Go!"

Adrian weaved past the fallen slaves as they tried to rise. With the ground shaking more violently, Adrian lurched from side to side like a sailor on a sea-tossed ship.

"Adrian!"

He turned toward the call. Little fingers probed between a cell's bars. He looked in. Randall held Regina close to the door. At least ten other prisoners sat on the floor, apparently tossed by the explosion. "Adrian, did you see what I did? I made more Adrians!"

"I saw that." He kissed one of her fingers. "Tell everyone to get ready. Someone's coming to let you out."

After lifting the cell's crossbar and throwing it down, Adrian hurried on and clambered up the staircase leading to the surface. When he reached the top and the trapdoor leading out, he crouched to avoid banging his head and extended the key toward the lock. The trembling ground shook his arm and the key, making him miss the hole.

From outside, someone shouted, "Arxad! Open that door!"

Adrian blinked. Marcelle?

Something pounded on the door with a loud boom. The panel vibrated. Wood splintered. Another boom sounded. The door cracked. Fire poured through narrow gaps and spread across the door's underside, chasing an expanding ring of char.

Adrian shifted backwards. A sudden tremor sent him tumbling down the stairs. When he caught himself with his hands on one wall and his feet on the other, he looked up. The door had burned away, and Marcelle stared at him, a flaming torch in hand.

She ran down the steps and hoisted him to his feet. "We have to get out of here!"

"I know!" Adrian hobbled to the dungeon level and waved an arm at the people funneling through the corridor. "March quickly but don't panic!"

Marcelle leaped to the last stair, pulled a baby from a woman's arms, and ran toward the exit above. "Get the children out first! I'll guard the door!"

Now standing at the top of the stairs, Marcelle handed the baby off to Elyssa and whipped out her sword. "Keep them coming!"

Arxad called out, "Bring one woman with each child! I will fly some to safety and return for more!"

A few seconds later, a beating of wings announced Arxad's departure.

"How many Tarks are up there?" Adrian called.

"Twenty or so, but they're shaken up. More are coming from the palace. Less than a minute till a battle starts. Now that Arxad's gone, it's not looking good."

"I'm on my way!" Adrian ran up the stairs behind a man carrying a toddler. When he reached the top, he stood at Marcelle's side, his sword tight in his grip. "Ready?"

She kissed his cheek, then turned toward the Tarks and growled, "Ready."

As the tremors heightened, former slaves continued pouring out from the dungeon. Now at least fifty Tarks massed a couple of dozen paces away, all with swords or spears in hand. They marched toward the dungeon at double-time speed.

Adrian shouted, "All men friendly to Mesolantrum rally to me! Find stones, sticks, anything!"

Randall, Captain Reed, and dozens of other men rushed out of the growing crowd of escapees. They scooped up whatever they could find on the ground, and gathered behind Adrian and Marcelle.

Edison Masters stepped to Adrian's side, a Tark sword in hand. "We're here, and we're ready."

"Then let's go." Adrian, Marcelle, and Edison charged into the horde of Tarks, slashing and hacking with their swords. Adrian whacked a spear's shaft in two, spun, and drove his sword into a Tark's gut. Marcelle ducked under a sword swipe and swung her blade across a Tark's leg, nearly cutting it off. Although Edison had shifted out of sight, his familiar grunts sounded from somewhere in the melee. Randall, Reed, and the other men flooded the battlefield, beating Tarks with sticks, pelting them with stones, and throwing punches.

A new tremor knocked many off balance. Obscenity-laced shouts flew. Blood spewed everywhere. Adrian hacked and hewed through the mob. A sword sliced through his tunic and ripped the bottom half off, taking a strip of skin with it. A spear point grazed his shoulder. A shaft bashed against his head. With each wound, he fought back even harder. Six dead Tarks. A slash across a throat. Seven. A thrust through a chest. Eight.

Two steps away, Marcelle copied his moves, driving forward slash for slash, thrust for thrust. When they punched through the pack, they spun and faced them again, their swords ready. Ahead, Tarks and former slaves fought spear and sword against fists and clubs. Although Adrian and Marcelle had thinned the ranks, the Tarks still held the advantage.

From above, Arxad descended into light, his mouth open and his claws extended. He would arrive in seconds.

Just as Adrian set his feet to charge, an enormous explosion boomed across the Enforcement Zone. Again everyone fell. A concussive wave sent Arxad reeling through the air.

Adrian rolled to Marcelle, grabbed her arm, and hauled her to her feet. As they balanced against the rollicking ground, palace turrets crumbled. Rocks and debris flew across their bodies, pelting their backs and shoulders. Flat stones embedded in the ground cracked and heaved upward. Flames spewed through the vents with loud squeals, igniting combatants' clothes and hair. Every gas lantern exploded, leaving the erupting flames as the only light in the field.

A moment later, the ground settled. The upwelling flames drew back into the ground like slurping tongues. Darkness fell over the area. The sound of a few pebbles skittering across stone faded to silence. Moans drifted from place to place. Otherwise, all was quiet.

In the distance, a stream of flames ignited a torch. A former slave standing next to Arxad carried the torch closer, bringing light to the field. He picked up another torch, touched the two together, and thrust one into the ground.

Adrian turned toward the palace. It remained standing, though much of the upper half had collapsed. He lifted his sword, his legs still wobbly, and searched for his father among the fallen men. With so little light and with dirt, debris, and blood covering nearly everyone, spotting him seemed impossible. He sucked in a breath and shouted, "If any Tark moves a muscle, it will be his last move!"

Arxad flew to an empty space in the midst of the battlefield and sprayed flames in a wide circle. As they fizzled, he roared, "And I will back up that promise with fire!"

Adrian nodded at Marcelle. "Are you okay?"

Blood trickling from her forehead to her nose, and a raw scrape running from cheek to chin, she nodded. "Everything hurts, but I'm okay."

Adrian walked toward Arxad, again shouting. "All friends of Mesolantrum may rise." He helped an escaped slave to his feet. "After that, all Tarks who wish to surrender may drop your weapons and rise with your hands above your heads."

While the emancipated slaves collected Tark weapons, Adrian walked from body to body, searching for his father. He found Captain Reed and hoisted him up. "Are you all right?"

"Not really." He limped toward another section of the battlefield. "I think I saw your father fall over here."

Adrian hustled to join him, sheathing his sword along the way. When they arrived at the spot, they found a huge flat stone lying on top of a man. Labored breaths wheezed from underneath. Gripping the stone with both hands, Adrian and Captain Reed heaved it off as if opening the cover of a book and let it thud to the ground. Edison Masters lay in the exposed spot. He took in a sharp breath and let it out slowly through his nose. "I thought you'd never get here. That blasted stone weighs a ton."

"Anything broken?" Adrian asked.

Edison prodded his ribcage with a finger, wincing. "Maybe a rib or two. It hurts to breathe."

"Just lie still," Adrian said. "We'll find a stretcher."

"When pigs fly." Edison reached up. "Give me your hand. That's an order."

Smiling, Adrian grabbed his father's wrist and helped him to his feet. "Can't keep an old soldier down, can I?"

"Never." Edison brushed himself off, again wincing. "Have you seen Frederick?"

"Not yet." Adrian looked at the demolished palace and swallowed through a lump. "I don't know if he had time to get out."

Marcelle joined them. "Where did he go?"

Adrian nodded toward the palace. "I sent him out through the archives."

"Not good," Marcelle said. "The pipeline ran right past that room."

Adrian kicked a pebble. "We'd better get started looking for him."

Captain Reed laid a hand on Adrian's shoulder. "Rest a moment, Son. I'll find some able-bodied men, and we'll get right to—" His brow lifted. "Well, speak of the devil."

Adrian followed Reed's line of sight. Frederick hobbled down the palace's rear steps. Covered with gray dust, he looked more like a ghost than a man. He waved an arm. "They need some help in there!"

"Stay put," Captain Reed said to Adrian. "Like I said, I'll get some men. We have a few who aren't ready to fall over."

As Reed ambled away, he passed by Frederick and whispered something. They both laughed quietly.

Frederick limped to Adrian's side. "The palace is in ruins. The upper floors smashed down into the lower levels. I found several dead bodies and carried a few survivors to the front courtyard. Captain Reed said I'm not allowed to go back in. Said I've done enough damage for now."

Adrian bumped his arm with a fist. "To yourself or to the palace?"

"Both, I suppose. I was just about to lay that guard on an infirmary bed when the explosion hit. The ceiling started collapsing, so I ran with him and made it out the front door just before the second floor crashed down."

"So he's alive, then."

"Yep. Looks like he'll be fine. Terrible headache, though."

Adrian breathed a sigh of relief. Knocking the poor man out nearly led to his death. At least one tragedy had been averted, though too many good folks had lost their lives. A tear crept to his eye, but he didn't bother to brush it away. So much pain. So much suffering. Why did all of this have to happen?

He looked out over the devastation. Men limped or crawled from place to place, some prodding Tarks with a spear or sword. It would take hours or even days just to put everything in order. Not only that, there was still Drexel to deal with.

Adrian exhaled. "So much to do and so little time."

"More than you know," Marcelle said, taking Adrian's hand. "We're going to get married at the king's palace." She lowered her voice to a whisper. "It'll be a fake wedding, part of a plan to trap Drexel. It's a long story, and maybe I should have asked first, but I had to make a quick decision. Besides, Professor Dunwoody kind of made the decision for me."

Adrian smiled. "Even pretending will be a pleasure, but how are we going to get ready in time?"

She poked his chest with a finger. "You and I will fly there on Arxad. We're supposed to be an exotic couple from a foreign land, so it won't be a shock that family members aren't present." She looked at Edison hopefully. "Besides, you have a lot to do here, right?"

"Of course." Edison laid a hand on his ribs. "And Estelle has to patch me up before I can do anything."

Adrian patted his father's back. "I was at our commune a little while ago. Look for Mother in the barn. I rode Primus here and left him at Old Pete's. And don't forget the bodies back at the portal chamber. Someone has to get them and—"

"Don't worry, Son. I'll take care of everything."

Elyssa ran up to Marcelle. "Jason found a Tark sword, and he's in the woods guarding rescued slaves. Some are hurt, so we were wondering what to do with them."

Frederick brushed dust from his tunic. "They're setting up an infirmary in the blacksmith's shop. I'll join Jason in a minute and help him lead everyone there. Once the worst cases are stable, we can take them to the healing river."

Adrian touched Elyssa's arm. "Please find a girl named Regina. She was among the prisoners. I would like her to come to the wedding with us."

"Do you mean she'll fly there with us now?" Marcelle asked.

Adrian nodded. "She displayed a Starlighter talent that might help us against Drexel."

"We'll need to get my bridal gown from Mrs. Longley's and suitable clothes for you and Regina." Marcelle gazed at the palace. "My father has emergency funds for my use stashed in a lockbox in his desk. I think it will be enough, assuming I can find it in the remains of the palace."

"Like Father said, we'll take care of everything." Frederick laid an arm around Adrian and Marcelle. "You two get cleaned up at the bathhouse. I'll find Regina, get your clothes, and meet you back here with her and Arxad. I'm sure I can break open a lockbox—with Marcelle's permission, of course."

She smiled. "Permission granted. It should be in the lower right-hand drawer. But what if you can't find it?"

"And what about the wounded slaves?" Adrian asked. "If I stay for a while, I can—"

Frederick elbowed Adrian's ribs. "Trust your big brother. Father and I will do whatever is necessary here."

"If you say so." Adrian hugged his father and Frederick, then kissed Elyssa on the forehead. "Tell Jason I'll see him soon."

Adrian and Marcelle hurried around the palace and into the village square. Dozens of people had emerged from their homes and gathered at the sentry station. People filed out of the palace helping others leave the building. Torches burned, men shouted orders, women carried buckets of water from the bathhouse to an area on the street where palace residents lay, most wearing frilly nightgowns, now torn and smeared with dirt and blood.

Adrian stopped. How could he fly away on Arxad at a time like this? With water from the bathhouse being used to scrub wounds, he and Marcelle wouldn't be able to—

"Stop, Adrian."

He blinked at her. "Stop what?"

She tapped his head with a finger. "I know what you're thinking. You can't carry the world on your shoulders. Let someone else help these people. You need to get ready to save the entire kingdom."

"The bathhouse looks too busy. I was thinking we could help them for just a few—"

"We can wash in Tarkton." She looked up at him. "How much time will it take to get there? An hour?"

He shrugged, pain and sadness not allowing him to smile. "I have no experience flying to Tarkton on a dragon."

She dabbed the sword wound on his abdomen. "On second thought, this wound needs to be cleaned immediately, but we don't have time to get to the healing waters and back."

Adrian rotated a sore shoulder, tearing his tunic away from another wound. He grimaced.

"Let's go." Marcelle tugged him toward the Enforcement Zone.

He let her pull him along. "Where are we going?"

"To Nelson's Creek. It's down the hill behind the dungeon. We can be there in a few minutes."

Adrian let himself smile. "I wonder if any sharks are there."

"Not sure, but I don't want any biting my backside. We'll bring Arxad and Regina along just in case."

✷ TWENTY-TWO ✷

DUNWOODY sat with Issachar in the carriage's rear-facing bench. Four white glow sticks lined the carriage's ceiling, providing enough light to see, though their glow had dimmed during the journey. The fading light had allowed for chatter during the early stages, then a slow progression toward slumber. Issachar fell asleep hours ago and still snored with his head drooping forward.

Now awake after a nap, Dunwoody stared at Cal Broder, supposedly Drexel, the man Marcelle accused of murdering her mother. Broder leaned against the side of the carriage—half awake, half asleep—Sophia next to him, leaning against the other side panel, her deep breaths signaling her sleeping state.

Dunwoody studied their faces. Of course, they anticipated a ceremony to honor the new governor of Mesolantrum and knew nothing about the wedding, though they would learn in time. For now, figuring out how to keep Cal on a leash was paramount. Preventing him from plying his hypnotic trade might be impossible, so minimizing the damage he could do seemed to be the only hope.

Dunwoody yawned. The rocking motion and the rapid clopping of hooves called him back toward slumber, but he couldn't give in. Three hours of sleep would have to do. Soon they would arrive, and he had to be fully awake to resist Broder's powerful influence.

After a few moments, Broder drew away from the panel and locked stares with Dunwoody—probing, searching. Dunwoody refused to blink. He didn't dare show any sign of weakness or intimidation. He had to conquer, stay in control. Broder was like an eagle with talons extended, ready to snatch its prey—an archivist familiar with every name, face, and position in the royal court. With such a victim under his control, Broder would have easy access to those holding government seats and thereby seize power that would soon become impossible to counteract. The key to stopping him would be to feign compliance, allow him some freedom to carry out his scheme while trying to foil his efforts from behind the scenes.

Dunwoody glanced at Issachar. The low light provided a view of his "immunity" mark. He had taken it willingly, which proved that his resistance to Broder remained weak. Even revealing to him that Broder was really Drexel provided no help. The fact that Marcelle claimed to see the transformation herself did little to alter his perception that Broder couldn't possibly be someone to whom he bore absolutely no resemblance. Still, giving Issachar the photo of his late wife did calm his fire. He gladly carried it along.

Looking down, Dunwoody couldn't catch a glimpse of his own immunity mark, the fake spot of greasy ash he had applied to his cheek, hoping Broder wouldn't remember that he hadn't made the mark himself. Standing in line while Sophia was looking on and then ducking away when she turned her back seemed to provide enough cover to convince Broder that he couldn't remember everyone he had touched.

A call of "Whoa!" and the jingling of horse tack roused the sleepers. When the carriage stopped, Dunwoody pushed a curtain to the side and peered out. Solarus's dawning rays cast an orange hue over the royal palace. Rising nearly twice as high as the governor's poor copy in Mesolantrum, the palace sparkled as if diamond crystals mixed in with the marble on its alabaster façade.

The door on Dunwoody's side flew open, revealing the carriage driver, a strapping man of about thirty. He extended a hand, smiling. "Ladies first."

Sophia rose, stepped in front of Dunwoody and Broder, and took the driver's hand. Wearing a recently purchased travel ensemble—tan skirt and white long-sleeved blouse, she allowed him to help her to the ground.

"Gents next!"

Dunwoody prodded Issachar's shoulder. "Shall we?"

He stretched his arms and yawned. "You two first. I'm still waking up."

"No sense dawdling." Dunwoody rose and stayed bent until he hopped out with the driver's help. He took a step away, pretending to gawk at the palace as he listened to the conversation inside the carriage.

"Remember to request the funds when I give the signal," Broder said.

"I'll remember," Issachar replied.

Broder appeared at the carriage door. He jumped to the ground and faced the palace with his arms crossed, apparently admiring the impressive sight.

When Issachar joined them, the driver smiled. "When shall I return?"

Issachar reached into his jacket pocket, withdrew several bills, and handed them to the driver. "Be a good fellow and return this evening after the festival."

The driver nodded. "Yes sir!"

"Since I am the official liaison," Dunwoody said, "allow me to lead the way."

They walked from the cobblestone street up a set of marble stairs with polished brass rails on each side, a path wide enough for ten horses striding abreast.

When they reached the top, a sentry at the door offered a nod. "Who is calling this fine morning?"

Dunwoody gave a half bow, then gestured toward Broder. "This is the new governor of Mesolantrum, Cal Broder. This young woman is Sophia Halstead, the governor's festival companion, and this other gentleman is Issachar Stafford, the head financial officer of Mesolantrum." He touched himself on the chest. "I am Dawson Dunwoody, the governor's personal liaison."

The guard's eyes widened. "Ah! We have heard the news of a most interesting succession—a peasant's appeal for justice."

"Correct. It's no surprise that the news is spreading quickly."

"And there will be a special event this evening, if I'm not mistaken."

Dunwoody nodded. "Honoring a new governor is quite special. I agree."

"I refer to the wedding." The sentry leaned to look around Dunwoody. "Did the couple come with you? Who are they, anyway?"

"They will be arriving by a special transport, and their identities are being kept secret for now." Dunwoody cleared his throat and took on a formal air. "We are here to meet with your protocol officer. I sent a Courier late yesterday, so I assume my arrival is expected."

"Of course." The sentry bowed and backed through the door. "I will send a Courier to announce your presence."

Dunwoody turned to his party and crossed his arms over his chest. "Now we wait."

"What is this about a wedding?" Broder asked.

"A couple is coming from another province to be wed in the palace, so I hoped to join their festivities with ours in order to ensure a large crowd for your introduction to the people."

Broder stared at Dunwoody. His eyes seemed to penetrate deeper and deeper as he whispered, "The father of the bride?" He glanced at Issachar, then quickly averted his eyes. "Never mind. It's a good idea. Though I would have preferred being informed."

"Informed. ... Of course." Dunwoody concealed a grimace. *Be vigilant! Guard your thoughts!* Broder had stolen a vital piece of information, and now all might be lost. What could be done to repair the potential damage?

"When we meet with the protocol officer," Broder said. "I can learn what needs to be done to accommodate multiple purposes."

"When *we* meet?" Dunwoody shook his head. "Such a meeting would be boring for you. Just details about who stands where, who speaks before whom, when to bow, that sort of thing. I will fill you in on your role when the meeting is over."

"What will I do while you're with the officer?" Broder asked.

"Once I get approval, I hoped Issachar would guide you and Miss Halstead on a tour of the palace. He is well acquainted with the history of the building and the city. It will be an educational opportunity that might enhance your ability to govern with knowledge and wisdom in addition to providing a bit of local seasoning for your planned statements to the crowd this evening."

"Yes, I suppose that would be a good idea." Broder's gaze drifted across the palace. "I wonder if the king would have a moment in his schedule to meet with me."

"A private meeting?" Dunwoody asked.

Broder nodded. "Is that a breach in decorum?"

"No. No. Of course not. I trust that he would welcome the opportunity to get to know a new governor." Dunwoody stroked his chin. Actually such a meeting might be beneficial. Since Leo had not been able to control King Sasser, perhaps His Majesty would reveal his secret for overcoming a male Starlighter. "It's short notice, so the king probably already has a full schedule today, but I suppose it won't hurt to ask."

A breeze kicked up, a sign that autumn's preview of winter had arrived. Broder pulled his cloak close and fastened a belt around it. "I think I will be able to convince the protocol officer to arrange a meeting."

Dunwoody nodded. "You have been able to, shall we say, exercise great influence with everyone you meet. You certainly possess a charismatic appeal."

Sophia's expression grew as cold as the breeze. "It is not charisma that people find convincing. It is dedication to helping people who cannot help themselves. Everyone who possesses a soft heart is attracted to such virtue."

Dunwoody forced a smile. Sophia's response proved that Broder had assumed complete control over her.

"You are too kind, Sophia." Broder pulled a beret from his pocket and pressed it over his head. "I hope my supposed charisma can help us arrange a private meeting with His Majesty."

The sentry reopened the door and gestured inside where a young man wearing a black uniform stood. "This Courier will take you to the protocol office."

Dunwoody led the way through the door, followed by Broder, who removed his beret as he entered. Sophia and Issachar trailed in single file. As they walked through a cavernous lobby, their shoes clopped on polished white marble.

The Courier spoke over the clatter. "The palace residents are excited about the festival tonight, so we are expecting a large gathering. I hear the chief of protocol is handling the details personally. It's not often that we are able to witness a wedding of such importance."

"Excellent," Dunwoody said. "This day promises to be filled with excitement."

They turned into a wide corridor where offices lined both walls. A rectangular plaque on each door provided a name for the business within—Department of Energy, Minister of Science, Department of Education, Regulation of Trade, Finance Officer, Exploration, and finally Protocol Officer.

The Courier halted and knocked on the door. "The emissaries from Mesolantrum are here."

"Excellent! Excellent! Send them in!"

Broder furrowed his brow. "The officer is a woman?"

"Yes. Her name is Kiera Jarten." The Courier opened the door and extended an arm inside. "You may enter."

Dunwoody stepped to the threshold and bowed to a forty-something woman standing behind a large wooden desk. "Madam Jarten, I am Dawson Dunwoody." After introducing the others in his party and guiding them into the office, he bowed again. "Since you and I will discuss matters that will likely bore your other guests, may I suggest that Issachar Stafford, our region's banker, be allowed the freedom to tour the public sectors of the palace? He has been here many times."

"Of course. I will issue passes for them that will alert the guards so that—"

"Madam Jarten," Broder said. "Please pardon the interruption, but might the king have time to meet with me today?"

"The king?" Madam Jarten raised a hand over her mouth. "I apologize for my outburst, but the king's schedule is filled weeks ahead of time, and he has cleared it for tonight's festivities, making the hours between now and then even more crowded." She seated herself in a leather chair and nervously straightened stacks of papers on the desktop. "I have much to do to prepare for tonight, so your original suggestion is the better one. You can start your tour in the library where the attendant will guide you through a most interesting series of videos and photographs that will provide a detailed history of—"

"Madam Jarten." Broder stepped up to the desk and focused his stare on her. "Kindly look at me."

She set her gaze on him. Her eyes locked in place and slowly took on a glassy sheen. "Yes?"

"Please arrange an audience for me with King Sasser. It is essential that I speak to him as soon as possible."

Nodding mechanically, Madam Jarten rose from her chair. "Wait here." Without another word, she walked around the desk and left the office. Her footsteps echoed from the hall and slowly faded.

"Well," Issachar said. "She certainly changed her mind in a hurry."

Sophia curled her arm through Broder's. "Like we all know, Cal has a charismatic appeal."

Dunwoody cleared his throat. "Tell me, Governor Broder, is it your intention to use this gift of charisma on the king?"

"Use it?" Broder glanced nervously at Sophia. "Well, I suppose so. If I have such a gift, it would be quite impossible to turn it off."

Dunwoody gave Issachar a momentary look. "What I mean is, do you plan to use your gift to try to influence the king in some way?"

"Of course he will," Sophia said. "Every governor hopes to curry the king's favor in order to benefit those under his governorship. A region whose needs are never in the king's ear is a region whose needs are never addressed."

"Well stated." Dunwoody nodded. Between the Starlighter and his appointed liar, the two made a formidable team. He would have to either divide them or accompany them to any meeting with the king. But how? Such a stratagem would be difficult to employ without arousing suspicion. Yet, meeting with the king could produce a benefit besides learning his secret to overcoming a Starlighter.

Perhaps Issachar, as the deposed governor, might appeal to the king for an immediate ruling concerning the succession law. Broder could be ousted from his new seat on the spot.

Madam Jarten bustled back into the office, her face awash in red. "Come quickly, Governor Broder. The king has graciously allowed a few moments to meet with you, but we must hurry."

Sophia locked her arm with Broder's. "Yes, let's hurry."

Dunwoody set a hand on Madam Jarten's shoulder. "Is it a breach in protocol for me to join the governor even though I am yet unannounced?"

"A breach?" Madam Jarten looked down for a moment, then shook her head. "I can think of no rules of etiquette that would forbid a multiple introduction."

"Then I suggest that we all go. I have never met the king myself, and since he has only a few minutes, the time taken away from our planning will be insignificant. Of course, we will have to work more quickly afterward, but meeting the king is well worth it." Dunwoody straightened his tunic. "Let's not keep His Majesty waiting."

Madam Jarten led the group through the corridor and across a massive ballroom. "I am taking you this way so you can see where the festivities will take place tonight." She swept her arm, pointing at the floor then toward the far side of the chamber. "We will have a red carpet running to a low stage where the priest will conduct the wedding ceremony. The couple will walk down the carpet in front of an expected crowd of one thousand."

"Will the priest also bless my inauguration?" Broder asked.

"Your inauguration?" Still walking across the expanse, Madam Jarten glanced at Dunwoody. "I will have to confer with those who invited the priest."

"Who invited him?" Broder asked Dunwoody. "You?"

"I did. He is a local monk who knows the couple. They asked for him."

After another moment, they arrived at a set of tall double doors, one of which stood open, revealing a wide floor leading to a huge desk and an ornate chair behind it. A man sat in the chair, his head low as he wrote with a quill pen on a page in a huge book, a magnifying glass in his other hand. Trim gray hair adorned his bare head—no sign of a crown anywhere.

"I must warn you," Madam Jarten whispered, "that the king prefers to converse with his guests without a protocol officer present. He wants to get to know you as you are, not with someone like me making sure you don't violate our customs."

Broder nodded. "I understand."

Madam Jarten stood just inside the door and bowed. "Your Majesty," she shouted, "the new governor of Mesolantrum is here with his entourage."

Dunwoody winced at her volume. The entire palace likely heard the call.

"Excellent." The king looked up, a deep squint accentuating his wrinkles. "Come. Come. I have only a few minutes."

Madam Jarten backed out of the room, whispering, "You're on your own."

Dunwoody stepped in front and led the "entourage" to within a few paces of the desk. He bowed low. "Greetings from Mesolantrum, Your Majesty. I am—"

"What?" The king raised an ear trumpet to his ear. "Speak up!"

Dunwoody suppressed a smile. So this is how the king resisted Leo. He couldn't hear the Starlighter's oratory. After taking a breath, Dunwoody shouted, "Greetings from Mesolantrum, Your Majesty. I am Dawson Dunwoody. Please allow me to introduce—"

"Bah!" The king waved a hand. "Enough of this protocol excrement. I'm sure grown-ups are able to introduce themselves."

Broder stepped forward and spoke with a loud, even tone. "My pleasure, Your Majesty. I am Cal Broder, the new governor of Mesolantrum, and I—"

"Cal Broder?" The king blinked, then squinted again, his trumpet still raised. "What kind of mother would name her son after a storybook hero?"

"A good mother, Sire," Sophia said, bowing. "A mother who dreams of her son following in the legendary Cal's footsteps as a courageous, noble, and sacrificial gentleman who risks his life for the betterment of those who need the help only he can bring."

"Well, well …" The king leaned closer. "Whom have we here?"

Dunwoody spotted a pair of thick spectacles close to the front of the desk. The king's poor eyesight was likely another reason he was able to resist a Starlighter's charms. Dunwoody stepped close, bumped the desk, and stealthily slid the spectacles into his pocket. "I apologize for my clumsiness, Your Highness."

"You need not. I am so blind I bump into things all the time." The king lowered his trumpet and probed the desk surface with his hand. "My spectacles are around here somewhere. I heard a young woman's voice, and I would like to see her."

"She is Sophia Halstead, Sire." Broder said. "She comes from—"

"Eh?" The king lifted the trumpet to his ear again. "Whose head?"

Broder raised his voice. "Sophia Halstead. She comes from—"

"Let her speak for herself." After laying the trumpet down, the king pulled out a desk drawer and felt inside. "She sounds very much like my daughter. I would like to see if their faces match as well."

Sophia walked around the desk and knelt at the king's side. "I am Sophia Halstead, daughter of Montague and Louisa Halstead."

The king set his palm on Sophia's cheek and drew her nearly nose to nose. "Ah! I see the resemblance!"

Sophia blinked at him. "Sire?"

"I knew your mother quite well. Her husband and my wife died within days of each other. I heard about your father's death from my gardener who once worked with him, so I invited your mother to join me at some sort of function. I don't remember which. In any case, she became my companion at several dinners, but when we realized that we were using each other's company to attend to our own wounds rather than establishing a true friendship, we parted ways." He let out a long sigh. "Pity. I should never have let her go. She is a fine woman, a fine woman, indeed."

Dunwoody firmed his lips. The situation was quickly deteriorating. An emotional plea would likely come next, but trying to intervene now would be too obvious.

"Your Highness," Sophia said loudly, "I get the impression that you do not know about her passing. Counselor Orion had my mother burned at the stake some years ago."

"What?" The king's face reddened. "On what grounds?"

"That she was a Diviner. A sorceress."

"Superstitious nonsense!" The king growled. "Why did this news never reach my ears?"

"I don't know, Your Majesty, but I assume the powers in Mesolantrum never sent a report, or perhaps sent one with a false name and accusation." Sophia inhaled a long breath. "As a family member of the unjustly executed, I requested that Cal Broder be elevated to the governorship. I trust that you are familiar with the law that allows such an appeal."

"Familiar with it? My father wrote it."

Dunwoody stepped forward, picked up the king's trumpet, and handed it to him. It was now or never. "Your Majesty?"

The king lifted the trumpet to his ear. "Yes?"

"Speaking of that law, since you know it so well, was the royal intention to punish the governor who would allow such a cruel injustice?"

"Of course. Such a governor should be disgraced before all eyes. He should never be allowed authority over a marshmallow roast, much less over who should live or die by fire."

Sophia raised a hand. "But, Your Highness, the law says—"

"The law was written," Dunwoody continued, "in such a way that an innocent governor could be deposed. In our case, the governor who allowed the execution is dead, and the governor being deposed by this law had nothing to do with the execution. In fact, he spoke against it in public and in private, so being innocent in the matter—"

The king slammed a fist on the desk. "How dare you question the validity of the law! It was written with such a possibility in mind. Justice for the family is far more important than whether or not a particular governor loses his seat of power. It is Mesolantrum's seat, the people's seat, and no individual has a claim on it. The governor who protested the execution, and not loudly enough, it seems, should have been honored to step down and deliver the seat to the designee."

Issachar stepped closer. "And I was, Your Majesty."

"What?" The king squinted once again and aimed the trumpet at Issachar. "Who are you?"

"Issachar Stafford." He bowed. "I am the governor who freely delivered the seat to Cal Broder."

"Then what's all this rubbish about how the law was written? It sounded as if an appeal was about to be raised."

"Perhaps I can explain." Broder walked around the desk and joined Sophia in a kneeling posture. "Your Majesty, I am sure that my spokesman wanted to clarify the application of your law. He merely raised the question in order to verify your intent."

The king nodded. "Ah! I see. That is reasonable, though poorly executed."

"We are all new in our respective roles." Broder scooted closer and looked directly into the king's eyes. "Because of our inexperience, I will need help from you."

"What kind of help?"

Dunwoody fingered the king's spectacles in his pocket. There was no stopping this runaway carriage now. The king's handicaps remained his only hope.

Broder nodded at Issachar. "Former Governor Stafford was working on exposing the corruption that led to Louisa Halstead's death, but it will be difficult to squeeze the pus out of the infection, if you will, without a clear mandate from the throne. Therefore, I ask that you confer upon me martial-law power and allow me to have access to one of your generals. Since the corrupt politicians might have some of the local military officers in their pockets, I will need a detachment that commands enough muscle to overwhelm any opposition I come across."

Dunwoody raised a finger. "Governor Broder, perhaps you would like to tell the king about your own position before you accepted the governorship."

"My own position?" Broder half closed an eye. "Whatever for?"

"Learning about your level of experience will help His Majesty decide which of his commanders is best suited to come to your aid."

"Yes," the king said. "Tell me about your previous position. I am most interested."

"Well ... I was ..."

Sophia took Broder's hand. "Cal is a humble man, Your Majesty, so he is hesitant to tell of his own exploits. Kindly allow me to do so in his place."

The king glanced at Dunwoody, then at Broder, a grave expression shadowing his face. "I believe the allotted time has been spent, and it sounds as if you would wish to tell me much more than I need to know."

Sophia's brow arched. "So will you grant our requests?"

The king set the trumpet on the desk. "You may see yourselves out."

"Our requests!" Sophia shouted. "Will you grant them?"

The king rose and gestured for Broder to rise with him. "I will consult with my advisors."

"Thank you, Sire." Broder took the king's hand and kissed his fingers.

Dunwoody cringed. Poor eyesight wouldn't protect the king from direct contact.

"I have one more request." Broder kept a grip on the king's hand and nodded at Issachar. "Go ahead."

Issachar cleared his throat. "As chief banker of Mesolantrum, it is my duty to inform you that corrupt officials have made off with large sums of the people's money, and the ship of state is floundering in the storm of changes. We will need a significant infusion in order to right the ship."

"I understand." The king wobbled in place. "It seems that I am suddenly not feeling well."

Broder released the king's fingers. "Shall I call for help?"

"No need." The king clapped his hands. Three men in Tark uniforms ran in from a side door and stood at attention, all with spears in hand and swords in hip scabbards. "One of you summon my physician," the king said, his voice weak and shaky. "One of you escort my guests to General Brock and tell the general to grant the new governor's request, and one of you help me to my chambers."

The shortest yet stoutest of the guards ran to the king, pushed a shoulder under his arm, and guided him to the side door. A second guard hurried out the main double doors, and the third took three steps closer to Dunwoody, then stood at attention again. "I will take you to General Brock."

Dunwoody wrung his hands. Broder meeting the general could be disastrous. He would have the entire kingdom in his pocket in a matter of hours. It seemed that the king knew something was wrong, but when Broder touched him, he lost focus. There had to be some way to warn him.

Stepping toward the guard, Dunwoody withdrew the king's spectacles from his pocket. "Excuse me, good fellow. It seems that the king left his spectacles here. May I catch up with the other guard and deliver them? It will take only a moment."

The guard gave the spectacles a cursory glance. "Those belong here. He has another pair in his chambers and another ear trumpet as well."

"Yes. Of course. I should have known." Dunwoody set the spectacles on the desk. "I have a gift from the people of Mesolantrum that I forgot to give him. May I deliver that?"

Broder shot Dunwoody a heated glare. "You didn't tell me about a gift."

"Well … no, I didn't. This was prepared for the king by school children before you assumed the governor's seat. This is my first opportunity to deliver it."

Broder nodded. "I understand. Very well, then."

"You may leave the gift here," the guard said. "I will see to it."

"You don't understand. This isn't a physical gift." Dunwoody glanced at Issachar, hoping for help.

The guard's brow arched. "Well? What is it?"

"It's a poem," Issachar said. "A tribute to the king. The children composed it with their teacher's help."

"Then recite it at the festival." The guard waved an arm. "Let's go."

Dunwoody set his feet. "It's a private message for the king from our citizens. A public airing would be inappropriate."

Broder touched the guard's shoulder. "We won't be needing him. It would be best if he concentrated on plans for the festival. Send him to the king and arrange an escort to the protocol officer."

The guard looked at Dunwoody, his eyes beginning to glaze over. "You may go. When you deliver the gift, ask the other guard to escort you to the protocol office. I cannot have you wandering around the palace. You might get lost."

"We both have to go," Issachar said. "The poem is a song … a duet. And besides, I know the way to the king's chambers. I brought financial reports to his steward several times."

"Yes, I remember you, Mr. Stafford." The guard gave them a nod. "Go ahead."

Issachar grasped Dunwoody's arm, and the two hurried silently from the room. As they quick marched through a corridor, Dunwoody whispered, "You seem to be thinking clearly now."

"Your idea worked." Issachar slid a small brass frame from his trousers pocket—a photo of a bride wearing a traditional wedding gown. "When Broder objected that you didn't tell him about a gift, I saw Drexel in his eyes. I heard Drexel in his voice. There's no doubt about it. The malevolence was like a fingerprint—unique and unmistakable."

"Good. Then my theory is correct that exposing him can break the hypnosis. We must alert the king before Drexel gains control of the entire military."

"But how? People here don't know Drexel, so they won't be able to recognize him."

"Then we'll have to employ a different stratagem."

"What stratagem?"

"One I will soon formulate." Dunwoody slowed to a walk, withdrew his Starlighter journal, and began leafing through the pages. "We will have to rely on wisdom from the past."

"Earlier you mentioned a wedding, and Drexel said something about the father of the bride. What's really going on?"

"I apologize for not letting you know more. Since you have been, shall we say, preoccupied, I wasn't comfortable with telling you my plan."

"Very well. What is it?"

Dunwoody pinched Issachar's lapel. "You are the father of the bride in a phony wedding. Adrian and Marcelle are on their way here to act as the blessed couple."

"Interesting, but how will that help us?"

Dunwoody touched a page in his journal. "If you'll remember, only dragon fire can kill a male Starlighter. That's how Marcelle vanquished Leo. So we'll have Arxad close by while the wedding takes place."

"Arxad? Where is he now?"

Dunwoody glanced upward. "Perhaps flying here with Adrian and Marcelle at this very moment."

"I see. Well, hiding a dragon is far easier said than done. How will we get him into the palace?"

"As I said, I am formulating the plan. I didn't say it lacked holes."

"Chasms, if you'll pardon me."

"Of course, as long as you'll help me shovel ideas into the chasm." Dunwoody flipped a page in his notebook and pointed at an entry. "Here is another potential hole. Although Drexel doesn't know our plan, a Starlighter is able to leech thoughts from the minds of those in his presence, which is why I kept it a secret from you until now. He has already learned from my mind that you are the father of the bride. This fact alone will alert him that Adrian and Marcelle are coming."

Issachar nodded. "Yet, he doesn't know that they will come here with a dragon. Therefore, since you and I are the only ones who know about Arxad, we need to stay away from Drexel until we spring the trap."

"True, my friend, but I fear that he might deduce our plan to call upon Arxad's assistance." Dunwoody heaved a sigh. "We must, however, press on. Perhaps the king will help us build a trap that Drexel cannot avoid no matter what he knows."

When they arrived at the king's chambers, Dunwoody cleared his throat. "Are you ready to perform our duet?"

"What do you have in mind? It has to be something that sounds original, something children would have written."

"Do you remember the ditty you and I used to sing together during our grade school years?"

Issachar groaned. "Not the barnyard song! We would have to do the animal noises."

"You're the one who mentioned a duet," Dunwoody said. "Do you have another one in mind?"

"No. I suggested a duet so I could come with you."

"Then practice your quacking, Mr. Duck. It's the only song we have."

✶ TWENTY-THREE ✶

ADRIAN clutched Arxad's spine and held on tightly. To the rear, Regina and Marcelle sat in the next gap, both hanging on to a spine. A rising Solarus provided a stunning backdrop, framing the two female riders in hues of orange and pink though not yet providing any warmth. Fortunately, patience and wisdom held sway last night, and they had taken a meal and slept for a while before departing. Everyone felt rested and energized, ready to fly toward their date with Drexel.

Arxad carried two garment bags in his claws, one containing Marcelle's bridal gown and a dress for Regina and the other Adrian's suit along with various toiletries they would need for cleaning up after the flight.

Below, clouds obscured the ground. Arxad had decided to fly above the misty bank to keep their approach secret, but the altitude and a brisk autumn wind raised quite a shiver. Earlier, they had merely washed their extremities and cleansed their wounds in Nelson's Creek instead of fully bathing. Adding wetness to the buffeting breeze would have chilled them to the bone.

Arxad curled his neck and breathed hot, dry air across Marcelle and Regina.

Regina laughed. "That feels good!"

"I am glad I could provide some comfort." Arxad's ears flattened. "According to the directions you provided, we should be close to our destination. I will drop below the clouds just long enough for you to verify our location."

"I'll do my best," Adrian said. "The king's palace should stand out well enough."

"Once we determine that we are within walking distance, I will search for a secluded place to land, perhaps a forest clearing. This will mean sharp drops and turns, so please prepare yourselves."

All three latched on to the spines more tightly. "Ready," Adrian said.

Marcelle and Regina echoed his call.

"Descending now." Arxad angled his wings. His huge body slowly eased down into the clouds. After several seconds, he broke through.

Although the blanket above veiled Solarus, dawn's rays provided enough light to see the landscape below. Adrian scanned the squared-off farmlands and humble cottages. Dirt roads divided the plots in straight though not quite parallel lines. The roads drew closer together as they converged upon a village where the buildings grew in height toward a massive edifice at the center.

"There's the palace," Adrian shouted, pointing at a twenty-degree angle to the right. "It's hard to be sure, but I think we're about five miles away. If you could land somewhere within a mile, we could walk from there."

"You could walk that far, but we dragons have a harder time with ground travel." Arxad shifted his direction toward the palace. "Hang on. I see a suitable place."

Once again, the passengers tightened their grips. Arxad ascended into the clouds and flew in the mist, preventing any view of the ground or sky. After several minutes, he folded in his wings and dove at a sharp angle.

When they broke through again, the castle came into view nearly directly below. They plunged straight toward it like a falling hailstone. Finally, Arxad stretched out his wings and caught the air, making his powerful canopies billow.

Adrian's body pressed against Arxad's back. Marcelle grunted. Regina squeaked. Beating his wings mightily, Arxad landed on the highest flat portion of the palace's roof, a patio nestled between two spires that seemed to sprout from the surface, wide at the bottom and pointed at the top, maybe fifty feet higher up.

"This should work well." Arxad lay on his belly and stretched out his neck. "I think the villagers will not be able to see me now."

"Perfect." Adrian slid down Arxad's side to the flat stone roof, then helped Regina and Marcelle dismount.

Marcelle pointed at one of the spires. "A door. Let's hope it's unlocked."

"Who could get up here to break in?" Adrian turned the knob and pushed the door open, revealing a downward spiraling stairway immediately inside. "Much too narrow for a dragon."

"I will stay here for now," Arxad said. "Considering the poor weather conditions, I assume no one will venture to the roof. When you find your compatriots and learn what is afoot, kindly return to me so that I may be informed."

Adrian nodded. "I'll see if we can find a leg of lamb or something for you to eat."

"Thank you. The dried fish from your commune and the few I caught in the creek were helpful, but they did not last long. After the infusion of pheterone, my metabolism rate is quite high, and the flight increased it."

"Then we'll try to bring the whole lamb." Adrian picked up the garment bags, withdrew a silver glow stick from a pouch on the side, and shook it. "Let's go."

He led the way into the spire and down the stairwell, holding the glow stick out in front as he followed the clockwise spiral. With every turn, the surrounding plaster-coated cylinder widened, as if the conical spire extended downward inside the palace.

After the sixth revolution, the stairway ended at a door. Adrian stopped, pulled it open a crack, and peered through the gap. A short corridor intersected with what appeared to be another corridor, maybe ten steps away. No one was in sight.

"Quiet now." Gesturing for Marcelle and Regina to follow, Adrian pulled the door the rest of the way and padded into the corridor. When the three had gathered, he sniffed deeply. A faint hint of perfume hung in the air along with moisture—warm and inconsistent. An indoor bath lay somewhere nearby. If he were to follow the sensations, they could probably find it and get cleaned up, but it would be better to locate Marcelle's father and Professor Dunwoody first. Then they could explore freely as special guests.

He whispered, "Wait here," walked to the end of the corridor, and peered around a corner. At the end of the new corridor, a man in a Tark uniform passed through an open set of double doors, closed them, and walked toward Adrian, a sword in a hip scabbard.

Adrian laid the garment bags down, unbuckled his sword belt, and took in a breath. This had to work.

He stepped into the open. "Excuse me, sir."

The Tark halted within a few steps, blinking. "Yes?"

Adrian extended the belt, the scabbard dangling. "I am a guest here, and I forgot to ask if I should leave my weapon somewhere."

"Registered guests are allowed to keep swords at their sides." The guard tilted his head. "Who are you, and why are you in the king's residence area?"

"Formal introductions can come later." Adrian offered a shallow bow. "I am to be wed here this evening, but I think the many hallways and turns have confused me."

"Ah! The special wedding guest! Of course. Of course." The guard scanned Adrian from head to toe. "It looks like you have had a long journey."

"I have." Adrian spied Marcelle creeping closer, Regina tagging along. He gestured for them to come. "My bride-to-be and my sister are with me, and we would like to find a place to clean up."

When Marcelle and Regina entered the corridor, Adrian touched each of them on the shoulder in turn. "My bride-to-be and my sister."

"I am Sergeant Wilton." The guard gave them a head bow, then eyed Marcelle. "Were you in a battle?"

"Please pardon my appearance." She brushed her trousers, then gripped the hilt of her sword. "I carry a weapon to ward off beasts. It was a harrowing journey filled with many dangers, so I suffered a number of wounds."

The guard chuckled. "The beasts in your path should run for their lives."

Marcelle's grip tightened, but her voice stayed calm. "Including the two-legged variety."

The guard cleared his throat. "Yes ... well ... in any case, after I escort you to the bath area, I will inform the other guests that you have arrived."

"The other guests?" Adrian asked.

"Four of them. The bride's father, the governor of Mesolantrum, the governor's liaison, and the governor's lady friend. I just escorted the governor and his friend to General Brock for some sort of briefing, and I was on my way to see about the king. He wasn't feeling well." The guard looked at Marcelle, narrowing his eyes. "Since your father is from Mesolantrum and you arrived in a separate conveyance, I assume you hail from a different region."

"I was born in Mesolantrum," Marcelle said in a formal tone, "but I most recently came from a faraway land. I assume we will be introduced at the wedding, so our story will be told to everyone at once." She sniffed her own shoulder and wrinkled her nose. "For now, however, we would like to get cleaned up, so if you could find my father and let him know we've arrived, I would appreciate it very much."

"Stay here, and I will fetch the bath attendants. Then I will inform your father." The guard pivoted and began walking away.

"What about checking on the king's health?" Adrian called.

"My understanding is that the bride's father is with the king, so I will be able to complete both tasks at the same time."

The guard passed through the double doors again. When they closed with an echoing click, Adrian turned to Marcelle. "Drexel's with one of the generals."

"I heard. That means it'll be us and a dragon against Drexel and the entire Tarkton army."

"And since Wilton made the attachment between you and your father, Drexel will figure out that we're here." Adrian rebuckled his sword belt and picked up the garment bags. "Let's keep moving forward with our plans and see what your father and Professor Dunwoody know."

Regina pulled Adrian's sleeve. "If you'll get me close to Drexel, maybe I can figure out what he's up to. I can gather tales from his mind."

"Good idea." Adrian laid a hand on Regina's shoulder. "We'll all get cleaned up and dressed so we'll look like dignitaries. Then we'll try to find Drexel."

Marcelle straightened her tunic. "I didn't bring anything besides my bridal gown. I expected to wear what I have on until I changed into it."

"If you ask, I'm sure they'll launder your clothes while you and Regina bathe."

"And then everyone will stare at the trousers-clad bride-to-be." Marcelle shrugged. "I suppose it's the only way that makes sense."

After several minutes, a stout woman with curly gray hair bustled through the double doors. "Here you are!" She stopped and took Marcelle's hand, then Regina's. "Come with me. You, too, good sir." As she led them through the doorway, she chattered nonstop. "My name is Nancy, the king's head concierge. We are so excited to have you as guests. I apologize for taking so long, but I sent two staff members to begin heating water for your baths. Water from the pump is cold this time of year, so it takes quite some time to get it to a comfortable bathing temperature even over a blazing fire."

They turned into a side alcove, passing under a high arch. Nancy pointed to the right. "The gentleman will go in there."

Adrian extended the garment bags. "Clothes for all of us are in these."

"Including my bridal gown." Marcelle touched her tunic. "Could you launder these clothes while I bathe? I can wear them until it's time for the wedding."

"I should say not." Nancy clicked her tongue. "I will find appropriate dresses for you and the little miss, and we'll look after your wedding ensembles as well. If anything needs cleaning or pressing, we'll take care of it." She took the garment bags and nodded toward each direction in turn. "Go on, now. You'll find a staff member inside to assist you, and we will bring your clothes when they're ready."

"Where will we meet after the bath?" Marcelle asked.

"Your bath assistant will escort you to the ballroom. You'll meet there."

Marcelle withdrew a small pouch from a garment bag and blew Adrian a kiss. "See you soon."

He grabbed the kiss out of the air and applied it to his cheek. "I'll count the seconds."

Nancy's smile broadened. "Oh, I just love weddings!"

After retrieving his own toiletry pouch, Adrian walked between two curtains and into a steamy room where a large mirror dominated a plaster wall on one side. Shelves lined the opposite wall, holding towels and various glass bottles. A thin old man wearing a black smock stood next to a white tub. He poured water from a metal pot, holding its wooden handle with one hand and supporting the bottom with a fibrous rag. As the water flowed, white vapor billowed, coating the mirror with a moisture glaze.

Adrian bowed his head. "How do you do? I'm the groom for tonight's wedding."

The man shook his head. "No hear," he said in a gravelly voice.

Adrian nodded. As he undressed, he took inventory of his clothing and accessories. With so many rips and holes in tunics and trousers, it was no wonder the guard suggested that it had been a long journey.

He felt for the crystalline wafer in an insert in his belt—still there and unbroken. In the next few hours it could come in handy.

After laying his clothes in a pile and setting his belt on a backless bench that abutted a wall, and after using a chamber pot in a small alcove, he picked up a bar of soap from his pouch and climbed into the tub.

The attendant snatched the soap. "Harsh." He walked to one of the shelves, grabbed a bottle half-filled with a semitransparent blue liquid, and poured most of it into the bathwater. "For the groom. Smells sweet. Softens skin."

Adrian nodded again and settled into the hot, soothing mixture. The attendant showed him a sponge and raised his brow. "You or me?"

Adrian pointed at himself, took the sponge, and dipped it into the water.

The attendant touched another pot at the side of the tub. "For rinsing."

After nodding once more, Adrian glanced at a series of hooks on the wall, probably designed for hanging garments. Maybe the attendant would bring his wedding attire and hang it there, but it wouldn't do any good to ask about it.

The attendant scooped up Adrian's dirty clothes and walked toward the curtains, calling, "Back soon."

For the next few minutes, Adrian scrubbed every inch of his body, careful to brush his wounds gently. The gash near his stomach still oozed a bit, so a bandage might be necessary to keep blood from seeping into his suit.

After washing his hair and rinsing, Adrian walked to a shelf, picked up a towel, and dried off. He wrapped the towel around his waist and fished a brush from his pouch. With moisture still thick in the air, vapor fogged the mirror, forcing him to brush his hair without a clear view.

As he continued, he glanced at the curtains every few seconds. When would the attendant return? He had said *soon*, but what did that mean? A few minutes? An hour? Maybe the typical palace resident soaked in a long, luxurious bath, a treat no one in the Mesolantrum communes ever enjoyed. There was always too much work to do.

When Adrian finished brushing, he sat on the bench. Warm air wafted up from a vent in the floor, caressing his legs. At least the wait would be comfortable. Maybe a huge furnace burned stacks of wood in a basement somewhere, supplying heat throughout the palace. In Mesolantrum, extane heaters warmed the governor's abode, but the gas was rarer here in Tarkton, so they probably resorted to a more primitive fuel.

For the next several minutes, Adrian alternately sat or walked around the spacious bath chamber, feeling the walls and their varying textures and temperatures as he painted a mental picture of the construction behind each surface. Apparently the room shared a wall with the ladies' chamber, the uniform temperature across the surface giving evidence that warm air circulated on the other side.

Adrian knocked on the wall. "Marcelle, can you hear me?"

A muffled voice replied. "Yes."

"Any sign of your attendant?"

"None. And we've been finished for a while."

"Put on a towel and meet me at the curtains to the corridor." Adrian walked to the exit curtain and peeked out. No one stood in the alcove or anywhere within sight.

Marcelle's eyes appeared between the curtains on the ladies' side. "I'm here."

"Have you heard anything about our clothes?"

"Nothing. Regina and I were just talking about it. When Nancy left, I asked her how long it would take, but she was evasive."

Regina's voice piped up from behind the curtain. "I read a tale in her mind. She was with a group of people in a big room, and they were all listening to a red-haired man speaking, but I couldn't understand what he was saying."

Adrian nodded. "That meeting was probably the real reason it took so long for her to show up in the first place." He tightened the towel and tucked the end at his waist. He then stalked back to the bench, fastened on his sword belt, and marched into the alcove. "Now I'm sure Drexel knows we're here."

"So what do we do now?" Marcelle asked, still behind the curtain.

"I have to find our clothes, then Professor Dunwoody and your father."

"You can't go looking for our clothes dressed like that."

"Do you have another idea?"

"Just one." After a few seconds, Marcelle walked out, a towel wrapped around her body from her armpits down to the middle of her thighs. With her own sword belt over the towel and her hair wet and slicked down, she gave him a firm nod. "We'll go together."

"What about me?" Regina walked between the curtains, a towel loosely hanging around her scant waist. "I can't stay here by myself."

"You'll come with us." Marcelle hiked Regina's towel up to her armpits, covering her body down to her knees, and tied it securely. "Let's go."

Adrian took Regina's hand and whispered, "Let me know if you sense anyone's thoughts. We need to find our clothes and avoid anyone who might be looking for us."

She nodded. "Okay."

The trio walked along a corridor, passing rooms with closed doors on each side. Regina angled her head from time to time, as if listening. After a few moments, she stopped at a door and laid a palm on it. "Nancy's in here."

Footsteps pounded nearby, loud and fast.

"Someone's coming," Marcelle said.

Adrian glanced left and right down the corridor, but the echoing sounds seemed to be coming from both directions. "No time to knock!"

* * * * * *

Drexel studied a map of the kingdom spread across a table in the palace's war room. Twin busts of King Popperell, Sasser's late father, held the map's edges, keeping it from rolling up. As Sophia ran a hand along one bust's pure white marble, it looked as if she were caressing the face of a ghost.

General Brock, a hefty, bearded man in his fifties, pointed at Mesolantrum, a region southwest of Tarkton on the map. "The cost of rebuilding is incalculable, so when I report to the king—"

"There is no need to report to the king." Drexel stared straight into Brock's eyes. "Am I right?"

The telltale glaze washed over Brock's pupils. "You're right. Of course you're right."

"Good. Now back to the problem at hand. I saw the devastation in your scout's photo tube, but the angles made it difficult to determine the extent of the damage."

"It's quite extensive." Brock touched the palace site. "The damage runs from here …" He ran his thick, hairy finger along a straight line, brushing his orange-and-black sleeve across the paper. "To here. The palace is roughly fifty percent destroyed, and my scout reports that the dungeon has been obliterated. The gas reserves have burned along with the distribution equipment. You have lost your most valuable trading commodity, and it will take months to rebuild your infrastructure. The upper classes will be without extane, so there will be no fuel to drive their pumps. They will have to fetch water from the public wells the old-fashioned way."

"Might your soldiers be able to come to our aid?"

"Of course I will send who we can spare, but the savages in the northern colonies have been massing at the border. They are of no concern if I have my full force on hand, but if I send more than a few to Mesolantrum, we could be vulnerable."

"I understand." Drexel focused on the dungeon area, a tiny gray dot on the map's white background. "My bigger problem is that these events are a sign that the returning slaves have escaped. They likely caused the explosions."

Brock's brow lifted. "Really? Diseased, half-starved slaves?"

"Not alone, to be sure. Certain people who went to Dracon to free them have returned, usurped the seat of power, and taken over. I saw two of the culprits in the photo tube, Edison and Frederick Masters."

"Then you will need a considerable force to take Mesolantrum back."

Drexel nodded. "Unless you can think of another option."

"You could simply wait here. It wouldn't take many men to enforce a blockade to quarantine the people within Mesolantrum. When the disease has run its course and most of your opponents have died, you could return and clean up the mess. By that time, perhaps the threat on the northern boundary will ease, and we will be able to send enough troops to enforce your will upon the survivors."

"Perhaps," Drexel said, "but the rebels have a dragon friend who will likely fight for them, a terrible lizard named Arxad. In fact, since Adrian Masters is here, I am concerned that he might have brought Arxad with him to try to destroy me, and I have sensed a powerful, nonhuman mind nearby, which gives credence to my suspicions."

"Why? What quarrel does the Masters family have with you?"

"Well …" Drexel glanced at Sophia. She gripped the bust tightly, as if nervous about the conversation, but there was no need to involve her. Avoidance of the issue might work as well as a lie.

"It would be unseemly for me to air Mesolantrum's political laundry here and unnecessarily sully a good name. I hope you will simply do your duty and guard the king and his palace from a potential insurrection. A wedding ceremony is a perfect ambush scenario. They might think I will be relaxed and unprepared for an attack, especially by a dragon."

"Indeed." Brock nodded gravely. "We have no experience with fighting a dragon. My men have courage, but in the face of a fire-breathing monster, I think they would run for cover with me close at their heels."

"Then we should consider how to prevent an attack from occurring."

Brock laughed. "Shall I construct a scarecrow for a dragon? Call it a scaredragon?"

"Amusing ..." Drexel paced. "If Arxad really is here, how could we know for certain? By what means would we trap him? He is quite clever."

"Rats are too smart for traps," Brock said, "so we kill them by poisoning the bait."

"Bait?" Drexel halted and stroked his chin. "If a dragon flew here after helping in a battle against my forces in Mesolantrum, he will be very hungry."

"No doubt." Brock folded his arms across his chest. "What do you have in mind?"

"Where would he get a substantial amount of food in a place he is unfamiliar with?"

"Our chef is preparing a feast. Surely this Masters fellow will guess that."

Drexel looked toward the planning room's closed door. "Then I should pay a visit to the chef. But assuming my suspicions are correct, I will need some kind of poison for whatever they decide to serve the dragon."

"Poison?" Brock shook his head. "I have some for the tips of arrows, but I have no idea if it's enough to kill a dragon. Besides, it is quite bitter. He would detect it long before consuming enough to kill him."

"How about a sleep inducer?" Sophia asked. "The palace physician should have several options."

Brock pressed his lips together. "I know of such a drug—odorless and tasteless. But we still won't know the proper amount to put him to sleep or how long it would take to work."

"Or how long he would remain asleep," Drexel added.

Brock laughed under his breath. "Well, that part won't matter. Once he is asleep, you can kill him."

"Spoken by a man who has never tried to kill a dragon."

Brock furrowed his brow. "What do you mean?"

Drexel touched his stomach. "The only spot vulnerable to a sword is a small region on the underbelly. Dragons tend to sleep on it in order to protect themselves. Even if it is exposed, you get only one try. If you don't plunge deeply enough, the dragon will awaken and kill you with a single blast of fire. Besides, we won't be the ones feeding him, so we won't have access to him when he falls asleep."

"I see," Brock said, nodding. "What do you propose?"

"The ideal situation is to capture the dragon while he is asleep. If I can be present when he awakens and is still groggy, I could absorb his power and become stronger than he is."

"How will you find him?"

"We will persuade Adrian Masters to tell us where Arxad is. All we have to do is capture his bride-to-be and threaten her."

"Very well." Brock walked toward the door. "I will procure the sleep drug."

"And I will visit the chef." Drexel followed the general, but Sophia pulled his arm, stopping him.

"Can we talk for a moment?" she asked.

Drexel glanced at her, then at the general. "Go ahead, General. Meet me at the kitchen with the drug."

"I'll see you there." Brock exited and closed the door.

Drexel looked at Sophia, tapping his shoe on the floor. "What is it?"

"Well ..." She ran a finger along his sleeve, following it with her eyes. "I was wondering, after this is all over and you're back in Mesolantrum as the rightful governor, what will you do with me?"

"Do with you? What do you mean?"

She looked up at him. "I mean, will I still be at your side?"

"Well, of course. I'm sure I will need a knowledgeable spokesperson who can manage the politics for me."

"By politics, I assume you mean deception."

"Politics and deception are practically synonyms."

"They have been synonyms, to be sure. Past governors of Mesolantrum have proven that." She firmed her lips for a moment before continuing. "I've been willing to lie in order to help elevate you to the governor's seat, but once you're in power, you won't need me anymore. That's why I asked about your plans for me."

"Ah! I see. A fair question." Drexel lifted his brow. "What office would you like? Head of our education initiatives, perhaps?"

She averted her eyes. "Do you really want to know?"

"Of course. Otherwise I wouldn't have asked."

"In the interest of complete frankness ..." She slid her arms under his outer tunic and around his waist, then kissed him softly on the lips. When she drew away, she kept her arms in place and pressed her body close. "I want to be your wife."

"My ... my wife?" Drexel's head grew lighter. His skin seemed to burn, starting at his hips where her body contacted his and radiating up and down. "I ... I don't know what to say. I am flattered, to be sure."

"Just speak the truth, as always." She withdrew a hand, grabbed his wrist, and pulled his arm around her back. "Do you find me desirable?"

"Well, yes, of course." Sweat dampened his forehead. "Only a fool wouldn't. You are a very attractive young lady."

Her smile widened. "Then show me. Here. Now. We can lock the door." She pushed her hand under his tunic again, then stopped. "What's this?" Blinking, she drew back, pinching a severed finger.

She shrieked and dropped it. "What? ... Whose?" She swallowed, her eyes blazing with alarm. "What did you do?"

Drexel reached out to her, but she shuffled back and swallowed again, steadying her voice. "Where did you get that finger?"

"Sophia, I ..." His throat tightened. "I ..."

He reached out again, but she slapped his hand away. "Don't touch me!"

"Sophia, why are you frightened? The woman who once owned that finger died many years ago."

Her face flushed. "Did ... did you kill her?"

Drexel bent over, picked up the finger, and slid it back into his tunic pocket. "Why do you insist on cornering me with such a question?"

"You did kill her, didn't you?" She backed away again and bumped into the map table. "Didn't you!"

He spoke in a matter-of-fact tone. "I severed four fingers from each hand and used them as genetic keys to open a portal to Dracon. If I hadn't done so, I wouldn't have been able to enter that world in my quest to ... to ..."

She walked slowly sideways, edging her way toward the end of the table. "To what?"

"To bring a slave child home so I could be viewed as a hero."

"So you could get a reward." Her fingers inched toward the king's bust. "You weren't really interested in rescuing any children."

Drexel raised a hand. "Sophia, don't try it."

"You'll kill me if I don't."

"I had not even considered killing you." Drexel aimed his palm at her. She knew about the murder, so she had to be eliminated, regardless of her value. "Until now."

She lunged for the bust and lifted it with both hands. As the map rolled up on the table, she staggered under the bust's weight and dropped it to the floor. She let out a scream.

Drexel leaped and slapped a hand over her mouth. As she struggled, her cries muffled by his palm, he concentrated on the connection point. His hand strengthened, allowing his grip around her face to tighten. Color drained from her cheeks. Energy surged up his arm, rippling through every muscle.

Sophia's cries faded. Now as pale as the bust, she sank to her knees.

Drexel released her and stepped back, but the energy connection between his palm and her body stayed intact. More power flowed. Ecstasy surged. He heaved in breaths, barely able to restrain a cry of exhilaration.

He doubled his concentration, drawing more and more of Sophia's life energy. Her arms shriveled to bones and prunish skin. Hair fell from her scalp and slid down her body. Her face shrank to a leatherlike mask, little more than a skull with bulging eyes and a mouth agape in terror.

She toppled to the side. Her arm snapped. When her face struck the floor, her jaw shattered. She panted, her tongue hanging out. Then after a final gasp, she breathed no more.

Drexel lowered his arm. His palm burned, but it felt good, so very good. Every muscle flexed with vitality. He clenched a fist, feeling the tightness in his fingers. With this kind of power, who could ever withstand him? Even though he could not lie, why would it ever matter? An invincible man could say whatever he pleased.

He picked up King Popperell's bust and set it on the table. Soon King Sasser would fall, but for now patience was in order. He nudged Sophia with a shoe. A rib cracked. Her bones were so fragile getting rid of her body wouldn't be difficult.

He knelt, grasped a sleeve and her skirt, and folded her crackling body in, careful to sweep stray hairs with it. When he finished, he rose to his feet, clutched a gathered portion of the material, and lifted the collection of bones and flesh with his newly energized hand.

Letting out a tsking sound, he walked toward the door. Such a pity. Sophia held great promise. If only she hadn't raised so many questions. But now her beautiful new outfit would become her shroud and coffin, unless the birds in the forest could find anything worth pecking.

✹ TWENTY-FOUR ✹

ADRIAN opened Nancy's door, ushered Marcelle and Regina in, and closed it behind them. Nancy stood next to a poster bed, laying the two garment bags across the mattress.

"Oh!" She covered her mouth and backed away toward the far wall. "What are you doing here?"

A parade of tromping boots hustled by the door and quickly faded.

"As if you didn't know." Marcelle drew her sword, marched straight to Nancy, and touched the point of the blade to her throat. "Who ordered you to delay our clothes?"

Nancy trembled. "Your wedding dress had a slight tear, so I mended it. I apologize for taking so long, but I wanted it to look perfect. And only moments ago I found a dress that might fit you and put it in your garment bag. I hoped you would take longer in the bath, since the wedding isn't until evening."

"If that's so …" Marcelle gestured with her head toward the door. "Who is out there now trying to find us?"

"No one. I heard that the king commanded his entire company of bodyguards to come to his chambers, so they're probably the ones who just ran by."

"Really?" Marcelle returned her sword to its scabbard. "I have a hard time believing that you would leave us so long without clothing or at least an explanation from an attendant."

"You're right. I should have sent someone with a message." Nancy wrung her hands. "I hope you'll accept my sincere apologies."

Adrian withdrew the crystalline wafer from his belt and laid it in his palm where he alone could see it. "Tell me again, Nancy, who were those people who just ran by?"

"Like I said, I assume they were the king's bodyguards, though I can't be sure."

The wafer shimmered with bright light. The radiance stung Adrian's skin but not badly. "Were you in a meeting with the new governor of Mesolantrum?"

She nodded. "Everyone in the king's staff attended a brief reception with him."

Again the wafer glowed brightly. Marcelle joined Adrian at his side and looked at the crystal.

"Did the governor tell you to do anything?" Adrian asked.

Nancy shook her head. "Nothing. It was just an introduction."

The wafer turned gray, then black.

"You're lying," Marcelle said.

"How dare you accuse me of lying!" Nancy let out a huff. "Two strangers from another land come to the king's palace, one of them a woman dressed like a thuggish man and wielding a sword, then they barge into my private room uninvited and half-naked and accuse me of lying!" She tilted her head upward. "We're not accustomed to such boorish behavior here."

"Boorish? Thuggish?" Marcelle touched the hilt of her sword, her face reddening. "Maybe another visit with this blade will get your forked tongue to work without spewing more lies."

"You are such a rude—"

A new voice crackled in the room. "Of course you will show your usual hospitality to these guests." Out of nowhere, a red-headed man appeared next to Nancy, a hand on his chest as he took on an orator's posture. "If these guests are who I think they are, they deserve all the respect and honor you can provide, so I ask only that you delay them as much as you can. Give them comfort, but ensure that they stay in the palace until I send someone to escort them to the festival hall."

The man faded until he disappeared.

"Drexel," Marcelle growled.

"Well!" Nancy rubbed her hands along her dress as if smoothing wrinkles. "I see that our guests are not only rude and boorish; they practice sorcery."

"Who is the sorceress?" Marcelle whipped out her sword. "The truth teller or the liar?"

"The woman who refuses to revere her femininity." Nancy's tone lowered to a spite-filled growl. "Everyone knows that a sorceress would wear trousers, wield a sword, or even prance around naked to seduce her victims."

"Seduce her victims!" Marcelle pointed the sword at her. "Listen, you snobbish hen! If you think—"

"Marcelle." Adrian grabbed her arm. "It's not worth it. We have too much to do." He slid the crystalline wafer into his belt. "Let's get dressed."

Marcelle threw her sword onto the bed and unbuckled her belt, a scowl still bending her features. "Regina and I will stay here while you dress at the baths. Since those guards are long gone, it should be safe to go there."

"Let's hope so." Adrian picked up his garment bag. "Back in a couple of minutes." He jogged out the door and hurried to the bath chamber. After taking a deep breath, he put on his wedding suit—a white flowing shirt overlaid by a tan vest with dark brown trim. Dark laces crisscrossed the vest from waist level to about two-thirds of the way up, leaving the neckline loose and comfortable. The trousers, also dark brown, fit loosely as well, allowing freedom of movement, which might come in handy in a fight.

He held the sword belt around his waist but didn't allow it to touch his clothes. With blood and dirt spattering the leather, it would surely soil the finery.

He unbuckled the scabbard, dropped the belt, and washed the outside of the scabbard. Inside the bag, he found a new belt and looked it over—no scabbard strap. He fastened it to his waist, slid the scabbard behind the belt, and put on the final article of clothing—a dark leather jacket with knobby buttons and a high collar.

After fastening all but the top button, he stepped in front of the mirror. The outfit looked great, but the sword balanced awkwardly, lifting the hem of the jacket. Still, it would have to do.

He retrieved the crystalline wafer, pushed it into his trousers pocket, and stowed his old belt on a shelf, covering it with his towel. He then hurried back to Nancy's room and knocked on the door. It opened seconds later, revealing Marcelle and Regina, both wearing satiny dresses that brushed the floor, Regina in deep purple and Marcelle in royal blue. Gold bands wrapped their biceps, and bell sleeves flowed down to their ankles. Nancy sat on the bed behind them, her arms crossed and her lips tight.

Marcelle walked closer to Adrian. Her dress fit snugly to her narrow waist, and her gait made the dress sweep elegantly with her gliding form. "How do you like it?"

Adrian's throat tightened. "I …" He coughed. "I think you look like an angel."

"An angel?" Marcelle spun in place, making her dress twirl. "I thought maybe I resembled Cassabrie and her blue cloak."

Adrian took her hand and kissed her fingers. "Cassabrie is a brilliant star, but you are brighter still. Your beauty is an artistic masterpiece."

"Well!" Smiling, Marcelle caressed the bodice. "I could get used to this dress-wearing business."

Regina gave her own dress a twirl. "I've never worn anything so beautiful!"

"And your smile makes you even more beautiful." Adrian stepped nearly toe-to-toe with Marcelle and whispered, "Any more revelations from our little Starlighter?"

Marcelle shook her head. "It seems that Nancy has learned to close her mind to Regina's probing. Seeing her thoughts come to life must have clued her in."

"Understood." Adrian stepped around Marcelle and walked casually toward Nancy. "Would you be so kind as to lead us to the king's chamber? We heard that Marcelle's father is there."

Nancy firmed her chin. "I most certainly will not."

Adrian glanced at Marcelle. Normally a refusal like that would have been followed by the zing of her sword zipping from its scabbard, but she simply crossed her arms and frowned.

"Then we'll have to provide a bit of persuasion." Adrian grasped Nancy's forearm and pulled her to her feet. "You lead. We'll follow. No one gets hurt. Understand?"

"Boorish thugs!" Nancy let out a huff and stalked toward the door, leaving Marcelle's garment bag on the bed.

"Wait." Adrian touched the bag. "Marcelle, do you need this?"

"Eventually. My wedding gown is in there."

"And your scabbard?"

"It's in the bag. I thought it would look tacky with this dress."

"We'd better take it now." He picked the bag up and draped it over his shoulder. "Let's go."

With another huff, Nancy walked out of the room and through the corridor. Adrian and company followed close behind. The hall widened and led down a marble stairway, then onto a wide expanse lined with busts resting on chest-high pedestals. Framed artwork hung on every wall, and full statues of nude and nearly nude men and women stood here and there, each one painted garishly, as if the colors had been chosen by a drunken clown.

Ivory tapers burned in candelabras on tables, shelves, and metal fixtures hanging from the ceiling, casting flickering light over the exhibits and making them look all the more eerie.

As they walked past a statue depicting a close dance between a green-and-purple man and a red-and-black woman, both dressed only in tiny loin cloths, Adrian said to Nancy, "Is this a museum?"

"Yes," she said coldly. "Some of our finest artwork resides here."

Adrian gave the dancing couple another glance as they passed by. "And you think we were strange for wearing towels."

"This is art, not a ribald display of prurient exhibitionism."

"Actually," Adrian said, "I think this defines the phrase you just used."

Nancy lifted her nose higher. "Do you think I care about the opinion of riffraff like you?"

"Not really, but this so-called art does give me some insight into how weak-minded people are so easily controlled."

"Humpf!" Pumping her fists, she picked up her pace, her considerable weight making her look like a flustered duck waddling to escape a whipping.

At the end of the room, a new corridor led into another section of the palace. Two guards stood at the arched entry to the corridor, each carrying a spear.

Nancy leaped ahead, shouting, "Help! These foreigners are threatening me!"

The guards pointed their spears at Adrian. "Halt!" one of them barked.

Adrian raised his hands. "This woman is mad! I am the groom for the wedding this evening, and she was escorting us to meet with the bride's father." He nodded at Marcelle, who dipped into a not-so-graceful curtsy.

"He speaks the truth, good sirs," Marcelle said. "We would be mad ourselves to think that we could barge through your palace with such threats while men like you are on duty."

"I know Nancy," the guard said. "She's not mad. She's got a good head on her shoulders."

The other guard nodded. "Solid as a rock."

A triumphant smile crossed Nancy's face. "Take them to the magistrate."

"Wait!" Regina stepped in front of Adrian and stared at the two guards. She twirled her dress, making the purple satin shimmer in the glow of hundreds of candles. "Michael and Raoul, brothers inseparable, listen to me."

The two guards gawked at her, their eyes wide. Nancy stared as well. Her smile wilted into a flat line.

Regina waved a hand. A woman appeared next to her, tall and stately.

"Hearken unto your mother," Regina said.

The woman, clothed in a simple dress of white linen, smiled. "My good sons, take these visitors straight to where they ask. How many times have I told you to treat guests with the utmost courtesy?"

"Yes, Mum," one of the guards said. "Right away."

The other guard waved a hand. "Follow us, please. The bride's father is in the king's receiving chamber."

"Are we no longer in the king's residence area?" Marcelle asked.

"No. It looks like you just came from that direction. We will take you there another way."

Marcelle glared at Nancy. "I see."

The image of the guards' mother vanished, though they didn't seem to notice. As they marched into the corridor, Adrian, Marcelle, and Regina followed. Nancy stayed put, her mouth agape as she watched them leave.

Still carrying the garment bag, Adrian touched Regina's head and whispered, "Good girl."

She looked up at him and smiled. "That was fun."

The guards led them into a huge room with high ceilings and a majestic pair of doors to the right, perhaps the palace's main entry. They turned left and followed a wide corridor that turned left again, then to the right. Finally, they stopped at a pair of oaken doors with brass knobs.

One of the guards knocked and called out, "The bride and groom have arrived!"

"Send them in!"

The guard opened the door, stepped out of the way, and nodded. "You may enter."

"Thank you." Adrian walked into a spacious room filled with thousands of books stuffed into wall shelves that lined the perimeter from the floor to twice his height. A few steps away, King Sasser sat in a cushioned rocking chair, rocking to the rhythm of his own humming, an ear trumpet propped at the side of his head. Marcelle's father and Professor Dunwoody sat in straight-backed chairs, both tapping their toes.

"Daddy!" Marcelle ran to her father and gave him a hug.

He kissed her cheek, his smile wide. "You look no worse for the wear."

Adrian bowed toward the king. "Greetings, Your Majesty. I am Adrian Masters."

The king waved a hand. "Oh, don't bother with such formalities here. This is my private chamber. Make yourself at home." He adjusted a pair of spectacles on the bridge of his nose and continued rocking, again humming a tune.

"I thought your bodyguards would be here," Adrian said. "We heard them running this way."

"They came to check on me for some odd reason, but I sent them away."

"I assume they were checking to see who was here," Professor Dunwoody said to Adrian. "Perhaps searching for you. If that's the case, then we should vacate this room soon."

"I understand." After introducing Marcelle and Regina, Adrian laid the garment bag over the back of an empty chair. "With all the humming and toe tapping, you three seem to be having a good time."

"Oh, yes," the king said. "These two taught me a new song. Cows and pigs and ducks, complete with authentic sounds. It's delightful."

Adrian smiled. "Well, we could use something to lift our spirits, so maybe one of you can sing—"

"No." Issachar cleared his throat, his face reddening. "Considering the trials awaiting us, we should address those immediately."

"That's fine." Adrian glanced at the door, still closed. No sounds emanated from outside. "First question—do you know what Drexel's up to?"

Professor Dunwoody rose to his feet. "We assume he is working on taking over the king's military forces, so we're considering a strategy to counteract him."

Adrian lifted his brow. "And that is?"

"Dragon fire might be our only reasonable option." Dunwoody looked toward the entry door. "Did you bring Arxad?"

Adrian glanced upward. "He's hiding on the roof, which reminds me, I need to get some food to him. His metabolism is like a furnace right now."

The king rose from his chair. "I will send for a feast."

"But I'll have to take it to him," Adrian said. "We can't let anyone else know he's here."

"Of course. Of course." The king set his trumpet down and clapped his hands three times. Several moments later, the door flew open, revealing a short man wearing a long apron and a chef's hat.

He bowed low, holding his hat in place. "Yes, Your Majesty?"

"Martin, what is the main course for the ball tonight?" The king raised his trumpet again.

Martin straightened and puffed out his chest. "A choice of ox steak, goose, or magna fish. All three will be succulent, tender, and flavorful."

"No doubt. No doubt. But what do you have in the most excess?"

"The magna fish, by far. The trawler crew caught fifteen, each weighing more than a thousand pounds."

"Excellent." The king returned to his chair and began rocking again. "Bring fifty pounds of it here at once."

"Of course, Sire, but I have not broiled it yet. This fish is best served freshly cooked, so I planned to wait for a while longer."

"Raw fish is very popular where I come from," Adrian said. "It's a delicacy."

"Magna fish is quite tasty, even raw …" Martin blinked. "But fifty pounds?"

Adrian rubbed his stomach. "We had a long journey."

"If you say so." Martin shrugged, bowed to the king, and left the room.

When the door closed, Professor Dunwoody began pacing, his hands behind his back. "We have informed His Majesty about Broder's rise to power, his abilities as a Starlighter, and his former identity as Drexel, including Marcelle's accusation that he murdered her mother. Drexel's attempts to influence the king were short-lived. Our king's visual and auditory handicaps have actually been a boon that came in handy when Leo tried to charm him."

"Indeed," the king said. "That rascal was a deceiver, to be sure, so being half blind and deaf had its advantages. I apologize for carting Leo off to Mesolantrum, but Orion assured me that he could handle him."

"We did handle Leo, thank the Creator," Dunwoody continued. "Unfortunately, Drexel appears to be more powerful than Leo, so a simple touch to your hand gave Drexel access to General Brock. We have concluded that Drexel is even now gaining control over the military forces."

Adrian tapped himself on the chest. "And he knows Marcelle and I are here. I'm not sure how he figured it out."

"Not good. Not good." Dunwoody stopped pacing. "Drexel's powers include the ability to gain secrets from unguarded minds, and I'm afraid I was lax for a moment with my own mind. Since Drexel lost control over Issachar, we should be able to contain any other secrets if we are vigilant."

"Does he know about Arxad's presence?"

"I don't think so, though he is smart enough to guess that Arxad might come. A dragon is our only real offensive weapon. He might not be able to defeat the entire Tarkton military, but if he can kill Drexel, perhaps the spell will be broken. The ideal scenario is to expose Drexel before any battle commences so that lives will be spared."

"How do you propose to do that?" Adrian asked.

The king rose again, his trumpet still in place. "We should carry on with the festivities as planned. This Drexel character likely knows that we realize what he is up to, so we must be wary. We don't know who among us is immune to his power, so we should stay away from him until the last moment."

Adrian set a hand on Regina's shoulder. "We have someone who can counteract Drexel's power."

"This lovely little lady?" the king asked. "What can she do?"

"She is a Starlighter."

"A Starlighter?" Dunwoody stooped and looked Regina in the eye. "Miss, have you developed an ability to display tales in such a way that the people in the tales look real?"

She nodded. "I did it just a little while ago. Two men thought their mother was there."

"Excellent! How long can you make a tale last?"

Regina shrugged. "As long as I want, I think."

"But you need a tale from someone's mind or one you have seen yourself. Am I correct?"

She nodded. "Or I can make someone I know move or talk, like I did with Adrian in the dungeon."

"Well, then," Dunwoody continued as he rose, "after I visit the protocol officer to complete the wedding plans, we'll go straight to the ballroom and conduct a rehearsal before the actual event."

"And have Regina watch," Issachar said. "She can replay the rehearsal during the event. The real Adrian and Marcelle will be free to be elsewhere."

Dunwoody clapped his shoulder. "Exactly my thoughts, my friend. It is clear that your mind is as sharp as ever."

"But where is *elsewhere?*" Marcelle asked. "What will we do?"

Dunwoody tapped his chin. "I think we won't know until we see the arrangement of the guests. Drexel will likely invite many soldiers, so it will be necessary to learn where he will stand. The soldiers might make a protective ring around him."

"That won't stop a dragon." Adrian looked at the king. "Is there a way to sneak Arxad into a hiding place close to the ballroom?"

King Sasser put his trumpet down and leaned back in his chair. "The easiest way to sneak something into the palace is to do so in plain view so that no one is suspicious. We'll bring him in through the front door."

"Then we'll ruin the element of surprise," Marcelle said. "Drexel won't come anywhere near Arxad."

The king adjusted his spectacles. "Not if the dragon is a prisoner, a conquered foe on display."

Dunwoody clenched a fist. "Brilliant! Arxad can feign weakness and be presented to the general, who can bring him bound in chains and muzzled, a trophy for the king. At the appropriate time, he can break loose and kill Drexel."

Marcelle shook her head. "No, no, no. We can't risk Arxad's life like that. The general might just try to kill him."

"A fair concern, but Drexel has an incentive to keep Arxad alive." Dunwoody withdrew his notebook, thumbed through it, and stopped at a page near the back. "Here it is." He cleared his throat and read from the page. "Although a male Starlighter is vulnerable to dragon fire, if he were to absorb a dragon's energy, he would be nearly omnipotent. Yet, in order to do so, he must face the dragon eye to eye, a dangerous proposition, so he must gain control of the dragon's faculties before attempting the feat."

Dunwoody closed the notebook and returned it to his pocket. "Although Drexel is a Starlighter, we should not assume that he knows these facts. We will have to ensure that he sees the value in keeping Arxad alive."

"Drexel knows," Adrian said. "Koren heard a white dragon tell him."

"Good. Good. That helps immensely." Dunwoody folded his hands at his waist. "Also, we must ensure that Arxad's bonds are fragile enough to break. If he were to be put into a cage, perhaps the general would think he is sufficiently subdued. He is more than capable of defending himself if necessary."

King Sasser looked toward the ceiling. "How big is this creature? We have a rolling cage for an elephant and a ramp to place over the front stairs."

"From snout to tail?" Adrian tried to imagine Arxad in comparison to an elephant, but the image wouldn't take shape in his mind. "I think he's quite a bit longer than an elephant, but he can curl up. That cage should do just fine."

Marcelle crossed her arms and took on a skeptical posture. "You'd better ask Arxad before you make all these plans. He's not one who would enjoy being on display."

"Of course," Dunwoody said, "but after reading his profound and thought-provoking words about protecting humans from harm in spite of their foolishness, I trust that he will participate in order to put a stop to this madman's schemes."

A knock sounded at the door. "It is Martin, Sire. I have the fish."

"Enter," the king said.

When the door opened, Martin walked in pushing a wheeled cart loaded with slabs of fish, one with a tail still attached. "Shall I slice it into serving portions?"

"We will take care of it, thank you." The king gave Martin a dismissive nod. "And we will look forward to tasting your broiled variety as well. I'm sure it will be delicious, as usual."

With a hint of a smile, Martin bowed and backed toward the door.

Adrian studied the chef's eyes—a bit fogged up. Might he have been in contact with Drexel? Adrian leaned close to the fish and sniffed it. Fishy and quite fresh. No sign of any tainting. It was probably fine.

After Martin left the room, Dunwoody clapped his hands and rubbed them together. "I'm sure the protocol officer is quite frenzied by now, so I will visit her to finish preparations. Adrian will take the fish to Arxad, ask him about our plan to bring him into the palace as a trophy, and then join the rest of us at a rehearsal where Regina will memorize every move. I'm sure the king can tell us where to go to stay out of sight for a while." He scanned the line of people in the room. "Am I missing anything?"

"Just one item." Adrian touched the top slab of fish, wet and slimy, then looked at his fine wedding suit. "Anyone have a basket?"

✷ TWENTY-FIVE ✷

ADRIAN sat against one of the roof spires while Arxad chewed a slab of fish. When he swallowed, a lump traveled down his scaly throat and disappeared into his abdomen. "Ah! That was excellent. And not a hint of tainting. Thank you for the much-needed nourishment."

"You're quite welcome." Adrian rose to his feet and picked up the empty basket. "So what do you think of our plan?"

"It is workable, but only if Drexel is not close to anyone who is aware of it."

"Well, one of us has to deliver you to Drexel. Since I've been heavily exposed to Cassabrie, I'm probably the best option. I am able to resist his probes, but maybe I should take you to the military barracks and avoid Drexel altogether."

"I agree. Let us carry out the plan. The sooner, the better."

Adrian exhaled. "It's dangerous. Very dangerous. I can't even begin to list all the potential hazards."

"Yet they are minuscule compared to what you and I have already faced." Arxad nuzzled Adrian's cheek with his own. "You are a courageous warrior, Adrian Masters, and I trust that the Creator will guide us through this fragile plan."

Adrian stroked Arxad's neck. "You never cease to amaze me. Your love for dragons and humans alike is an inspiration."

"As is your willingness to risk your life for those you love and for strangers. Your example is the very reason I feel ready to do what you ask."

"So now I have to put you in bonds." Adrian touched Arxad's snout. "We found a muzzle the zoo uses for its alligators, and the elephant cage has chains built into its floor. The king arranged to have everything transported to a forest clearing not far away, and a team of horses is waiting there. I'll make sure the bonds are weakened so you can escape."

"Leave them strong. I am sure Drexel will inspect them. I will be able to burn the muzzle with fire through my nostrils. If the cage has a wooden floor, I can burn that as well. I will be free in moments."

"You're taking a big risk."

"You are marrying Marcelle." Arxad let out a throaty laugh. "Who has the greater risk?"

Adrian grinned. "Okay, now you're a comedian." He pointed toward the northwest. "The clearing is about a mile and a half in that direction. Let's see if we can get there without anyone noticing us."

Once again Adrian climbed aboard the great dragon's back. When he settled between two spines, they flew from the palace roof and headed straight toward the clearing. Fully rested and fed, Arxad beat his wings furiously and zoomed toward an oblong gap in the trees. Between the palace and the wooded area, a narrow cobblestone road weaved around boulders, connecting the king's abode with the forest. The journey back to the castle, even with a caged dragon in tow, wouldn't be too hard.

When they arrived in the clearing, Arxad landed next to a wheeled cage with iron bars at the sides and top, as well as thick sheets of metal at the front and back. Four bridled horses tied to a stake in the ground reared up and whinnied loudly, but when Arxad's wings stopped beating, they settled and merely stared as they shifted in their harnesses.

Adrian slid down, grasped one of the vertical bars, and shook it. It held firm without a hint of a rattle. The cage's wooden floor, resting on the axles about three feet off the ground, housed four iron rings deeply embedded in the grain with a thick chain leading from each to an open manacle. The king had arranged everything perfectly.

A muzzle and two keys lay on the floor next to one of the rings. Adrian picked up the muzzle and ran a finger along the leather surface. With ropes for laces, it was flexible enough to fit around any large snout, but, like the wooden floor, a dragon could burn through it, especially one as powerful as Arxad.

Adrian scooped up the keys and used one to unlock the rear gate. The entire sheet of metal swung downward on a trio of hinges. The top edge landed on the ground with a clank, making a sturdy ramp. Adrian jogged up the ramp and waited inside. "I suppose this one's for the manacles," he said, displaying the second key. "We'll have to fasten them or else the ruse won't work."

"Agreed." Arxad shuffled up the ramp. With every lumbering step, the metal bent and shimmied. One horse reared again while the others snorted and stamped their hooves. When Arxad pushed his body inside and curled on the floor comfortably, Adrian squeezed around him and checked to make sure the key opened each manacle before fastening them to his limbs. When he finished, he tromped down the ramp and heaved it closed.

After locking the gate, he walked to the side of the cage and grasped two bars. "Comfortable?"

"Not at all. It seems that contorting myself in this manner is causing my digestive system a bit of turmoil." Arxad curled his neck and rested his head on his body. "This position is a little better."

Adrian picked up the muzzle again and tucked it under his arm. "I can wait to put this on if it will help."

"I think it would." Arxad's ears drooped. "Let us tell the people who receive me that you have given me a sleep-inducing drug. With this deception, you can say that you felt safe to haul me without the muzzle. While I pretend to sleep, you can put it on in their presence, thereby increasing their confidence that it is safe to bring me into the palace."

"That sounds good." Adrian walked to the front of the cage, unfastened the lead rope from the stake, and strode ahead. "Let's go."

With a loud jingle and a few snorts, the horses pulled the cage. At first, the wheels squeaked and groaned, but once the speed increased to a quick march, the noises settled until only the clopping of hooves on stone remained.

After a half hour or so, Adrian stopped the horses at the entry gate to the military quarters, just a stone's throw from the palace's front steps. A guard dressed in the customary orange and black hurried to the gate and opened it, his eyes wide. "Is that a dragon?"

"Indeed it is. It's a gift to King Sasser, a trophy signifying our conquest of Dracon."

The guard gestured with a shaky hand toward the closest building. "Take it to the general. I'll tell him you're here."

"Will do." While the guard ran ahead to the building, Adrian pulled the lead rope and led the horses through the gateway. By the time he arrived at the quarters, a bearded man stood at the door with the guard. His multitude of stripes gave away his rank.

The general gave Adrian an across-the-chest salute. "I am General Brock. By your manner of dress, I assume you're the groom."

"I am." Adrian bowed, intentionally withholding his name.

Brock took the lead rope. "Then allow me to lift your burden. We wouldn't want any further risk of soiling your garments."

The guard laughed. "I almost soiled mine when I saw that dragon. I thought he'd have a muzzle."

"Oh. Right." Adrian showed them the muzzle. "I'll put it on him now. I gave him a drug that put him to sleep. He's harmless."

"Yes," Brock said. "Please do so. We wouldn't want to try to put it on him when he wakes up."

Adrian walked around to the side of the cage, reached between the bars, and wrapped the muzzle around Arxad's snout, making sure the laces ran across one of his nostrils. Arxad's neck and head stayed limp. He was doing a great job pretending to be asleep, and a snore that began as a rumble in his belly and huffed out in hot breaths through his nostrils added to the effect.

As Adrian tied the laces, he glanced back at the general. "I mentioned this to your guard. If I may make a request, I would like for the dragon to be brought into the palace ballroom as the wedding ceremony begins. It will be presented as a trophy to King Sasser."

The general joined him. "It's quite a risk to expose the king to such danger."

"He'll stay asleep for a long time." Adrian tied off the laces. "Check the chains. They're good and strong."

Brock reached in and shook one of the manacles, making the chain jingle. "This will be a fine tribute to our good king."

Adrian hid a sigh of relief. "Good. I'll go now and—"

"Wait." Brock extended his hand, palm up. "I'll need the keys."

Adrian touched his trousers pocket. "I thought I would keep them until after the wedding."

Brock laughed under his breath. "I am not about to haul a dangerous creature into the king's presence unless I am in full control. If I end up having to slay this beast, I want access to him. Also, it will help assure those I call upon to haul him into the palace."

"I understand." Adrian fished out the keys and handed them over. "I'll see you at the wedding."

Adrian walked slowly in the midst of the ballroom's gathering crowd. Wearing a monk's robe that hid his scabbard in the belt underneath, he pulled the hood low over his brow and drifted close to a bronze statue of a soldier on a horse. Marcelle waited there, dressed in similar garb. She had changed to her wedding gown for the rehearsal, which she now wore under the robe.

While a trio of pipers near the entry played soft background music, Drexel and King Sasser stood on a low stage at the front of the room, their hands folded at their waists. The king wore a simple crown of gold, not much more than a wide circlet, and robes that draped him in ivory and purple. His spectacles slid down the bridge of his nose, but he quickly pushed them back into place. His ear trumpet sat on a small table near the edge of the stage, perhaps four paces away from his side.

Drexel sported a form-fitting military uniform of Mesolantrum origin, perhaps a sign that he hoped to command forces while maintaining loyalty to his own region, or perhaps this was all he could buy on short notice.

Adrian searched for Sophia, but she seemed to be nowhere around. Without his designated liar nearby, Drexel would be more vulnerable. She would probably show her face eventually.

The incoming crowd assembled in two groups, leaving a red-carpeted aisle in between, a clear path from the door to the stage. Everyone who entered focused on Drexel, and he on them. He seemed to be preying on their minds as if devouring their resistance to his influence. One by one, the citizens of Tarkton were coming under his control, and with every mind that acquiesced, the plan to subdue him grew more and more fragile.

Two other "monks" stood near the entry door, one at each side, Professor Dunwoody and Marcelle's father. Adrian scanned the incoming stream of guests. When would General Brock call for his "trophy" to enter? Or perhaps Drexel would do the honors, assuming that Brock had informed him by now.

Soon, a herald carrying the king's banner marched along the red carpet, stopping every few paces to blow a bugle. Each blast worked to quiet the crowd.

During one of the bugle calls, Adrian leaned close to Marcelle and whispered, "Have you seen Regina?"

"She's in place." Marcelle's gaze wandered to a balcony above the stage. Behind a white wooden railing, Regina sat in a chair facing the door, perfectly motionless as if imitating a statue. "Where's Sophia?"

"No clue." Adrian again scanned the crowd for her, but she was still nowhere in sight.

When the herald reached the stage, the entry doors closed, and he turned and faced the crowd. After placing the banner pole in a stand and tucking the bugle under his arm, he withdrew a scroll from his tunic and rolled it open. "By order of King Sasser and in honor of our neighbors in the province of Mesolantrum, from this year forth, today will be known as Mesolantrum Day, recognizing their extraordinary feat in subduing the dragons of Starlight, a world known to us as Dracon, and rescuing the slaves who suffered there in chains. After one hundred years of bondage, the surviving slaves have returned, and on this inaugural Mesolantrum Day, we give honor to the new governor, Cal Broder, and celebrate his benevolent rule over the province."

When the herald rolled up the scroll, applause erupted. Drexel bowed his head a number of times in response. As the applause ebbed, he stepped to the front of the stage and spread his arm toward the door.

"Here it comes," Adrian whispered. "Be ready for anything."

Marcelle elbowed him. "Shhh!"

King Sasser picked up his ear trumpet and set it in place.

"Your Majesty," Drexel said, "as tribute to your own benevolent rule, I have a gift for you, a trophy that will seal our triumph in the minds of everyone for years to come."

The entry doors flew open. The cage rolled in, pushed by several Tarkton soldiers. Inside, Arxad lay with his neck and tail curled, his head hidden by a wing.

Gasps rose from the crowd. As the cage rolled on, squeaking under Arxad's weight, people on both sides of the aisle backed away.

"There is no need to fear," Drexel said. "He has been drugged, and although you cannot see his head, I assure you that his mouth has been tightly closed with a muzzle so he won't be able to breathe fire. We decided against killing the beast for now, because we wanted to put him on display and demonstrate that we were able to conquer the species that enslaved our people for so long. In due time, however, we will dispatch him and perhaps stuff him for permanent display."

Adrian nodded. So far, so good. But why would Arxad hide his head? Showing the muzzle made for good theater. Something had to be wrong.

Marcelle whispered, "He's faking sleep very well."

"Too well." Adrian eyed Arxad's back. It rose and fell in a steady rhythm. "He's worrying me."

"He ate too much, maybe?"

"Not too much for a dragon. The fish was ..." Adrian's throat tightened. The fish must have been drugged after all! Since Arxad didn't detect any tainting, the drug must have been odorless. How stupid not to test it!

After catching his breath, Adrian let out a weak, "Someone really drugged him."

As gasps followed the cage's progress, Marcelle whispered, "We're in trouble."

"We'll just have to stall until he wakes up. Whatever the drug was, it didn't kill him."

Marcelle growled under her breath. "You mean it hasn't killed him yet."

"Keep the faith. Stay with the plan."

"But the plan's falling apart. We have to do something else."

Adrian nodded. "If you come up with a better plan, go for it."

The soldiers pushed Arxad to the left of the stage, still in plain sight of all. More soldiers streamed in and formed a line near the walls, surrounding the guests. General Brock walked in and began a quick march up the aisle. When he reached the front, he bowed to the king.

King Sasser pointed his trumpet toward the general. "Why this show of military strength?"

"Your Majesty, it has come to my attention that forces not loyal to your rule have threatened to disrupt the festivities, so I have summoned my men to stand guard in order to ensure a peaceful ceremony."

A new round of whispers erupted. Adrian added his own. "Another stab to our plan."

"It's falling apart piece by piece," Marcelle said.

The king set the trumpet down and pushed his spectacles into place. "Thank you, General."

When Brock reversed course down the aisle, King Sasser waved a hand. "Let us commence with the wedding. The bride and groom have requested that the monastery priests conduct the rituals." He walked to a pair of high-backed chairs at the rear of the stage and sat down.

Dunwoody and Issachar, disguised in their cloaks, nodded from the rear of the chamber. Issachar exited and closed the entry doors, while Dunwoody began a slow walk toward the front, chanting in a foreign language. The plan was for Issachar to hail the carriage and wait nearby with it in case they needed a quick escape. Because of his age, Marcelle didn't want him to stay in the event that a battle ensued, not to mention the fact that he had succumbed to Drexel before.

"I have a new plan." Marcelle grasped Adrian's wrist. "Just trust me and play along."

"What are you going to do?"

"Talk to Regina. But no fighting unless you're with me. I promise." She pulled her hood low over her brow and walked slowly toward a side door. When she reached it, she nodded at a soldier. He opened the door, waited for her to pass through, and closed it again.

After a minute or so, Marcelle, still dressed in a monastery robe, appeared in the balcony with Regina. The two whispered for a moment, then Marcelle gave Regina a vase and exited through a door at the rear of the balcony area. With every eye focused on Arxad, it seemed that no one noticed Marcelle's comings and goings.

Dunwoody now stood near Arxad's cage, out of Drexel's line of sight. Maybe Dunwoody would try to awaken Arxad, but he would have to wait for a distraction of some kind.

In the balcony, Regina locked her stare on the main door, the vase now perched on the balcony railing. The pipers began playing a march, not Mesolantrum's traditional wedding processional, but it was pretty enough. At the door, a perfect replica of Adrian entered, his face straight ahead as he walked toward the stage.

Drexel sat in a chair next to the king, staring at the images. His cheek twitched. He seemed to be trying to probe the replica, unsuccessfully of course, but at this point he probably wouldn't raise an alarm. Perhaps he guessed that the wedding participants would be well prepared to guard their minds.

King Sasser patted his robes as if searching for something. The spectacles no longer sat on his nose.

With every gaze focused on the phantom groom as he waited on the stage, Adrian looked toward the door. Replicas of Marcelle and her father stood there, Marcelle wearing a stunning gown of alabaster lace and silk and a semitransparent veil draped over her face. With gold bands around her biceps, gold trim lining the plunging sleeves, and bronze medallions linked together to fashion a loosely fitting belt, she looked like a warrior goddess.

A crash sounded. Adrian swiveled toward the noise. The remains of a vase lay scattered next to an empty pedestal. He glanced at the balcony. Regina exhaled hard, the vase no longer on the railing. Yet, if it had merely fallen, it would have landed on the stage. She must have thrown it toward the pedestal.

Adrian rose to tiptoes and eyed the entry door. Marcelle still stood with her father, but something had changed. The gold band on her right bicep had disappeared. She had taken it off after the rehearsal to give her sword arm freedom to maneuver. This was the real Marcelle! Whatever she had in mind, it probably involved attacking the man who murdered her mother. Still, she said she wouldn't fight without him. That left only one option. He would have to get into position to join her.

The pipers shifted to a different tune. As the real Marcelle and her father's image marched down the aisle, keeping pace with the slow rhythm, Adrian weaved through the crowd toward the stage. A few people refused to budge, forcing him to take a meandering route.

Now near the side of the stage, Adrian edged closer to Arxad. His body continued its rhythmic rise and fall. The real Dunwoody, still dressed in monk attire and standing just beyond the cage, gave Adrian a glance but nothing more. They couldn't converse without raising suspicion.

When Marcelle stepped up to the stage with Issachar Stafford's replica, Dunwoody climbed a set of stairs at the stage's side and stood in front of them. In a disguised voice, he called out, "Who gives this woman to be married to this man?"

"I do." Issachar placed Marcelle's hand in the hand of Adrian's image, then walked to a spot at the opposite side of the stage and watched.

Adrian stepped closer and eyed the bride and groom's contact point. Of course Marcelle couldn't really hold the image's hand, but she was doing a good job faking it. Only the most astute onlooker could tell that their hands weren't really touching.

Drexel leaned forward in his chair, squinting. Unfortunately, he *was* an astute onlooker. Whatever Marcelle had in mind, she needed to reveal her plan soon. The dark Starlighter would figure out the charade in mere moments.

Dunwoody stepped between Drexel and Marcelle, apparently trying to block his view, and opened a large book over his palms. "Today we are gathered to celebrate the uniting of this couple in holy wedlock."

Rising to his feet, Drexel scowled. Adrian slowly pushed back his robe to grasp his sword. It would take only a few seconds to leap onto the stage and whack off the deceiver's head, but the attack would have to be a complete surprise or else his Starlighter powers would give him an advantage.

While Dunwoody continued the traditional wedding introduction, Adrian glanced at Marcelle. She kept her gaze averted from Drexel, apparently trying to keep him from probing her mind.

Adrian looked again at Arxad, still sleeping only two steps away, though now his wing had shifted, uncovering his snout. Someone had sliced through the muzzle's laces, leaving it hanging loose. Maybe Dunwoody managed that feat while everyone was distracted. Arxad's eyelids fluttered open, then closed again.

Sliding his feet inch by inch, Adrian closed in on Arxad. He reached back and felt for a draconic body part and pinched it hard. Arxad's breathing shifted in rhythm. His eyelid opened a slit, revealing a fiery orb, but his body stayed motionless, save for the continued rise and fall of respiration.

Adrian inched closer to the stage. Dunwoody had neared the end of the traditional introduction, and the surrounding guards seemed to be settling into complacency, though Drexel stood erect, bending to the side to get a view of Marcelle. With Arxad now stirring, the time to attack had arrived.

Clutching the hilt, Adrian eased ever closer. Since Marcelle was unarmed, he would have to do this himself. He drew his sword, taking care to keep it hidden under the robe as it slid noiselessly. When the tip cleared his scabbard, he looked at Marcelle again. Her eyes shifted his way, and she gave him a nod.

Drexel jerked his head toward Adrian. Adrian threw off his robe, leaped onto the stage, and drew his sword back to strike. Drexel thrust a hand forward and pointed his palm at Adrian.

Adrian's muscles stiffened. He froze in midswing, his arms locked in place and his feet fixed to the stage. Drexel kept his stare on Adrian and called out, "This wedding is a sham! The participants are phantoms! General Brock, see to the king's safety! Check every guest and find the real Marcelle immediately! She will look exactly like this woman in the bridal gown!"

Able to move only his eyes, Adrian watched as chaos erupted. Soldiers stormed into the crowd, looking at each woman amid shouts and shifting bodies. A trio of guards leaped onto the stage, whisked the king down the steps, and hustled him out of the room. He called out, "No! Wait!" but the guards paid no attention.

Marcelle kept her focus on Dunwoody and began reciting her vows, "I, Marcelle, take you, Adrian, to be my lawfully wedded husband."

Adrian's legs buckled. He fell to his knees. It seemed that energy flowed from every pore, but he had to resist. As he concentrated, Cassabrie's voice flowed through his mind. *I am simply trying to prepare you for a future event that exceeds this one in wonder and importance.* Yes. He was prepared. He could resist, but for how long?

Marcelle's voice returned. "To have and to hold from this day forward."

Arxad's head lifted, probably unnoticed by everyone except Adrian, but it swayed as if he were drunk. The muzzle separated and fell to the cage floor.

"For better or for worse, for richer, for poorer, in sickness and in health."

Adrian clenched his teeth. What was Marcelle waiting for? And Dunwoody? Even unarmed either of them could break Drexel's concentration. Adrian glanced up. Regina waved her arms as if trying to conjure a new image, but her grimace indicated frustration at the effort of maintaining the current images at the same time. Maybe Marcelle was waiting for the Starlighter to create a distraction, something that might thwart the soldiers, but she couldn't wait much longer. Time was running out.

Drexel shouted, "Also look for someone who is projecting these images! I suspect a female!"

"To love, honor, and cherish, from this day forward."

Drexel sneered at Adrian. "You resist quite well, but you will soon break. When we find Marcelle, you will both be shriveled enough to share the same coffin."

"Till death do us part!" Marcelle lifted her dress, drew a sword from a scabbard strapped to her thigh, and charged at Drexel. She swiped at his neck, but he ducked just in time to avoid the blade. With a backswing, she whacked at his chest, tearing his tunic, ripping into flesh, and slicing into ribs.

The blade lodged in place. Blood poured from the wound. Drexel backpedaled, jerking the sword from her grip. He quickly righted himself and returned his glare to Adrian, again raising a hand to keep him frozen in place. "Take her!" he shouted.

Soldiers rushed toward the stage. Four grabbed Marcelle, two holding each arm as they pulled her back. She screamed, "Broder's a fraud! He murdered my mother!"

Dunwoody shouted at General Brock. "She charges the new governor with murder! He must be sequestered!"

"No!" Drexel yelled. "You saw for yourself that Marcelle tried to murder me!" He grasped the hilt of the sword, jerked it out of his chest, and threw it down. Blood sprayed for a moment before easing to a trickle.

Murmurs erupted from the crowd. A woman cried out, "He must be an angel!"

The general pointed at the guards who held Marcelle. "She's the dangerous one! Don't let her go!"

A chorus of gasps sounded from the entry doors. Ten identical Marcelles rushed into the chamber and ran up the aisle, each wielding a sword and shouting, "Till death do us part!"

The crowd drew back on each side, many falling into each other. Marcelle jerked free, grabbed her sword, and melded in with the other Marcelles. They surrounded the stage with their swords pointed at Drexel. A dragon barged through the entry and leaped into the air. Beating his wings, he flew in a circle near the high ceiling, spewing flames.

Wedding guests stampeded toward the door, along with many soldiers. Adrian looked up at Regina. Her eyes followed the dragon's flight, apparently guiding the phantom.

Dunwoody lunged at Drexel. Drexel shifted his arm away from Adrian and aimed his palm at Dunwoody, sending him flying as if slammed by a charging bull. Dunwoody crashed onto the main floor, his back slapping the marble. He slid for several feet and lay motionless.

The release made Adrian stumble backwards. He fell off the stage and rolled to Arxad's wagon.

Arxad whispered to him, "Reach in and remove the mirror from my underbelly."

Adrian squinted. His vision pulsed between clarity and a blur. Forcing his body to all fours, Adrian slid an arm between two bars and groped for Arxad.

From the stage, Drexel called out, "Marcelle, all of your heroic men have fallen, and I am able to kill any of them from where I stand. Surrender yourself to me, and I will release them unharmed. I will allow them to return to Mesolantrum as my prisoners, but they will live."

Silence ensued. Adrian found the mirror attached to Arxad's belly and pulled, ripping it off his skin. Arxad let out a yelp, then covered his face with a wing.

Adrian swiveled his head toward the stage. Drexel glanced at Arxad, then looked up at the phantom dragon, still flying in an orbit near the ceiling.

"Where is the Starlighter? I know you must have one among your allies." His gaze shifted to the balcony. "Aha!"

Drexel aimed his palm at Regina. She gasped, stiffened, and immediately withered. Within seconds, her frail body wrinkled, her eyes bulged, and her hair began falling out.

"Stop!" Marcelle called, her voice resonating.

Drexel released Regina and pivoted toward the front of the stage. Marcelle stood alone near the edge of the stage's bottom step, her gown's skirt now ripped away, exposing short trousers and an empty sheath strapped to her thigh. Every wedding guest and soldier, including General Brock, had fled, leaving the ballroom a cavernous chamber that echoed the slightest sounds.

"Get ready to throw the mirror to her," Arxad whispered. "I am too weak to help."

"What will it do?"

"Protect her. Are you strong enough?"

"I hope so, but I can barely move."

Drexel picked up Adrian's sword and walked slowly toward Marcelle. "I could simply absorb your life energy and turn you into a bag of bones, but I think I would like a bit more out of you."

Marcelle squared her shoulders. "Coward! You murder women and children!"

"And what will you do about it?" Drexel set the point of the blade against her chin and laughed. "As long as I maintain power, I have nothing to fear. Fifteen years ago I sliced eight fingers from the hands of a helpless mother, and I have answered to neither god nor man for it. I'm not worried about threats from you or any other weak female."

She spat in his face. Her scarlet cheeks and fiery eyes screamed a volley of obscenities, but only a hiss escaped her clenched teeth.

"I see that our conversation has ended." Drexel withdrew a handkerchief and wiped the spittle from his eye. While sliding the handkerchief away, he suddenly thrust the sword. Marcelle leaned back but not in time. The point struck her chest and tore her gown's bodice, though the blade bent and wouldn't pierce her skin.

Marcelle leaped backwards. Heaving shallow breaths, she covered the hole with a hand and glared. "That's the only chance you get." She pointed her own sword and lunged.

He raised a hand and stopped her in midstride. She bent forward and pushed with her legs, but she couldn't seem to move even an inch.

"Now," Arxad whispered.

Adrian summoned all his strength and tossed the mirror to Marcelle. It struck her shoulder and rolled down her back to the floor.

Marcelle dropped to her stomach, snatched the mirror, and aimed it at Drexel.

He stared at his reflection, blinking wildly.

Adrian crawled up onto the stage and struggled toward Drexel on all fours, just a few seconds away from the scoundrel, if only he would keep his attention averted.

Drexel's hair color transformed from red to dark with gray speckles, and his skin tone turned more rugged.

Marcelle climbed to her feet and again tried to trudge toward him. As she leaned forward once more, she pushed but made no progress, as if pressing against an invisible wall—a stalemate.

Adrian slid closer, almost within reach. If he could break Drexel's connection, Marcelle could attack with fury.

General Brock shouted from the entry door. "The dragon's gone!" He and twenty or more men charged, all brandishing swords or spears.

"Help!" Drexel shouted. "Arrest Marcelle at once!"

Brock halted halfway up the aisle and stared at Drexel. "Who are you?"

"Cal Broder!" He pointed at Marcelle. "This sorceress is casting a spell on me!"

Brock waved a hand. "Take her!"

Adrian struggled to his feet and shoved his body into Drexel. Drexel tried to jump out of the way, but Adrian grabbed his leg and held on, pain throttling every nerve. He didn't dare let go. Marcelle couldn't battle Drexel and Brock's men at the same time.

Marcelle spun and parried an attacking sword with her own, knocking the soldier back. The men formed a semicircle around her and closed in. Whenever one attacked, she blocked the blow. Still wearing her wedding gown's bodice, she pivoted through a 180-degree arc, slapping blades and spears.

Drexel laid his palm on Adrian's head. "I assume your energy will restore me."

With all his might, Adrian twisted Drexel's leg, groaning with the effort, but it wouldn't turn. Adrian's arms fell limp. He could no longer budge. It seemed that no matter how much he resisted Drexel's power, life itself leaked out through his skull. Darkness poured across his vision, and he fell into unconsciousness.

✻ TWENTY-SIX ✻

MARCELLE batted a blade away, then another, then another. She sliced a soldier's wrist, drawing a spray of blood. A finger flew from another soldier's hand. Her bodice sparkled with gold and ivory, though now spattered with scarlet.

On the stage, Adrian clung to Drexel's leg, his energy sapped. Drexel laid a hand on Adrian's head and said something too quiet to hear.

Marcelle grimaced. Drexel would drain him dry in seconds. Even with the endurance gained from Cassabrie's indwelling, he couldn't hold out much longer.

General Brock shouted. "Attack! All at once!"

"I'm coming, Adrian!" Marcelle sprang into a backflip that sent her flying onto the stage. She landed on both feet, whipped the sword around with all her might, and sliced the blade through Drexel's throat. In a fountain of blood, his head toppled off and fell with a splash. His body dropped to its knees, then keeled over limply.

Instantly, Drexel's head altered to its former state, complete with salt-and-pepper hair though without his handlebar mustache. His eyes blinked, and his mouth moved, but only a trickle of blood came out.

Soldiers surrounded the stage, their swords and spears pointing at Marcelle. "Surrender!" Brock called. "You can't get away!"

Marcelle grabbed a fistful of Drexel's hair and lifted his head. As she gasped for breath, her heart pounded. Images of her mother's autopsy flashed in her brain—the deep gashes, the bloody stubs on her hands, the pale, lifeless body. Finally, her mother's murderer had paid the price. A thousand nightmares had been vanquished. "Here is the man who murdered my mother. He was an imposter."

Blinking, Brock shook his head hard, as if casting off spiderwebs. The other soldiers carried on similar movements, some rubbing their eyes, others wobbling in place as if off balance. "What madness has bedeviled me?" Brock muttered.

"The bedevilment is over." Marcelle dropped Drexel's head. "I make no apologies for killing the devil who caused it, but now that he's dead …" She let her sword fall to the stage. "I will submit to a trial. I appeal to the mercy of King Sasser."

"Pallance," Brock said, "pick up their weapons and treat them with gentleness. Five of you stand guard while I escort the king here. The rest of you put your weapons away. The injured may report to the infirmary."

As swords slid into sheaths, Marcelle knelt next to Adrian and turned him to his back. He breathed in unsteady gasps, his face gaunt and pale and his lips a bluish tint. She pushed his eyelids up. His pupils had rolled out of sight, revealing bloodshot whites.

Professor Dunwoody groaned from the ballroom floor. "Oh, my head!" Two soldiers helped him rise. Once he had balanced himself, he limped up the steps and stopped at Drexel's body and severed head. Drexel's fingers twitched, then curled into a fist. Blood oozed from his neck stump though not the gushing flow anyone would expect.

"He's still alive," Professor Dunwoody said.

Arxad growled as he rose to his haunches and squeezed his body against the bars. "My strength is returning. Let me out so I can end his life for good."

"Do you have the energy to breathe fire?" Marcelle asked.

"I think so, if I can get close enough."

Pallance, a hulking freckle-faced man with a cleft in his chin, knelt at Adrian's other side, visibly trembling as he glanced between Marcelle and Drexel. "Am I to assume that this dragon is friendly?"

Marcelle nodded. "To all who are good and noble. If you would get Arxad out of that cage, we would both be grateful. He is too weak to escape on his own."

"Well …" Pallance shuddered. "I think we'll keep it that way unless the general says otherwise when he returns. Besides, he has the keys."

Marcelle looked at Arxad. "Adrian doesn't seem to be doing any better. Can his energy be recovered from Drexel?"

"Male Starlighters are able to reinfuse energy into their victims," Arxad said, "but Drexel is not able to function. Although Adrian's body will regenerate its physical losses over time, it is possible that absent life forces could leave him in a vegetative state, similar to your existence when he carried you while your spirit resided here."

Marcelle lifted Adrian into her lap and ran her fingers through his sweat-dampened hair. "Do you mean his spirit might be inside that foul beast right now?"

"Perhaps. I have little experience with male Starlighters, so I am merely guessing. If, however, I were to burn Drexel, it is possible we could lose Adrian in the process."

"Then we can't. We won't." Marcelle rocked Adrian, tears trickling down her cheeks. "Don't worry, my love. You carried me in your arms for miles and miles. I won't forsake you now." Images of Adrian drifted into her mind's eye. He leaned back in a chair, his eyes vacant and his mouth limp as she fed him softened cereal from a teaspoon. When some dribbled down his chin, she dabbed it with a napkin and hummed the tune she played on the pipes during rainbow twilights while Adrian beat on a deerskin drum, his arms strong and his hands thrumming with vigor. He was so healthy then, so filled with life. And now?

"No. ... No!" She shook the image away. "It won't be that way! It can't be that way!" She leaned her head back and shouted at the ceiling. "Creator! Help Adrian! Please, please help him! He surrendered to you. He trusted in you. Don't forsake him now."

She lowered her head and wept, whispering, "And I surrender, too. I'll take care of Adrian no matter what happens, till death do us part, but I beg of you to make him whole."

From a side door, Regina staggered in, bald and bug-eyed. With her hands extended, she felt her way toward the stage. "Adrian!" she called, her voice shattered by grief. "Help me! I'm blind again!"

"I'll get her!" Professor Dunwoody hobbled down the steps and hurried across the ballroom floor. He knelt in front of Regina, wrapped his arms around her, and held her close. "Come, dear girl. I will take you to Adrian and Marcelle."

She pulled back and felt his cheeks. "Who are you?"

"It's Dunwoody. Remember?"

"I'm blind, Dunwoody." Her face twisted as she wept. "I could see. The Creator gave me my sight back. ... But now ... but now it's gone. ... I tried to make the dragon right away ... but it was so hard. ... I was too late. ... Is the Creator punishing me?"

"Of course not, dear." Professor Dunwoody rose and led Regina by the hand to the stage. After helping her up the steps, they knelt close to Adrian and Marcelle. "It seems that Drexel has also stolen much of this little Starlighter's energy."

"I can't see," Regina cried. "I can't hear anyone's tales! I'm in the dark!" She let out a wail. "Oh, Creator! Help me! I don't want to be all alone again!"

"That foul beast!" Arxad huffed a small wad of flames that burned a section of the cage floor. A chain's mooring popped loose. Arxad flailed until the others tore away. Seconds later, the cage's floor collapsed, allowing him to shove the bars over his head with his wings.

Three of the soldiers fled while two others backed slowly away.

"Cowards!" Gasping for breath, Arxad beat his wings, hopped up to the stage, and skittered to the gathering, his chains dragging behind him. "Drexel has absorbed the life energy of two precious humans, but I have no idea how to extract them."

"Yet someone does, my old friend." A breeze blew open the double doors. As if drawn by the wind, a dazzling young woman walked through the opening, long red hair flowing across her shoulders and a shimmering blue cloak trailing her graceful strides. Wearing a radiant white dress, she seemed to glow with her own brilliance.

The remaining pair of soldiers ran out a side door and slammed it, leaving the ballroom without a guard.

Marcelle felt her mouth drop open. "Ca … Cassabrie?"

Staying silent, Cassabrie stooped, picked up a fallen sword, and studied the bloodstained blade. As her brow furrowed, every quiet second seemed infused with meditative sorrow. Finally, she whispered, "It is so sad." Her soft words echoed throughout the chamber, as if unable to be quenched by space or time. "The sons of men give what is priceless to receive what is worthless—blood for prestige, life for license, integrity for a chair that sits higher than another. Eternity is but a heartbeat away, yet they spend their frail moments purchasing what can never last." As each phrase resonated, every eye focused on her. The most powerful of all Starlighters had come, and no one could break away from her hold.

She straightened and waved a hand. "Marcelle, Arxad, Dawson. I release you. We have work to do."

"Cassabrie." Marcelle reached out, her voice quivering. "Can you help Adrian and Regina? I know how much you loved Adrian."

"And still love him." Cassabrie dropped the sword to the red carpet and glided closer. "Whether or not I can help depends on a number of factors."

"Name them." Marcelle sniffed, trying to quell a sob. "I'll do anything."

"One difficulty lies in the fact that Regina's body was reconstituted from the soil of Starlight. I'm not sure she can be fully restored again. Regarding both of them, the first step depends on the willingness of two creatures who have done very little in the way of sacrifice. They have been wandering in search of Drexel, and they have arrived, but we shall see if they will be of service." Cassabrie turned toward the door. "Come in."

Two smoky forms entered, hovering a few inches off the carpet and drifting toward the stage.

"Hiram?" Marcelle swallowed. "Bodnar?"

Thinner and more nebulous than before, both apparitions floated to within a few paces of Cassabrie, speaking in unison. "Where is the evil soul we have been searching for?"

"He is here." Cassabrie turned toward the stage again. "One of the most evil beings to take a breath now lies without the ability to move. You may take him and feed off his energy, but I ask that you find any other spirits dwelling within him and expel them to the outside world."

In a pair of cyclonic spins, Hiram and Bodnar lifted to the stage and settled over Drexel's body and head. When the snatchers combined, their smoke turned black, making their vortex look like spinning tar. Growls emanated, spiced with obscenities. Drexel's face spun in the tornadic coil, first with an angry sneer, then with terrified eyes. After a few seconds, his face shattered, and the spin absorbed every fragment.

Soon, the smoke faded from black to gray to white. The vortex split into two halves, leaving a pile of clothes where Drexel once lay. The spinning slowed in each half, and the amorphous forms took on human characteristics—arms, legs, and face. When they stopped, Hiram and Bodnar stood on the stage, both dressed in the same clothes they had worn in the earlier visions and looking as normal as any human, though they both blinked and wobbled in place.

Marcelle stroked Adrian's head. "Where are you, my love? Where are you?"

"He is here." Bodnar walked over to Adrian and knelt at his side. "And now I perform my penance." He pressed his mouth over Adrian's and exhaled—once, twice, three times. With every breath, Bodnar grew darker and more transparent. Smoke replaced skin. Eyes became swirls. Finally, Bodnar returned to his snatcher form, gray and nebulous.

Adrian's eyes fluttered open. He looked at Marcelle, his lips pale. "I'm … I'm back."

"Adrian!" Marcelle pulled him close and kissed his cheek. Crying, she stroked his hair again and again, her throat too tight to squeeze out another word.

Bodnar drifted away, his smoky form bent. "I am glad I could help."

"Well, my friend," Hiram said, laughing, "it seems that you're a hero." He turned toward the door. "Have fun guarding that stupid portal or whatever is left for you to do. I'm going to start a new life."

Professor Dunwoody grabbed Hiram's sleeve and slammed a palm against his chest. "Where's Regina?"

Hiram smirked. "I consumed her. She's part of the energy that restored me."

Marcelle looked at Cassabrie. She stood calmly at the bottom of the stage steps, still glowing with brilliant light. "What can we do?" Marcelle asked.

"Very little that hasn't already been done." Cassabrie walked up the stairs, each step graceful and fluid. "Darkness and light cannot coexist. Although darkness rules for a season, light always overcomes in the end."

Hiram let out a snort. "Trite platitudes aren't worth—" His eyes widened. He clutched his shirt, his arms quaking violently.

Professor Dunwoody backed away. "What's happening?"

"The natural order of things." Cassabrie stepped over Adrian and stood next to Bodnar. "Be ready to perform one final act of penance."

Hiram's face paled. His lips turned blood red, and his hands shriveled into bony appendages, like forked sticks at the ends of branches. His shoes burst open. His toes lengthened and spread across the stage floor like crawling roots. His body thinned and stretched out, becoming taller with every second.

"Now," Cassabrie said. "Collect this tree's fruit."

Bodnar floated toward Hiram and melded with his body in a dark spinning cloud, veiling all but Hiram's face. Hiram's mouth opened in a silent scream. A misty proboscis plunged into Hiram's throat. As it came out again, bringing with it three distinct shapes, Hiram's body dissolved into a twirling cylinder, gray and indistinct. After a few seconds, the cylinder exploded, sending puffs of smoke scattering through the air.

Backing away, Bodnar spun in stripes of black, white, and gray, like ribbons whipping in a swirling wind.

"Release Regina's energy," Cassabrie said. "You may keep Hiram and Drexel for yourself."

The white ribbon reeled out of the vortex and spilled over Regina's head. Like creamy milk, it coated her scalp and cascaded down her face and shoulders. Red hair sprouted and grew several inches.

Regina blinked, then laughed. "I can see! I can see!"

"There is another soul in here," Bodnar said as he continued spinning. The gray ribbon reeled out and collected in a column. Within seconds it formed an image of Sophia, transparent and nude. She looked at herself, then gasped, crouched, and covered her torso with her arms. "What happened? Where am I?"

Cassabrie whipped off her cloak and draped it around Sophia, covering her. "I will explain during our journey to see the Creator and hear his judgment."

"His judgment? Why? Cal deceived me. He controlled—"

"Silence." Cassabrie waved a hand in front of Sophia's face. "She who is willing to be deceived should not be surprised when a deceiver fulfills her wishes."

Sophia rose and stood erect, her eyes glazing over and her hands clutching tightly to the cloak.

Bodnar continued spinning. Blackness infused every particle of his smoky swirl. The smoke took on a sheen that reflected the glow emanating from Cassabrie. The swirl absorbed the radiance until the vortex shimmered, like dawn's rays on water. Soon, it morphed into Bodnar's form, now glowing from his face and every other uncovered part of his body.

Cassabrie reached a hand toward Bodnar and Sophia. "Come with me. We can no longer stay here."

"Cassabrie?" Adrian said as he pulled away from Marcelle and climbed to his feet. "Why can't you stay?" He grasped Marcelle's hand and helped her rise. "Or at least come back for our wedding?"

Cassabrie's smile seemed to light up the entire palace. "These two are fragile so I have to take them to the Creator's abode right away to await his judgment. The Creator allowed me to come here because of a desperate need and two cries for help. Since the calls have been answered, and all enemies have been vanquished, my time here is complete."

"Do you mean if we had called for your help earlier, we could have avoided a lot of this pain?"

Cassabrie laughed. "Not necessarily, Adrian. Every faithful cry is answered, but not always with direct intervention. Often suffering is an unpleasant gift from the Creator. Perseverance in suffering builds proven character. Proven character results in selfless sacrifice, and selfless sacrifice leads to a lifetime of service to the Creator. Without that, where would we be?"

Professor Dunwoody raised a finger. "What happened to Hiram?"

"Oh, yes. Hiram." Cassabrie nodded thoughtfully. "Hiram and Bodnar were the root cause of the death of Starlight. One has turned to the light, and the other has borne the poisonous fruit of his labors, and he will journey through darkness for all eternity. We can rejoice in both mercy and justice. It is as if Alaph and Beth have resurrected here today, giving me hope that they have reunited in spirit."

Cassabrie turned and walked with Bodnar and Sophia along the red carpet and out the door.

Adrian wrapped Marcelle in his arms and held her close. "Are you all right?"

"I hope so." She laid her head on his shoulder. "I need a minute to think."

Regina hugged Adrian's waist. "I can't hear tales anymore. Not from either of you."

"Well, that's interesting." Adrian looked at the door. "I guess Koren really is the last Starlighter."

Marcelle nodded. "Just like Cassabrie said."

Adrian rubbed the top of Regina's head. "Look at all that beautiful red hair!"

Regina shook her head hard, letting her tresses fly. "Isn't it wonderful?"

"Well, my new sister, you'd better be ready for a good brushing when we get back to our mother."

"Our mother," Regina repeated with a smile. "I love hearing that!"

King Sasser's voice boomed. "What is the meaning of this?"

Adrian and Marcelle pivoted as one. The king stood with General Brock at a side entry, the king smiling as he squinted through a pair of spectacles and held his trumpet to his ear. "What a mess! Where should I send the bill for cleaning it all up?"

General Brock laughed. "This warrior maiden did most of the damage herself!"

"You're telling me." Marcelle ran a hand along her bodice. "Look. Blood all over it." She then touched a hole over her chest. "This rip, though, is a good reminder that Arxad's scale saved my life."

"I guess we should stay long enough to help clean up," Adrian said. "After all, this was our party."

"Think nothing of it." King Sasser gave Brock the trumpet, joined Adrian and Marcelle, and spread his arms across their shoulders. "General Brock filled me in on the details. It seems that you not only liberated the slaves from Dracon, you also eliminated a murderer and a potential usurper who would have enslaved the entire kingdom. Go home. Rest. Get married and have children." He grinned. "As long as you name one of them after me."

"What's this?" Professor Dunwoody said from the stage. He picked up a book from Drexel's clothing and opened it. "Ah! Uriel Blackstone's journal! What a magnificent stroke of luck!"

"That's great, Professor," Marcelle said. "A priceless treasure for your archives."

"I should say not!" He limped down the stairs and presented it to Marcelle. "As his closest surviving relative, it is yours."

She opened it to the first page and read the handwritten inscription out loud. "To Tibalt, and to any of my beloved descendants who might read this journal, blessings to you. Inside these pages you will encounter many mysteries, some of which I described to the best of my ability, but they were too wonderful to put into words in a succinct manner. Unfortunately, I lack a Starlighter's power to conjure actual images, though you will find a few crude drawings here and there. Someday I hope we will be together in the Creator's abode where I assume my tongue will be loosed and my thoughts released to tell vivid tales for all eternity." Marcelle brushed away a tear. "Yet, be on guard, my loved ones. Although I might have risen to the stars, I will be watching over you, and if the Creator allows, I will come and visit you if the need arises. I will ever be your loving father, Uriel Blackstone."

Marcelle closed the book and hugged it to her chest. "I wish I had known him." She sniffed back a sob. "To see him die trying to save Koren was so painful. I wanted to run to him and ... and ..." She broke down and wept.

Adrian took her into his arms and patted her on the back, breathing quiet shushes.

"Yes ..." Dunwoody shifted from foot to foot. "Well ... I suppose I should find Issachar. He is probably quite worried about us by now. And I must send a Courier to find Fenton Xavier and cancel an ambush he was planning in case we happened to fail." Again limping, he hurried toward the door.

"Tell you what." Adrian took Marcelle's hand and led her to Arxad. "Once our good dragon feels up to it, we'll fly back to

Mesolantrum and have our wedding there. I'll wear my old bodyguard uniform, and you can wear your favorite battle trousers. We'll invite the rescued slaves and all our friends on Starlight. Let's fill the Cathedral with everyone who wants to see us the way we really are."

"The Cathedral?"

"Sure. Why not?"

Marcelle gave him a coy smile. "I have a better idea."

"Name the place and time. I'll be there."

"It's a date." Marcelle picked up her gown's skirt from the floor, bloodstained and ripped. "Though I have to admit this dress looks more like me than ever."

✷ TWENTY-SEVEN ✷

ADRIAN smoothed out a sleeve of an old-style military uniform, his pristine white gloves a stark contrast to the dark blue material and the brass buttons closing the cuff. This perfectly pressed outfit belonged to his father, a heftier man now than he was when he wore it for special occasions during his years as a Mesolantrum soldier. What a great honor to wear it now as a groom.

Standing a few paces from the outer wall of the amphitheater, Frederick fastened a polished scabbard to Adrian's belt and patted the attachment point. "There. You look about as good as an ugly guy like you can get."

"Thanks a lot." Adrian punched Frederick's arm. "I should've left you in that pit."

"Shhh. Watch your words." With a sword dangling at his own hip, Frederick nodded toward the nearby walkway. "Witnesses to your threat."

Dozens of Mesolantrum citizens streamed toward the amphitheater, some glancing at the pair of brothers and smiling, all holding unlit candles of various shapes and sizes. A stunning rainbow provided a backdrop in the sky. Everything was coming together perfectly. The beautiful spectrum promised a rainbow celebration no one would soon forget.

Jason broke away from the flow and ran to them. "Look." He stopped and opened a black velvet box, revealing a pair of gold rings resting on white silk. "Just in time."

"Whew!" Adrian touched one of the rings. "Let's be sure to send a letter of thanks to King Sasser. These are a very generous gift."

"Elyssa's already working on one." Jason smiled. With no sign of the horrific bruise around his neck, he looked as good as new. The healing waters in Starlight had done wonders to repair his body. In fact, during the four days since the fake wedding, everyone who had suffered injuries in recent battles traveled to that river to bathe. For some reason, the water didn't heal as quickly as it had earlier, but a few washings proved to be enough to seal cuts, fade bruises, and soothe aching muscles.

Adrian closed the box. "Take them to Father. He's been worried sick about getting them in time."

"Will do." Jason opened a door in the wall and disappeared in the corridor leading to the amphitheater's arena.

Frederick stepped back and looked Adrian over. "You okay? I mean, are your emotions under control?"

"If you're talking about the tears I shed at the funerals, if you had known them like I did, you—"

"Hey! Don't worry. I'm not giving you a hard time. I shed a few myself. I'm just wondering how you're going to react when you see Marcelle in a few minutes."

"Okay. Sorry." Adrian inhaled deeply. Attending two funerals during the past few days had taken an emotional toll. On Starlight, they honored Cassabrie, Lattimer, Tamminy the dragon bard, and all from that world who had perished during the struggle to liberate the slaves, while on Major Four, they honored Uriel, Tibalt, Gregor, Ollie, and a number of other fallen soldiers and escaped slaves. Many tears had flowed, becoming a salted river of grief.

Adrian looked at the forest on the horizon. Solarus's lower arc was now brushing the tops of the trees. The time had come. "I'm ready."

Frederick clasped his arm. "Then let's go."

Adrian followed Frederick into the doorway Jason had entered and walked along a narrow corridor of plaster and stone toward the amphitheater's arena, the passage that tournament combatants used. The cool dampness, along with a view of the sea of faces in the tiered seats ahead, raised a shiver. In mere moments, a hundred pairs of eyes would lock their stares on him, making him the center of unwanted attention. Fortunately it would be short-lived. When the bride appeared, she would become the main attraction.

When Adrian and Frederick crossed the grassy strip separating the seats from the tourney ring, Jason joined them, and the trio formed a line at one side of the circle. They faced a gap between two seating sections. Now that the ceremony was only moments away, just a few stragglers filed in through the gap and hustled to vacant spots in the stair-stepped gallery.

A waist-high stone pedestal stood near the gap within view of the audience. Similar to a book stand, its flat surface lay empty. Adrian squinted at it. No one had mentioned its purpose. Maybe it would become clear soon.

Adrian shifted from side to side, his feet cold and tingling. His two brothers fidgeted to his left as if reflecting his nervousness. As dusk approached, Elyssa walked around the front of the seats lighting an array of candles on head-high stands. Using a brass pole with a flaming wick on the end, she touched candles at five-pace intervals, some embedded in multitiered candelabras, some burning in single candlesticks. Although fading sunlight remained, the candles provided an excellent atmosphere—mysterious and exciting.

Rescued slaves, young and old alike, along with many members of Mesolantrum's peasant class populated most of the seats, though a few of the more noble nobles sat sprinkled in among the poorer folks. Their chosen manner of dress seemed to blend well, both in color and texture, a far cry from the separation of classes at this same venue not many days ago when the divide between the nobility and peasantry was as obvious as a dragon wearing a top hat. Now their humble array and smiling faces wove together, creating a tapestry of multicolored unity, a beautiful sight indeed.

At the opposite side of the tourney ring, no one stood in the space where Marcelle's bridal attendants should have been. She insisted on having no bridesmaids but didn't explain why, though the most likely reason wasn't hard to figure out. Her penchant for offending the females in the noble class had made her something of a pariah. Of course, she could have asked Regina, Elyssa, and Shellinda, but they had become friends only recently. Since Marcelle didn't mention them, it seemed best to avoid the issue.

A glimmer on his sleeve caught his attention, not noticeable until this dusky hour. His entire suit sparkled with shimmering crystalline dust collected from the shattered Reflections Crystal. His groomsmen, Frederick and Jason, also sported tailored suits that sparkled in the candlelight. It had taken Koren a few hours to collect all the tiny shards and attach them to the material, but the effect was worth the trouble.

Adrian searched the crowd. Several former slaves sat together—Erin, Tamara, Tamara's brother Scott, Penelope, Vanna, Orlan, and Cassandra among others. Nearby, Randall's mother, Lady Moulraine, sat next to Meredith Cantor, both laughing and chatting quietly.

When Elyssa lit the final candle, she laid the pole in the grass, walked up to the first row, and sat next to Professor Dunwoody, Regina, and Shellinda.

A hush descended. After a few moments, Koren walked in, escorted by Randall and Wallace, each carrying a candle. Wearing a dazzling white dress and her blue Starlighter cloak, Koren sat with her escorts near Elyssa in the first row.

Seconds later Adrian's mother and father walked in side by side. As they strode at a lively pace, they both beamed. Father's suit and Mother's long flowing blue gown sparkled with crystalline shards.

After Mother sat in the first row close to one of the aisles, leaving a few spaces open between her and Elyssa, Father walked to the front, gave Adrian a brief hug, and occupied the best man's position.

When the guests had taken their seats, Counselor Orion walked in from the access corridor, his head low and his shoulders sloped. Carrying a large book under his arm, he stopped in front of the ring and cleared his throat. A new hush fell across the audience, and every eye trained on him.

"As you all know," Orion said, his tone somber, "I normally officiate and sanction weddings in Mesolantrum, but recent events have given me reason to doubt my qualifications to hold this sacred office. After this ceremony I will take a leave of absence in order to go on a spiritual pilgrimage, but before I go, I will provide Governor Stafford with a detailed list of officials who have acted corruptly, as well as their crimes, including my own. I only hope that the new powers will consider my repentance and the fact that I have bequeathed my entire estate toward building new cottages for the former slaves and toward their sustenance in the existing communes during the construction period.

"When I return I will submit myself to arrest by whomever the governor appoints as the new seneschal. Since the former seneschal was the ringleader in much of the corruption within the palace walls, it seems fitting that the collapse of those walls ended his life."

Orion lifted the book, showing the cover to the audience. "This is the Code, the copy that we kept under glass at the Cathedral for many years. No one could peruse its pages or glean from its wisdom, and Prescott destroyed all other copies in our region. Now, in honor of the liberation of Starlight, I announce the liberation of our land as well, a liberation of mind and spirit. No more will the Creator's thoughts be withheld. We will make copies for every man, woman, and child so that each mind may drink from the Code's healing waters. May its light spread to every region of our world."

He tucked the book under his arm and took a deep breath. "Overseeing this union will be my final act as counselor until I return, though I will decline actually performing the ceremony. At the request of the father of the bride, the officiating priest will remain a mystery until the appropriate time, though some of you know him quite well."

Orion walked to the side of the arena, opened the book, set it on the pedestal, and climbed to the top row where he sat alone. Regina and Shellinda leaped from their seats and ran up to Orion's row. The girls sat with him, one on either side, each holding one of his hands. He smiled and clutched their hands gratefully.

The crowd again grew silent. Adrian stared at the gap leading to the outside path, now dimming in the twilight. He forced his legs to stay calm. Only a few moments remained before the most amazing woman in the world would appear and walk into the arena. What would she be wearing? All the other suits and dresses had been paid for by the king's personal funds, but Marcelle had remained coy about hers. Would she really opt for trousers, or would she wear a traditional white gown? There had been plenty of time for a new gown to be made or the old one to be repaired and laundered.

Professor Dunwoody rose from his seat and strode into the tourney ring carrying a minstrel's lyre. He positioned himself next to Jason and strummed the strings, giving each note time to resonate and die away. When the final string sounded, Adrian's mother rose to her feet. Everyone else did the same. Notes from the lyre played Mesolantrum's traditional wedding march—soft and slow. A silhouette stepped into the amphitheater's gap, veiled by the evening's dimness. The audience took a collective breath and waited.

A strong voice called out. "Adrian Masters, I love you." Like a lightning flash, radiance exploded around a feminine form.

A chorus of *oohs* and *aahs* rose from the audience, a hundred people gasping as one.

Wearing a full-length white gown with a long train, both covered with glowing crystals, Marcelle walked into the arena, escorted by her father. A veil shifted in front of her face, so thin, if not for the movement, it would have been invisible.

After a few steps, she called out, "The Creator deserves all glory for helping us liberate the slaves of Starlight."

Again her gown burst with light, hundreds of crystals sparkling.

"Everyone in both worlds should honor Cassabrie as the blessed liberator of Starlight."

Her voice carried with a clarion resonance, and a new splash of radiance streamed from her shimmering gown.

"Koren and the dragons of Starlight should be considered as friends and allies forever."

As Marcelle drew closer to the tourney ring, Adrian's own clothes began to pulse with light. The shards on the groomsmen did the same, as if echoing Marcelle's proclamations.

Finally, she and Issachar stopped in front of Adrian. "It would be the highest blessing I could receive if my choice for my bridal attendant would be able to take her position, even for a few moments." She looked toward the darkening sky. "Dear Creator, I would cherish those moments forever."

Her dress again exploded with radiance. The glow spread throughout the amphitheater, making the entire area brighter than ever.

When her gown's glow settled to the strength of a single lantern's light, she waited. After several seconds, she pulled in her bottom lip and bit it. Finally, she gave her father a nod, tears glistening in her eyes.

Issachar spoke with equal clarity. "To officiate this wedding, I have chosen a priest unknown to most of you. He is very old and comes from far away, but as a mediator who rescued our entire race from destruction, I'm sure you will recognize and affirm his authority to perform this sacred ceremony."

From the darkness above, a growling voice called out, "Who gives this woman to be married to this man?"

Arxad flew in an orbit overhead, then landed gracefully in the grass bordering the tourney ring. He shuffled into the ring and settled next to Adrian, his neck extended and his snout aimed at Issachar.

Issachar looked to each side and toward the entry gap. Then he sighed. His lips quivering, he said, "I—"

"Wait!" a woman called from the gap.

Everyone turned. Surrounded by dimness, two human forms entered the arena. One climbed into the seats and sat in the back, while a female hurried toward the ring. When she entered the bride's glow, she cried out, "Marcelle! My dearest!" She wrapped Marcelle in her arms.

Marcelle pushed away, her mouth hanging open. "M-M-Mother?"

"Yes, my darling." She pinched the shoulder of Marcelle's gown. "Is this mine?"

Tears streaming, Marcelle nodded. "My new one got ruined."

"Thank you for honoring me in such a lovely way."

Marcelle clasped her mother's pale hand. "I asked the Creator for this blessing, and I can hardly believe it's coming true." Tears streaming, she lifted her mother's hand and kissed it. "Will you be my matron of honor?"

"Oh, yes! Of course!" As she embraced Marcelle, they both trembled. "Thank the Creator for this miracle." She then hugged Issachar and kissed him tenderly. "My gracious husband," she said as she drew back, "I wish I could spend hours with you, but Cassabrie says we have only a few moments. She showed me how to create a body for myself here—" She wiggled a handful of fingers. "—even how to restore my hands, but it will perish soon. Then I have to return to the Creator."

"Cassabrie taught you?" Marcelle asked, swiveling her head. "Where is she?"

Her mother nodded toward the entry. "Outside on the path. She said she would wait for me there."

"I'll be right back." Hiking up her dress and exposing bare feet, Marcelle ran up the aisle and out of sight, her gown's glow following her. For a few seconds darkening twilight settled in the arena. It seemed that everyone held another collective breath. Dunwoody skulked to his seat and sat quietly, as if the slightest sound would fracture the moment.

Soon, light flowed in, followed by Marcelle leading someone by the hand as she hurried through her words. "Of course you should come inside. We told you we wanted you to come."

Wearing her flowing cloak, Cassabrie stumbled along behind Marcelle's pull. "I thought I would watch from a distance. It is unseemly for a former rival to be a distraction at your wedding."

"Nonsense." When they reached the ring, Marcelle stopped and looked Cassabrie in the eye. "You were once a rival, but I have no fear of that any longer. I know Adrian's heart is mine, and mine is his, and I renounce any thought that old distrust will divide us, two headstrong women who ought to be best friends." Her gown burst with new radiance.

"Best friends?" Cassabrie caressed Marcelle's cheek. "You and me?"

Marcelle covered Cassabrie's hand with her own. "Your wisdom set me straight. Now that you're …" She licked her lips. "Now that you're dead, will you be able to keep me straight?"

"No, Marcelle. The Creator allowed us to come because of your desperate cries. Even now we must hurry and leave this world forever. Yet I trust that the Creator will continue to bring light to your mind in new and wonderful ways."

A tear dripped from Marcelle's chin, sparkling as it fell. "Can you stay long enough to be my bridesmaid?"

Cassabrie stepped back and curtsied. "Marcelle, my best friend, it will be an honor."

"Thank you." Marcelle guided Cassabrie to her place at the edge of the ring opposite Adrian and his groomsmen, then stepped between her mother and father and faced Arxad. Brushing away tears, she nodded. "We'd better hurry."

"Very well." Arxad's ears perked upright. "I repeat, who gives this woman to be married to this man?"

Issachar smiled broadly. "Her mother and I do." He pivoted and took a seat in the front row next to Captain Reed.

When Marcelle strode to the side of the ring where her mother stood, her mother adjusted the gown's train. Then, Adrian and Marcelle faced each other, as if preparing to do battle in the ring.

Arxad extended his neck and brought his head close to the groom. As he breathed, warm air brushed across Adrian's cheeks. "I will begin with a brief monologue," Arxad said, "and then proceed directly to the vows. I understand that you each wish to speak them without the usual prompting."

Adrian nodded. "If it is acceptable."

"It is." Arxad drew his head back and lifted it high. With only a remnant glow from Marcelle's gown, he looked like a tall, lurking shadow. "Faithful residents of Mesolantrum, both long-term and newly arrived, the past few days have been filled with turmoil and terror. In fact, I understand that many in your village still hide in fear of a conquered disease and of the presence of a dragon in their land. They lack understanding that there is no fear in love and that no creature is inherently evil. Humans and dragons alike are corrupted by their own actions, not by their existence or by the actions of their progenitors. To believe that a creature is somehow sullied by being a certain species or because of who gave him birth is the root of all bigotry. It is the heart of superstitious fear.

"And now we have the opportunity to cast out such fear by the joining of two humans who have risked their lives to unite two worlds. They began with a hatred of my own kind, even beginning their journey by killing one of us, and now they celebrate the day of their union by allowing a dragon to oversee the tying of their bond. Such is their commitment to the advancement of knowledge, wisdom, and love for all creatures, whether they look like their own reflections or are covered with scales. It is this brand of love we lift up today, for each of you, Adrian and Marcelle, will change over the years, perhaps becoming wrinkled, toothless, or crippled. Yet your love will endure, not taking into account the physical losses as the fires of true love burn within, love for each other's hearts and minds, love for the light within that the Creator bestowed, and therefore love for the Creator himself, for it is the Creator who bestows all good that dwells within, whether in humans or in dragons."

The crystals in Marcelle's gown brightened, as did those in Adrian's suit, casting radiance across Arxad and the wedding party.

"Now," Arxad said, glancing between Adrian and Marcelle, "come together and speak what is on your hearts."

Frederick withdrew his sword, walked to Marcelle, and laid the hilt in her hand, then retreated to his former position.

Adrian slid out his own sword and walked toward the center of the ring. Marcelle approached from the opposite side. When they met at the center, they stopped and gazed at each other, then intertwined their sword arms, his forearm against her chest and her forearm against his chest, leaving a gap between their upright blades that allowed a view of each other's eyes.

Arxad shuffled to a spot near the center and spread out his wings as if creating a backdrop for the vows. "Proceed."

Adrian's legs trembled. Marcelle looked so beautiful, her smile brighter than Solarus. Her auburn hair shone like dawn's glory. She was simply dazzling.

Their plan was for him to recite vows that he had written two days ago, but her mesmerizing beauty seemed to extract every word from his mind, as if a Starlighter had cast a hypnotic spell and left him in a stupor. But he had to say something. This was the moment he had looked forward to for so long.

Steeling himself, he cleared his throat. "Marcelle, I remember when we first became friends. We were quite small, and our families were at Nelson's Creek. I splashed water in your face, and you responded by punching me in the nose."

The audience laughed. Adrian smiled with them, and the outburst of communal joy calmed his nerves.

When the laughter settled, he continued. "We glared at each other for a few seconds, then I offered you my hand. You shook it and stared at me through narrowed eyes. Then you retrieved a handkerchief from your mother, dipped it into the creek, and dabbed the blood trickling from my nose. You said, 'Do you want to be friends?' I think I just nodded. That's when you said, 'Then we shouldn't try to hurt each other.'"

His throat caught, but a swallow loosened it. "Marcelle, those words still echo to this day. They were the reason I couldn't fight you here in the tournament. They were the reason I carried you for so many miles on Starlight. And they are the reason I stand before you now, asking you to be my forever friend. I promise that I will never intentionally hurt you, whether with the words I speak, with the actions I perform, or even with the thoughts I ponder in my mind.

"More than this, I will use every word, deed, and thought to build you up and never tear you down. As you asked me not long ago, I will always be at your side to fight against evil forces together, for we will be inseparable partners in the Creator's service, with blades sharpened to cut our foes and never each other. My heart is yours. My mind is yours. My body is yours. Never to be given to another save to the Creator himself. Whether in calm or in storms, whether in wealth or in poverty, whether in health or in sickness, I will keep this vow until death do us part."

The shards in Adrian's suit blazed with light—pulsing as if ready to burst.

Marcelle ran her fingers along his sleeve, pausing to touch one of the lights. "I don't need these crystals to know that you speak the truth, Adrian Masters. Your word has always been truth … though my own words have sometimes diverged from that path, my actions have sometimes hurt those whom I claim to love, and my words have been sharpened daggers designed to cut with bitterness and rub salt into the wounds. Even though I have stabbed you as well, you never responded in kind, thereby exposing me for what I was."

She drew back from their arm link, reached under her neckline, pried Arxad's scale loose, and showed it to Adrian. "I thought my bravado would protect my broken heart. I thought wielding a sword and tracking down my mother's murderer would take my mind off the torture I felt inside. I thought putting on trousers and battle tunic would disguise the fragile, needy little girl that never fully grieved for her beloved mother."

Tears sparkled, reflecting her gown's brilliant glow. Her face twisting with emotion, she laid the scale on Arxad's clawed hand. He pried the mirror loose from his underbelly, replaced it with the scale, and gave her the mirror.

She showed Adrian the reflective side, then pointed it at herself. "This is what I needed, to see who I really am inside and heed the words of the inscription. It says, 'Your heart is reflected by the light you shine. How great is your light when you sacrifice all you have for those who have nothing to give.'"

She pushed the mirror into Adrian's hand. "Adrian Masters, you have shown me that light. You gave, and you gave, and you gave, while I caused you nothing but trouble."

"But Marcelle, you—"

She pressed a finger on his lips. "It's my turn, dearest one. My vows. My heart." She again curled her sword arm around his and pressed close. "And I give you my heart, Adrian, a reflection of my soul. At times I will be a warrior battling at your side, and we will conquer evil together. We will slap hands in triumph and sing songs of victory. But at other times, I might be a little girl who needs you to comfort me and protect me. Then we will sit in quietness with your strong arms enveloping me in your loving embrace. We will sing quiet hymns that remind us of the Creator's love and how he heals wounded souls."

She took a deep breath, brushed away tears, and squared her shoulders. "With all my heart, I promise to stay at your side, to build you up with words of strength and blessing, to bind your wounds of body and mind, to be a woman you long to be with, and to be for you a warm abode—your hearth, your home. No other man will rest against my bosom. No other man will satisfy my longings. I will honor, trust, and cherish you, whether you are carrying me or I am carrying you. I, Marcelle, will be your wife, until death do us part."

The crystalline shards again burst with brilliance. Adrian's suit flashed in response, as did those of the groomsmen.

Arxad bobbed his head. "Now the rings, please."

As Adrian and Marcelle took a step back from each other, Edison placed two gold rings in Arxad's palm.

"I will now add my own touch to this portion of the ceremony." Arxad breathed over the rings, then passed the daintier of the two to Adrian. "To reflect the warmth of your love."

Adrian caressed the ring's smooth surface—hot, but not scalding. He reached for Marcelle's hand and slid the ring onto her finger. "This is a symbol of our unbreakable bond, and with it I pledge myself to you."

Arxad passed the thicker ring to Marcelle. She slid it onto Adrian's finger and said, "Unbreakable, to be sure, and a bond willingly taken. I am yours forever."

"Now turn to face the witnesses," Arxad said.

When they turned, Adrian's mother rose from her seat and walked into the ring carrying two candles. After Arxad lit both with his breath, she handed one to Marcelle's mother and whispered into her ear. She nodded and smiled.

Arxad lifted his head again. "It is my understanding that in many human wedding ceremonies, the couple's parents light a candle together to show that two lives have become one. Today, however, Adrian and Marcelle have chosen to alter the tradition, hoping to symbolize their desire to spread their light and love to everyone. Also, they will not leave in a recessional march. As you likely heard when you were invited here, the newly united couple will stay for a rainbow-night celebration and mingle with all of you—their family and their friends, both new and old."

The two mothers walked into the audience and began climbing the stairs. Along the way, they stopped at each level and touched their candle flame to the unlit candle held by the person sitting at the end. That person passed the flame along to the next person, and that one to the next. Soon, dozens and dozens of candles lit up the amphitheater.

When the two mothers returned to their places, Arxad's voice boomed. "Because Adrian and Marcelle have pledged their love and faith to each other and sealed their vows in the giving and receiving of rings, by the authority vested in me as a priest of Starlight and as a designated surrogate for the counselor of Mesolantrum, I proclaim that they are husband and wife together. What the Creator has joined, let no man or dragon put asunder." Using his wings, he pushed Adrian and Marcelle closer to each other. "Adrian, you may now kiss your bride."

Adrian sheathed his sword. Marcelle gave hers back to Frederick. Then, Adrian lifted her veil. Laying a hand on the back of her head, he drew her close. Just before their lips touched, she breathed, "Twenty heartbeats" in a soft whisper. When they kissed, warmth surged across his skin and coursed throughout his body. With their bodies pressed together, Adrian counted their heartbeats, now seemingly beating as one. His suit lit up. Her gown flashed with brilliance. The light seemed to create an aura all around.

When the count reached twenty, Adrian pulled back and whispered, "I love you."

"And I love you." As their crystals brightened once again, Marcelle's voice lowered further. "Are you wondering if I'm wearing trousers under my dress?"

He glanced at her lace-covered legs. "Are you?"

"Well ..." She grinned. "That's for me to know and you to find out."

He winked. "I intend to."

She opened her mouth in mock surprise, but when Arxad used his wings to turn them toward the audience, she pressed her lips together, still grinning.

"Ladies and gentlemen," Arxad called, "I present to you, Adrian and Marcelle Masters."

Cheers erupted. Many clapped, making their candle flames shake.

Cassabrie led Marcelle's mother to the center of the ring. "I apologize for breaking protocol," Cassabrie said, "but we must leave immediately."

Marcelle caught her mother's hand. "I love you, Mother." They hugged and kissed briefly. "I'll see you again someday."

"You will, indeed, and I look forward to your arrival." After kissing Issachar, she spread out her arms. A breeze whisked into the arena and swirled around her body. Her hands fragmented, and her skin sloughed off and drizzled to the ground. "Issachar and Marcelle," she said, "I have seen the Creator face-to-face, and he is pleased with both of you. Thank you for loving me even after I left this world."

Cassabrie, too, began dissolving in the breeze. "Good-bye, Marcelle. Thank you for giving us this blessing. After tonight, there will be no more visits from those who have departed this life, so the next time we see you will be when we meet in the Creator's abode."

Within seconds, they crumbled into two piles of dust. The breeze swirled around the piles and ushered the particles into the sky.

Everyone stared in silence. Adrian set a hand on Marcelle's shoulder. No new tears spilled. Her smile said it all. She was content. Her mother was safe and happy, and they would be together again someday.

Professor Dunwoody rose from his seat, strummed his lyre, and shouted. "It's time to celebrate! The bride and groom get the first dance!"

Adrian bowed toward Marcelle. "Shall we?"

She curtsied, this time with perfect grace. "I would be honored."

While Professor Dunwoody played a soft ballad, Adrian and Marcelle danced a waltz, swaying gently. After a few moments,

Issachar cut in, and Adrian danced with his mother. When the song ended, Dunwoody let out a whoop. "Now let's liven it up, shall we?"

Jason ran to the first row, picked up a set of bamboo pipes, and tossed them toward Marcelle.

Laughing, she caught them, looped the strap over her neck, and looked at Adrian. "Are you ready to play?"

"You know it!" Adrian called to Jason, "Where are my drums?"

"Right here!" Jason lifted two small barrels covered with deerskin. "Let's make some music!"

Frederick waved an arm. "Everyone come into the arena!"

As the crowd filed down the steps, including Regina and Shellinda pulling Orion along, Jason brought the barrels and two stools to the center of the ring. Adrian and Marcelle sat on the stools, facing each other. Marcelle lifted the pipes to her lips and began playing a lively tune while Adrian pounded out the rhythm on the skins.

Children gathered around and danced. Adults joined in. Scott swung Tamara in a wild spin. Elyssa and Wallace joined hands and swayed to the rapid beat. Adrian's father and mother pressed their cheeks together, their fingers intertwined as they rocked slowly from side to side. Professor Dunwoody joined hands with a pair of children, and they formed a growing circle of children and adults, including Koren, Randall, Orion, and Captain Reed, all dancing while they slowly orbited the tourney ring.

Adrian inhaled deeply. The aroma of freedom smelled so good. This was truly a rainbow night. Showers had watered the land, showers of liberation that allowed the colors of Mesolantrum to spring forth, to live together in peace and harmony.

He nodded at Marcelle. "How about a song?"

She drew her lips back from the pipes. "Do you have one in mind?"

"The one your father sang at your mother's funeral."

She bent her brow. "You still remember it after all these years?"

"I'll never forget it, but let's inject some joy into it." Adrian rose from his stool and slid the drums to Jason. "Take over."

Marcelle played the first measure on the pipes, lively and fast. Jason slapped the deerskins with a steady rhythm, bobbing his head with the beat.

When Marcelle began again, Adrian took in a deep breath and sang with all his heart.

> Starlight I see at night beyond my mortal view;
> Daylight revives my sight and wakens me anew.
> O let me dream of homeland's shores awaiting my return;
> O let me fly in skies so high and let my passion burn.
>
> The chains of death I toss behind and run to catch the wind;
> The chains of breath I now embrace and fill my lungs again.
> To sing of starlight, take me back to set my people free,
> So they can breathe the air I found, the love 'tween you and me.

Music and dancing went on and on. Other adults took turns singing folk tunes and traditional anthems. Children chanted silly poems, spreading laughter and gaiety from smile to smile. Frederick set up a bowl filled with Mother's "Party Punch," a secret recipe blending three fruit juices and an assortment of spices. No one ever turned down a cup of its sweet goodness.

Adrian let out a contented sigh. It seemed that all fear of the disease and all fomenting distrust had fled. Drexel was dead and gone. The slaves were free. Liberty had been restored in both worlds.

After a few hours, the celebrants began filtering out and making their way home. Singing gave way to quiet conversations and dancing to embraces and clasps of hands. Family and close friends lingered, including Koren, Elyssa, Randall, Captain Reed and his family, and a few commune members.

As midnight drew closer, more celebrants departed until only Adrian's parents, Frederick, Jason, Regina, Shellinda, Elyssa, and Koren remained, along with Marcelle's father, all now sitting at the center of the tourney ring while Arxad settled on his haunches within reach.

One lone man still sat at the amphitheater's top row. Dressed in a hooded overcoat, he watched quietly from the darkness. Earlier, Adrian had tried to talk to the mysterious guest, perhaps the same person who had entered when Marcelle's mother arrived, but he waved Adrian off without a word.

"So," Edison said to Adrian, "will you tell us your plans now? Where will you go? A honeymoon journey? Are you planning to live at the commune for a while?"

Adrian blew out a tired breath. "We have some money left over from Marcelle's cache, so we thought we'd take a carriage to the sea and rent a cabin on a wilderness beach. After that?" He shrugged. "We'll have to come back to the commune until we save some money. The palace won't be ready for anyone to live in for months."

"Because the palace is in ruins," Issachar said, "I have no access to my funds, or I would pay for your honeymoon and a place to stay for a while." He nodded at Arxad. "I've told everyone else this. Right now, I'm bunking with Randall in his father's getaway suite at the Manor Hotel. Fortunately it is well away from the gas line and remained intact. Although I have been reinstated as governor, Randall will inherit the rule when he is of age. By that time, I hope to have our huge mess cleaned up. Eventually our province will become a model for the kingdom."

"And I will work with Koren to clean up Starlight's mess." Arxad lifted his brow. "Were you able to find the crystal that imprisons the other male Starlighter?"

"Leo?" Issachar smiled. "He is now burning in a Cathedral fireplace. Since we no longer have a snatcher to feed him to, he will remain there."

"Excellent." Arxad shifted his neck and looked at Adrian and Marcelle. "You are welcome to come with me to Starlight. The Northlands palace has plenty of room, and Koren would welcome you. Since it is now safe to keep the Northlands portal open, it will not take long at all to travel between our worlds."

"Yes," Koren said. "We would love to have you. Since Deference and Resolute have physical bodies, we can all have a great time together."

Adrian slid his hand into Marcelle's. "Thank you. That sounds perfect. When we get back from the sea, we'll probably go there for a while."

"Yes, thank you," Marcelle said. "You both are wonderful friends."

"Indeed they are." The voice came from an upper row. The man in the overcoat strolled down the stairs, pushing back his hood as he drew closer.

Jason shot to his feet. "Uriel Blackstone?"

He ambled into the tourney ring. "I'm glad you recognized me, but I prefer to be known as Orson."

"Daddy!" Koren jumped up, slid her arms around his waist, and rested her head on his chest. "You're here! How is it possible?"

"A gift from the Creator." While patting Koren's back, Orson laid a hand on his cheek. "As cold as this heartless body feels, I'm sure I look like the walking dead." He chuckled. "I suppose I *am* the walking dead. I heard Cassabrie tell you that after tonight no one else will be visiting from the grave, so I suppose my time here is limited to the waning moments until midnight."

When Koren drew back, Adrian rose and extended his hand. "I'm glad you could come."

"My pleasure." Orson shook his hand. "I greatly enjoyed the ceremony."

Adrian kept the clasp intact for a few seconds, hoping to send some warmth into Orson's cold-as-death skin.

Marcelle embraced Orson. "I figured out that you're my great-grandfather. I'm proud to be a descendant of the man who gave his life to free the slaves."

"Yes," Arxad said, dipping his head low. "Without you, my old friend, the dragons of Starlight would still be ruled by darkness, and slavery would be a millstone around those in chains as well as their masters."

"Your words do me a great kindness." Orson reached into his coat's pocket. "Yet I didn't come to collect blessings. I came to bestow them." He withdrew a long brass key and a rolled-up sheet of parchment. "Since Tibalt died while …" He choked up, and his voice pitched higher. "If this body had more fluids, I would likely be weeping right now." After taking a breath, he continued in an even keel. "There is no need for sadness. I have seen Tibalt in the Creator's abode. I just grieve over all that he suffered because of my own passion to liberate my fellow humans."

"He chose to do so willingly." Adrian spread out his arm. "We all did."

Orson nodded. "And that's why I am here. I began this quest for liberation long ago. With so many failures, I started to think it was a madman's dream, and at times I thought I might be that madman, but now I have seen the dream's fulfillment. You, Marcelle, Arxad, Koren, Jason, Elyssa, and so many others made my dream come true. Since my daughter is well supplied with a castle and servants, I bequeath to you all that I have remaining." He laid the key and parchment in Adrian's hand. "On this page you will find a map that shows the location of a house I built in the Forbidden

Zone. I checked, and it is still there. It will require some repairs, but it is structurally quite sound. The map will also reveal where I hid a cache of valuables—precious metals I collected along with a modest sum of local currency. I trust that it will be sufficient for you and Marcelle to begin a new life together."

"But we don't deserve—"

"Shhh." Orson closed Adrian's hand around the gifts. "What you deserve is up to the Creator. I give these out of gratitude, and I trust that you will share the bounty with all who participated in the liberation of both Starlight and Major Four. Surely two worlds have been set free from bondage. The Lost Ones have become the Found Ones. My greatest dream has come true."

"Thank you, Orson." Adrian clasped his shoulder. "On behalf of all who followed in your footsteps, I express my deep appreciation and admiration for your willingness to shine a light, even when everyone else cowered in the darkness. You are an inspiration to us all."

"And you are very kind." His smile quivering, he took a step back. "I leave you with this, a poetic song of sorts. As you might have heard, I enjoy simple rhymes that children can understand and remember. Please sing it to your children and your grandchildren until they know it by heart. Let us hope that the light will continue to shine from generation to generation, and the darkness of bondage will never again creep into our worlds."

Another breeze blew in and swirled around Orson as he began singing in a gentle tenor.

> I'm not afraid of darkness now;
> I trust in powers big and strong.
> Creator give me light today
> To do what's right and not what's wrong.

It's wrong to hate or lie or steal;
It's wrong to live by lust and greed.
It's right to love and tell the truth;
It's right to give to all who need.

And now Creator hear my prayer.
Allow your light to shine from me,
To fill all souls with light and love.
To break their chains and set them free.

The wind swept across Orson's skin and peeled away layer after layer. "Good-bye, my friends. This is the end of my story and the beginning of yours."

Adrian and Marcelle joined hands. Everyone formed a ring around Orson's disintegrating body, including Arxad, who completed the circle with his outstretched wings.

"Good-bye, Orson," Adrian said, loudly enough for all to hear. "I promise that we will all shine your light, and we will teach your song to those who come after us, just like you did. May the Creator help us to fulfill these vows, today and forever. Amen."